THE TIGER'S FATE

Chronicles of an Imperial Legionary Officer

Book Three:

THE TIGER'S FATE

MARC ALAN EDELHEIT

Chronicles of an Imperial Legionary Officer BOOK THREE: THE TIGER'S FATE

First Edition

I wish to thank my agents, Andrea Hurst and Sean Fletcher, for their invaluable assistance. I would also like to thank my Beta Readers: Barrett McKinney, Jon Cockes, Norman Stiteler, Nicolas Weiss, Stephan Kobert, Matthew Ashley, Melinda Vallem, Brett Stewart, Brett Smith, Jon Quast, Greg Schell, Tim Andrew Adams II, Chris Cox, Gary Furrow, Mario Rivera, Michael Reeves, Michelle Klein, Paul Klebaur. I would also like to take a moment to thank my loving wife who sacrificed many an evening to allow me to work on my writing.

Editing Assistance by: Hannah Streetman, Audrey Mackaman
Cover Art by Piero Mng (Gianpiero Mangialardi)

Cover Formatting by Telemachus Press

Dedication
To My Loving Wife, Elizabeth, who put up with many
lonely evenings so that I could finish this novel.

The Tiger's Fate is book 3 in the series. Why not start at the beginning?

Book One: **Stiger's Tiger**
Book Two: **The Tiger**

Excerpt from Thelius's Histories, The Mal'Zeelan Empire, Volume 3, Book 2.

THE MAL'ZEELAN IMPERIAL LEGION

Pre-Emperor Midisian Reformation

The imperial legion was a formation that numbered, when at full strength, five thousand five hundred to six thousand men. The legion was composed of heavy infantry recruited exclusively from the citizens of the empire. Slaves and non-citizens were prohibited from serving. The legion was divided into ten cohorts of 480 men, with First Cohort, being an over-strength unit, numbering around a thousand. A legion usually included a mix of engineers, surgeons, and various support staff. Legions were always accompanied by allied auxiliary formations, ranging from cavalry to various forms of light infantry. The Imperial Legion was commanded by a legate (general).

The basic unit of the legion was the century, numbering eighty men in strength. There were six centuries in a cohort. A centurion (basic officer) commanded the century. The centurion was supported by an optio (equivalent of a corporal) who handled minor administrative duties. Both had to be capable of reading and performing basic math.

Note: Very rarely were legions ever maintained at full strength. This was due primarily to the following reasons: retirement, death, disability, budget shortages (graft), and the slow stream of replacements.

The most famous legion was the Thirteenth, commanded by Legate . . .

Post-Emperor Midisian Reformation

Emperor Midiuses's reforms were focused on streamlining the legions and cutting cost through the elimination of at least half of the officer corps per legion, amongst other changes.

The basic unit of the legion became the company, numbering around two hundred men in strength. There were ten twenty-man files per company. A captain commanded the company. The captain was supported by a lieutenant, two sergeants, and a corporal per file.

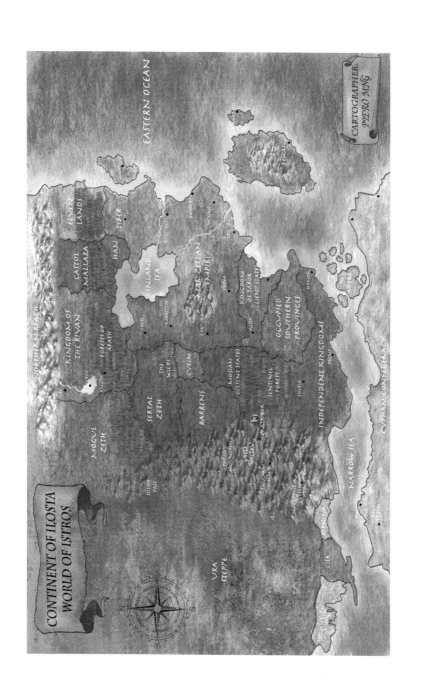

PROLOGUE

General Treim guided his horse off to the side of the road, pulling up to a stop in front of the tribune, who was clearly waiting for him. Colonel Aetius, who had been riding at the general's side, turned his horse after Treim's and stopped alongside his general. The steady tread of hundreds of hobnailed sandals on weathered paving stone was the backdrop behind the two senior officers. Yokes in hand, helmets hanging from ties about their necks, and covered shields strapped to their backs, the tired and weary men marched by.

The tribune executed a perfect salute, which Treim responded to with a simple wave. He was tired from a long, forced march. As ordered, it had taken the old general seven hard days to get here, and he was eager to be out of the saddle. He had received his orders following the successful conclusion of a small campaign before the city Anesia. Had he not forced the enemy to battle and defeated them, he would have had to abandon the city and its population of two hundred thousand. Of late, the Cyphan Confederacy had taken too many of the empire's cities. It had felt good to give them a real drubbing.

"General," the tribune greeted using the old tongue, which immediately put Treim on guard and drew all of his attention to the man. The old tongue was only spoken at court. "The emperor commands your presence."

"Tribune," Treim said, using common. Without looking he could tell that Aetius had stiffened in his saddle. "What is your name?"

"Tribune Handi," he replied smoothly, flashing a smile that the overly-painted ladies of court likely found charming.

Everything about the officer before him was too perfect for the general's taste. Even the young man's smile irritated him. Treim very much doubted that the officer before him had ever done any hard soldiering.

"Tribune Handi," Treim said, sounding the man's name out. He was unfamiliar with the family. It bothered him little. He had been probing to see if the tribune was from a friendly house. Had the emperor sent an enemy to greet him, he would have been on his guard. Instead, he decided that Handi was a nobody, and no cause for concern. There were a thousand nobles just like him. Treim idly wondered how the man had obtained such a high rank serving the emperor directly. Either his family was extremely wealthy or he had a powerful mentor. Perhaps even the emperor had taken a liking to him. Treim decided he would require more information on this man. Later this evening, when time permitted, he would ask his spymaster to make some inquiries.

"Tribune Handi," Treim started again sourly, "I am weary from a long march. Surely the emperor will excuse me long enough to make myself somewhat presentable. I would not wish to offend his majesty's sensibilities."

"I am afraid my orders were to bring you straightaway, sir."

"Colonel." Treim turned to Aetius with more than a little irritation. "Locate the space allotted for our legions. See that our men set up the marching camp."

"Yes, sir." Aetius offered a salute, just as Lieutenant Marius, one of the general's many aides, rode up. He was returning from delivering a dispatch and handed over the reply to the general after a hasty salute.

Treim pocketed the dispatch. He would read it over later when there was some privacy.

"Marius," Aetius said, "the general will be visiting the emperor. See to the general's needs."

"Yes, sir." The lieutenant's head had snapped up at the mention of the emperor, and he straightened in the saddle, apparently becoming aware of the tribune for the first time. He was dusty and grimy like the rest of the army, but the youthful officer's eyes were now lit up with the prospect of potentially seeing the emperor.

"Lead on, tribune," Treim said, stifling a yawn.

The tribune turned his horse and led both the general and aide off the side of the road. They wound their way through the maze of camp follower tents that hugged the massive encampment and concentration of the emperor's best legions.

As expected, the camp smelled awful, but Treim was pleased to see that basic sanitation was being practiced. With so many people in such a confined area, the smell was something to which one eventually became accustomed. Men, women, and children moved aside and watched the officers pass. The streets were crowded. A large number of merchants had set up shop with the hopes of preying upon the men of the legions and turning a profit. As long as they did not gouge too terribly and paid off the camp prefects, those who would share with the generals would be permitted to stay.

Off-duty legionaries weaved their way through the streets, stepping aside as the party rode by and offering salutes. Treim knew there were six legions and a number of allied auxiliary formations present. That kind of military concentration attracted a lot of camp followers. Treim would be adding an additional four legions to that number and sixteen auxiliary cohorts. The flower of the empire's military was being gathered here with the purpose of striking back against the Cyphan. It had taken some time, but the military machine of the empire was finally grinding forward. Other legions, which had been stationed along the frontier, were also being brought in. Recalling the legions would cause some problems with the fringes of the empire, but it could not be helped. The empire would deal with any troublesome neighbors once the Cyphan had been dealt with.

The camp eventually gave way to the fortified encampment of the legions, one positioned after another. From what he could see, each legion had its own fortified marching camp. The one he was being led to was that of the emperor, who had mustered the Praetorian Guard. The praetorians were the emperor's personal guard, an over-strength legion, numbering close to ten thousand. The men who served with the Praetorian Guard had previously served with distinction in the regular legions before being recommended. Theoretically speaking, they were a crack force, one capable of giving a good accounting of themselves in the field. However, most had not seen any action, other than the occasional assassination of one of the emperor's foes, in many years. With their flashy armor and purple cloaks, they certainly looked impressive. Treim had a feeling the praetorians had long ago gone soft. Sadly, in the general's estimation, the praetorians were a political force to be reckoned with. Whoever paid the most owned them.

A smart emperor always paid them well, for if someone gave them a better offer, the empire could find itself abruptly with new leadership. Such things had been known to happen. It was one of the reasons why Treim had no desire or aspiration to be emperor. He was content to simply serve with distinction and honor. If he'd had his way, he would have already retired. Instead, the Cyphan Confederacy had had other ideas.

The praetorians standing post on the camp gate saluted smartly. The general was waved through by the gate officer without even having to sign in. Unlike the men in the streets before the gates, these men would know who he was, or perhaps they simply knew his escort, the tribune.

The tribune led General Treim through the neatly ordered streets of the praetorian camp toward imperial headquarters. The High Command would be here also. Treim made a mental note to remember to speak to them. He badly needed replacements. All four of his legions were understrength, not to mention his allied auxiliary cohorts. The last time they had seen any replacements had been before the winter campaign against the Rivan.

Treim swept his eyes across the training grounds and was pleased to see the praetorians drilling. There were at least three companies hard at it, with sergeants shouting orders and hurling profanities at their men. Perhaps, thought Treim, they might just be ready for a fight. Then again, he understood, only time would tell.

"This is where I will leave you, sir." The tribune stopped in front of an elaborate tent and dismounted. Several praetorians were stationed around it. Two slave boys ran forward to take the horses of the general and his aide as they dismounted. Treim paid them no mind as he stretched out his back. It had been a long, dusty ride, and he wished he'd had time to clean up before meeting with the emperor. There was no point worrying about spilt wine. The emperor knew his value as a fighting general and would just have to accept that his loyal servant was a little saddle dirty.

The tribune spoke to the praetorians. One of the praetorians, a lieutenant, stepped into the tent. A moment later, the emperor's personal steward, Thelonius, emerged. He clicked his tongue at the general's appearance. Treim shrugged in reply. Thelonius was an old man, gray-haired and stooped by age. Despite the steward's decrepit appearance, his mind was as sharp as any sword. He had served the imperial household faithfully for years. Treim knew the man well and respected him.

"No time for a bath?" the steward asked with pursed lips.

"I was commanded to attend," Treim informed him and nodded toward the tribune. "You could even say I was plucked right off the road."

"Tribune Handi," the steward said, "thank you for discharging your duty so faithfully."

The smartly dressed tribune offered the general a salute. He stepped off and away from the emperor's tent, leading his horse. Treim watched the man go and was tempted to frown, but kept his face impassive. He did not need to make any fresh enemies before he knew which way the wind was blowing.

"A social climber," the steward whispered. "A current favorite of his majesty, but no one of consequence."

"How is he today?" Treim asked in a whisper, referring to the emperor.

"He is in an excellent mood," the steward informed him. "Especially now that his most successful general has arrived."

"Good," Treim said, with some relief. The emperor's mood had a tendency to shift more easily than Treim's adopted teenage daughter. "Can we get this over with? I need a bath and some sleep."

The steward led him into the tent, but not before telling Lieutenant Marius to wait outside. The lieutenant looked crestfallen. Treim knew he would get over it. The general turned and entered the tent. He discovered the tent was full of senior officers, all waiting in attendance upon the emperor, who sat upon a raised golden throne along the back wall. The emperor was saying something to one of the officers when the steward announced him.

All eyes turned upon Treim. Some were friendly and others most definitely not so.

"Ah," the emperor said with a smile. He gestured impatiently for the man he had been speaking with to step away. "Our most successful general has finally arrived to the party we are preparing for the Cyphan dogs."

General Treim made his way up to the emperor, who was garbed in flowing, royal purple robes. A crown of delicate golden leaves rested upon the emperor's prematurely balding head. Even though the emperor was only in his thirties, he looked much older. The office weighed heavily upon him. Treim went to a knee and bowed his head. The emperor held out a hand to him. Treim dutifully kissed the ring of office.

"Rise, my faithful general," the emperor said. Treim stood and took a couple of respectful steps backward. There were two praetorians standing to either side of the emperor. Their eyes were upon him, ever on the lookout for trouble, for in the empire no one was above suspicion. "We were gratified to receive word of your victory before the gates of Anesia."

"I am pleased to serve," Treim said neutrally. Standing off to the emperor's right was Haranos, his secretary. Garbed in the plain robes of a freedman, he looked harmless. However, he was anything but and had a fearsome reputation for disappearing some of the emperor's more dangerous foes. Harananos nodded a greeting to Treim, but said nothing.

"I look forward to the day we crush the Cyphan," the emperor said, cracking a smile. He paused. The crowd of officers seemed to hold their breath as the emperor gazed around the tent. Treim knew something important was coming and so did those gathered.

"I am pleased to announce," the emperor continued, "General Treim will lead that effort. General Treim shall command the combined might of the empire when we next go into battle."

"Me?" Treim asked with more than a little surprise, though with his recent successes he knew he shouldn't be. Treim had assumed the position would have been filled by someone more senior to him. He wondered if the emperor was jesting, for the man was known for flights of fancy and moments of terrible jest. Was this one of the latter? The general sensed it was not and his mood darkened. The emperor should have had the common sense to consult his opinion in private and ask rather than just announce it. What if he had refused? Could he refuse?

"You doubt your own capability?" the emperor asked, gently mocking him.

"I had not expected such an honor," Treim admitted, struggling to gather his thoughts. He had no doubts when it came to his ability as a general and leader of men.

"I expect you shall deliver great honor to your family, empire, and emperor," Harananos said quietly.

"I will endeavor to do so," Treim said, feeling even more tired than before, resigned to his new office and the responsibility that came with it, for in his hands now rested the fate of the empire. There would be no immediate rest for him. The High Command would wish much of his attention. With the bulk of the enemy army only thirty miles away, Treim would have to become rapidly familiar with the forces under his command. He suspected that the Cyphan would not allow the empire to continue to concentrate her legions unimpeded.

"Excellent." The emperor turned to the assembled officers. "Leave us. You may congratulate General Treim later. I wish to speak with my general in private."

The command was unexpected, and a number of general officers hesitated before respectfully offering bows and exiting the tent. The emperor waited patiently for the thirty or so officers to file quietly out. Treim wondered what was so important that the emperor wished to speak with him in private. Surely such a talk could have waited 'til later in the evening, when the business of the day was done.

"Tenya'Far," the emperor called. "Not you. Stay, if you will."

Treim turned. He had not realized that an elf was present. Tenya'Far had been standing off to the side of the tent, almost in the corner. The general's eyes narrowed. What was an elf doing attending the emperor?

"You too . . . leave us," the emperor commanded to the two praetorians after everyone else had exited the tent. They looked about to argue, but then bowed respectfully and left.

Treim noticed that Harananos had remained. The secretary had not moved.

The elf, with the appearance of a youth of no more than twenty years, approached and stood next to Treim. Despite his youthful appearance, Treim felt a sense of great age in the elf. The general looked over at him and felt uncomfortable in Tenya'Far's presence. The elves had long abandoned the empire, but were still nominally considered an ally, even if they had turned their backs on their former human friends. Where things stood now, the elves left the empire alone and the empire refrained from bothering them. The only other elf Treim had ever come across in service to the empire was the one that Ben Stiger dragged around with him. He tried to remember the name of Stiger's pet elf, but could not. The general's thoughts darkened as he thought on the officer who had once served him with distinction. Treim regretted having sent him south. In the disaster that had befallen the southern legions, Ben Stiger had been lost along with many other fine men.

"We have received word from a garrison to the far south," Harananos explained once the tent had emptied.

"I did not think we had any forces left behind the lines," Treim said.

"We did not either," Harananos admitted. "It came as quite a surprise. A messenger won his way through to report that the garrison of Vrell has managed to hold out."

"Vrell?" Treim asked. He had never heard of the place.

"It is a large isolated valley, guarded by Castle Vrell. I understand it to be an extremely well-fortified position, a real tough nut to crack," the emperor said, speaking up. "General, you will be gratified to know that Ben, our mutual friend, now commands the garrison. He has over a thousand men and has stated his intention to hold at all costs."

"Stiger!" Treim exclaimed. He grinned broadly. "The Cyphan will never take that castle from him, unless they are willing to pay for it in rivers of blood. Ben Stiger is a very determined officer."

"I think we both know how determined he can be," the emperor said, suddenly looking tired. Treim well knew of the young Stiger's childhood friendship with the emperor. It was probably the only reason the entire family had not been executed. Thoughts of Ben's father, Marcus Stiger, brought a wave of regret. The elder Stiger was one of the most skilled generals the empire had ever put in command of a field army. It was a shame that Marcus Stiger would never again be permitted to serve. He was essentially a prisoner on his own estate outside of Mal'Zeel, permitted to live only by the emperor's grace.

"Well," Harananos said, "there is a complication. The young Stiger found the eagle of the Thirteenth."

"The Thirteenth?" Treim said. "The Vanished? He found the lost eagle?"

"Yes, he did," the emperor said, "and that is the problem."

"I do not see how." Treim was confused. "It is just an eagle. All he has to do is hang onto it until we can fight our way south. If this castle is so well fortified, there should be little problem with him holding out."

"It is a bit more complicated than that," Harananos said. "This here is Eli'Far's father."

"That's the elf who follows Stiger around, right?" Treim asked, glancing over at Tenya'Far.

"My son," the elf admitted, speaking for the first time. There was no hint of emotion in his expression and tone. As with any elf he had ever met, Treim found Tenya'Far inscrutable.

"We need to send Stiger aid," Harananos said. "Should Vrell fall, the empire is doomed."

"That is why," Tenya'Far stated, "I am taking a force of elven fighters to relieve Legate Stiger."

"What? I don't understand," Treim said, his mind racing. He could not see how a remote, isolated valley could hold the key to the empire's survival. "Elven fighters? Legate? We have not used that title in centuries. We call them generals now."

"General Treim," the emperor said, leaning forward from his golden throne, "as commander of my armies, it is time you were told of the Compact."

"The Compact?"

"Yes," Harananos said, "an alliance made over two thousand years ago."

The general glanced over at Harananos. He had a bad feeling about what was to come.

ONE

Stiger took the reins of his horse from the legionary who had led the animal out from the castle stables. Nomad nuzzled Stiger playfully, nudging him in the shoulder. He patted the horse's neck. A final parting gift from father to son, Nomad had served him well. He was a good horse and one of the few things Stiger was grateful to his father for.

"We have quite a ride ahead of us, old boy," Stiger said as a bitterly cold wind whipped through the castle courtyard, rustling his thick blue cloak. A flurry of freshly fallen snow was sent swirling into the air by the gust. "It will be a bit of a cold ride, but nothing we've not seen before."

The castle courtyard was bustling with activity as riders readied themselves. Though it was an hour after dawn, the courtyard was still heavily shadowed, thanks in part to the massive walls of the castle. A few feet away, Thane Braddock, along with his aide Garrack, checked their mounts. The dwarves, though short and squat, were wider than a man had a right to be. Stiger had learned that they were incredibly strong. The thane's personal guard had already mounted up and were waiting. Each one of Braddock's guard looked hard as a nail and ready to act at a moment's notice. They were also heavily armed and armored, more so than a legionary.

Like their thane, they wore capes and horse-haired helms that were dyed a deep, rich purple. Stiger had learned the color purple, much like that of his emperor, was reserved for the thane himself and those of his clan. Naggock, the captain of Braddock's guard, sat astride his pony, watching closely whomever came near his charge. With black hair tied back in a ponytail and a cold disposition, Naggock was smaller than most of his kind. There was an air of confidence and competence about him.

The dwarves were mounted on stout mountain ponies that they had brought with them. Manes braided much like their riders' beards, the ponies bulged with muscles. Stiger had never seen their like. Though smaller than the average horse, these animals were impressively powerful. They would have to be, Stiger thought, to handle the weight of a dwarf and his armor. Dwarves, though smaller in stature than a full-grown man, were much heavier.

"We breed them to be strong," Braddock had told Stiger proudly upon his arrival at the castle. "Most find use as draft animals, but these have been raised for war."

Looking for some attention, Nomad nuzzled Stiger again, drawing him back to the present. He scratched the horse's neck. Next to Eli, the horse was one of the few constants in his life.

"Okay, boy," Stiger chuckled at Nomad's enthusiasm. He dug into a saddlebag where the feed was stored and pulled out a handful of oats, which he fed to the greedy horse. "Easy now."

Stiger found most dwarves difficult to tell apart. They were just too similar in appearance. Their thick beards that grew up to their cheeks obscured facial features that would have made them much more readily identifiable. He was sure they could easily tell one another apart, but he had a difficult time doing so. On the other hand, it was a simpler matter to separate the clans. Each one could be identified by a specific color or pattern scheme on their cloaks and tunics that was unique to the clan. Simply put, dwarves stood apart from other dwarves in dress and took enormous pride in their clans, which Stiger had learned were more like an extended family.

Amongst themselves, dwarves were also very competitive. So much so that Stiger and his legionaries had been introduced to a dwarven sport called nose ball. Braddock had explained that the friendly sport was a way for his people to let off steam. Stiger and his legionaries had been treated to an exhibition game, though from what Stiger could see, there had been nothing even remotely friendly about the match. The game had been exceptionally violent, as each side worked to possess the ball, an inflated goat's stomach. The object of the game was to advance the ball down the field toward the other team's goal line. The only rules were that you could not throw a punch, kick, pull a weapon, or use your hands. Everything else was fair game, including body-slams, head-butts, and even the use of one's teeth. Stiger suspected the reason the game was called nose ball was on account of the many broken noses.

Unfortunately, the game was catching on amongst his legionaries. Stiger was considering banning the sport, as it was beginning to send a steady stream of injured players to the hospital ward, which affected his strength totals.

Stiger pulled out another handful of oats, fed it to his ever-hungry friend, and then checked the saddle straps to ensure that they were tight and secure. He was far from surprised to discover that they were loose. He tightened them. From painful experience, he knew that Nomad had the regrettable tendency to take a deep breath and hold it while being saddled. When the horse finally exhaled, the result was predictable: loose saddle straps. Stiger had learned to wait for a time and then readjust the straps.

Lan and his cavalry troop would act as Stiger's personal escort. They were busily readying themselves and their horses, tightening straps, securing saddlebags, checking shoes, and a number of other tasks. No longer would he enjoy the freedom of unescorted travel. Lieutenant Ikely and Centurion Sabinus had steadfastly insisted upon this precaution. No matter how much Stiger disliked the idea, he had not even bothered to complain. There was no point. His men needed him and that was that.

Stiger paused in tightening the strap on his saddle bag, securing the oats. Despite what Atticus's letter claimed, Stiger was unsure just what would happen when he was able to reestablish communication with the empire. Would the emperor accept what he had done? Would the alliance with the dwarves be repudiated? He finished securing the saddle strap and then patted Nomad's neck.

"You are a good horse. When we return, I will find an apple for you."

Eli led his horse out of the stables, followed by Marcus and Taha'Leeth, the stunningly beautiful elven princess from the small band who had recently joined them after rebelling against the Cyphan Confederacy. Stiger saw another elf, likely Taha'Leeth's escort, also emerge. He was still troubled by the glamour Taha'Leeth had tried to pull on him and knew for damn sure he could not yet afford to trust her. Until she proved herself worthy, he would be watching. Trust had to be earned.

A hearty laugh echoed across the courtyard and Stiger's attention was drawn to Father Thomas, who was already mounted and talking casually with Centurion Vargus. Next to the paladin on a dappled mare was Sergeant Arnold, who no longer walked with a severe limp. Father Thomas had healed the grizzled sergeant of his crippling injury.

The two had since become inseparable. The formerly irreverent troublemaker from the supply branch could regularly be seen with his nose buried in the High Father's holy book or openly discussing theology with the paladin. Arnold had actually turned polite and respectful. Incredibly, he no longer swore. Not only did Arnold now present like a model legionary, shaved and well-groomed along with a flawlessly maintained kit, the sergeant had even become helpful. He voluntarily tended to the wounded in the hospital ward or stepped up to lead supply runs down into the valley, helping to return the food stores confiscated by the late Captain Aveeno. The man's transformation was remarkable. Stiger was worried that the transformation was too quick to last.

"I would very much like to work with Arnold and help him to study the good word," Father Thomas had said a few days back. "He has much to learn, and I have much to teach."

"Are you sure about this, Father?" Stiger had countered. "Arnold does not strike me as the most reliable man."

"All men have their faults," Father Thomas had replied. "Everyone is sinful, but none are beyond redemption."

With more than a few reservations, Stiger had granted the request to detach Arnold from duty, allowing the man to spend additional time with the paladin.

Stiger patted his horse again as Nomad sniffed at the pocket in his cloak, apparently with hopes of finding a hidden treat, perhaps a coveted apple or pear.

"Sorry, old boy," Stiger said with mock sadness. "No more treats today."

Vargus, who was in command of Second Cohort, chuckled in reply to something the paladin said. The centurion was one of the elected members of the Valley Council. The two of them seemed to be getting on grandly, Stiger thought sourly.

Stiger had ordered Vargus to ride with them down into the valley, where his presence hopefully would smooth over any lingering hard feelings. At the very least, Vargus would be able to act as an intermediary. Only a few weeks had passed since Captain Aveeno's reign of terror had come to an end. Aveeno had been corrupted by the dark god Castor, bringing suffering to the people of Vrell through the hands of the garrison. It had led to hard feelings on both sides, as the people of the valley had become hostile. There had even been a few attacks on the legionaries of Aveeno's garrison.

Since Stiger had liberated the valley and restored the Compact, apparently the attitude toward the garrison had completely changed. No matter what Vargus and the other valley officers said now about the feeling of the people of the valley, Stiger was concerned about how he and his men would be received. In Stiger's experience, someone always tended to harbor a grudge. It was better to be safe than sorry, and so Vargus was coming along.

All in all, Stiger reflected taking in the bustling activity in the courtyard, it would be good to get away for a few days, though even the thought of making the trip made him uncomfortable. The Cyphan and their army were encamped just outside the gates. Though the pass was choked with snow and any direct assault seemed unlikely, he was still concerned about something happening during his absence.

"Good morning, sir. Are you excited about getting away for a few days? It should be quite something seeing Thane's Mountain and an abandoned dwarven city."

Stiger turned to find Lieutenant Ikely. Over the last few weeks, his executive officer had shown his mettle in battle and more than proved himself in Stiger's estimation. Ikely had grown from an inexperienced officer to a respected leader of men and, Stiger reflected, a friend.

"Lieutenant," Stiger greeted, rubbing the back of his neck. He had slept poorly and his neck was sore. Funny how he could sleep like a baby in the field, but not in a bed.

"We will be here when you return, sir," Ikely said, clamping his lips together to keep from grinning at his commanding officer, clearly knowing full well that Stiger was discomforted by leaving the defense of the castle in another's hands.

"I know you will," Stiger replied gruffly and with much practiced ease pulled himself up onto Nomad. He shifted position to get comfortable, the hard saddle leather creaking in the cold morning air. Nomad took a couple of eager sidesteps before Stiger took firm hold of the reins and brought the animal under control.

Stiger glanced around the courtyard and up at the walls, where the sentries walked their rounds, ever watchful of the enemy. Though it felt longer, it had been almost three weeks since Stiger and his men had fought their way back to the safety of the castle. Stiger's campaign against the Cyphan had been hard and costly, but it had bought enough time for the first heavy snows to arrive and block the pass. The deep mountain snows made it nearly impossible for the enemy to even contemplate assaulting the walls of Castle Vrell.

It bothered Stiger that he had been forced to fall back before the enemy. Sure, he had been outnumbered, but it still irritated him just the same. He'd had no choice. He could have either delayed the Cyphan for a time and fallen back, or fought and been destroyed.

Now that the bulk of Braddock's army had joined him and was encamped on the valley side of the castle, Stiger was eager to make the Cyphan pay. Braddock, thane of the dwarves, had brought nearly fifteen thousand dwarven warriors. Between the legionaries and the dwarves, there was no doubt in Stiger's mind that together they could defeat the army camped before the castle. Unfortunately, that would have to wait 'til spring, when the snows melted.

There were now more than eighteen thousand on hand to hold the walls against an enemy army of similar size. Stiger understood that any type of action was unlikely, and the enemy did not appear to have any intention of making a move until the weather improved. From what could be observed, the enemy had gone into winter quarters.

Stiger intended to send some scouts over the mountains soon. Eli was training a new set of scouts and evaluating those from the cohorts of the Thirteenth. One of the elves who had come with Taha'Leeth would be remaining behind to oversee their training while Eli was away.

"Should the enemy do anything, send a messenger without delay," Stiger said.

"They will not catch us napping," Ikely assured him, hand resting comfortably upon his sword hilt. "Of that be you can be sure."

"We should have a constant presence on this side of the valley, both mounted and foot patrols. Impress upon the men that they are to venture up and into the trees along the slopes, looking for any sign of the enemy making an attempt to sneak men over the mountains. Though, to be honest, in this miserable weather I rather doubt they would even attempt such an enterprise."

"If we find any evidence of the enemy," Ikely said, "I will dispatch a sufficient number of men to hunt them down and alert you."

"Good," Stiger replied, trying to think of anything else he might have forgotten. He had already gone over this and more with Ikely and Sabinus last evening. He was confident both men would do their jobs. But despite his confidence in them, he couldn't shake the bad feeling he had about leaving.

He glanced up at the steel gray clouds, moving leisurely above the castle walls. It did not seem like a good day for a ride.

"Looks like more snow," Stiger said. If it had not been for Braddock's insistence and Delvaris's scroll, he would not be making this trip into the valley. Stiger's hand involuntarily went to the pocket of his cloak, where the scroll was tucked safely away. To say the contents had disturbed him was an understatement.

"It does, sir," Ikely agreed, glancing upward. "It is a shame Braddock would not consent to a delay of a day or two."

"Better to get it over with in bad weather I suppose," Stiger said. "That way the enemy is unlikely to try anything."

"About Sabinus," Ikely began, clearing his throat. "He technically outranks me."

"You are in command of the castle," Stiger affirmed, looking down on his lieutenant from his horse. Sabinus was the centurion who had arrived leading the First Cohort of the Thirteenth Legion. "He commands the three cohorts from the Thirteenth. You have the garrison and the 85th. You also have Lieutenant Brent to assist you. I expect you and Sabinus to work together. Should the enemy make any kind of move, you have over-all command."

"Yes, sir," Ikely said, straightening up. Stiger could still read the concern and uncertainty in the young officer's eyes. He knew Ikely would eventually outgrow such feelings and develop more confidence when dealing with other officers of equal rank. He had already developed confidence on the battlefield, so now it was only a matter of time and seasoning. This would be a good experience for him.

"I have seen you handle men in a fight," Stiger said, softening and lowering his tone so that only the lieutenant could hear him. "Unfortunately, I have not seen Sabinus in action. You have my trust and my friendship."

Stiger reached down and offered a hand to his lieutenant. Ikely took the firm grip and shook.

"I will see you in four days' time, sir," the lieutenant said, stepping back. "Good travels."

Stiger was the legate now, at least according to Emperor Atticus's letter. All three cohorts from the Thirteenth believed it and Stiger felt compelled to act the part. He straightened up in his saddle and cast one more look down upon his executive officer before he nudged Nomad forward toward Eli. His friend pulled himself up onto Wind Runner's back. Eli's horse was a rare forest breed that was highly prized amongst horse traders for intelligence and sure-footedness, qualities that were a must in the forest.

Eli greeted Stiger with a measured, sidelong glance. Taha'Leeth, her red hair and beauty contrasting starkly against the drab morning, offered Stiger a small, tight smile before returning to a conversation she was having with her companion, one of the two other elves who had recently joined them. It took Stiger a moment to recall his name, Aver'Mons. The elf had arrived with Taha'Leeth and been present when she had tried to influence him with a glamour, a power that all elven females possessed. When he had lived amongst the elves, a few had used their power to twist his heart cruelly until Eli had put a stop to such nonsense.

"I sense you remain conflicted," Eli stated in a low tone, leaning toward his friend. "You must go. We both know that."

"Yes," Stiger replied evenly, with a glance over at the barred gate that led to the Sentinel Forest, where the enemy was camped. He had shared the contents of Delvaris's scroll with Eli and no one else, for Stiger had feared the reaction of others. In fact, Delvaris had warned him not to share it with anyone other than his closest companion. *An elven ranger we both know and love.*

How Delvaris had known his closest friend would be an elf troubled Stiger immensely, and Eli ardently insisted that he had never met Delvaris. It was one of the reasons Stiger was bringing the scroll with him. He did not want anyone to discover it in his absence, as it might raise some very uncomfortable questions.

"You cannot stay," Eli said with conviction. "The scroll makes that much clear. Besides, our new allies would take offense. We cannot afford that."

"All to look at this holy relic called a 'Gate,'" Stiger said quietly, so only Eli could hear. He did not want to offend his allies, who were mere feet away. After Braddock had arrived at the castle, the thane had told him about the World Gate, a doorway to another world. The damn thing apparently did not even work, which was one of the reasons why Stiger had not wanted to go. Only Braddock's determined insistence and Delvaris's letter, along with Eli's prodding, had convinced him to make the trip to Thane's Mountain.

"The dwarves take this very seriously," Eli responded with a reproachful look. "Perhaps it might have been wiser to learn more of the Compact before you tied us to it."

Stiger took note of the tone of disapproval and the gentle rebuke. He could not disagree, but at the time it had seemed necessary. A thought occurred to him.

"This World Gate Braddock keeps speaking of, you have heard of it before now," Stiger demanded, looking at his friend intently. "Haven't you?"

Eli was silent a moment, his eyes deep and unfathomable. Stiger refused to be put off. He returned Eli's timeless gaze in a way that was intended to tell his friend to stop beating around the bush and answer the question.

"Though we thought it lost or perhaps even destroyed," Eli said in a hushed tone, "my people are well aware of its existence."

"It is important then?" Stiger asked.

Eli nodded curtly.

"Then why did you say nothing?"

"I had hoped it was destroyed," Eli said with a shrug. His friend glanced down at the reins he held lightly in his left hand and was silent a moment before looking back up at Stiger. "Though it is difficult to be sure what now lies on the other side . . . " Eli hesitated for a moment, as if he wanted to say something more but had reconsidered. "This Gate, as you have been told by Braddock, leads to other worlds. It is now sealed and cannot be opened. Should it ever be opened, it could lead to much that is evil." Eli paused once again and looked away. When he turned back to Stiger, the look in his eyes was intense. "Then again, it could lead to much that is good."

"Legate," a voice boomed across the courtyard, cutting into their conversation. It was Braddock, who had mounted up. "Would you ride at my side and honor me with your company?"

"Of course," Stiger replied and nudged his horse forward, regretfully leaving Eli behind. He shot his friend a look that said they would resume this conversation later. Eli shrugged in reply.

"Good morning, Thane Braddock."

"Though I be Thane of the Dvergr, Braddock will do," he replied to Stiger. "We stand little on ceremony."

"Instead our cup overflows with passion," Garrack snorted, with no little amount of amusement.

"Very true," Braddock chuckled. He leaned toward Stiger. "My people have much passion when it comes to personal Legend. Honor, if you will. Sometimes we can be a very prickly bunch."

"What happens when honor is seriously affronted amongst individuals?" Stiger asked, suspecting the answer.

"An honor duel is usual result," Garrack answered in his rough common.

"To the death?" Stiger asked and received a nod in reply. "And when honor amongst clans is affronted?"

"A blood feud," Braddock replied unhappily, his mood souring. "Such can lead to war between the clans. I admit, it is a failing amongst my people . . . one that I strive to correct. Even so, I have forbidden such disputes and unpleasantness. All injuries to Legend have been put aside upon my direct edict. We focus on the Compact and destroying the Cyphan." Braddock was silent a moment before waving a hand. "I find such talk tiresome. We have a long ride ahead of us. Shall we proceed?"

Stiger nodded and glanced quickly around the courtyard. Everyone had mounted up. They were looking toward Stiger and Braddock expectantly. It was time.

"Open the gates!" Stiger called to the sentries standing by the internal gates that led to the valley. The sentries stepped forward and struggled for a moment before they were able to release and swing the heavy wooden gates outward.

Watching the gates open into the tunnel that led under the walls and to the valley, Stiger was reminded of all that had occurred over the past few weeks. When he considered everything he had been through, it seemed so surreal. It had begun with Castor's minion, right here in this very castle. Thoughts of the Twisted One and the minion he and Father Thomas had defeated freeing the valley darkened his mood somewhat. Stiger had had more than his fair share of encounters with servants and minions of the dark gods. He prayed that there would be no more.

A legionary horn blared from the battlements, calling to the legionary and dwarven military encampments on the other side of the walls. The muffled sound of a horn replied. This would be the first time Stiger had gone down into the valley proper. He felt a sudden sense of eager anticipation, and with it, his mood lightened considerably. For the next few days, he might even be able to relax, something he had been unable to do for some time.

Lieutenant Lan gave the order to start forward. He led his troop, which rode into the tunnel in a double column. Braddock's personal guard went next, with two of their number remaining to follow closely behind the thane and Stiger. Naggock shot Stiger a sour look before starting down the tunnel. Stiger nudged his horse forward. He, Braddock, and Garrack entered the tunnel together. The rest of the oversized party came after them. The noise inside the confined space of the tunnel was deafening as the metal-shod hooves of the horses clattered and occasionally sparked off of the worn paving stone.

Within seconds they emerged out onto the road, which had been cleared of fresh snow by the prisoners Stiger had taken during his campaign against the Cyphan. Castle Vrell sat directly on the summit of the pass, and the view before them could be described as breathtaking. Stiger could see clear across to the other side of the snow-coated valley, where the tops of the mountains disappeared, swallowed up by the clouds.

For a moment, both he and Braddock slowed their horses to admire the view. The road before them meandered right down into the heart of the valley, where small towns and villages could be seen several thousand feet below. With farms on either side, a small river snaked its course across the northern end of the valley.

"You should see the view from my palace at Garand Kalgore," Braddock said. "It is very far from here, but the city is so high that on a clear day you can see the tops of these very mountains. It is magnificent. One day you will come and see for yourself, yes?"

"I would like that," Stiger said as they continued forward.

Before them, along both sides of the road, a military encampment spread outward from the walls of the castle. A thundering cheer greeted Braddock and Stiger. Dwarves in the thousands lined the road, formed up by unit, cheering themselves hoarse as they took in the sight of their thane, the leader responsible for restoring the Compact. With the high walls of the pass, smoothed and shaped by ancient dwarven hands, the cheering seemed much louder than it otherwise would have been.

"BRADDOCK . . . BRADDOCK!" the dwarves shouted in unison. "BRADDOCK . . . BRADDOCK!"

"Striking," Braddock commented to Stiger with obvious pride, "are they not?"

Stiger had to agree. The dwarves were turned out and neatly assembled in ranks, brilliantly colored clan banners and standards flapping boldly in the cold wind. Officers and clan chiefs stood to the front of their respective commands, each waiting their turn to respectfully greet their thane. They saluted as the party slowly rode by, with Braddock occasionally stopping to introduce a chief or an important officer. All the while, the dwarves in their neatly ordered ranks cheered and chanted madly.

Whenever another dwarf came near, Braddock's personal guard slowed their horses, reining in to pull alongside and closer to their thane. Naggock always remained within spitting distance of the thane, and his eyes more often than not were on Stiger.

Braddock raised his right hand, the one not holding the reins, and waved as they passed by the cheering multitudes. It seemed to Stiger that the thane was in his element, as if such displays were commonplace. He had seen the emperor have a similar effect on the people in Mal'Zeel. Stiger doubted that he could ever be as comfortable with such adulation. He was just a soldier, doing his duty to the empire.

A powerful-looking dwarf, wearing engraved plate armor completed with a richly cut dark green cloak and a greenish dyed horsehair-crested helmet, stomped directly into the road, blocking their path. Naggock snapped a harsh order and two of Braddock's guards used their horses to check the dwarf's path. The thane pulled on his reins, stopping his pony. With a wave, he ordered his personal guard aside.

The dwarf with the green cloak stepped forward and went to a knee before his thane. Braddock said something in his own language and the dwarf returned to his feet. The thane then turned to Stiger and introduced Tyga, Chief of the Rock Breakers.

"I am honored to meet the Legate of the Thirteenth," Tyga said in his own language, which was translated by Braddock. "Your coming has been foretold by the Oracle and long awaited."

"It is my honor to greet you, Tyga, Chief of the Rock Breakers," Stiger replied formally. Tyga, like the other dwarves he had met, looked short, stocky, heavily-muscled, and wider than a man had a right to be. Tyga's long blond beard was neatly and tightly braided with small black bands. His forearms, where they emerged from his armor, were heavily marked. Stiger took this as evidence of years of arms drill. The chief's eyes were a deep, piercing blue that seemed to miss nothing. He moved like a confident warrior, and Stiger instinctively understood that Tyga was one dwarf to be respected.

"I believe I chart my own course and destiny," Stiger added after a brief delay.

Tyga shot Braddock a look upon the thane's translation and then seemed to ask a question of the thane. Braddock chuckled and replied briefly. Eyes narrowing, Tyga cracked a grin at Stiger as he stepped back and out of the road. Braddock nudged his horse forward and they continued on their way.

"What did he say?" Stiger asked, looking curiously on Tyga and his dwarves as they rode by.

"Tyga asked if all humans were so sure of themselves."

"What did you tell him?"

"That you had a right to be," Braddock replied.

A formation of gnomes waited, drawn up in ranks, at the end of the dwarven encampment. None wore armor, but all were armed with small swords that appeared to be a few inches shorter than a legionary's gladius. The gnomes were half the size of a dwarf and twice as skinny. They looked even more similar to one another than the dwarves did, with short, cropped black hair and small, beady, black eyes. Most disturbing to Stiger was that gnomes had no pupils. They all wore simple gray tunics that were belted at the middle. They stood silently and watched as the party passed them by. Braddock made no effort to introduce their leaders.

Stiger estimated that there were at least two thousand of the strange, mean little creatures.

A few days before, Stiger had met one of their leaders, Alagg. Although the gnome had been irascible and seemingly incapable of sitting still for longer than a moment, Stiger had done his best to greet him cordially. Alagg's reply had left Stiger simmering with anger. Braddock had then taken pains to explain that gnomes were incapable of niceties and the proper decorum expected of civilized beings.

"It is best simply to ignore them," Braddock had advised. "Killing them does no good, trust me."

Near as Stiger could tell, the gnomes acted as engineers for the dwarves, though he suspected they were more than that. The little creatures had built several impressive catapults on the castle walls, which had been put to immediate use against the Cyphan.

Within a matter of minutes of the bombardment starting, the enemy host had wrongly thought that they were safe from missile fire, had abandoned their camp and pulled back farther into the trees. They had since relocated their entire camp, which had amused the gnomes greatly.

Only the enemy's sentries, standing watch at the edge of the forest, could now be seen. Accordingly, the gnomes were now hard at work erecting machines they claimed would have even greater range. Stiger had decided that their enthusiasm to wreak destruction upon the enemy made up for their disagreeable dispositions.

The party passed through the dwarven camp and on into the legionary encampment, which had been set up just beyond. It was a traditionally fortified marching camp, complete with gate, walls, towers, and a defensive trench. The road cut right through the encampment, and the party soon found themselves riding into the camp proper. Sabinus had turned out all three cohorts, who were lined up in neat ranks, silently standing to attention. To Stiger's critical eye, they looked damn fine.

Sabinus stood near the middle along the road with several other officers. Standing before First Cohort, he saluted smartly as Stiger and Braddock rode up. These were men of the Thirteenth Legion, the Vanished. They stood in ranks, armor and kit perfectly maintained, unit standards fluttering in the breeze. Stiger was their commander, their legate.

Second and Third Cohorts had been raised and maintained in secret by the residents of the valley, but First Cohort was another matter. Stiger still had difficulty believing all that had been revealed to him. However, he had come to accept that these men had been magically preserved and held in stasis for hundreds of years. They were volunteers, from the entire Thirteenth, who had willingly gone into magical stasis for a time in the distant future when they would be desperately needed. Now was that time.

The remainder of the legion, Stiger had learned, had settled in the valley and intermarried with the locals. The people of the valley had since taken great pains to secretly maintain the two cohorts. For more than three centuries, they had kept the valley safe from external threats. In secret, the residents of the valley honored the Compact, even as the empire had long forgotten its commitments.

First Cohort was an over-strength unit, more than double the size of a normal 480-man cohort. These were veterans from Delvaris's legion. Men who had fought under the general himself. Unlike the modern legions, which were organized into files, those in Delvaris's day were organized into centuries, which were eighty-man units capable of independent action and commanded by a centurion.

Stiger had met a number of the officers from the First and reviewed several of the cohort's centuries. Every man from the First spoke an older, slightly accented version of common. They also spoke the old tongue as if born to it, which Stiger figured they had been. Stiger shook his head slightly, still having some difficulty coming to accept that a dwarven wizard had preserved them in "stasis," as Garrack had called it, for so long a period of time. It was incredible.

Stiger returned Sabinus's salute with a nod and pulled Nomad up short. Braddock continued on, allowing Stiger some privacy with his subordinate. Sabinus stepped forward.

"Do you wish to inspect the men?" the primus pilus of the First asked.

Stiger glanced first at Sabinus, who had asked the question, then around as he briefly considered the offer. After a moment, he shook his head, declining. "We have a long road ahead of us this day."

"Any final orders then, sir?" Sabinus asked.

Stiger felt somewhat uncomfortable in the man's presence. He had initially thought the veteran centurion was measuring the new legate against Stiger's ancestor, perhaps even challenging his ability as a capable military leader. However, after prolonged contact over the last few days, Stiger had begun to suspect there was something more to it than that.

"Nothing more than what was discussed last evening." Nomad took a couple of nervous steps, which Stiger countered by taking the reins sharply in hand.

"As ordered, I will support Lieutenant Ikely," Sabinus affirmed, clearly attempting to set the legate's mind at ease. He stepped back and offered another smart salute. "Until you return then, sir."

Stiger returned the centurion's salute.

"The men look fine," Stiger called loudly to Sabinus, so that many of those nearest would hear. He nudged Nomad forward into a slow walk. "Are they ready to fight?"

In answer, a roar rose up from the ranks as the legionaries cheered, just as the dwarves had. Stiger punched his fist up into the air. The men shouted louder. Stiger was satisfied. If they fought half as well as they looked, he would be even more pleased.

He increased Nomad's pace to a trot and in a few moments had caught up with the thane. Amidst the cheering, a chant began to form. It took a moment for it to catch and then all of the legionaries were shouting madly away.

"DELVARIS . . . DELVARIS!"

Stiger frowned. A chill sped down his back that was not borne of the cold morning air. Did they view him as Delvaris reborn?

"It is not just my people . . . " Braddock glanced sympathetically over at Stiger and shrugged.

Stiger said nothing further as he and Braddock rode out of the fortified encampment and found another camp beyond. Stiger glanced around in amazement at the camp followers. Women and children eagerly lined the road, cheering just as loudly as the men they had followed. Not all were human. Many were dwarven or gnomish.

"And so," Braddock commented with a smile as they left the camps behind and looked at the open road lying before them, "our journey finally begins."

Two

Stiger dismounted, feet crunching in the snow, much of which had been shoveled off the street and piled up against the buildings. At least an inch from the previous evening's snowfall remained. Stiger glanced around the village of Bridgetown, which consisted of ten small, one-story dwellings, a centrally located tavern, and a handful of barns with snow-covered grass thatch roofs that were well maintained. A number of houses had small pasture pens attached and caged hen houses out back. Stiger found the little community appealing in a quiet sort of way.

Braddock and Garrack slid off their ponies. Stiger took a moment to stretch out his back and then looped Nomad's reins around the hitching post before the tavern, which Vargus had recommended as a good place to stop for a short lunch and drink. Braddock handed his reins off to one of his personal guards and gazed around with his hands upon his hips, nodding as he did so.

The residents of the small village cheered madly at their arrival. Judging by the number of horses tied up, people from some of the surrounding villages and towns had traveled to see them. Word had clearly spread about their journey to the abandoned city under Thane's Mountain, known to the dwarves as Old City. Braddock seemed to be enjoying himself immensely, though the display of public adoration left Stiger feeling awkward. Motivating soldiers was one thing; civilians were another and, as such, reserved for politicians.

The tavern keeper, holding aside the door, bowed low as Braddock stumped by and inside. The thane's personal guard had already searched the humble establishment and had positioned themselves at strategic locations around the tavern. Garrack followed his thane inside, but not before saying something to Naggock, who stood outside by the door.

Stiger pulled his pipe and a small pouch with some tobacco from one of his saddlebags. He tucked both in his cloak pocket and then looked around. He found Lan a few feet away. The lieutenant had dismounted and secured his horse to a post. Marcus was doing the same for his horse next to the lieutenant. Stiger called Lan over to him.

"Lieutenant, make sure the men eat their rations. They are not to go exploring the town."

"You think these people are hostile towards us, sir?" Lan asked, glancing around at the cheering mob. "They certainly don't appear threatening."

"I do not wish to take the chance that someone is nursing a grievance," Stiger replied, glancing around for Vargus. The column stretched out and around the side of the tavern. He could not see the centurion and wondered where he was. The streets were narrow, made more so by the people crowding around. Stiger could not see Eli either. "Keep the men close together and under control. No games of chance, fraternizing, or drinking. Find Vargus and send him to me."

"Yes, sir," Lan replied with a salute. "I will see to it."

Eli rounded a corner, weaving his way slowly between horses and people. He rode up to Stiger and dismounted smoothly. The elf grinned with a closed-mouth smile as he tied Wind Runner up to the hitching post.

"No doubt you find all this terribly amusing," Stiger said.

"I find it refreshing."

"How so?" Stiger crossed his arms suspiciously.

"They are not trying to kill us," Eli said. "It wasn't too long ago that any civilian we ran into in the north would attempt to kill us given the chance. Yes, I would say this is a definite improvement."

Declining to take the bait, Stiger gave Eli a flat look before rolling his eyes and turning away. He made his way into the tavern, nodding to Naggock as he passed by. The dwarf shot him a look that could curdle old milk, but did nothing to bar his way.

Stiger found Braddock and Garrack inside, both seated with jugs before them. Eli followed. They cleaned their boots on the scraper by the door and hung their cloaks on pegs. Stiger removed his riding gloves, tucked them beneath his armor, and surveyed the interior.

The tavern was a small affair, barely large enough for the five tables that crowded the common room. A small fireplace with a low-burning fire provided some warmth. There was no bar at which locals could sit and be served, only a closed door that presumably led to the kitchen. The door opened slightly and a pair of children peered curiously out, only to be shooed back by a plump middle-aged woman Stiger took to be the proprietor's wife.

The jugs the dwarves had been given were usually used for pouring instead of drinking. The thane called on Stiger and Eli to join them. They took a seat across the table from the two dwarves on a single well-worn wooden bench, which scraped along the floor as Stiger pulled it out.

"A fine place, this," Braddock commented. "You have no idea how long it has been since I've been in a good drinking establishment."

"Yes," Garrack grunted, taking a pull from his drink. "Journey to Vrell was long."

"When I was but a youth, my father brought me to this valley," Braddock commented wistfully and fell silent for a moment, as if he were reliving a fond memory. "Back then, there were not nearly so many humans living here. It has been eye-opening to see the change."

The tavern keeper emerged from the kitchen with two plates and a hunk of venison on an old, dull, metal platter. He set them down before Braddock and Garrack and then looked over at Stiger and Eli. He was a large man in his middling years, beginning to go soft around the belly. His nose had the look of having been broken multiple times and was slightly mashed off center to the right. He wore a badly stained and well-used apron over a gray tunic and coarse brown pants, no doubt worn only in cold weather. Stiger noted the man's arms were scarred and heavily marked. He had the manner and look of a retired veteran.

"Two jars of ale for the legate and his elven friend," Braddock ordered. The tavern keeper shuffled back a step when he realized that Eli was not human. Quite accustomed to such reactions, Eli paid him no mind.

"The legate?" the tavern keeper then whispered, eyes widening as he turned his attention to Stiger. "Then it is really true? You are the legate?"

"He is," Braddock boomed heartily, using his dagger to cut off some meat. "Before you sits the descendent of Delvaris."

"Sir." The tavern keeper straightened up into a position of near attention. "Legionary Malik, Second Cohort, retired these past eight years, sir. It is my deepest honor to serve you."

Eli shot Stiger an extremely amused smirk, but thankfully said nothing.

"Thank you, Legionary Malik," Stiger replied, shifting slightly on the bench. "You have a fine establishment here."

"I will bring you ale," Malik replied, puffing up at the compliment. He headed off, limping slightly into the kitchen and closing the door behind him.

"Treat you as a god," Garrack said, taking a heavy pull from his jug of ale and wiping his lips with the back of his forearm. Ale dribbled down into his beard. It did not seem to bother him any.

"I am but a man," Stiger replied evenly. "I have no wish to be hailed as a god."

"I should think not," Braddock said thoughtfully. "Such behavior would be unseemly. You are the legate of the Thirteenth and restorer of the Compact. For that you should be hailed."

"That may be so," Stiger growled, not liking the direction the conversation was taking. "But I am still a man."

Taking a bite of meat from his knife, Braddock eyed Stiger speculatively for a moment before nodding in agreement. "You are a man, if an uncommon one at that."

Malik returned with two smaller glass jars of heated ale, which he set before Stiger and Eli. He looked over at the rapidly dwindling meat, which the dwarves were heartily tearing into. "I will bring you both some meat. We also have some spiced potatoes, dried grapes, and fresh bread. Unfortunately, there is no butter."

"That will be acceptable," Stiger said and then hesitated. "Do you have an apple? I promised my horse one."

"I have some jarred fall apples," Malik replied. "Will that do?"

"Yes," Stiger said, somewhat pleased. "Nomad is not a very discriminating eater."

The tavern keeper left them, hesitating at the door to eye his four patrons before disappearing into the kitchen. The door banged closed behind him.

Stiger took a pull of his heated ale. He was parched from the ride and chilled. The warmth was welcome. It was also quite tasty. He noted pleasantly the ale was not the watered down swill you might find in other establishments outside of the valley.

"Old City is under Thane's Mountain?" Eli asked, eyeing the dwarves. He had not yet touched his drink. "We have an old map showing a road leading into the mountains. I take it the road leads to the city?"

"The road no longer exists," Braddock answered, chewing as he did so and talking out of the side of his mouth. "It used to travel to the mountain. The forest has long since reclaimed it."

"This Gate," Stiger said, eyeing Eli a moment, recalling their earlier conversation back at the castle. "It is the prize, is it not? It is the reason the Compact was formed?"

"Yes," Garrack answered, setting down his jug. "Gate is greatest prize of all, though very dangerous."

"That is an understatement," Braddock said.

"Yes," Eli confirmed quietly, looking over at his friend.

"The Dvergr race," Braddock said, "is not native to this world."

"What?" Stiger asked, looking between Braddock and Eli. "What do you mean not native to this world?"

"Though we now call this world our home," Braddock continued, "our home world, Thas'Goran, is many Gates' and worlds' distant. You see, this world once had two Gates.

Sadly, the one my people came through was destroyed. There is no going home for my people . . . ever."

"You are saying that there are many other worlds then?" Stiger's head spun at the thought. Though some faiths taught that there were worlds beyond counting in the heavens, Stiger had never truly believed. Until now, he had found such concepts preposterous. The heavens were beyond the reach of men.

"Yes," Braddock affirmed.

"Then the priests of Bhallen are right?"

"That is a name I've not heard in a great long time," Braddock said, leaning back. "Bhallen, the lesser god to Antigus?"

"Who?" Stiger asked, looking over at Eli in question. His friend shrugged.

"It matters little," Braddock replied with a negligent wave of his hand. "My people have long memories and honor all friendly gods."

"My thane," Garrack interrupted and spoke for a bit in his own language to Braddock.

Braddock nodded and replied.

"He says that humans have short collective memories," Eli translated for Stiger, reminding him that his friend had learned the language of the dwarves. Stiger considered that, should time permit, it might not be a bad idea for him to learn their language as well. When the snows melted and it came time to fight, knowing the dwarven language could prove critical.

"You speak our language?" Braddock asked of Eli, leaning closer. He received a nod in reply.

"You have met others of our race?" Braddock pressed with a grave expression.

"I have not been personally introduced," Eli replied. "However, I was present, as a child, when emissaries from your people were presented to the Elantric Warden."

The two dwarves began speaking excitedly in their own language.

"Unfortunately," Eli said to them, clearly following what they were saying, "I do not know where their lands reside. You must understand, it was very long ago, perhaps seven hundred years."

"It is still good to hear," Braddock said. "We have lost contact with the clans that went north. It had always been our hope that they found a home and prospered. When this unpleasantness is over, we will send a delegation to the Warden. Surely she would know where our brothers and sisters reside."

"I believe that very possible," Eli replied.

Braddock was silent a moment before turning back to Stiger. "Sadly, your people have forgotten much."

Stiger could not disagree.

"Though humans came to this world long ago, your people arrived more recently," Braddock continued.

"My people?" Stiger asked. "What do you mean?"

"Your people . . . not humans of this world already here . . . legion humans came to this world just before World Gate was closed," Garrack said, struggling with his common. "Helped us hold long enough to close World Gate."

"Yes," Braddock said, getting a faraway look in his eyes. "Your people worked with mine to end the war, at least on this world. Our two peoples fought side by side, holding off the Horde long enough for the Gate to be shut and sealed. Human legionaries stood shoulder-to-shoulder with those of the Bloody Axe. It was a magnificent and heroic stand."

"Surely," Stiger said, having difficulty accepting the tale, "there would have been some record of this, some history that my people would have remembered?"

Braddock said nothing, but looked to Eli as he took another pull from his jug.

"If I recall," Eli said, speaking up and looking over at Stiger, "you people venerate the founders of your empire?"

"Yes," Stiger admitted, wondering where Eli was going with this. "But that is nothing more than legend, no better than mythology."

"Is it?" Eli asked, raising a thin eyebrow curiously. "Is it truly?"

Stiger sat back, sucking in a breath. He placed his drink down on the table and was silent for a few moments as he considered his friend. "Surely you do not mean to say Rome is real? Romulus and Remus were real?"

"You are children of Rome." Braddock ran a hand through his beard. "Hohhak the Historian recorded the story of the last days of Tanis and the sealing of the Gate. In his great work, he tells some of the history of the legion of Rome that fought at our side. If you like, I can have the history translated for you?"

"Rome is real?" Stiger could not believe what he was hearing. With everything else he had learned in the last few weeks, he felt that this should not surprise him, and yet it did. The news rocked him. As a child, like every other, he had learned the story of Romulus and Remus and the place from whence they came . . . Rome. Here for the first time was a real connection to the myth and legend. They were suggesting—no, insisting—that Rome was real. It was incredible . . . almost unbelievable.

"Yes," Eli said softly. "When the World Gate was sealed, your people, unable to return home, settled with some of the other humans of this world. Soon after, they began to build their own empire based upon the one they knew, Rome."

"How long ago was this?" Stiger asked, wondering why Eli, in all of the years they had spent together, had never spoken of this before. They would definitely be speaking on this later.

"Over two thousand years have passed since the World Gate was sealed," Braddock replied in a grave manner. "We are fast approaching the day when it can be unsealed and the Way made open. That is what we must keep from happening. That is the true purpose of the Compact and our alliance."

Malik returned with two plates of steaming venison, dried grapes, and a loaf of bread. One of his children was holding a plate of spiced potatoes. Malik placed them before Stiger and Eli. He then returned to the kitchen, ushering his child before him. Stiger took the opportunity to remain silent as he absorbed what had just been imparted and considered what he would say next.

The door banged open and with it cold air poured into the common room. Vargus entered, along with Father Thomas. They quickly closed the door. Father Thomas hung his heavy cloak on a peg and moved over to a table near the fire.

"Sir, you asked to see me?" Vargus said, coming up.

Stiger had nearly forgotten that he had requested the centurion's presence. He eyed Vargus for a moment, then nodded.

"Join us."

Vargus hung his red cloak next to the others. He took a seat at an adjacent table, pulling his gloves off as he did so and laying them on the table with a nonchalant attitude.

Vargus smiled politely, but not genuinely, as he looked over at the legate.

"You know of this Gate?" Stiger asked of him bluntly.

"Of course," Vargus replied. "It is why the Thirteenth is here."

"And you did not feel the need to mention it?"

"I am sorry, sir." Vargus's eyebrows drew together. "I thought you already knew."

"The empire has garrisoned this valley for years," Stiger said, taking another direction to his questioning. "Why not come out and announce who you are? Why keep your presence a secret?"

"Orders, sir," Vargus replied. "We were only to reveal ourselves when the conditions were right. General Delvaris left specific instructions. You fulfilled those conditions. That was why the Tomb of the Thirteenth was unsealed and the valley cohorts were free to come forward."

"Some things are best forgotten until they are needed," Father Thomas spoke up.

"You too?" Stiger asked, eyeing the paladin sharply.

Father Thomas simply returned Stiger's look, but offered up no more.

"What of your people?" Stiger asked Eli. "Are they part of the Compact too?"

"No," Braddock spat angrily, before Eli could manage a reply. "His people are not. They hid in their forests and did nothing whilst our two peoples bled and died."

"Is that true?" Stiger asked, looking over at his friend. Why was he finding this out from others?

"My people stood apart," Eli said with some hesitation, meeting Stiger's gaze. "We have our reasons, though I stand with you now."

Stiger felt irritated at Eli's response. He eyed his friend a moment and looked back to Braddock. Tonight, when the time permitted and they were alone, he would speak frankly with Eli. It was time his friend answered some hard questions.

"So, there is another enemy beyond the Gate?" Stiger asked. "On the other side, another world like our own? This Horde?"

"Yes," Braddock answered. "That world is called Tanis. When the World Gate was sealed, Tanis was overrun."

"Castor and the Cyphan, they know it is here and they want to open it."

"That would be a good assumption," Braddock said. "It is why we defend the valley. It is the heart of the Compact. The Gate must never again be opened. The Way must stay blocked."

Stiger glanced down at the table. The pieces of the puzzle were coming together and he did not at all like the picture that was emerging. He looked up and over at Eli, who was enigmatic as could be, before turning back to Braddock.

"Then my people can never go home?" Stiger said, feeling somewhat disappointed. To see Rome, a city he had until recently thought only a place in legend and mythology, would be one fantastic journey.

"Home, you say?" Braddock said with a scowl. "Neither can mine. This world, what your people call Istros and mine Istria, is our home now."

"Is home now for both our peoples," Garrack said, pointing a thick finger at Stiger. "We fight Last War for our home and future."

"Malik, old boy." Vargus grinned as the tavern keeper returned, limping back into the room with a large, fresh pitcher of heated ale.

"Vargus," Malik exclaimed with a pleased smile. "It's been too long. You should visit more often."

"Do you have any of that good wine your brother makes?"

"I do," Malik said as he refilled drinks. "I have some warming now. I will get you a jar."

"Bring some for Father Thomas too," Vargus replied, turning to the paladin. "I am confident you will find it very satisfying. We make exceptional wine here in the valley."

"I have already become quite fond of your wine," the paladin said and then directed himself to Malik. "Some mulled wine would be heavenly, my son."

Malik retreated and returned shortly with two small jars of heated wine, which he placed before Vargus and Father Thomas. The tavern keeper quickly retreated back to the kitchen, the door banging behind him.

"Malik is a good man, sir," Vargus informed Stiger. "He was one tough legionary. Took a crippling wound clearing out some of the lesser races."

"Lesser races?" Stiger asked. He had heard Braddock mention the lesser races before.

"Enough talk such as this," Braddock announced, holding up his jug. "I propose a toast. Together we will crush those Cyphan dogs!"

Stiger lifted his jar along with everyone else and took a sip.

"We see Gate," Garrack said. "Then crush Cyphan into dust, salt fields, raze cities, and piss on graves."

"My pioneers should already be hard at work cutting the enemy's supply," Braddock said with an evil grin.

Stiger set his drink down on the table. "Your pioneers? What do you mean?"

"I dispatched some of our finest pioneers shortly after we met," Braddock explained. "The road to Vrell is long. My boys should have already begun hitting the enemy's supply line."

"It is long road." Garrack grinned with agreement. "Cyphan army will begin to go hungry soon."

"How?" Stiger asked, wondering how the dwarves got out of the valley. Had they gone over the mountains?

"Old City was a great mining center," Braddock explained, taking another drink from his jug. "These mountains once ran rich with ore. Now they are mostly tapped out, but the mines and tunnels remain. The enemy believes falsely that Grata'Kor is the only way in or out of the valley. In a few weeks, when they are hungry, together we will strike."

"You should have consulted me." Stiger became angry. Braddock had planned everything out without him. If Braddock could send a force out, the enemy could send one in the same way.

"I am thane!" Braddock roared. "I do as I wish."

"And I am your ally," Stiger replied quietly.

Braddock took a deep breath, meeting Stiger's gaze. After a moment he nodded, conceding the point. "Yes, we are allies."

"The enemy could use the same tunnels?" Stiger asked with no small amount of concern.

"Unlikely," Braddock said. "They are known only to dwarves and very difficult to find."

"Even if Cyphan find," Garrack added, "is confusing maze, not know way to go."

"They come out deep into the forest, well away from the road," Braddock assured him. "My people have hidden the entrances well. They are impossible to locate."

"Like by the monument to the Thirteenth?" Stiger asked.

"Yes," Garrack said. "Tunnels are hidden. Our warriors patrol."

"Are there any that lead into Castle Vrell?" Eli asked. Stiger found he was keen on learning the answer to that question.

"Yes," came the response from Garrack, after a moment's hesitation.

"Will you show us the tunnels?" Stiger asked, eyes narrowing. "They will need to be patrolled and guarded carefully." Garrack looked to Braddock.

"They are already patrolled by warriors from my clan," Braddock stated, as if that were the end of the matter. "There is no need for your concern."

Stiger's anger mounted once again. Eli shot him a warning glance that spoke volumes. Stiger disregarded it. His new allies were not as forthcoming as he felt they should be. The empire and dwarven nation were equal partners in this venture. If he did not stand up for himself now, Braddock would see the humans as the inferior party, and Stiger forever after would be dealing from a position of weakness. The issue needed to be pressed to its fullest.

"When were you going to tell me about them?" Stiger asked, looking directly at Braddock.

Braddock said nothing at first, but returned Stiger's gaze with equanimity. The thane slowly took another drink, set the jug carefully down, and leaned back on the bench, which creaked loudly.

"We were not," Braddock admitted, a hand coming up to stroke his neatly braided beard. Garrack looked over at his thane with a warning glance. Braddock did not seem to notice. "No one but my fellow dwarves knows of the tunnels."

"How can we be allies if we cannot trust one another?" Stiger asked bluntly, pointing an accusatory finger at Braddock.

"It has nothing to do with trust," Braddock replied.

"That was how you were planning on retaking the castle, wasn't it?" Stiger felt the pieces of the puzzle coming together one after another.

"It was," Braddock said and then leaned forward toward Stiger, resting a heavy elbow on the tabletop, gaze intense. "We came before your people and claimed this land as our own. No matter how long humans have lived in this valley or squatted in Grata'Kor, this land is still ours. Never forget that."

Stiger leaned forward also, anger becoming hot rage. Eli placed a warning hand upon Stiger's forearm, but he angrily shook it off and directed his full attention on the thane. "My mistake then. I thought we were equal partners in this enterprise you call the Compact. You don't need us."

Braddock hissed, looking over at Garrack in outrage. Clearly the thane was not accustomed to being spoken to in such a way.

"Legate!" Vargus exclaimed in alarm. "They are our—"

"Hold your tongue, centurion," Stiger snapped, not bothering to look over at Vargus. His entire attention was fixed upon Braddock. "If this alliance is to have a chance, the thane and I need an understanding."

Braddock turned back. Stiger could read the wrath and anger in the dwarf's eyes. The thane's free hand clenched and unclenched.

Garrack unexpectedly burst out laughing. It was a deep belly laugh, which exploded into the silence of the small common room. Both Braddock and Stiger almost jumped.

"What is so funny?" Braddock demanded with an irritated look.

It took the other dwarf a moment to bring himself under control. Garrack said something in his own language, stifling another laugh as he did so. Braddock at first looked shocked, then glanced over at Stiger and then back to Garrack before his expression cracked. A smile appeared.

"What did he say?" Stiger asked.

"I never thought to meet another as determined, hard-headed, and difficult," Garrack translated. "With you both . . . leading alliance . . . enemies stand no chance."

Braddock began to laugh as well and soon both dwarves were roaring away, speaking in their own language. The thane thumped Garrack on the back.

"He is right, you know," Eli said with no little amount of amusement. "You are determined, hard-headed, and difficult, even for a human. There are times you have the will of a boulder. You can be quite unmovable when you desire to be."

The dwarves laughed even harder at that. Stiger shot Eli a sour look.

Braddock pounded the table with much amusement. The thane wagged a finger in Stiger's direction, then raised his jug of ale. "I think we should drink to our mutual obstinate nature and the destruction of our enemies."

Stiger cracked a smile, finally becoming faintly amused. It was hard to stay angry when the other party was dying with fits of laughter. Besides, Stiger understood the truth. He was a difficult person and so was the thane. In an odd sort of way, he felt a kinship to the dwarf.

"To difficult people!" Stiger said, raising his own jar.

"To the destruction of our enemy!" Braddock roared. "May we both one day piss on their graves."

Everyone in the tavern drank.

"To allies!" Garrack roared, holding his jug up.

Everyone drank once again.

"Tavern keeper!" Braddock suddenly roared. "More ale!"

Malik appeared in a hurry with the large pitcher of ale. He set about refilling his customers' drinks and then hastily retreated to the kitchen.

"One more," Braddock said standing. "I salute our alliance, for it is made of equal parts."

Stiger looked up at the thane before standing himself. Everyone else stood with him.

"I also salute our alliance, for together we will grind the bones of our enemies into the dust."

Braddock nodded at that, and together they both drank deeply. Braddock wiped his lips with the back of his forearm. He set down his jug hard on the table and offered his hand to Stiger, which was accepted. The dwarf's large hand swallowed his own.

"Eat." Braddock pointed to Stiger's untouched food. "We have a lot to see and do today, for as my father once opened my eyes by showing me the World Gate, I too shall do the same for you."

He stomped out of the tavern, grabbing his cloak on the way out. Stiger watched the thane go, thinking on what Braddock had just said.

Garrack stepped around the table, punching Stiger gently on the arm as he stepped by, a grin visible through his thickly braided beard. "When we get back to Grata'Kor, I show you tunnels myself. Good?"

Stiger nodded, and with that, Garrack followed his thane out of the tavern.

"Well!" Father Thomas exclaimed. "And here I thought tangling with the minion of Castor was exciting. It is never dull around you, is it?"

"Never," Eli said with an amused look.

Stiger rolled his eyes and, without saying anything further, sat down. He took out his knife and began carving up the now cold meat. Eli sat as well, as did Father Thomas and Vargus. Malik brought out food for the other two and together they ate in silence, Stiger thinking on his alliance with the dwarven thane. He wondered whether or not he could fully trust his new allies. Stiger supposed that only time would tell.

Twenty-five minutes later, the party rode out of the village and onto the snow-packed road that led toward the extreme northern end of the valley. Taha'Leeth pulled her horse up alongside Stiger as they passed the last of the cheering people. She cast a look his way, as if she wanted to say something, but there was a hesitation in her manner.

"Yes?" Stiger asked as he negotiated Nomad around an extraordinarily large slush-filled pothole on his side of the road.

"They . . . " she began in elven and then stopped, switching to common. Taha'Leeth shot a glance behind them. "Those people, they adore you."

This elicited a frown from Stiger, who, having passed around the pothole, pulled his horse back next to hers. Stiger took a moment to consider his response before he spoke.

"No," he said with a hard look. "They do not love me."

"They cheer for you, no?" she said. "This is the same thing, is it not? They treat you as a conquering hero."

"No," Stiger said with an unhappy look. "They do not."

"I do not understand," she said, eying him carefully.

Stiger returned Taha'Leeth's gaze and found her eyes, for some reason he could not name, extremely sad. Her fiery red hair was a marked contrast to the snow-covered countryside around them. She was by far the most beautiful woman he had ever seen.

Stiger had found that most elves had eyes that seemed to dance with barely concealed amusement and mischief.

Hers, on the other hand, were not only deep, but hard. Yes, Stiger thought to himself, there is a terrible sadness there, mixed with a steely resolve. Now that he thought on it, Aver'Mons also had a grim hardness to him that matched hers. Taha'Leeth's people, until recently, had been slaves of the Cyphan. Stiger had difficulty imagining what it must have been like for such a proud people as the High Born to have been brought so low. How much had she suffered?

"I have seen a Cyphan general cheered the same way," she said, and Stiger suddenly realized that he had remained silent as he studied her.

"It is not like that," Stiger said with a heavy sigh. "Though they think they do, those people do not cheer me."

She frowned but said nothing in reply, waiting for Stiger to continue.

"They cheer an ideal," Stiger said, his voice growing cold. "They cheer the ideal my ancestor and the dwarven Oracle set for me."

"Not the fulfillment of your Compact?" She raised a delicate eyebrow at him.

"That too," Stiger said, with a trace of a frown. He did not feel like saying more and so he remained silent. They said nothing further for several minutes as their horses plodded along.

"Are you Delvaris reborn?" she asked him plainly, her look, though doubtful, was clearly curious. Had it been Eli asking, Stiger would have suspected that the question was meant to tease and poke fun at him. Taha'Leeth, on the other hand, was looking for an answer. She was serious, grave even.

"No," Stiger said, scratching at his jaw. "I am simply me, nothing more, nothing less."

"I see," she said, contemplating him with a sidelong look. "You do not wish to be treated so?"

"No," Stiger replied, feeling weary of the conversation. "I most certainly do not."

"You do not wish to be a great man?"

Her last question caught Stiger completely by surprise. He pulled up on the reins of his horse, bringing Nomad to a halt. She stopped her horse also. Those behind were forced to ride around the two. Eli gave both of them a quizzical look as he passed them by, but thankfully said nothing.

"I just want to be me," Stiger said as he regarded her, and he meant it with the entire force of his being. It was important to him that she understood. "I desire to serve both my family and empire faithfully." Stiger paused and then added, "I asked for none of this."

"And yet," she said, the sadness in her deep eyes seeming to creep into her voice, "here you are, the hope of your people."

"Yes," Stiger said bitterly and nudged Nomad back into a walk. "It seems that I am."

Starting her horse forward, she matched Stiger's pace.

"You make choices you think best serve your family and empire?" she asked, an intense look in her eyes.

"Yes," Stiger responded, wondering what she was getting at. "I do. Though we will have to see what comes of those I've already made. I have no idea how they will play out. I do what I can and hope everything will work out . . . It usually does."

"There is greatness in your actions," she said, and pulled in a deep, almost shuddering breath. "Though I at first doubted it, I feel it. I truly do." She nudged her horse into a trot and left Stiger behind, watching her as she caught up to Aver'Mons, who rode just ahead. She said something to him and he glanced back in Stiger's direction. It was not a friendly look.

"Elves," Stiger muttered to himself and continued on.

Just beyond the village, they came to a bridge that forded a small, fast-moving river, which they had seen from above earlier in the morning. The bridge was wooden and barely wide enough for a wagon. Due to the snow and ice, they dismounted and walked across.

Thankful for the bridge, Stiger glanced down over the side and into the water below as he crossed. He judged the depth to be around four feet, likely the result of years of silt buildup around the pylons. The fast-moving water was crystal clear, and he could see right down to the rocks littering the bottom. But from the looks of it, the depth increased dramatically just a few feet out.

Once beyond the bridge, the road climbed a short way to a low ridgeline. The ridge extended outward in both directions for a least a quarter mile before curving back toward the river's edge. Near the summit of the rise, Stiger pulled Nomad to a stop.

A strange feeling had come over him. He felt like he had been here before, in this very spot. Stiger rubbed his jaw and tried to shake the feeling off, to no avail. Perhaps, he considered, it just reminded him of a place he had been in the north? Glancing around, Stiger's military mind recognized the defensive nature of this ground, especially if an army was contesting a river crossing. The feeling of having been here before became much more acute, growing stronger. He could almost visualize defenses lining the top of the ridgeline. After a moment, he snapped his fingers. Yes, he decided, this reminded him of his first battle. As a lieutenant, his legion had been tasked with securing a river crossing and fighting up a similar ridge. It had been bloody going, but they had done it and pushed the Rivan out of their defensive position.

"What is it?" Eli asked, wheeling his horse around and walking Wind Runner back to Stiger. As usual, his friend had sensed something was not quite right with Stiger. Taha'Leeth and Aver'Mons rode by. She gave him an odd, almost knowing look as she passed, her horse kicking up snow with each step. When Stiger had lived amongst the elves, he had learned their females were surprisingly perceptive. Some had even been reputed to read the emotions of others. Had she sensed his troubled thoughts, or was it something else?

"Nothing," Stiger replied and nudged Nomad into a walk, desiring to avoid discussion on the subject. Stiger's first battle had occurred before the two of them had met, and Stiger wanted to put it behind him, leaving it in the past where it belonged.

Braddock and Garrack were reaching the top of the rise as Stiger started forward once again. The thane pulled his pony alongside.

"This is where it happened," Braddock said, gesturing about with one hand while holding the reins with the other.

"What happened?" Stiger asked, looking over at the thane with a hooded expression.

"This ridge is where Delvaris made his stand with the Thirteenth," Braddock explained. "He fought here in defense of the Compact and held it long enough for my father's army to arrive."

Glancing around, Stiger recalled the vision the sword had shown him, of a mortally wounded Delvaris confronting a minion of Castor. The vision had helped Stiger and Father Thomas defeat the minion they had faced. The sword had also spoken to him, as if it were alive. The chill that ran down his back returned. He shivered slightly, glancing around with understanding. He was looking upon a battlefield, and it no longer felt or reminded him of his first battle. Stiger glanced down at Delvaris's magical sword. Was it the vision the sword had shown him that made this place seem familiar? Or was it something else?

Uncomfortable with such thoughts, he increased Nomad's pace, intent on leaving the ancient battlefield behind.

Yes, the sword hissed in his mind and Stiger nearly jumped in his saddle. *Remember this place . . .*

THREE

The dwarves led the party toward the northern end of the valley. They passed through several more villages, where the locals turned out to greet them just as enthusiastically as those in Bridgetown had. Some older men even dressed themselves in ill-fitting legionary kit that they had used in their youth. These stood to attention as best they could and saluted Stiger. He offered them a respectful nod. More than a few shed tears at his passing or seemed overcome with feeling. They cheered him with Delvaris's name.

Stiger did not feel worthy of such attention. That was what bothered him. That and they viewed him as Delvaris reborn. Stiger was being treated as a returning hero and yet he had done nothing to deserve their adoration other than being selected by fortune and birth to restore the Compact.

"They have long awaited your coming," Vargus informed him. "You are more than just the legate. To my people you are a symbol that their faith in remaining vigilant mattered."

"How do you feel about that?" Stiger asked of him, somewhat sour after they had ridden through another village.

"The gods in their wisdom foretold of your coming," Vargus answered. He looked over at the legate with a level look. "But I think you are just a man, like any other. The gods have simply favored you more than most."

Stiger returned Vargus's look before facing front. He was silent for a time as he considered the man's words. Truth be told, Stiger felt as if he had become caught up in something greater than himself. He was not sure that was such a good thing. All he wanted was to be a soldier of the empire and serve with honor. He felt trapped, deeply ensnared in a strange prophecy he did not yet fully understand. Worse, his actions would have a serious impact upon the empire he served and loved. That could very well end poorly for him.

Should the emperor not support the decisions he had made, his family line could come to a premature end. By tying himself to the Compact, he had already bound the empire to the dwarves and, in that alliance, his own family's fate. Besides service to the empire, family honor was everything to an imperial noble. The thought worried him more than he cared to admit. Stiger's family was an old one. He could trace his roots back to the founding of the empire. Old or not, he feared it would not be enough to counter the emperor's wrath.

Stiger's only consolation was the scroll from Emperor Atticus. The empire already had a long-standing treaty with the dwarven nations. Stiger had only reinforced it. It was some comfort, but he was unsure how it would all play out. He took a deep breath and ran his hand through Nomad's mane. With the events of the past few weeks, he found he could no longer deny that the gods had plans of their own for him. No matter the potential costs to his family, he would just have to do what he considered to be in the best interests of the empire and hope for the best. Gritting his teeth, he resolved to do just that.

"You are correct, centurion," Stiger replied, sparing Vargus a grim smile. "I am but a man."

Vargus looked over at his legate, but said nothing further. Stiger returned the centurion's gaze until the large man looked away to maneuver his horse around a deep rut in the road.

He was but a man.

Stiger looked ahead toward the northern end of the valley. Snowcapped mountains rose above the tree line. Thane's Mountain towered above them all like an older brother. Sourly, Stiger wondered what additional surprises waited for him there.

The road soon became little more than a logging track after they passed through the last of the settlements. It took them up from the base of the valley to the hills, and then to the slopes of the mountain and into the tree line. Stiger found it odd how the hills on this side of the valley were not cultivated for vineyards or grazing.

He was not a farmer, but he suspected it had something to do with the shade. Thane's Mountain towered over them, casting its imposing shadow across this part of the valley, and it was only early afternoon. He realized it must block the sun for a good portion of the day, though perhaps, he thought, watching the dwarves ride just ahead, the real reason was that the dwarves had prohibited cultivation here.

In the shade of the mountain, without the sun to provide some warmth, the cold intensified with the elevation. The track climbed steeply, which soon became no more than a path, barely distinguishable from a game trail. As the trees and brush closed in, they were forced to dismount and walk their horses in single file, one behind the other. Eli for once stayed with the party and did not wander off into the woods, though Stiger suspected he badly desired to do so. Eli led

Wind Runner right behind Nomad and Stiger. Taha'Leeth, Aver'Mons, and Marcus were somewhere to the rear. Braddock and his dwarves, knowing the way, led the party onward.

The pace was a good one, and Stiger found himself perspiring, even as the biting wind blew around him, rustling the brush and stirring the leafless limbs above. Father Thomas walked his horse just behind Eli and after him came Sergeant Arnold. Thomas and Arnold were involved in a deep discussion on the meaning of a particular passage in the High Father's holy book. Arnold and the paladin had been discussing it for the last forty minutes. Arnold was struggling to fully grasp the meaning, but by this point, even Stiger had a position on the gist of the passage. The discourse reminded Stiger of his youth and time spent before the family tutors. His tutors had droned on and on without letup for hours at a time. When the young Stiger had drowsed, they had awoken him painfully with a reed switch. Those were not particularly fond memories.

Feet crunching in the churned-up snow, Stiger had heard more than enough on the good book for one day. He wished the trooper walking his horse directly ahead would move a little faster. For a moment, Stiger considered ordering the man to stand aside so he could pass, but then changed his mind. Listening to a little prattle on the High Father's good word wouldn't kill him. Besides, Eli might suspect his real motivations for ordering the legionary aside and find it somewhat amusing. When Eli found something funny, he would inevitably revisit such moments, usually at an inconvenient time. Stiger had no intention of indulging his friend's sense of humor and so he continued on, careful to let no hint of irritation show.

The trail they had been following opened up to a long, wide, peaceful-looking meadow that was covered in untouched snow. To the left and right, for over a mile in either direction, the trees stretched outward in a near-perfect line. The meadow reached forward from the trees, rising every thirty paces in a gentle grade to what looked like a series of natural shelves or terraces, with each one slightly higher than the last. The meadow ended abruptly at a sheer cliff face that seemed to rise right up out of the ground, climbing vertically a thousand feet or more, before disappearing into the clouds. Stiger had never seen anything like it. They had reached Thane's Mountain.

Braddock and the other dwarves waited a few feet beyond the edge of the tree line. Stiger made his way over to the thane. Braddock's bodyguard moved grudgingly aside, though only after Naggock, the captain of thane's bodyguard, barked an order to allow him to pass. Eli followed, leading his horse after Stiger.

"This land is not natural," Eli said quietly to Stiger, stopping him. "It has been shaped by deliberate labor."

Stiger looked around. The snow-covered meadow appeared to be quite natural. Eli saw his look, rolled his eyes as if it were obvious, and then dug his boot into the snow, moving it aside until he hit the bottom layer, which was a mixture of ice and snow. After a moment, he scrapped enough clear to expose stone beneath.

"Paving stones," he said, arching a knowing eyebrow at Stiger.

"Very perceptive, elf," Braddock said, turning to face Stiger with a broad smile. "Welcome to the trading side of Old City."

"I don't understand," Stiger admitted. There was nothing to see other than the snow-covered meadow, cliff face, and tree line.

"Exactly," Braddock said, his smile, partially hidden beneath his beard, growing larger. "Garrack?"

Garrack shouted out something in his own language, which sounded like a brief chant. The view of the meadow wavered before Stiger's eyes, as if it were a mirage on an extremely hot day, and within a heartbeat was gone. There was an audible gasp and a few oaths from Lan's troopers. Stiger took a step back. Where there had been nothing now stood around thirty large block-shaped buildings wreathed in snow. These had been constructed on the stone terraces that Stiger had thought natural just moments before.

Beyond the buildings and cut into the face of the cliff itself were two massive granite gates that were each at least sixty feet tall and thirty-five feet wide. There were images carved into the doors themselves and the surrounding cliff face. Stiger let out a slow breath as he took it all in. The entire cliff face had been carved full of dwarven images. It was the most impressive piece of stonework Stiger had ever seen. There were dwarves intricately carved into the stone farming, mining, tending to animals, working a forge, scribing, forming up under arms . . . It went on and on and seemed to be telling some kind of a story.

The scale and intricate nature of the carvings were incredible to behold and reminded Stiger of some of the victory pillars and arches in Mal'Zeel, each of which told the story of a victorious campaign. Those were insignificant compared to this. His jaw dropped at the sight and he looked over at Eli, who appeared just as impressed. Stiger thought this had to be one of the great wonders of the world, and no one other than the dwarves knew about it. Well, no one else until now.

"Welcome to Thane's Mountain and Garand Thoss," Braddock said with a knowing grin. "Otherwise known as Old

City, once home to over two hundred thousand dwarves. Now that you have seen it, the illusion will no longer work on you."

"Impressive, is not?" Garrack asked.

"That word does not adequately describe what I am seeing," Stiger replied without even bothering to look over. He was transfixed by the sight before him and longed to examine the cliff face closer.

"Garand Thoss is small city." Garrack barked out an amused laugh. "One day you come to real city like Garand Tyrell. Then you see true dwarven wonders."

Stiger looked over sharply at Garrack, wondering if the dwarf was joking.

"Come," Braddock said, mounting up. "This is nothing compared to what you are about to see."

With a glance thrown to Eli, Stiger mounted up and nudged Nomad forward after the dwarves. As they neared the first of the rundown buildings, Stiger noticed a wide road down the center that led straight up to the colossal gates. It was almost like a main thoroughfare. The road had been shoveled clean, and surprisingly there was no evidence of snow or ice gracing the wet paving stone. As they clattered onto the road, Stiger was sure the temperature was below freezing. He could not understand how the dwarves kept the slick stone from freezing over into a solid sheet of ice. When he turned to ask Eli, he saw that his friend had dismounted and was kneeling down, feeling the stone, having removed a glove to do so. Stiger pulled Nomad to a halt and wheeled around.

"Cold." Eli looked up at Stiger with raised eyebrows. "Enough so to freeze."

"Gnomes very clever." Garrack stopped, having seen their reaction. He said something in his language to Braddock, who replied in kind, also pulling up short.

"Beet juice?" Eli asked in surprise, straightening up. "Beet juice keeps it from freezing?"

"A type of sugar beet they found," Braddock explained with a shrug. "The juice is squeezed out and then mixed with saltwater. It melts ice and keeps the water from freezing until it gets too cold, and then everything freezes, no matter what they put on it. We use sand at that point."

Braddock wheeled his pony about and continued on, with Garrack at his side.

Stiger dismounted and moved his feet across the wet stone. It was stained a slight purplish red. Marveling at the ingenuity, he quickly mounted back up.

"Very clever," Stiger commented, nudging his horse forward.

Eli pulled himself into the saddle and they continued on, following the dwarves along the main road as it cut between the buildings. Though the walls were thick, the stone buildings showed signs of succumbing to age and a distinct lack of maintenance. A few had crumbled in upon themselves, leaving only a shell of thick stone walls, but most were still intact. Studying the buildings, Stiger was unsure of their purpose. With no windows and wide door-less spaces in the middle, they did not resemble any type of house or tenement he had ever seen. The walls of each were at least three feet thick, which was one of the reasons why they still stood, despite the years of clear neglect.

"Storage," Eli said, as if he had read his friend's mind. "They constructed these buildings so that foreign traders had no reason to enter their city. Dwarves are an extremely private and secretive people."

"More so than elves?" Stiger asked with a sidelong glance at his friend. "I find that hard to believe."

"Think what you will," Eli replied, nodding toward the massive gates they were nearing. "Elves don't lock themselves under mountains."

"No, you just confine yourselves to the depths of the forest and kill any unwelcome trespassers," Stiger said with some seriousness.

"Try living my years and you might one day understand the appeal of keeping strangers out to achieve a bit of solitude."

Though Eli had made the quip as a lighthearted comment, Stiger pursed his lips as he contemplated his friend. Eli had lived many lifetimes and would continue to do so long after Stiger was gone. That bothered him more than he cared to admit, for Stiger would have long joined the shades before his friend even reached his middling years. Contemplating one's mortality against another's near immortality was never a satisfying experience.

"Is that why you hang around me?" Stiger asked with a sudden grin. "For some peace and solitude?"

"I think we can both agree that you attract far too much trouble for me to ever achieve true peace and solitude," Eli answered. "Besides, we are in the wrong profession."

"It really depends on your perspective," Stiger countered. "When the legions are finished, there is peace, if enforced at times."

"Does that cover the rebellion here in the south?"

"The job isn't done yet."

"What isn't done?" Taha'Leeth asked, having come up on Stiger's right. Behind her was the other elf, Aver'Mons. He was silent and grim as he studied the gates they were approaching.

"Nothing," Stiger said, not wishing to include her in their conversation.

"The captain . . . " Eli said with a mischievous smile. Stiger knew trouble was coming. "Ah . . . the legate and I were having a debate about peace and solitude."

"As a soldier, he will not find much," Taha'Leeth said seriously.

"That is almost exactly what I just told him," Eli grinned, putting on a full showing of his teeth.

"Dear gods," Stiger groaned dramatically. "Now I have to contend with two instead of one."

"Do you find working alongside elves that much of a burden?" she asked him, a serious look upon her beautiful face.

"Only one elf tries my patience," Stiger replied. "He is a very difficult person to be around and obviously not as pleasant as I find your company, my lady, apart from our initial introduction, of course."

She cocked her head at him, then glanced over at Eli, who shrugged. She looked back to Stiger, eyes narrowing.

"You jest with me," she accused him. "You jest?"

"It means he likes you," Eli said, drawing a sharp look from Stiger. "You had best watch yourself, my lady. He may name you a friend one day, as I do him."

Stiger's head snapped up as the dwarves ahead abruptly stopped. A double line of dwarven warriors, some thirty strong, marched out from one of the numerous side streets in between the trade buildings. These warriors wore yellow and brown. Stiger had not seen that particular pattern with the dwarven army. Their capes and horse-haired helmet crests were bright yellow, and their rounded shields, held to the side, were painted a dark brown.

Braddock's guard moved forward to interpose themselves between these warriors and their thane. For a moment, Stiger thought this might mean trouble, but the formation halted their movement, left-faced, and came to a position of attention. The officer in command of the formation stepped forward, approaching Braddock. He was allowed through the ring of the thane's personal guard. The officer dropped to a knee before his thane and spoke something in the dwarven language.

Stiger attempted to move himself closer, but was not permitted by the tense guards. One held out his hand and with a shake of his head communicated to Stiger that he must stop. Garrack saw and snapped something at Naggock, who turned and barked what sounded like a harsh order. With an unhappy expression, the guard allowed Stiger through. Garrack wheeled his pony around and rode back to Stiger.

"These our escorts into city," Garrack said, pulling his pony to a stop. "From Hammer Fisted Clan. They hold Old City while we campaign."

"I see," Stiger said, continuing to observe the exchange between Braddock and the dwarven officer a few feet away. "What are they discussing?"

"Good wishes from Clan Chief Hrove and news," Garrack answered, seeming to be completely unconcerned. However, Stiger was not wholly convinced. Something about the abrupt appearance of this formation worried him. It was almost as if they had intentionally meant to surprise the thane's party.

"I see," Stiger said. "Why do we need an escort?"

Garrack looked at him, clearly shocked by the question. "Is required! Is Legend!"

"Legend?"

Garrack frowned, apparently trying to think of the right word. "You call honor."

"You mean the escort is an honor, an honorable thing that is expected?"

"Yes," Garrack said with a firm nod and pleased look. "Is honorable."

The dwarven officer stood, stomped back to his men, and barked out what Stiger took to be a string of orders. The formation of dwarven warriors shifted position, with the clear intent to march before the thane's party. Braddock's guard closed in about their thane, with Naggock riding just ahead of Braddock. He sat stiffly in his saddle, purple cape fluttering with the wind. The dwarven officer in charge of the escort shouted an order and the column began to move again. Braddock turned in his saddle and gestured for Stiger to ride beside him.

"Hrove, Chief of the Hammer Fisted Clan, will undoubtedly greet us before we pass through the gates," Braddock informed him. "It will be good for you to meet one of my most valued advisors."

Stiger nodded but said nothing as they continued onward to the gates. More dwarven warriors appeared on either side of the road in groups and small formations. As if on a silent cue, they dropped to a knee as Braddock made his way past. There was no cheering as before, just silence.

"Since my warriors have marched with the army, the Hammer Fisted Clan has taken up the responsibility for Old City and the World Gate," Braddock explained. "Hrove is no serious warrior. However, thankfully he has officers who are more than competent. He is business-oriented and good at making his clan wealthy, which is not a problem for my people. We strive to be successful in any undertaking. Hrove is just better at it than others. His clan is very wealthy." The Thane paused and scratched at an itch in his beard. "He is also good at irritating some of the other chieftains. In fact, you might say he excels at it."

"He can be trusted then?" Stiger asked, eyeing the silent warriors of the Hammer Fisted Clan with some concern.

"I would not have left him to hold Old City and the World Gate if he had not proven himself worthy of my trust," Braddock said with a frown. Stiger studied Braddock a moment. He could not help feeling that there was more to it than that. The thane had already concealed the existence of secret tunnels from him. What else was he not sharing?

With an impossibly loud groan, the gates to the mountain began to open outward, revealing a large tunnel. The gates looked to be very thick. It seemed impossible that they were made completely of stone. As the gates slowly swung open, large internal steel support arms became visible. Watching the process, Stiger began to wonder if the dwarves ever did anything on a small scale.

Even before the gates had ceased their movement as they opened, a delegation of three dwarves marched through and out to greet their thane. Two were competent-looking warriors. The third wore no armor, but instead a fine brown tunic and yellow cloak. He led the other two as they made their way forward. The escort moved aside and the officer in charge bowed deeply as the delegation passed him by, making for the thane.

Braddock waited patiently, Garrack having returned to his side. The three dwarves went to a knee before Braddock, who spoke briefly to them. They stood as if they had been granted permission to do so. The one in the lead, whom Stiger took to be Hrove, said something, and there followed a sharp, heated reply from Braddock. Hrove's gaze flicked in Stiger's direction. The dwarven language sounded very guttural to Stiger, as if the speaker were perpetually angered. More words were exchanged and Braddock replied almost harshly this time. There was a brief silence before the clan chief bowed his head in apparent acceptance and stepped aside.

Braddock dismounted, as did his bodyguard.

"We dismount here," Garrack announced with an unhappy look. "Horses and your escort will be put up at gatehouse just inside and after entrance tunnel. They wait there for our return."

Stiger dismounted and moved several feet from Braddock, then beckoned Lan. Eli slid off his horse.

"Sir?" Lan asked. Vargus was with him. The two dismounted. Father Thomas and Sergeant Arnold rode up behind them.

"It seems we will walk our horses into the mountain," Stiger said. "You and your escort will be put up at a gatehouse just inside. Vargus, you will stay with the lieutenant and act as a liaison with the dwarves if needed."

"Sir," Lan protested, "you should really have a personal escort."

"The elves, Father Thomas, and . . . " Stiger hesitated with a glance over at the paladin, "and Sergeant Arnold will be accompanying me. That should prove a sufficient escort, I would think."

"Ah, yes, sir," Lan replied, clearly unhappy that more men were not going with the legate.

Stiger was about to say more, but decided against it. If he was not safe with a paladin and three elven rangers, a few more men would not matter. He glanced over at Braddock, who was conferring with Hrove, and scratched his jaw idly, feeling somewhat uneasy. He could not shake the feeling that something was not right. Perhaps he was just being paranoid as a result of the recent fighting and the pressure he had been under over the past few weeks.

"Centurion." Stiger turned to Vargus. "Do you know this Hrove and his clan?"

"No, sir," Vargus replied. "Our dealings with the dwarves have only been through our emissary or the rare visit by

Garrack. Their nearest settlements belong to the Stone Breakers and are over seventy miles through the mountains. It is a difficult journey in the best of weather, and though the dwarves have easier routes to take, we do not know of them."

"I see." Stiger considered his next words carefully. "I want both of you to keep your eyes open for trouble. Make sure you post a watch and keep the men under control. We can afford no incidents with our new allies. Is that understood?"

"Yes, sir," Lan said.

"There will be no trouble, sir," Vargus assured him. "We will see that the men behave."

Stiger nodded and was about to turn away when Vargus shifted slightly, as if he wanted to say more.

"If you have something to say, then do so."

"Sir," Vargus said. "I served as the valley emissary for two years. That involved traveling to the nearest dwarven settlement to confer. I got to know them well. I can tell you that dwarves are a warm and honorable people. You have nothing to fear from them."

"I hope you are right." Stiger turned and began leading his horse forward toward Braddock, with Eli following. Behind him, Lan ordered his men to dismount.

Braddock glanced back as Stiger approached, his expression indecipherable. Garrack stood to the thane's side and looked just as implacable. Hrove, on the other hand, appeared furious. The dwarf cast a superior and judgmental look upon Stiger.

"Legate Stiger, I have the honor to introduce you to the Chief of the Hammer Fisted Clan, Hrove Uth'Al'Maggo, Large Councilor, and my personal adviser. You may simply call him Hrove."

Hrove looked to Garrack as the dwarf translated the words, and then his eyes went to Stiger. There was no warmth there. The dwarf bowed very slightly. The look of fury dimmed somewhat as Braddock spoke in his own language to Hrove.

"Thane just introduced you," Garrack translated, "as Legate of Thirteenth, heir to Delvaris, restorer of Compact, and noble lord of empire."

Stiger bowed just as slightly to Hrove in reply.

"Would you please convey my deep honor at meeting the noble and honorable chieftain of the Hammer Fisted Clan?" Stiger was tempted to add to the compliment, speaking on Hrove's business dealings, but decided against it. He did not know enough about dwarves to understand fully how that would be received. So he left it at that.

Braddock translated. Hrove nodded and replied.

"Hrove says is honor to meet you, legate," Garrack said.

Hrove waited for the translation to be completed and then barked out what seemed to be an order to his men.

"Very good then." Braddock turned to Stiger. "It is time for you to see what dwarves can do when we put our minds to it."

Hrove, with his warriors before him, led them through the massive gates and into the mountain. Stiger was impressed as they entered the large tunnel behind the gates. A double row of support columns on either side of the tunnel rose to the ceiling, at least sixty feet in height. The stone floor was worn smooth from years of use. Large stone fire pits, set several feet apart, provided ample lighting. It was enough to see that the walls were carved from floor to ceiling with intricate dwarven reliefs. Several gnomes moved about, keeping the fires well fed. They stopped what they were doing to stare as the party passed them by.

Stiger assumed that the reliefs depicted dwarven history, but he could not be sure. He noticed small dark holes periodically set into the walls at varying heights. When looking up, he could also barely make out what appeared to be trap doors above and several large metal portcullises suspended by heavy chains, ready to be lowered if needed. He saw large dark holes set right above the fire pits and he realized they were vents to channel the smoke out of the tunnel.

"Impressive defenses," Stiger commented, recognizing the murder holes set strategically about. He was confident there were some defenses he could not see due to the dim light.

"We are now in what could be considered an extension of Grata'Jalor," Braddock explained. "This is part of an ancient citadel designed to protect both the city and World Gate. It has never fallen to an enemy. Should one make it through the gates, they will have a very difficult time of it."

"Another castle then?" Stiger asked, recognizing the similar dwarven naming convention to Castle Vrell.

"One of last resort," Braddock explained. "As such, it is most powerful in defense. Grata'Jalor would be much more difficult to overcome than Grata'Kor."

After about a five-minute walk, they came to another large set of granite gates, just as large and impressive as the first set. These stood open, and beyond them, Stiger could see why Grata'Jalor made such a formidable defensive structure.

Passing through the last set of gates, they entered an unbelievably giant cavern. Stiger and everyone else came to a complete stop at the sight that greeted them. Hundreds of rounded support columns, each the size of a house, climbed upward toward the ceiling, disappearing in the darkness above. Though Stiger could not see the darkened ceiling, which was perhaps more than a thousand feet high, large beams of light flooded downward, illuminating much of the interior of the cavern. He held a hand up against the light, squinting for the source, and realized that he could see clouds and sky. The dwarves had carved a set of massive, open skylights that bathed the cavern in muted but natural light. It was an incredibly impressive achievement, but what proved even more exceptional was the castle that sat in the middle of the cavern, less than a quarter of a mile away. It was ringed by a wide, dark chasm, much like an aboveground castle might have a moat. From this distance, he could see no water and had a sneaking suspicion that there was none, just a very long drop-off.

A single lonely drawbridge lay across the chasm. The walls and battlements of the castle looked to be twice as high as those of Castle Vrell. Movement could barely be seen on the walls as sentries walked their rounds. The castle's keep rose upward, towering above the walls. Stiger did not even want to contemplate how one would begin to try to take such a formidable position. Like Castle Vrell, he reasoned, the best way to do it would be from the inside.

"The walls of Grata'Jalor," Braddock announced proudly. "My ancestors labored for centuries on them. Beyond the citadel, on the other side of the great chasm, lies the ancient city of Garand Thoss. You are much honored today, for few outsiders have seen this place."

"I thought Castle Vrell would be a tough nut to crack." Stiger whistled softly and looked over at Eli to see his friend's reaction. The elf looked drawn and pale. Stiger thought he detected a slight sheen of sweat on his friend's brow. Though it was slightly warmer inside the mountain, it was still cold.

"What's wrong?" he asked Eli quietly, as he noticed that Taha'Leeth and Aver'Mons appeared to be similarly affected.

Eli shook his head, indicating that he did not want to speak on it.

"Escort remain here," Garrack announced, interrupting Stiger before he could ask more of Eli. The dwarf was pointing to a structure that stood off to their right, one he had not noticed. It was a two-story building that looked to have a stable on the first floor and some type of barracks on the second. Yellowed light shown dimly from several windows and a number of chimneys sent smoke lazily skyward toward the great open skylights.

Stiger could see a number of dwarven ponies tethered to hitching posts out in front. Hay had been thrown down in front of the ponies.

"Your men be fed and horses cared for," Garrack said.

"Lieutenant," Stiger called, leading Nomad back to Lan. "This is as far as you go. Detail men to take our horses. You will be staying over there."

"Yes, sir," Lan said, clearly disappointed that he would be going no farther. Vargus led his horse up. He had an odd look on his face as he studied the walls and battlements of Grata'Jalor.

"Remember to keep the men on a tight leash." Stiger looked back at the thane, who was speaking again with Hrove. "Braddock said we would only be staying the night, so I will see you in the morning."

"Yes, sir," Lan said.

"Send a dispatch back to Lieutenant Ikely," Stiger ordered. "Inform him of our progress and the location of the mountain entrance should I be needed."

"I will see to it, sir."

Several of Hrove's warriors who had been part of their escort stomped over. They began speaking in their own language and gesturing toward the building Garrack had indicated. Stiger handed his reins to Lan and patted Nomad lightly on the side. He untied a saddle bag that contained his pipe and other necessities, including a change of clothes. He slung it over his shoulder.

Lan shouted orders for several of his men to get the others' horses. Stiger's free hand came to rest on his sword, and he felt the familiar and reassuring electric tingle course up and down his arm. At first he had worried about the tingle but now had come to welcome it. The dim light of the cavern seemed to lighten slightly, and Stiger was able to see more. He supposed his eyes were finally adjusting.

"I have never seen the World Gate," Vargus said, drawing Stiger's attention. "I have heard enough that I do not wish to. Dwarves rarely give outsiders a chance to see their holy sites or cities."

Stiger considered the centurion before he nodded his understanding. He then turned and made for Braddock, then paused. He sensed a soft humming, perhaps even a vibration. Stiger almost jumped when he realized it was coming from his sword in his scabbard. What was it doing?

Power, the sword whispered to him, in a hiss that at times Stiger felt was almost menacing. This time though, Stiger thought he detected an eagerness, almost akin to a hungry man anticipating a good meal. *Power . . .*

"Legate," Braddock said, drawing his attention away from the weapon. The thane and everyone else thankfully seemed unaware of the humming, which had abruptly died off.

"Hrove will be leaving us," Braddock said as Stiger came up to him. "He has duties to attend to. We will continue on our own."

"Really?" Stiger was surprised that the chieftain would not be joining them. After all, weren't the city and Gate his responsibility? The dwarven thane was visiting and Hrove was not coming? It seemed damn odd.

"Yes," Braddock said with a deep, unhappy breath. "There has been an incursion of the lesser races in the lower recesses of the city. Hrove's warriors are flushing them out and back into the mines. He wishes to personally oversee the process."

"Lesser races?" Stiger asked.

"Orcs, goblins, and some other unsavory creatures," Braddock explained. "When the city was abandoned, the lesser races moved in and made it their home. They fouled our great city with their presence. Upon our return, my war band drove them back to the depths. In time, we will push them completely out of the mountain."

Stiger had never seen a goblin, but as a youth he had once seen an orc at the great games in the capital. The orc, more animal than person, had towered over the six criminals who had been sentenced to fight the beast to the death. It had been an impressive struggle. Unarmed, the orc had managed to kill four before being taken down by the surviving criminals, who had been armed. Upon their victory, the criminals had been granted their freedom. It was an exciting fight, and the city had talked of it for weeks after.

"There is nothing to worry about," Braddock assured him confidently. "Grata'Jalor and the World Gate have never been left unguarded. My people have always had a presence here."

There was a clatter from behind and Stiger turned to see his escort being led off. It almost seemed as if Hrove's warriors were treating his as prisoners. Watching Hrove and his dwarven warriors lead Stiger's legionaries away caused him to frown. Once he saw the Gate and got back to Castle Vrell, he could return to his duty and focus exclusively on the enemy. He did not care to understand dwarven politics and had no wish to be caught up in them. Imperial politics were enough for him.

Stiger turned back to Grata'Jalor in time to see a few small figures appear on the drawbridge. They threw something that looked suspiciously like a body into the chasm and watched it fall for a brief moment before disappearing once again out of view.

"What was that?" Stiger asked.

"Gnomes disposing of the remains of one of the lesser races," Braddock said with an uninterested shrug. "We are still cleaning up."

"Where is the Gate?" Stiger asked of Braddock. He fairly itched to get this over with.

"The World Gate lies at the heart of Grata'Jalor." Braddock pointed across the chasm.

POWER! the sword roared in his head, and Stiger almost staggered under the force of it. *I sense great power . . . at long last our time is coming.*

FOUR

Step after step, Stiger followed Braddock downward. Booted feet echoed harshly off the bare walls as they descended the spiral staircase into the bowels of Grata'Jalor. Oil lanterns had been hung every few feet, providing just enough light to see. Stiger found that he needed to be careful, as his hobnailed boots slid slightly on the stone steps, well-worn from centuries of use. More than once he had been forced to steady himself with a hand on the wall.

Grata'Jalor had a feeling to it of immense age that almost seemed to weigh heavily upon the air itself. Surprisingly, the deeper they went, the warmer it became. Though chilly, the temperature had risen to the point where Stiger was considering removing his cloak and gloves.

Braddock came to a halt at a landing. Two sentries from the Hammer Fisted clan dropped to a knee at the sight of their thane. They were older dwarves and their beards were quite long, touching the ground as they kneeled. Both looked to be seasoned warriors. Behind them was a closed steel door, which had been painted a dull black. The door was remarkable, not only for being metal, but also having no visible handle by which to open it.

The thane exchanged a few words with the sentries before one stood and banged on the door. The other sentry

80

stood and moved aside. He assumed a position of attention against the wall. Stiger noted that the sentry eyed the humans with a hostile look. Where most of Braddock's army had treated the legionaries with respect and openness, it seemed Hrove's dwarves were resentful of human intrusion upon their mountain.

A small recessed panel slid back in the middle of the door, revealing the eyes of a dwarf on the other side. He looked into the room and asked a question, which was immediately answered by the one who had banged on the door. The dwarf hesitated and peered into the room to study them, then withdrew. The panel was slammed back in place. A series of bolts being thrown could be heard on the other side. The heavy door slowly and painfully began to screech its way open.

When it had swung wide enough, Stiger could see a dwarf throwing his weight into the other side, while six others stood with their weapons out and shields forward, ready for trouble. It was the kind of thing the legions would have done in an encampment at night whenever a gate was opened to admit someone. Stiger approved of their vigilance. At the sight of their thane, they sheathed their weapons and stood respectfully aside.

The dwarves watched the humans and elves with hostile looks as they walked by, but said nothing. All wore the colors of the Hammer Fisted clan. Stiger felt a sense of foreboding as he glanced back at Eli. His friend still looked strained, almost as if he were suffering from a fever. Stiger had never seen Eli this way and was becoming concerned. Eli noticed his look and offered up a half-hearted grin.

We will speak on this later, Eli signed in ranger speak, using his hands.

"Legate," Braddock said, stopping just ahead, a very solemn look in his eyes. There was an open doorway, and through it Stiger could see a much larger room that was extremely well-lit. "What is beyond this doorway represents the heart of the Compact, the reason our peoples banded together in alliance. As long as the alliance remains strong, we remain strong."

"I understand," Stiger said, returning the thane's look with a level gaze of his own.

"No, I am afraid you do not fully understand," Braddock said. "Though in time you will."

The thane stepped aside and motioned for Stiger to go before him. Several of Braddock's guard had entered and stood waiting. Three remained with the thane. Stiger took a deep breath, broke Braddock's gaze, and stepped through the doorway.

A wave of warmth washed over him as he crossed the threshold. He found himself on an oval-shaped balcony that overlooked a large natural cavern. A metal railing ran around the outer edge of the balcony and a staircase led downward to his right. It curved along the outer wall of the cavern as it descended to the floor below.

Stiger's eyes were immediately drawn to a large yellow-ish ball of fire suspended in the air near the ceiling, around which numerous stalactites hung. The ball of fire crackled, hissed, and popped, though surprisingly it generated no smoke. It was this fireball that bathed the cavern in light.

The hair on Stiger's arms stood on end as he gazed up at the magically conjured light. He hesitated a half step before continuing up to the railing. Placing both hands upon the banister, he looked down and froze, not quite believing what he was seeing.

The base of the cavern floor had been leveled and smoothed. A circular ring of dull-gray stone pillars, perhaps a hundred feet in diameter, were planted in the floor. These stone pillars rose to a height of at least ten feet and were each around five feet apart. In the exact center of the ring were two enormous rounded pillars of the same height, though twice as thick and set fifteen feet apart. They looked to be made of some sort of a crystal and throbbed with a dull blue light that Stiger found uncomfortably similar to how his sword at times glowed. The pillars were emitting a low hum that filled the cavern with a steady background noise. Yet it was not the pillars that captured Stiger's attention, but a massive creature.

He knew instinctively what it was, but had trouble believing it. Impossibly, a dragon, curled up around the two glowing pillars, was sleeping just below him on the cavern floor. Like a bird, the dragon's head was tucked under a wing and was only partially visible. The heavy breathing of the magnificent creature rose and fell above the background hum of the two central pillars.

Stiger was afraid to breathe, lest he awaken the dragon. Gazing down, he felt that it was one of the most beautiful and deadly things he had ever seen, black on the top and gray underneath. He had difficulty determining the exact length, though he figured it was likely far larger than some of the sailing ships that graced the oceans. The claws alone were the size of a full grown man.

"Currose," Braddock breathed as he came up behind Stiger.

"What?" Stiger asked in a near whisper, not daring to take his eyes off of the sleeping dragon, which flexed a powerful claw.

"Her name is Currose," Braddock explained.

The rest of the group moved onto the balcony. Eli came up beside Stiger.

"Have you ever seen the like?" Stiger asked of him.

"It cannot be," Eli exclaimed quietly and switched to elven, addressing Taha'Leeth and Aver'Mons. Stiger followed what was said.

"That is a Greater Drak, correct?"

Taha'Leeth came to the railing and sucked in a startled breath at the sight of the massive dragon below them. "Impossible as it seems, it is a Greater Drak. I have seen others of her kind, but not for some long years."

"Bless me," Father Thomas exclaimed, coming to the railing.

"Holy sh—" Sergeant Arnold caught himself mid-curse and then made the sign of the High Father. He planted both hands firmly upon the metal banister. "When I joined, the recruiter swore up and down I would see everything there was to see in the world. I am starting to think he was right."

"Whoa." Marcus took an involuntary step back from the railing. Stiger looked over at his scout corporal and his eyes narrowed. He had not given Marcus permission to come along to see the Gate and had expected him to remain behind with Lan and Vargus. Eli had likely instructed him to follow along and stay out of the way. For some reason, the elves were keeping Marcus close. Ever since they had retired to Castle Vrell, at no time had the scout-turned-ranger been left alone. It was another thing to speak to Eli about.

"Currose is one of a pair," a voice to their right said in fluent common. "Two of the last of their kind."

All eyes turned upon an extremely tall, thin, and pale man who was making his way up the steps. He was fair looking, with near perfect features, and wore a long, gray robe that was richly cut. The robe thoroughly concealed his feet, giving the impression that he glided up the steps. His pupils were silver, along with his beard and hair, which fell down his back and around his shoulders. The man's hair had certainly not turned silver from age. He had the appearance of being in his prime. The tips of pointed ears emerged from his hair, and at the top of his head sat a delicate black and gray crown.

Stiger looked over at Eli to ask why an elf was in a dwarven fortress, when he saw his friend twitch with astonishment before bowing deeply. Taha'Leeth bowed also, and a fraction of a second later, Aver'Mons did the same. Stiger had never seen Eli offer such respect to anyone, even his own father.

"What is another elf doing here?" Stiger asked, putting to word his thoughts.

"I am no elf," the man snapped with some irritation mixed with amusement.

"Ben, this is a First One," Eli said in a low voice, still bowed and waiting for acknowledgement.

"Yes," the newcomer said, his voice a near hiss. "I am of the Noctalum, the First Race."

Stiger noticed that all of the dwarves bowed as well, with the exception of Braddock. He simply inclined his head slightly, and in return got a wave of acknowledgement. The elves and dwarves straightened back up.

"These know their betters," he said. "You humans apparently do not."

"Legate," Braddock said in a hard tone. "This is Menos, caretaker of the World Gate. Long has he resided in this holy place."

"It is an honor to greet you, Menos," Stiger said carefully. He did not like the caretaker's tone and was not sure whether to be irritated at the condescension directed toward him.

"I should think it is," Menos answered, tilting his head in much the same way that Eli did. He made a show of sniffing the air. "Long has it been since a human walked here. Long has it been since I tasted one of your . . . and yet your scent . . . it is—"

"My scent?"

"Yes, your stench, you wretched creature," snapped Menos, now with clear irritation, stepping closer to him. "There was a time your people feared mine."

"Menos," Braddock interjected. "We—"

"Braddock, I was under the impression that humans are short-lived." Menos leaned closer to Stiger and continued to sniff. Stiger could not ever recall being sniffed by anything other than one of his family's hounds. The experience was unsettling.

"They are," Braddock answered slowly. The thane was clearly puzzled and looked to Garrack in question. Garrack gave a half shrug.

"I have met this one before." Menos stepped back.

"If I had met you," Stiger growled, becoming hot, "I am sure I would have remembered." He had tired of the game Menos was playing.

"I agree," Menos replied with a frosty look.

"Legate," Garrack said quietly, almost reverently. "Noctalum are first race gods made, ancient beings, with much power. They honored and favored by gods."

"Yes, we are an ancient people," Menos said, with a distant look to his eyes. "So ancient that, at one time, we walked with the gods themselves, and strove to learn all they were willing to teach."

"You knew the gods?" The question had burst out before Stiger could stop it.

"Human," Menos said, casting Stiger a disdainful look, "your tiny brain cannot even begin to comprehend what we are, what we have done, and are yet capable of doing."

"Perhaps it is his ancestor you recognize?" Braddock suggested, drawing Menos's attention. "He is of the bloodline of Delvaris, the one the Oracle prophesized."

Menos turned back to Stiger. He stepped closer and dropped his voice to a hissing whisper that only Stiger could hear. "Delvaris, yes . . . yes, I knew your ancestor, as I also know you."

Menos abruptly stepped away, moving to the railing of the balcony, where he looked down upon the dragon. "You have seen Currose. She and her mate, Sian Tane, have guarded this World Gate for nearly two millennia."

Wary of Menos, Stiger eyed the caretaker suspiciously. He was not sure what he was dealing with here and, as such, decided to remain silent. Stiger saw no harm in letting this drama play out. Then what Menos had revealed finally hit him. There were two dragons. He looked back over the railing. Where was the other one? There was a large closed metal door against the far wall of the cavern. It was big enough for a dragon to move through.

"Sian Tane is out hunting, while Currose provides the eternal watch," Menos explained, as if he had read Stiger's thoughts. Turning to look back at the group of visitors, his pale silver eyes sought out Stiger. "Together they guard this World Gate in fulfillment of the Compact between our races."

So, Stiger thought with a quick glance over to Braddock, there are other races that are also part of the Compact.

"Below us lies the greatest of treasures. The World Gate is a pathway to both place and time. There are factions that would do anything to possess it." With a long, thin, almost frail-looking hand, Menos gestured toward the two pillars around which Currose was entwined. "We must do everything within our power to prevent their ambitions from becoming reality."

"If you mean to keep it sealed, then why not simply destroy it?" Stiger asked. "Would that not achieve the same purpose?"

"My people created the World Gates. We will not destroy them," Menos snapped and then took a breath, as if calming himself. "Besides, the gods in their infinite wisdom have prohibited such an act."

Stiger shifted slightly as he considered the caretaker's words. If it had been left up to him, he would have found a way to destroy the infernal thing. Stiger had only the caretaker's word on this. But what if Menos was right? Stiger was not of the mind to anger the gods, the ones he honored at least. He figured Castor was not too happy with him, but that did not much matter to Stiger. He had put his trust in the High Father's hands and had faith that the great god would look out for him. It was as simple as that.

Stiger looked away from Menos and glanced down over the railing again at the World Gate. How would the High Father react if he took steps to destroy the Gate? What misfortune would be sent his way? Did he even risk thinking such thoughts? Did he dare test the High Father's displeasure? Seven levels, he thought. How would you even go about destroying such a magical device? How would you get past the dragons?

Stiger's mood soured. If the gods had prohibited destruction of the Gate, then it must be defended. He knew without a doubt that would involve him and his men. Then a thought occurred to him. By holding Castle Vrell, he was already defending the Gate.

"How does it work?" Stiger asked.

"A wizard is required to open the Gate," said a harsh voice behind them, which was followed almost immediately by an unnatural giggle.

Ogg stepped through the doorway, the metal guard on the bottom of his staff clicking on the stone as he moved. Braddock's nearest bodyguard took a step back from the beardless dwarf, a distasteful expression on his face. Ogg paid him no mind.

"That and the planetary planes must be properly aligned," Ogg explained. "For our world, this occurs every two thousand years. Once opened, the World Gate remains linked to its counterpart for the next two thousand years. When the connection is broken, well, the dimensional planes do not align properly again for another two thousand." Ogg walked to the metal railing and glanced casually over before turning back to Stiger. "This World Gate leads to a world called Tanis. That world has a second Gate that leads to another world and that world then leads you to a place called Earth, where your people's ancestral homeland, Rome, resides."

"Rome?" Stiger was still having difficulty believing what Braddock had told him. He had always assumed that Rome was more myth and legend than reality. After all, no one knew where it was located, which made sense in a strange sort of way, especially if the legendary city was locked away on another world.

"Rome," Ogg confirmed firmly, before turning to Menos and inclining his head slightly. "Menos, it is a pleasure to see you well."

"Wizard." Menos chuckled. "You are as impertinent as ever."

"Would it be more appropriate if I were not?"

"Why must we keep the Gate closed?" Stiger had to know, suddenly feeling the urge and call of Rome. Seeing another world sounded interesting. Visiting Rome would be incredible. What wonders awaited such a traveler? Then again, what horrors awaited as well? Armies of the dark gods?

"There is a war," Ogg said simply.

"A war unlike others," Menos added with a tone of sadness.

"The gods themselves war," Ogg continued after Menos fell silent. He looked over at the paladin with a flat look. "There are several factions, ours being the High Father's. Instead of direct conflict amongst themselves, the gods use the peoples and races of entire worlds to do their fighting."

"Should the gods clash directly," Menos added, "it is believed that such a direct confrontation would prove the universe's undoing."

"Why?" Stiger asked. "Why do they fight?"

Ogg giggled. "There are those who believe the gods grew bored and entertain themselves in this way."

"We do not know." Braddock threw a disapproving frown in the wizard's direction. "It could be as simple as good versus evil, but the gods are mysterious. Perhaps the paladin could add more?"

Stiger glanced over to Father Thomas, who looked a little hesitant.

"The High Father does not speak to us paladins directly," Father Thomas began slowly. "It is more of a nudge or push here and there. What we have gathered and believe is that the gods are in a struggle for dominance. On this world, the majority follow the teachings of the High Father and his alignment. As such, our alignment primarily has dominion here."

"On other worlds he does not have dominion then?" Stiger asked. "Is that what you are saying?"

"Tanis is one such world," Ogg said. "Or it was nearly two thousand years ago."

"Tanis was overrun," Menos explained.

"The Horde," Taha'Leeth whispered, drawing Stiger's attention.

"Though the struggle had already reached here," Menos continued, "your people, the dwarves, gnomes, elves, and others sought out this world as a place of refuge. To keep Istros from sharing the same fate as Tanis, the World Gate was sealed."

Stiger was silent as he considered this. Everything he had seen and learned over the last few weeks had tested his basic understanding of the world. His thoughts churned with the implications of what they were telling him.

"Why is this not common knowledge?" Stiger asked. "Why have I not heard of this before?"

"For some races, it is well-known," Ogg said, his gaze flicking toward Eli. "For others, some things are best forgotten. Your race, for example, serves differing alignments and, as such, cannot always be trusted. Steps were taken to ensure knowledge of the World Gates was, over time, forgotten by your people."

Stiger did not like the sound of that, though he knew from personal experience that what Ogg said was true. Some humans followed the dark gods. These were most definitely not part of the High Father's alignment.

"Braddock mentioned that the other World Gate was destroyed." Stiger changed the direction of his questioning. "I thought you said the gods prohibited that?"

"We believe it to be destroyed," Ogg answered with a brief glance in Taha'Leeth's direction before returning his eyes back to Stiger. "Even if it survived, that World Gate resides at the bottom of the Narrow Sea. Destroyed or not, it is inaccessible."

"The struggle of the gods still continues elsewhere?" Stiger asked.

"We believe that to be true," Ogg said, a tiny maniacal giggle escaping his lips. "The struggle has lasted many millennia, and there is direct evidence that it continues."

"Castor is part of another alignment then?" Stiger asked with a snap of the fingers, recalling the corruption of Captain Aveeno and the battle with the dark god's minion in Castle Vrell.

"That is correct," Menos answered. "When the World Gate was sealed, some of Castor's followers were stranded here, including those of the lesser races."

"Orcs and goblins are on Castor's side?" Stiger's brow furrowed as he considered this.

"Some undoubtedly are," Father Thomas answered. "To some degree, the gods allow free choice."

"You knew about the Gate," Stiger accused Father Thomas, rounding on the paladin. "Yet you said nothing."

"Though I knew of it, I did not know of its location. It was moved and has been lost for close to two thousand years. My order has been looking for it for a very long time. So, apparently, are the Cyphan."

"Then the Cyphan are of Castor's alignment too?"

"No," Taha'Leeth spoke up. "They are of Valloor's alignment and in competition to Castor, as they also compete with the High Father."

"Valloor?" Stiger asked. Valloor was the primary god that those of the Cyphan Confederacy worshipped. Valloor was considered a neutral god. There was even a temple honoring him in Mal'Zeel. The empire honored most gods, with the exception of the dark and evil ones.

"We may not have seen the last of Castor," Ogg said with another giggle. Stiger chilled at that statement. The last thing he wanted was to encounter another minion of the Twisted One.

"Then we need to be on our guard," Father Thomas said. "Castor works by infecting the minds of the weak and susceptible."

"So the High Father wants the Gate to remain closed?" Stiger asked Father Thomas.

"That, my son," Father Thomas said carefully, "is not so clear."

"What do you mean?" Ogg's gaze shifted to the paladin. "The Gate must remain closed or the Last War will come here, again."

"Will it?" Father Thomas looked over at Menos.

"Two thousand years have passed since the World Gate was last opened," Menos said. "There is no telling what now lies on the other side."

"We know what is waiting there," Ogg snapped irritably.

"Do we?" Menos challenged.

"The High Father's alignment could now rule on Tanis," Father Thomas said. "A great deal of time has passed."

"It would seem," Stiger suggested, following the back and forth, "that if Castor and Valloor are interested in opening the Gate, then that might not be the case."

"We do not know that they desire to open the World Gate," said Menos. "They may wish to prevent such an event from coming to pass. At the appointed time, a choice will have to be made. Whoever has control of both the Key and World Gate will make that choice."

"The Key?"

"Long ago your emperor was entrusted with the Key that unlocks the World Gate," Menos explained. "At the time, it was believed that by keeping the two apart the world would be safer. With hindsight, I wonder if perhaps we made a mistake."

Stiger paled at this, thinking of the emperor. The Cyphan were after the Key. It was why they had invaded the empire, for both the Key and Gate. Or perhaps they were just interested in the Key to prevent the Gate from being opened. Stiger knew that, with the condition of the southern legions, anything could have happened. Should they be defeated, there was not much standing in the way of the heart of the empire. He looked down at the stone floor and ground his teeth in frustration. Here he was stuck in Vrell, penned inside a valley, when perhaps the real struggle that needed fighting was at the heart of the empire. He knew without a doubt the emperor was in danger, and worse, there was no one to warn him.

"Do not worry," Braddock said, misunderstanding Stiger's thoughts. "We will take the war to the Cyphan soon enough. Together we will make them pay."

"Let us descend and see the World Gate," Ogg suggested abruptly.

"Yes." Menos turned toward the stairs, intent upon leading the way. "It is also time you saw a dragon up close."

FIVE

Marcus peered over the balcony to the cavern floor below as the others began to make their way down the stairs. He had hung back, observing and listening as Stiger spoke with Menos. He bit his lip at the sight of the sleeping dragon and just shook his head. This was something that in all of his wildest dreams he had never expected to see.

I've come a long way, Marcus reflected, his eyes running over the massive creature below. A hand came to rest upon his shoulder and he turned to see Eli.

"Stay up here," Eli advised, giving a friendly squeeze before letting go. "I gave you permission to come because I felt you needed to see what is here."

"I will stay out of trouble, sir." Marcus was relieved he was not going down to see the dragon. He was just fine with watching from a distance.

"I know you will," Eli said with a funny look before turning and joining the others. There was almost a regretful expression in Eli's eyes as the elf turned away.

Marcus watched Eli go, wondering what was wrong. Ever since they had entered the mountain, the elves had been a little out of sorts, almost as if it pained them to be underground. He could sympathize with them. Marcus enjoyed the wide open spaces aboveground to those below. Despite the grandeur of the dwarven labor, Marcus could not help but feel that life belowground was drab in comparison to that above.

At this, his thoughts turned to himself. He was no longer a simple company scout. He wasn't even the same person he had been just a few months earlier. Eli had been a big part of that change, for which Marcus was very grateful.

Marcus was now a ranger, or so Taha'Leeth had named him. It meant a great deal to him. Eli had assured Marcus that when they returned to the empire, he would be offered an opportunity to join the emperor's ranger corps or, if he wished, spend some time with the elves. Though Eli had not tried to influence him, it seemed to Marcus that the lieutenant was more desirous that he elect the latter option. Marcus wondered what it would be like to live amongst Eli's people. Just being offered the chance was a tremendous honor.

Since his return to Castle Vrell, one of the elves had taken pains to be with him at all times. They had tried to make it not too terribly obvious, but Marcus had noticed just the same. It was almost as if they were watching out for him, like a parent does a young child. They had also worked to keep him busy. Marcus considered that they were trying to keep his spirits up and off of the ordeal he had just been through. After all, he had just lost most of his fellow scouts and friends to the Cyphan.

Whatever their motivation, he was grateful for their attention. It had proven more than a simple distraction. All four had each spent some time testing him to learn the full extent of his abilities. There had also been some instruction on improving his deep meditation technique, which was designed to help him better understand the world around him. This was somewhat different than listening to the forest, and they had encouraged him to meditate whenever the opportunity presented itself.

And so, Marcus found himself alone on the balcony. Even Braddock's guard had gone down to the cavern floor. At first, he was tempted to watch, but then changed his mind. He considered working on his meditation technique, then decided against it. He had brought his pack with him. Pulling out his camp blanket, he selected an isolated spot on the balcony that was off to the side and would not be in the way of anyone who walked by. He carefully set the blanket on the floor and then sat down upon it, leaning his back against the cool stone wall of the cavern. Though the cavern was warmer, the stone was still cold to the touch. Everything under the mountain seemed to be either cool or wet or a combination of both.

Marcus closed his eyes. Ever since their return to Castle Vrell, he had been having difficulty, sleeping fitfully. He supposed he was still tired from the weeks of constant action. Deep down, he understood that losing most of the other scouts of the 85th had taken its toll on him. Davis and Todd were the only ones left. Perhaps it was the loss of so many friends . . . Marcus tried to relax, at first intent upon taking a nap. In the legions, you learned to sleep when you could. Before he drifted off, a thought occurred to him. He wondered . . .

Marcus sat up straight, eyes closed. He controlled his breathing and focused. If he had been in the forest, he would have opened himself up, listening to the living woods around him. It had felt natural and relaxing. Under the mountain, he attempted the same deep state, taking in the sounds and smells around him, reaching outward with his mind to feel . . . to touch . . . was there anything there?

At first he could feel nothing . . . touch nothing. There was only blackness and he almost gave up, but then he began to . . . sense the weight of the mountain and the rock around him. Marcus was surprised that the texture of the rock varied in so many interesting ways. He knew that there were different types of rock, but never so many. Fascinated, he went further, feeling out hollowed spaces, caverns, tunnels, deep mines, the ancient bedrock, the flowing river of fire rock just beneath the mountain, burning red hot. It was glorious, amazing, and frightening all at the same time, and yet a completely different feeling from the forest. He could not sense the voice of the mountain as he could the forest, a presence that was almost physical but not. It was just . . . well, plain different. Perhaps he was not delving far enough?

Marcus pulled himself in deeper in an attempt to hear the voice of the mountain. Instead he bumped into two powerful minds that blazed hotter than the sun. He had never felt anything like it. Both were very close. He could sense the edge of their emotions as if it were a new taste. Then he realized that the minds, both terribly complex with an incredible feeling of great age, wisdom, and knowledge, were of two dragons.

Marcus could not explain how he knew exactly, but he did. He suddenly became conscious that one of the dragons was aware of his presence. A deep anger flared. There was a tremendous push, and he was thrust violently away. His mind was carried far. Then he sensed something else, to the south, another powerful mind. It was dark, vile, twisted, and corrupt. There was no other way to describe it but evil. He shuddered, feeling cold, alone, and afraid. Marcus felt a sense of deep despair and dread as it became aware of his presence and turned on him, drawing him in, much like a fisherman reeling in a catch. Marcus was trapped. He could not pull away as it drew and pulled him in and away from his body, and he felt himself begin to grow colder. He struggled mightily, but with no success. He began to panic.

A hand clamped down hard on his shoulder and Marcus was abruptly ripped back to his body and reality. Blinking, he was hauled roughly to his feet and found himself staring directly into a pair of deep silver eyes. It was extremely disconcerting, and Marcus shuddered under the intensity of the caretaker's gaze. Menos had somehow pulled him back.

"Do not attempt that again," Menos warned, poking a hard finger into Marcus's chest.

Marcus blinked, disoriented. Feet were pounding up the stairs. He turned his head and saw Stiger reach the balcony, followed by Eli and the others. The floor suddenly vibrated, and from over the edge of the balcony there was a great scraping noise, followed by a deep, primal, guttural growl. The floor of the balcony shook with the impact of something smacking the cavern wall below. The cavern seemed to groan and dust billowed down from the ceiling. Several stalactites broke free and crashed to the floor.

Menos released him and stepped to the balcony railing as the massive head of Currose appeared, looming above, staring directly down upon Marcus with silver eyes that blazed with anger. Her head was the size of a small house. Marcus made the mistake of looking into the eyes of the dragon and found he could not look away, let alone blink. It was as if she could read his soul. His heart hammered as he felt pressure upon his mind. A great fear welled up inside of him. He wanted to scream and run for safety but could not move. The dragon's mouth opened, revealing an impressive set of fangs and several deadly-looking rows of serrated teeth. Steam escaped from around her nostrils as she took a deep breath and exhaled it out in a blast of heated air.

"Foolish human," the dragon hissed aloud, speaking common. "You play with earth-sense, a power you do not understand. Have you no wisdom?"

Caught in the deadly gaze of the dragon, his body was frozen, rooted to the floor. He screamed silently as the dragon's mind brutally invaded his own, digging and pushing though unwanted thoughts, searching for something. Tears rolled down his face as the dragon pried loose his memories one after another and examined them. The torment continued, and his body shook with unbelievable pain. Then, as suddenly as it had begun, the dragon released his mind. He was free.

Marcus screamed in agony as his muscles gave way. He collapsed upon the stone floor in a heap, breathing heavily. Tears freely streamed down his face as he cried unabashedly. He had never known such torment and shivered at the memory of the pain.

There was shouting. Marcus struggled to raise his head. After a failed try, he was successful. Stiger and Eli had their swords out. The legate was facing the dragon, a terrible rage contorting his face and his sword alight with blue fire. Marcus had heard of the magic sword, but he had not seen it at work.

The dragon's head reared back and she screamed in outrage.

"Rarokan?" the dragon roared, the noise deafening in the confines of the cavern. A gout of flame leapt several feet from her mouth before being sucked back inside. "Human, you dare threaten me?"

"Currose." A voice snapped like the crack of a whip. It took Marcus a moment to realize that it had been Menos. The dragon looked to the caretaker. "These are friends of the Compact. We do not treat our allies this way."

A growling noise escaped from the dragon's throat as she considered Menos. Currose ground her teeth in what seemed to Marcus to be frustration, and her head swung back and forth.

"Legate, put that abhorrence you call a sword away," Menos ordered curtly. "We will not destroy the Compact this day."

Marcus pulled himself to his knees and watched as Stiger hesitated a moment before angrily sheathing the weapon. The legate glared at the dragon with a look he might have given a man on parade who did not measure up to his standard.

"You do not harm my men," the legate snapped at the dragon. "Nor do you threaten them."

"Currose," Menos said, "this is the Legate of the Thirteenth."

The dragon snapped her teeth a couple of times before she leaned forward toward Stiger, sniffing as she came right up to the balcony. Marcus could not believe that Stiger stood his ground as they came face to face. The legate did not move an inch, nor did he flinch.

"I have met this one before," Currose said.

"He is the descendent of Delvaris," Menos said.

The dragon cocked her great head slightly before pulling back. "Very well, I leave this matter in your claws. I will return to my watch." The dragon spared Marcus a look. "Foolish human. Have a care, for you meddled with that which should not be disturbed."

Then her head and neck withdrew out of view from the balcony. There was the sound of scraping once again, and the balcony floor vibrated as the dragon settled down before finally becoming still. Dust continued to rain down from the ceiling in a fine mist.

"That was unwise," Menos said, turning to Marcus. "Without proper training, there are things your mind is not capable of handling. What were you thinking?"

Marcus stood, if a little shakily. He had a pounding headache and his vision was swimming. He held his forehead in his hands for a moment until the worst subsided.

"What did you do?" Stiger snapped at him, demanding an answer.

"I tried to listen to the mountain as I do the forest, sir." Marcus attempted to come to a position of attention and failed. He staggered slightly and was forced to catch himself with a hand to the cavern wall.

Ogg abruptly giggled, and surprisingly Eli chuckled along with him. Marcus noticed the legate grimace unhappily at Eli.

"He has mountain sense?" Braddock asked, abruptly looking over at Eli for confirmation.

"It would seem so," Eli said, eyeing Marcus with what he took to be an extremely pleased look.

"Impressive," Taha'Leeth said, eyeing Marcus curiously before glancing over at Eli. "The gods favor you greatly, ranger."

"Mountain sense is a very rare trait amongst our people," Braddock said. "Who taught you?"

"That would be me," Eli admitted.

"You?" Braddock asked with astonishment written on his face. "How can an elf teach something only dwarves know?"

"To be fair, you taught me the ways of the forest," Marcus said. The headache was receding. "I just used it here and found something a little different."

"Rock Friend." Garrack stepped forward and gave Marcus a friendly thump on the shoulder that was a little too powerful. Weakened from his encounter with the dragon, Marcus almost collapsed. Garrack caught him by an arm and held him steady. "Among my people you are now Rock Friend. You have great gift from gods. Is occasion for drink. Tonight we share friendly drinks."

Marcus was almost afraid of what a friendly drink entailed, but it sure sounded better than confronting a dragon. "I could sure use a drink."

"What exactly is this mountain sense?" Stiger asked.

"Your ranger can sense the mountain with his mind," Braddock explained. "Perhaps one every generation or so is born with this gift. It is used to find new caverns and veins of ore for mining. Occasionally, when someone is strong enough, they can sense more."

"More?"

"They can sense all living creatures under the mountain." The thane turned a curious look on Marcus. "To provoke such a reaction from Currose, he must be strong with the ability, that is sure."

There was a huffing sound from below and greasy black smoke rose up in several short blasts.

"It is time for you to leave," Menos said curtly before turning and walking down the steps. Over his shoulder he looked back briefly at Marcus. "You have tested Currose's patience. Do not do it again, for we may not be there to save you."

Then he was gone, descending the steps to the cavern floor. Marcus felt chilled by the words of the caretaker. He knew without a doubt that he had been extremely lucky.

"Legate Stiger," Braddock said, "perhaps we should retire for the evening to Old City. We have a place prepared for you, along with some food."

"Lead on," Stiger said, with an unhappy look over at Marcus.

Braddock said something to Naggock in dwarven, and several of the thane's guard started through the doorway.

Braddock followed, with Naggock a step behind. Stiger went next, trailed by Father Thomas and Sergeant Arnold.

"I thought you promised you would stay out of trouble." Eli stepped by Marcus, amusement dancing in his eyes. The elf paused a moment and clapped him on the shoulder before he too stepped through the doorway.

Taha'Leeth looked as if she wanted to say something, but appeared to change her mind. Together with Aver'Mons she stepped through the doorway and left only Garrack and Marcus on the balcony.

Marcus was able to stand much better now. Garrack leaned down and scooped up his blanket and his pack.

"How about we both go and get drink now?" Garrack suggested with a grin. "We both get very drunk. Is not every day you piss on dragon and survive, no?"

There was a very loud and disgusted grunt below them. A gout of flame shot up into the center of the cavern, level with the balcony. The heat of the blast was almost enough to singe.

"That might not be a bad idea," Marcus agreed hastily, retrieving his belongings from Garrack.

SIX

Stiger cracked his neck and then stretched it out as he walked. They had left Grata'Jalor and made the short journey from the castle to the city. On the back side of the castle, a drawbridge over the chasm took them to a large tunnel that led to the city, where they emerged on a ledge high above the cavern that housed Garand Thoss. A road wound downward to the city itself several hundred feet below them.

Garand Thoss had been built inside an adjoining cavern that, much like the one that housed Grata'Jalor, had been painstakingly carved out by hand. Glancing up toward the skylights, Stiger judged it to be late afternoon. The light from above was beginning to wane, casting darkness and shadow across the city below. There were only a few lights visible. From what Stiger could see in the gloom, the city was large and mostly empty.

The city itself, though long-abandoned, was a grand testament to dwarven skill at construction and engineering. Several stories in height, massive steepled buildings rose from a variety of smaller structures on the cavern floor. Where humans would use wood, brick, and plaster, the dwarves seemed to prefer stone. As a result, all of the buildings had a very solid look to them. Yet despite that, Stiger felt that they looked elegant as well.

Braddock explained that only a portion of the city was visible, as the rest extended down into the mountain itself. As they made their way along the road and came closer to the crumbling buildings, it surprised Stiger that such a great city had been abandoned. He had difficulty imagining an imperial city being left in such a way.

The thane and his escort led them off the road and into a portion of the city that appeared to be settled. They passed by several armed patrols of dwarves, all wearing the yellow and brown of Hrove's clan. When Braddock was not looking, Stiger thought he detected dirty looks cast their way. Though, to be honest, it was hard to be sure, what with dwarven beards. Still, Stiger found his sense of unease growing and wondered if it was just his imagination. Perhaps he was simply on edge because he was so far under the mountain. He found it very unnatural and suspected the elves felt the same way too.

They found a couple of gnomes waiting for them, standing patiently just before a tunnel that led downward and out of the massive cavern. The gnomes provided each of them with a lantern. No words were exchanged, and without any thanks to the gnomes, Braddock and his dwarves led them onward through a confusing maze of endless dusty passageways and staircases until they came to one that was nominally lit by oil lamps. The lamps had been hung from hooks in the ceiling every thirty feet or so. The passageway had also been swept clean and was free of dust and cobwebs.

"This is the Calgan District. It was once a thriving residential neighborhood," Braddock explained. He stopped and turned to face them. There were numerous doors located to either side of the passageway, all freshly painted with bright solid colors. The painted doors were the first real bit of color that Stiger had seen in the abandoned city.

Everything else had been drab, shrouded in dust and simply left to decay into ruin.

"Our cities are clan-based," Braddock said, standing in the center of the passageway and addressing them. "Think of them as individual kingdoms, with each clan having their own distinct lands. One clan will not trespass on another's without permission. Sadly, we are a quick-tempered people. I intend to change that. Garand Thoss will be an open city for all clans. It will be a model for the future of my people."

"You mean to populate this city with members from all clans?" Stiger asked the thane.

"It is my dream," Braddock explained with passion. "The first of our settlers from at least half a dozen clans have arrived. Most are second and third sons, with no opportunity to inherit. They come with royal grants to make a life for themselves and their families. More will come, seeking a fresh future, a new start."

"That is a noble effort," Stiger said, thinking on what Braddock was trying to accomplish by repopulating this dead city.

"Perhaps not in my lifetime, but surely in my son's they will reclaim this city," Braddock said brightly. "Garand Thoss will prove to be a symbol that one day all Dvergr will look to as an example."

"In that you are stronger working together than apart?" Eli hazarded.

"Yes, exactly." Braddock looked over at the elf with an extremely pleased look. "That is my dream."

"One day long from now," Eli said, "I hope that I am able return to see your dream fulfilled."

Braddock looked at the elf for a heartbeat and nodded. "Once a thing is done . . . it is easy to forget. On that day, you will tell all who care to listen how this city was once a crumbling ruin? You will remind them of the greatness it took to rebuild?"

"I will," Eli said gravely. "I swear it."

"Then I shall issue a proclamation. Upon my word, I will bind future generations to grant you access to Garand Thoss."

"I am honored," Eli said, inclining his head to the thane.

"The honor is mine," Braddock replied with a faraway look in his eyes. "I will have my proclamation entered into the Great Record this evening. You shall receive a copy."

Stiger looked between the two. Braddock was a determined leader. He would do everything possible to repopulate this city. Stiger could almost envision the thriving metropolis rising from the ashes of a long-dead city. He, like Braddock, would not live to see the dream come to fruition, but Stiger knew Eli well. As promised, he would one day return. It might take five hundred, maybe even a thousand years, but if he were able to do so, he would return. Should it succeed, Eli would witness the fulfillment of Braddock's dream.

Braddock addressed the group. "Two of our settlers from my clan have offered to host you and your companions."

"We are grateful for their hospitality," Stiger said, suspecting that playing host was important to dwarven culture. Stiger would have been happy to make the long ride back to Castle Vrell, though he could not admit that to Braddock.

A lot of work waited for him. He had to assess and assimilate the three new cohorts. Stiger intended to personally evaluate their ability and then build upon it with more training, if needed. There was always room for improvement. Stiger also had to begin preparing for the coming campaign against the Cyphan. There were hundreds of details that needed attending to, the most important being how to feed and supply his men. That meant determining what supplies were needed, both in consumables and equipment. As legate, Stiger was now the equivalent of a general, though his men numbered less than a full legion. He had to start thinking like one, and for the coming offensive with the dwarves, he needed to be prepared. That would require a lot of planning.

Seemingly satisfied with Stiger's response to stay, Braddock turned and led them farther down the passageway, until they came to a purple door, which stood open. Two smaller dwarves were waiting for them. They dropped to a knee before their thane and were quickly permitted to rise.

At first Stiger thought one of the two was another beardless dwarf, like Ogg. Then Stiger realized he was a she. Both dwarves were much younger than Braddock. The male's beard was only half the length of those Stiger had seen serving with the army. Both wore nicely made blue tunics with gray pants, though the male had on a purple vest that matched Braddock's clan colors. They also wore comfortable-looking sandals. A few words were exchanged and the two were introduced as Garran and Tema, a newly married couple from the city of Garand Nuwaga. Neither spoke common. Everything had to be translated by Braddock. Stiger expressed that he felt honored to be their guests. Both seemed pleased and bowed respectfully.

"Eli'Far speaks our tongue," Braddock announced, sounding abruptly weary. "We Dvergr prefer to feast in the morning. I have arranged a state feast. If you have need of me, speak to Garran; otherwise I will see you in the morning."

With that, Braddock turned and left, but not before snapping an order to Naggock. Two of Braddock's personal guard were left behind. They took up a position at either end of the passageway. Eyeing the two guards for a moment, Stiger worried if they would be needed. Was it the lesser races they guarded against or their own kind? The question was a troubling one.

Tema led them through the doorway and into a short hallway. Stiger went first, the elves next, followed by Father Thomas and Sergeant Arnold. It deposited them in a large common room. A tapestry separated the hallway from the common room. Tema held it aside for them to enter. Garran closed the door behind them. Stiger could hear bolts being thrown on the door. Tema smelled faintly of roses and offered him a friendly smile, which he returned as he stepped by her and into the common room.

A wave of warmth and light washed over Stiger. The room was so well-lit that he and the others had to shield their eyes for a moment until they adjusted. The bright light came from a handful of lanterns that were set in mirrored recesses along the walls. The mirrors appeared to amplify the light. It was an ingenious system, and if the opportunity permitted, Stiger planned on studying them closer.

In general, the common room was not what he had expected. Unlike the rest of Old City, it was clean and well-kept. A thick patterned rug took up the entire floor. There were cushions and pillows arranged on the floor that were meant for reclining. Thick, brightly colored, and patterned tapestries hung from the walls, completely covering the cold stone. A small table and two chairs sat in a corner. On it was set a large platter heaped with fruits, breads, and a large, round cheese wheel. A pitcher and several mugs had also been left on the table. There was even a vase with fresh-cut roses. Stiger wondered where they had gotten the flowers. It was the middle of winter.

"Bless me," Father Thomas said, as he stepped into the room. "Isn't this cozy."

Stiger glanced around and found he could not disagree. The overall effect combined to give the room a warm feeling. He liked it. Several hallways led from the room. A draft of warm air caught his attention and he noticed for the first time that there was no fire or even, for that matter, the telltale smell of smoke. He saw several small holes set in the walls where the tapestries had been pulled aside and hung by large hooks. Stiger stepped over and put his hand up to the hole. He marveled at the warm air that blew into the room.

Tema stepped forward and lifted the tapestry off of the hook. She let it fall back into place and said something, which he did not understand. She gestured emphatically toward the wall and then replaced the tapestry on the hook once again exposing the hole.

"She says that if it becomes too warm," Eli translated, "simply block the heating hole with the tapestry."

Tema launched into speech again, directing herself to Eli. Garran stood by her side and smiled broadly at his guests.

"She welcomes us to their humble home and requests we kindly take off our boots and place them here," Eli translated. Tema was pointing to a bench near the entrance to the hallway that led to their front door. Under the bench there were two well-worn pairs of boots. "She also says that rooms have been set aside for us and there are two washing rooms available for our use."

"That's a step in the right direction," Stiger said. He very much desired to remove his armor and perform a proper toilet. "Eli, please thank them for their hospitality," Stiger added as he moved over to remove his boots. The others began to do the same.

Eli translated and the two dwarves nodded with pleased expressions.

Once they had removed their shoes, Tema and Garran showed them their rooms. Stiger had his own, but the others were forced to share. The rooms were simple and without beds, with only pillows and a set of neatly folded quilted blankets. The walls, like the common room, were covered in tapestries. A thick, multicolored rug covered the stone flooring. Holes in the walls delivered warm air to each room.

The sound of running water greeted them before they entered the washing room. Water emerged from a hole in the wall and ran rapidly through a trough before disappearing out through another hole. It was a simple aqueduct system, similar to what the empire used in their cities to deliver water. In the empire, only the wealthiest could afford their own running water by purchasing a grant from the imperial household. The grant permitted them to tap directly into the aqueducts that carried water into Mal'Zeel. Those less fortunate had to settle for the communal troughs, basins, or fountains.

It was not uncommon to see the communal water supplies packed with slaves drawing water into barrels and jars to be carried back to residences. Stiger's family estate drew fresh water directly through lead pipes connected to the main aqueduct into Mal'Zeel. There had never been a period as a child where he had been forced to draw his own water. The water, like Garran and Tema's, flowed right into his home.

The dwarves had placed several large bowls and pitchers on a small wooden table for use in the washroom. On another table lay a pile of neatly folded towels, along with a bar of coarse soap. There was a small, grated drain in the floor. Tema warned them not to drink from the running water, as it was not fit for consumption.

They were then shown where Tema and Garran's side of the house was, including the kitchen with additional food. That side was fully furnished, with tables, chairs, and furniture. The two young dwarves were proud of their home and it showed. Before retiring, they politely asked if anything else was required.

Stiger went to his room and carefully removed his armor, starting with the sword first. Touching the hilt, he felt the familiar, comforting tingle. He paused, examining the scabbard and running his hand along one of the lacquered dragons. Before today, he had never thought to encounter a dragon or learn that Rome was real. All of it had been a shock, but it was the sword that worried Stiger. It seemed at times almost alive. He considered speaking to Father Thomas about it, but then dismissed the idea. For some strange reason that Stiger could not fully explain to himself, he did not yet feel comfortable talking to the paladin about the weapon. Was it that he was afraid of what he would learn? Or was it something else, far darker? Sighing, Stiger placed the sword in a small recess set into the wall. He spent some time cleaning his armor with a towel and small brush, then stacked it neatly in a corner.

Reduced to his tunic, he padded for the washroom and found one of them empty. He could hear the others out in the common room. The water was bitterly cold, but the entire house was comfortably warm. Like any other imperial noble, he appreciated cleanliness. Stiger bathed quickly. Once clean, he toweled himself off and put his tunic back on.

Stiger made for the common room, where he found Eli and Taha'Leeth speaking in low tones. They looked up at his approach. Both were pale, strained, and clearly uncomfortable. There was no one else about. The others must have retired to their rooms. Stiger suspected it would not be long before someone joined them.

"The washroom is available if you wish to use it, my lady." Stiger desired to speak with Eli alone. What he had to say was not for others to overhear.

"Thank you," Taha'Leeth said, picking up on the less-than-subtle hint and left them alone.

Stiger waited until her footsteps could no longer be heard. "How much of this did you know?" he asked Eli bluntly.

Eli said nothing, which only confirmed Stiger's suspicion. He felt a hollow feeling in the pit of his stomach. Once again, Eli had withheld something of critical importance from him.

"And you never thought to tell me?" Stiger's anger began to rise. He was at a loss for why his best friend had concealed something so important. The anger blossomed into a full rage. All through the weeks of fighting, Eli had said nothing.

"How much did you know?" Stiger demanded again.

"Most of it," Eli admitted quietly. "I knew of the World Gate and the war."

"Why not tell me?"

"I had hoped it was not time, that this burden would fall on someone else's shoulders."

"So you decided to keep me in the dark?" Stiger asked harshly. "Because of wishful thinking?"

Eli said nothing, but instead looked away.

"I thought you were my friend."

"I am."

"Then you should have told me! You should have trusted me as I trusted you."

"Would it have made any difference?" Eli asked hotly.

"It might have," Stiger growled. "We could have gone searching for the dwarves and restored the Compact."

"The dwarves long ago retreated and locked themselves away in hidden cities like this one. I had no idea where they were." Eli looked up, meeting Stiger's angry gaze. "They found us all the same. It has worked out rather well."

"That is not the point!" Stiger seethed with anger.

"Would you have believed me? If I had told you more on the dwarves? How much more difficult would it have been had I told you of the World Gate and the war between the gods? Would you have believed me then?"

Stiger said nothing as he considered Eli's words.

"Yes, I knew the dwarves had the World Gate. No, I did not know where it was. The dwarves and the Noctalum moved it from its original location and hid it away. Yes, I knew of the Compact and its purpose, but I did not know of the Thirteenth's connection to it all. There are some things I just do not know. I ask you again, would you have believed me?"

His friend had a point, but Stiger was too angry to concede it. Eli should have told him and trusted in their friendship. Stiger had long since learned to trust Eli, but knowing his friend had hidden much from him, he considered for the first time that his faith was perhaps misplaced.

"You remained silent," Stiger said, "even after the dwarves found us and I shared the contents of Delvaris's scroll with you."

Eli said nothing but looked down at the floor, avoiding Stiger's angry gaze.

"How can I ever trust you again?" Stiger asked, the heat leaving him in a rush. He felt drained by his friend's betrayal. "How will I know that you are forthcoming and not holding something back like Braddock? Something important?"

"You can trust me." Eli had a stricken look upon his face. "I am your friend."

"Can I?" Stiger demanded. "Are you really?"

"If you doubt that, Ben, then you are a fool," Eli snapped, anger plain in his voice. He was about to say more when they heard steps in the hallway leading to their rooms. Instead, Eli turned away for his room without a backward glance. A few moments later, Stiger caught a glimpse of Father Thomas leaving one of the washing rooms at the end of the corridor. Had the paladin overheard their argument? He decided after some thought that he did not care.

Stiger sat alone at the table in the common room. The others had long since gone to bed. It was late and he was tired. It had been an exceptionally long day. Stiger was angrier than he cared to admit. He was also in a terrible mood, which the others had sensed. They had left him to his brooding.

He and Eli had been through a lot together. For the life of him, Stiger did not understand how Eli could willingly keep such things to himself. Eli did have a point, though, and Stiger very much doubted that he would have fully believed had everything been revealed in advance. It was one thing to tell someone of the impossible and another for them to see it and discover for themselves. Still, Eli's behavior troubled him greatly.

What else are you hiding?

Besides his fight with Eli, Stiger was troubled about all he had learned. He was caught up in something that was far beyond his control. He did not wish to be part of it, and yet he felt like a puppet. All he wanted to do was serve his empire. The gods, the Compact, the World Gate, dragons, wizards, and magic . . . Stiger desired no part of that. His life had been so much simpler when he had been a lowly infantry officer serving in the legions, without some grand destiny that had been planned out in advance.

What he had learned about Rome intrigued him. He had to admit that it would be fascinating to travel to the fabled city that his empire only knew from legend, tale, and song. Stiger had been told by Braddock it would be his choice whether or not to open the World Gate, as the Oracle had prophesized it apparently in such a way that the exact meaning was fiendishly cryptic and hard to completely understand. Before Ogg had left them, the wizard had even admitted that he did not fully understand the Prophecy and he had spent years studying it. Stiger had wanted to read the Prophecy, but it turned out the dwarves did not have a copy in Old City. Braddock promised to send for one, but it would not arrive for some weeks. So, Stiger was relying on the words and recollections of others who did not fully understand what the Oracle had written. It was not a comforting thought. In fact, it was downright frustrating, maddening.

Stiger wondered what exactly lay on Tanis's side of the Gate. Two thousand years was a long time. He was sorely tempted to find out, more even than he cared to admit. On top of all of his other worries, this was a burden he surely did not need.

Stiger sipped some ale from his mug. It was extremely good, though he found he was not really able to appreciate it. His worries were eating away at him. The empire was in deep peril and the emperor was in danger. There was no telling what was happening beyond Castle Vrell's walls. Like a toy ship in a glass bottle, he was stuck in Vrell, and all the while the empire was burning. It was extremely frustrating. Stiger felt helpless, and that made him angry.

"Is it your habit to drink alone?"

Stiger straightened up from a slouch and turned to see Taha'Leeth. There was no telling how long she had been there. It could have been mere moments or longer. Stiger shrugged. He did not care.

"May I join you?" She came over to the table.

Stiger shrugged again.

She took the free chair and sat opposite from him. She was still wearing her woodland green and brown leathers. His dark mood lifted slightly as her beauty and fiery red hair brightened the room. Taha'Leeth poured herself a drink before leaning back. She sat for a while, staring at her mug as the silence in the room stretched.

"When I was a child, my family lived in a peaceful place." She took a light sip from her mug before placing it back on the table, both hands encircling it. "It was my home. The only home I had ever known. Elves had dwelt there for years beyond counting. We called it Dela Cor'tal. It was the most wonderful place imaginable, with ancient trees many hundreds of hands high with the lifespan to match an elf and so thick around you would find it impossible to believe."

She stopped talking and her eyes lost their focus. She seemed to be looking inward, remembering. Her focus returned and Taha'Leeth's eyes found his.

"Dela Cor'tal was a peaceful place. We were a peaceful people, who threatened no one. We had asked for no trouble, nor desired any, but the war came just the same." Her tone turned bitter. "It changed our nature as a people. Our gods demanded that we fight. We dutifully heeded their call and fight we did."

Knowing elves, Stiger suspected that no elf had ever told another non-elf this tale. Coming out of his funk, he listened with rapt attention as she continued.

"The war eventually shattered my people and scattered us over many worlds. We suffered unimaginable heartache. Dela Cor'tal was overrun, and those beautiful, ancient trees burned, along with my childhood." She paused for a moment, taking another sip from her mug and swallowing before continuing. "We felt betrayed by our gods, and so we abandoned them. We sought a quiet world, a place that knew not of the Last War and the struggle of the gods. In our long search . . . we found Istros. I led my people here."

Stiger's mind reeled. It meant she was much older than Eli, for if Stiger understood correctly, the World Gate had last been opened over two thousand years ago.

"Why are you telling me this?"

"We thought that by running, we could eventually find a world free of the war, but that decision was wrong."

"That is why Eli did not know of your people, nor you his," Stiger said. Another piece of the puzzle clicked into place. "You came through the other World Gate. Eli's people came through the one the dwarves have."

"Yes," she admitted sadly. "In our haste for safety and sanctuary, we destroyed the other World Gate, hoping to leave the war behind. We thought we could defy the gods. We were wrong. Our punishment was slavery and servitude."

"To the Cyphan?"

"First to the Bandu, then another, and finally the Cyphan. They are all the same, but with different names."

She was silent for several moments as she took another sip. Stiger could not help but feel sorry for her and her people. The pain in her voice was palpable.

"Eli'Far's people, though of the same blood, are similar to my people . . . yet different," she continued. "Do not judge your friend too harshly. By not sharing all he knew, he was protecting you, as he works to shield his own people."

Stiger considered her words, and both were silent for some time.

"What if we do destroy the dwarves' Gate?" Stiger asked. "We could roll the dice and take the risk that it will work out in the end."

"I fear," she took a deep breath, "the punishment for doing so would be far worse than mere slavery and servitude."

Stiger was silent, thinking. The more he thought it through, the more he was coming to the conclusion that he had little choice. Stiger had always honored the High Father and the other friendly gods, but he had never been truly devout. He had trusted that as long as he honored them, prayed, and made an occasional offering, they would mind their own business and share the occasional blessing. He had been mistaken. They wanted much more from him.

"I have no choice," Stiger admitted, staring down at the drink in his hands. "Is that why you are telling me this?"

She laughed lightly, and with it the pain seemed to leave her voice. Stiger found her laugh to be attractive. "Have you not been listening? We all have a choice."

"With all choices there are consequences then," Stiger said. "Is that what you are getting at?"

"My people made a choice, a poor one, and we paid dearly for it. You, I sense, are undecided. You wrestle with your own."

"My decision could not only ruin me, but the world and my empire as well," he said. "If I understand things correctly?"

Taha'Leeth nodded gravely.

"This dwarven Oracle prophesized that I am the one to decide whether the World Gate opens or stays shut," Stiger said. "It is not a choice I care to make."

"You are one of several who may make that choice," she said. "The other alignments have their own champions."

Stiger had suspected as much. It was why both Castor and Valloor had made their moves for the Gate. He had already worked out that the other alignments also had to have the ability to open the World Gate. If Stiger was the High Father's choice and champion, who represented the other factions? Might he have to confront those champions? It was not, Stiger thought sourly, an exciting prospect. "How do I know which one is the correct path?"

"That is for you to decide," she said.

"You are not being helpful."

She flashed Stiger an amused smile as he took a pull on his drink. Stiger set the drink down on the table and frowned unhappily.

"If the gods sentenced your people to slavery," Stiger said, looking back up at her, "then how is it you were able to throw off that yoke? Won't your people be punished again?"

Taha'Leeth did not immediately reply. Her eyes searched his and then studied his face. Stiger was transfixed by her eyes. Like other elven females, they were deep and seductive, but with Taha'Leeth, it was more, something different. Stiger was sure it was not simply the allure of her beauty. Stiger had lived with the elves in their forests to the north. She made the other elven girls he had known seem drab by comparison. Oddly, he felt a connection with her at some primal level. It was not her beauty, of that he was sure. In her eyes, he saw pain and suffering. Was that it?

"When my people were first punished," Taha'Leeth began slowly, "we suffered terribly at the hands of humans. I suffered . . . "

A solitary tear ran down her cheek. Stiger wanted to reach out and brush it away, offer her some comfort, but could not bring himself to do it.

"I suffered more than I care to admit," she said, and steel came into her voice. "I will not bore you with the details, just that I have come to hate your kind with a passion not borne of this world."

Stiger did not like the sound of that but did not stir or interrupt her. This was Taha'Leeth's story to tell and he wanted to hear it.

"I had a vision many years ago, long before you were born. It was after a terrible time. I had been brought so low I considered taking my own life. Amongst elves, suicide is one of the worst imaginable sins, but I was beyond caring. As I was about to end my life, one of the gods we had abandoned, Tanithe, came to me. In that vision, I saw that one day my people would be freed and that we would be forgiven." She paused and nearly sobbed. "Yet . . . Tanithe also revealed to me that I alone would have to make another choice for my people to be forgiven. To atone, I would have to sacrifice all that I am and will be."

"Why you and you alone?"

"As punishment for my actions, for it was I who saw to it the World Gate was destroyed. I, who hated humans more than any other, would have to forgive, to choose . . . to . . . choose . . . " She stopped abruptly and wiped another tear away. "I would have to surrender my feelings of loathing, disgust, and contempt . . . "

"Your choice?" Stiger asked, eyes narrowing. "You have already made it?"

"I have," Taha'Leeth admitted solemnly, which was followed by a near sob, before she recovered herself.

"Your people coming north," Stiger realized with sudden surprise. "Your people are now free again as they once were."

"It is more than that. Don't you see?" she said in a voice that was almost pleading. "Tanithe showed me the one in my vision who would help me choose a new path for my people. He showed me you."

"Me?" Stiger asked in alarm, leaning back in his chair. Now the gods were showing visions of him to others. Could this get any worse?

"Eli had told me much about you, but I did not believe. At first I thought I could control you, twist you to my will."

"The glamour?"

"Yes, and I was wrong to try. So, I gave in to what I was shown. I surrendered not only myself, but my soul. I have committed myself and my people to the High Father's cause."

Stiger frowned. "Will he accept you back?"

She tilted her head and looked at him in a curious, almost amused manner.

"What makes you think we were ever originally with the High Father?" she asked, finishing her drink and looking at him. Stiger was stunned by her admission. No wonder Eli's people had not joined the Compact and stood apart.

Taha'Leeth stood, pushing back her chair, and stepped around the table to him. Stiger felt his heart quicken at her nearness. She looked down upon him in a contemplative manner.

"Such passion bound up in such a short lifespan," she said, a hand caressing the side of his face. Stiger almost pushed her hand away, but the touch was like fire upon his skin. His heart beat even faster. Elven women had always had such an effect upon him, but not as much as Taha'Leeth was having now. She traced his scarred cheek with her index finger.

"Despite your gruff exterior, you are a good man, Ben Stiger." Leaning down, her lips brushed his cheek. "Though you do not fully understand yet, I have made my choice, and for that I thank you. In return, I have given you a great gift that I desperately fear one day both of us may regret."

Taha'Leeth straightened, looked down upon him for a moment. Then she turned away and left for her room.

Stiger suddenly felt very tired and more than a little frustrated. He could still feel the spot where her lips had brushed his cheek. What gift? he wondered. Elves were incredibly frustrating. Why could they never come right out and say what they meant?

Stiger finished his drink, stood, and retired to his room with the hopes of getting some sleep. Thinking on what she had just told him, he had his doubts that sleep would come easy.

"Why can't things ever be simple?" Stiger asked his empty room as he prepared to bed down for the night.

SEVEN

Stiger's eyes snapped open. It took him a moment to remember where he was. Light seeped into the room from underneath the tapestry hanging over the doorway. He could hear booted feet out in the hallway, and they were coming nearer. He rubbed at his eyes and then remembered that boots were to be left at the door. Something had happened.

Stiger sat up as the tapestry was pulled aside and light flooded into the small room. Shielding his eyes, Stiger saw Garran holding a lantern and looking apologetic. A legionary was behind him, one of Lan's troopers, judging by the long cavalry sword dangling from his side. The dwarf said something that appeared to be an apology as Stiger climbed to his feet. The trooper braced to attention at the sight of the legate.

"What is it?" Stiger demanded. He knew that being disturbed in this way boded ill. He wondered how long he had been asleep. It was difficult to tell time under the mountain, though Stiger felt somewhat rested. He must have managed several hours at least, which was good.

"Sorry, sir," the legionary said, stepping around Garran and entering the room. He handed a dispatch to Stiger and then stepped back. "From Lieutenant Lan, sir."

"I see. Garran, can you light my lantern?" Stiger asked and gestured toward the extinguished lantern. Garran lit it from his own lantern. He turned up Stiger's lantern so that shortly there was plenty of light to see by in the room. Garran bowed respectfully and then retreated. Stiger held the lantern up as he read the dispatch and then looked up.

"Did you see the fires?" Stiger asked the trooper.

"No, sir. The lieutenant went with a dwarf to see them. He then returned and wrote the dispatch. The lieutenant said to tell you that some of the fires looked quite large."

Stiger did not want to hear that. It meant a village or two, perhaps even a town, had been raided. This was the last thing he needed, especially now when he was away from his command.

"Do you know what time it is?"

"Sometime before dawn, sir."

Stiger cursed and began gathering his things. He should have been out there, where he could do some good, not here under the mountain in a dead city.

"The lieutenant ordered that the troop be made ready. He said to tell you he will be prepared to ride when you arrive, sir."

"Very good," Stiger said. "Go wake the others. They are in the rooms adjacent to this one."

"Yes, sir." The trooper left.

Stiger started to dress. As he was beginning to don his armor, Eli appeared.

"What is wrong?" Eli asked.

"A raid is underway in the valley. It appears the Cyphan got over the mountains," Stiger growled, pangs of anger from last night's argument resurfacing. He took a deep breath and let it out as he tightened the straps and tied them securely, looking away. "We are leaving."

Eli nodded and disappeared, letting the tapestry fall back into place.

Less than ten minutes later, Stiger strode into the common room, saddlebag in hand, sword hilt in the other. He found the trooper waiting with a dwarven warrior from the Hammer Fisted Clan. The dwarf eyed Stiger curiously as he approached. Garran and Tema stood off to one side. The others were not in the common room as of yet, but Stiger could hear them getting ready.

"What is your name?" Stiger asked the trooper.

"Legionary Talcus, sir."

"Report to Lieutenant Lan that we will be on our way shortly."

"Yes, sir." Talcus turned to his escort and gestured back toward the passageway. The dwarf nodded his understanding, and in moments both had gone. Stiger was about to ask Garran to find Braddock when the thane arrived with Garrack, who appeared extremely tired. Both wore only their tunics. They looked as if they had just been woken from a sound sleep.

"I heard about the fires," Braddock said first, with a grave look. "It cannot be more than a handful at most. The mountains are difficult to cross, especially at this time of year."

"I agree," Stiger said, thinking of the forbidding peaks that hemmed in the valley and of the recent heavy snows that should have made them nearly impassable. "I intend to deal with them and make sure they never come back."

"Good," Braddock replied.

Something occurred to Stiger. "Do you suppose they may have found a way into the valley through the tunnels and mines?"

Braddock looked over to Garrack, who shook his head firmly.

"We patrol mines and tunnels around Grata'Kor well," Garrack said. "We have word first if enemy in mines."

"Garrack is right," Braddock said. "No one is better underground than a dwarf. They would not have been able to evade our patrols. The Cyphan had to have come over the mountains to access the valley."

Stiger nodded, hoping they were right. If they were wrong . . .

Eli and Taha'Leeth emerged, along with Aver'Mons. Father Thomas arrived a moment later with Sergeant Arnold on his heels. Both were dressed and alert.

"Garrack will take you out of the mountain," Braddock said with a solemn look. "We will feast and break bread together another time."

"I would like that," Stiger said and found that he meant it. He was beginning to like the gruff thane.

"We have business here with Hrove," Braddock continued. "As soon as it is concluded, I will return to the army, likely by nightfall. Once this mess is settled, we will begin planning our offensive, *together*."

"I look forward to it," Stiger said, eager to be on his way but pleased that Braddock had emphasized the word "together."

"It is good you saw the World Gate," Braddock said, after a slight hesitation. "Now you know what we fight for."

"Yes," Stiger said, catching a look from Taha'Leeth. He frowned, thinking on their conversation the night before, then nodded to Braddock. "We fight to protect not only our people, but this world. I understand."

Braddock offered Stiger his hand.

"I will see you soon." Braddock stepped back.

Stiger glanced around at those gathered and ready. He was about to turn to leave when he realized someone was missing.

"Where is Marcus?" Stiger asked of Eli, who, in surprise, looked to Aver'Mons. They exchanged a few words in elven before the other elf pointed at Garrack.

"Ah . . . about that," Garrack said with an uncomfortable cough. "He's not in best shape, but will recover. He join us where horses are, though he may need be carried and lashed to his mount. I have already seen to it."

Stiger thought he could detect the strong air of ale about Garrack and frowned. Braddock shot a hard look at Garrack, who simply shrugged.

"It seemed like thing to do," Garrack said apologetically. "Pissing on dragon is not done every day. He needed drink."

"Right then," Stiger growled and turned to the others. "Let's go."

Crossing the drawbridge from Grata'Jalor, Stiger could see his cavalry assembled and ready. The men were holding their horses by the reins, waiting for the order to mount up. Stiger was surprised to see a large number of dwarven warriors, all from the Hammer Fisted Clan, watching them. There were perhaps as many as two hundred dwarves, all armed and in armor.

"Sir," Lan greeted as Stiger and the others joined them. "Dispatch rider just arrived for you."

Vargus was speaking heatedly to a cavalry trooper, who was holding the reins of his horse. Foam and sweat dripped from his horse's mouth, rump, and sides. He had clearly pushed his horse hard, which in the dark suggested that the raid was perhaps more serious than Stiger had thought.

Moving quickly on horseback in the dark was dangerous. Stiger ground his teeth in frustration. He pushed his way through the horses and men toward the dispatch rider, who, seeing the legate, turned with a relieved look as he braced to attention. Vargus scowled slightly when he saw Stiger.

"About time," Stiger thought he heard the centurion mutter under his breath. Stiger let it pass.

"Dispatch, sir, from Lieutenant Ikely." The trooper handed over the dispatch he had been holding, shooting Vargus a wary look as he did so. It was apparent the trooper had been unwilling to surrender the dispatch to the centurion.

Breaking the seal, Stiger scanned the contents. Several farms and villages had been attacked at the southern end of the valley around sunset. From the height of the castle walls, the burning buildings could clearly be observed. Ikely had dispatched Second Cohort, which had been out on a training march. He had also dispatched a troop of cavalry for a reconnaissance and placed Third Cohort on alert, prepared to march at short notice. Though the fires looked bad, Ikely speculated that a small force of rebels had made it over the mountains and was causing limited damage, burning whatever they could.

"You are from Lieutenant Cannol's company?" Stiger asked the dispatch rider.

"Yes, sir."

"Good job. Get your horse watered. Then walk her back to the castle. I don't think the lieutenant will be pleased if your mount comes up lame." The horse looked too blown for any further riding.

"Yes, sir, thank you, sir." With a wary glance over at the centurion, the trooper turned away and led his horse over toward a trough of water near the stables.

Stiger handed the dispatch to Vargus to read and sought out Lan. No matter how the people of the valley had greeted him on his way out to Thane's Mountain, he understood that their trust still had to be earned. If he did not handle this right, the people would begin to question his competence. If that happened, he would lose respect of the valley cohorts too. Then he would be in serious trouble.

"Where's my horse?"

"Sergeant Mills has it over there, sir." Lan pointed.

"Have the men mount up," Stiger ordered.

"Mount!" Lan shouted. Armor and bridles jingled as the men of the troop pulled themselves up onto their horses.

"Happily fed and watered, sir," Mills said, handing over the reins. The sergeant was holding his own mount as well. "I also made sure to put rations in your mess kit."

"Thank you, sergeant," Stiger replied, checking the tightness on Nomad's saddle straps. They were not loose.

Mills pulled himself up onto his own horse. Stiger saw that the others who had gone with him to see the World Gate had already mounted. Not surprisingly, Marcus was present. The ranger swayed slightly in the saddle and looked far from fit for a long ride.

"When did he get here?" Stiger asked, nodding toward Marcus.

"About ten minutes before you, sir," Mills replied with a sour look. "A couple of dwarves half carried, half dragged him. Says he and Garrack had a bit of a rough night, sir. Smells like a cheap tavern, he does."

"With everything he's done over the past few weeks, I'd say Marcus has earned himself a drink or two." Stiger patted Nomad affectionately on the neck as his horse nuzzled him in greeting.

"Two?" Mills questioned with a disapproving look. "Smells like he fell into the barrel, sir."

"He might have needed it. Marcus had a run-in with a dragon."

"A dragon?" Mills asked, disbelief creeping into his voice. "Are you pulling one over on me, sir?"

"I wish I was," Stiger breathed and swung himself up and into the saddle.

"Legate," Garrack called, approaching.

Stiger wheeled his horse about to see the dwarf. Nomad sidestepped as Garrack came closer. Stiger pulled sharply on the reins, stilling the animal.

"You see to valley," the dwarf told him with a serious look. "We meet you back at Castle Vrell when you return."

"I will see you then, Garrack." Stiger flashed an amused smile. "Thank you for returning Marcus, though I rather suspect the ride will be tough on him."

"Marcus good human," Garrack added with a matching smile through his beard. "Me fault he is drunk. You humans no hold drink like Dvergr. You not punish?"

Stiger shot a look over at Marcus, who, in the dim light of the massive cavern cast by nearby fire pits and torches, certainly looked to be in a terrible state. He was having difficulty staying in the saddle and was holding on for dear life as a trooper held his reins.

"I will not discipline him. He is a good man," Stiger affirmed.

"He has good Legend," Garrack said, with a pleased smile. "I share drink with him again."

Stiger leaned down from his horse and offered the dwarf a hand. They shook briefly.

"Lieutenant," Stiger called, seeing the cavalry had formed up into a double column. "Time to go."

"FOORAAWAARD," the lieutenant hollered, which echoed distantly off the walls of the great cavern. With a clatter, the column started forward toward the gates that led out of the mountain. The dwarves followed them. Stiger could not tell whether they were escorting him out or making sure that no humans wandered off, save the dispatch rider who was still watering and resting his horse.

The ride to the front gate was a short one. The doors were already open, and Stiger discovered that he had been missing fresh air as a cold winter gust cut through the tunnel. The abandoned dwarven city had smelled of mustiness, dampness, and decay. Though the wind was bitterly cold, the clean air was like a welcome old friend. He tugged his cloak tighter about himself as they rode by the last of the large fire pits and out through the gate into the early morning gloom.

The column came to an abrupt and uncertain halt. Stiger, riding at the rear, kicked his horse forward and around the side, rapidly riding up to the front of the column, where he found Lan and Vargus, eyes fixed forward toward the other end of the valley.

The sight that greeted him was shocking. It appeared as if the entire southern end of the valley were on fire. The horizon was a haze of deep orange from the glowing flames, with several distinct fires and an extremely large one. It had to be a town, Stiger realized.

Back at Castle Vrell, Stiger had studied the map of the valley carefully. If he recalled correctly, the largest town on the southern end of the valley was Riverton. It was the town where Lan had met with the valley council. On the map, a small river ran just north of the town. He had been told that there was a flour mill located there too that ground much of the valley's wheat.

From past experience, Stiger knew that it probably looked far worse than it was. Though he could not be sure, it was likely several bands of men burning whatever they could. In the dark of night, the fires could have been set by just a handful. Once the people of the towns and villages had gone to sleep, the enemy could have snuck in, set several fires, and then hoofed it. Without facts, Stiger realized this was all speculation. It might actually be the result of a substantial raid, in which case he would have a much more serious problem on his hands.

Stiger ground his teeth in frustration. This was his fault. A good commander knew his ground. He should never have agreed to join Braddock until he had ridden through the valley himself, assessing the slopes and possible ways to get across the mountains. Clearly the patrols he had dispatched had not proven sufficient. Stiger realized belatedly he needed a better understanding of the ground, a visual one. Now he was going to pay for it.

Though the damage was likely minimal and only affecting the civilians of the valley, the enemy had just dealt him a blow he would have some difficulty correcting. They had just proven that they could easily strike inside the valley. Not only would the raid cast some doubt on his competence, but it would ultimately require him to spread his forces out across the entirety of the valley. The slopes would have to be more heavily patrolled, as the enemy could not be permitted a repeat raid. This would limit the time available for training and preparation for a spring campaign. It would also eat up a lot of his personal time. The castle would have fewer defenders on hand, though with the dwarven army, holding Castle Vrell should not prove to be a problem.

Damn them! Stiger smacked his hand down upon his thigh in frustration, causing Nomad to sidestep nervously.

Gazing on the fires at the southern end of the valley, Stiger knew he must appear decisive and in control. He had to capture or kill as many of the raiders as possible. Stiger preferred to capture at least a few. That way they would be able to determine how and where the enemy had made it over the mountains. If they could not get a prisoner, then it would be up to the elves and his scouts to determine where the enemy had crossed over.

Damn them!

"That's Riverton," Vargus breathed in stunned disbelief.

"The southernmost town, right?" Stiger asked, understanding the significance for the centurion and feeling sympathetic to the man.

"My home."

Stiger pulled out his dispatch pad and charcoal pencil from a pocket in his cloak. Using what little light there was, he scratched out orders for Ikely. This raid also presented an opportunity, one he intended not to waste.

"Legate," Vargus said, snapping out of his shock. "We must get moving."

Stiger ignored him as he continued to write to Ikely. He explained he was riding toward the southern end of the valley to take direct command. He ordered Ikely to deploy the entirety of Lieutenant Cannol's cavalry. Cannol was to report to him at or near Riverton. He also ordered the Third Cohort to begin marching after Second Cohort. He hesitated a moment and ordered the 85th to march as soon as practical.

Stiger knew the 85th. They were his company. He had trained them, and after weeks of difficult fighting, they were all hardened veterans. They were men he could trust and rely upon. He did not yet know the true worth of Second or Third Cohorts. These were valley-trained men. He had assurances from Vargus and the other valley officers that they were good, but their effectiveness was still a question in Stiger's mind. Could they be trusted in a fight? Would they hold or run? Those were questions that he did not know the answers to. This was the perfect opportunity to begin testing them and their capabilities. Though Stiger knew the real test would only come in a standup fight or battle. Chasing a handful of raiders around the valley would not tell him all he needed to know, but it would be a start.

"Sir!" Vargus said in an angry tone. "My family is there."

Stiger had just ordered an additional eight hundred men out, not counting Second Cohort. When added to the total, Stiger would have a little over twelve hundred men in the field.

He continued to write. Ikely was to remain at the castle, with Brent. At no point was he to leave it, even if Stiger called for the First Cohort. The remnants of the garrison were to remain in possession of Castle Vrell. Stiger reminded Ikely that the raid on the valley could be a diversion. The enemy might be preparing a direct assault on the castle itself. He was to remain vigilant. If needed, he was to request assistance from the dwarven army commander until Braddock returned, which he expected to be this evening.

"Sir, are you listening to me?" Vargus demanded. "My cohort is marching south. We need to meet up with them."

Stiger finished writing, having added a request for confirmation of receipt at the end. Stiger spared the centurion a short look. He well understood the man's concern for his home and family. His loved ones could be dead or injured.

"Lieutenant." Stiger turned to Lan. He sealed the orders and, leaning over, handed them to Lan. "Select two of your best men. They are to deliver these orders to Lieutenant Ikely."

Lan immediately called for two men, passed them the orders, and told them to make for the castle at best possible speed. They set off, thundering over the stone toward the path down to the valley.

"I've ordered the cavalry out," Stiger explained to both Lan and Vargus. "We will need their eyes if we are to catch the bastards who did this. Third Cohort and the 85th will march as well. First will remain in reserve at the castle 'til we know more."

"Can we get moving now?" Vargus demanded with a thunderous expression.

Stiger bristled at the man's tone. It was insubordinate. Stiger swallowed a harsh reply. He had need of the man. Vargus was concerned for his family, but that did not excuse the disrespect. Alienating the man now would hardly serve his purpose of gaining the full assistance and respect from those of the valley, not to mention the most from Second Cohort.

"We are going to set a good pace," Stiger informed them. "We will ride two miles and then walk our horses one mile and repeat."

"What? Sir, I—"

"It will do us no good if our horses are blown by noon," Stiger growled, locking gazes with the centurion. "We have a lot of ground to cover. We will get there quicker if the horses do not go lame."

Vargus looked as if he wanted to say more, but bit off whatever he was going to say.

"Yes, sir," the centurion replied and averted his gaze.

"Lan, get the men moving."

"FOORAAWAARD!"

EIGHT

"This is the village of Tedge," Vargus informed Stiger. The two were riding side by side to the front of Lan and his troop. The sun had been up for several hours. Large pillars of smoke continued to rise into the sky in the direction they were riding. The elves, Father Thomas, and Sergeant Arnold were at the other end of the column. Eli had been avoiding him, keeping company of his own kind. Stiger was in a terrible mood, and it suited him just fine as he rode with Vargus.

The dirt road, somewhat muddy from the last snow and subsequent melting, showed evidence of recent passage by a large body of men. Stiger surmised that Second Cohort had passed through ahead of them. Imprints of hobnailed sandals gave it away.

"And those men?" Stiger asked as they neared the outskirts of the village. Around thirty armed men stood on lookout.

"Retired members of Second and Third Cohorts," Vargus explained with a wave of his hand. "Men like Malik, who are too old to serve or have given up their place to a youngster. They act more as a reserve militia should the worst come to pass."

Stiger absorbed that as he studied the village of Tedge, which had been built in a circular manner. He had seen similar villages in the heart of the empire, where the houses were grouped together in the center. The fields and animal pens spread outward like the spokes of a great wagon wheel. There were no defensive walls. The road cut right through the village.

"Much of the male population of the valley served at one time or another," Vargus added. "It is considered a badge of honor."

"If need be, how many can report under arms?" Stiger looked over at the centurion, eyebrows raised. "How many can still march effectively?"

Vargus took a deep breath before answering, thinking it over. He blew it out slowly. "Perhaps as many as five hundred, maybe a few less."

"And of those who can't march, but could still pick up a sword and serve?"

"I would expect another two thousand," Vargus answered, looking back over at Stiger. "What are you thinking?"

"Once we go over to the offensive against the Cyphan, it would be good to know that Castle Vrell is in capable hands."

"You would leave the castle in the hands of old men then?"

"It would allow us to deploy our maximum strength," Stiger explained. "The Cyphan are a determined enemy. I have a feeling we will need every sword."

"Vargus!" a man greeted as they rode up to the first of the buildings. Several others came over to watch as the cavalry troop rode into town. Like the other villages they had passed through, there were no cheers. The civilians were grim. "Your cohort came through here no less than two hours ago."

Vargus pulled his horse up to a stop, as did Stiger. A few of the locals had joined the five armed men who greeted them. All were older. The man who had hailed Vargus was in officer's kit. Stiger figured he was in his fifties.

"Legate," Vargus said formally, "may I introduce you to the mayor of Tedge, Centurion Severus Tilanus?"

"Retired," Tilanus added, and then what Vargus had said hit home. His eyes widened. "This is the legate?"

"Legate Stiger," Vargus said in a flat tone. "Child of the Delvaris line, as the Oracle prophesized, our bloody Tiger."

Tilanus snapped to attention, which looked a little odd, as the man's armor no longer fit very well. Stiger frowned at both what Vargus had said and Tilanus. The centurion-turned-mayor saluted him.

Stiger returned the salute and leaned forward in the saddle, stretching out his back. "Do you know what happened up ahead?"

"Yes, sir," the retired centurion answered with a grimace. Tilanus had several broken and rotted teeth. "Orc raid."

"Orcs?" Vargus exclaimed. "They've not come out of the mountains on a raid for over twenty years or more."

"Something stirred them up," Tilanus said. "Swept out of their valley and right down into ours."

"Orcs? Are you sure?" Stiger asked, sitting up straight in the saddle. He had thought this a raid by the Cyphan. Lan and Eli rode up, along with Father Thomas. The lieutenant had stopped his troop.

"We've had people come here for shelter. A few of 'em were from Riverton. They said they saw orcs."

"Has my family come through?" Vargus asked, clearly hopeful.

"Sorry, no," Tilanus said and then brightened. "Though the Riverton militia apparently turned out and fought off the raid. At least that is what we've heard. Many who came here lost their homes to the fire and were seeking shelter."

"Never thought to see them orcs come back out of their mountains to raid," one of the retired legionaries standing with Tilanus said. "They can be right trouble."

"A trading party came through just last week," Tilanus added with a frown. "It was that old fellow, Othag. You know the one. Peaceful as can be. There was no hint of any trouble, even said he would be back in a month."

"You trade with these creatures?" Stiger looked askance at Vargus.

"Yes," Vargus admitted with an unhappy look. "Relations with the local tribes have been pretty peaceful. Occasionally they will send a trading party into the valley. They have ore and uncut gems to trade for food and ale. They can't get enough of our ale and call it fire water."

"We have an arrangement with local tribes," Tilanus explained. "They don't bother us and we don't bother with them. It's been a good arrangement, at least up until now."

"As long as a priest is not around to stir things up, orcs are pretty docile. It has been near twenty years since we've had to mount a punitive expedition," Vargus explained to Stiger. "Since then, there has been no trouble."

"And you trade with them?" Stiger asked again, not quite believing what they had just told him. "Aren't they just little more than animals?"

Vargus shrugged. "Usually they don't venture out of their caves, unless they want to trade. They fight enough amongst their fellow tribes that they don't need trouble from us."

"They did not enjoy our last punitive expedition," Tilanus said, with a trace of pride in his tone. "I was there and we pasted them real good. Thought they would never come back in my lifetime. Guess I was wrong."

Stiger looked over at Eli, who returned his look. They both seemed to be thinking the same thing. This could be no coincidence. The timing was just too suspicious. It had to be part of something larger.

"Orcs tend to follow the dark gods, like Castor," Father Thomas said, drawing Stiger's attention. "You can expect more trouble."

Several of the men around Tilanus shuffled uncomfortably, with one making the sign of the High Father. Stiger glanced unhappily over at Father Thomas before turning back to Tilanus.

"Do you know their numbers?"

"No, sir," Tilanus replied. "Only that the Riverton militia managed to drive the raid there off."

That was the good news so far, Stiger thought. It meant the raiding party, or parties, were likely small. If they were few in number, the situation was manageable. Though with everything he had just learned about the World Gate, Stiger could not help feeling that much more was afoot. Father Thomas's comment had not helped either. He would have to be watchful.

Stiger looked up at the sky, which appeared to be clouding up. The sun was nearly directly overhead, though it was providing very little warmth, as the temperature was dropping. He judged it to be around noon. The men needed to be fed and the horses watered before continuing. A brief stop at this village before they pushed on was not a bad idea. Stiger hoped it would not snow again, though it looked likely.

"Is there somewhere we can water our horses?" Stiger asked of Tilanus.

"Yes, sir, in our village square we have a water trough." The retired centurion leaned to the left to get a better look at the troop of cavalry. "Though with these numbers, some of your men may have to work the well a bit."

"We need to continue on to Riverton," Vargus insisted, turning to look at Stiger. "We can't stop now."

"The horses need watering and a break," Stiger said with an edge. He hated having to explain himself. He softened his tone slightly, as he understood Vargus's motivations for haste. "The men need to eat also, and your cohort is already ahead of us."

"Yes, sir," Vargus said, clearly unhappy.

Regardless of the man's desires to get to Riverton as fast as possible, Stiger was beginning to become concerned with his attitude. He looked back down the road in the direction they had just come. A fork in the road a mile back led to Castle Vrell. He hoped the 85th and his cavalry were not far behind, because Stiger wanted them with him. Should Vargus refuse his orders at some point in the near future, things might get sticky.

"Lieutenant," Stiger said, directing himself to Lan, "we will water the horses. Make sure the men eat their rations. I plan on stopping here no longer than thirty minutes."

"Very good, sir," Lan replied, his eyes flicking over to Vargus before returning to Stiger. "The horses could use a rest and water."

"Centurion," Stiger ordered to Tilanus, "lead on."

They found Riverton in ruins. From a distance, Second Cohort could be seen moving about the town. Stiger realized they must have helped the survivors extinguish the last of the flames, which had torn savagely through the town. Very few buildings had been left standing. Most were charred ruins.

Those that had survived the maelstrom of fire looked oddly out of place, in a lonely sort of way. The stench of smoke and scorched wood was pungent, bitter, and nearly overwhelming. It also mixed with another stench. Stiger had encountered it before: the sweet, sickening smell of burnt flesh.

Second Cohort had brought their supply wagons with them. They found these covered wagons parked just outside of town, a precaution against a stray ember. A century of men had been left to guard the wagons. The centurion in charge saluted Stiger as he rode past. The look on the man's face was grim, hard. For all Stiger knew, like Vargus, Riverton was the man's home. Stiger returned the salute and continued without stopping.

On the outskirts of town, Stiger saw the first body. It was not human. He pulled up when he was alongside the remains. The body was that of an orc. He had never seen one up close and estimated the creature must have stood over six feet in height. The skin was pasty greenish in color. Intricate tattoos worked their way across its animal-like face, neck, and arms, disappearing beneath a solid but rough-looking steel breastplate.

From what he could see, the orc was heavily muscled, with hair that was dyed white and had been limed back. The canine-like jaw with thick, yellowed tusks was open in a silent death scream or perhaps a roar of rage. Stiger could not decide which one. A javelin was sticking out of the creature's belly, just under where the breastplate ended. The throat had also been slit, and thick greenish blood had dried around the wound, leaching down to the dirt, where it had congealed.

"They will pay for this." Vargus spat on the corpse and kicked his horse forward, trotting the rest of the way into the town, leaving Stiger behind.

Stiger glanced over at Lan, who had also stopped to study the body. The lieutenant appeared a little shaken. Their eyes met, and Lan looked uncertainly back down on the body.

"These creatures can be killed," Stiger assured him. "The evidence is there before you."

Lan swallowed and nodded. "You are right, of course."

Stiger spared the dead orc another look before he nudged Nomad forward into a slow walk. He continued into the town with the troop following. The troopers gave the dead orc a good look as they passed it by.

Stiger found Vargus in the town center on the common. Vargus was with two other legionaries and a sobbing woman, who was being comforted by the centurion. They were sitting on a charred support beam that had collapsed, along with the building it had once held up.

Stiger dismounted, holding the reins in his hands. He rubbed at his tired eyes. The ruins around him represented the life's work of the people of this town. Stiger had seen such sights before, usually enemy towns and villages, some of which had even been burned by his own hand. A life in the legions exposed one to the ugly side of the world, the one few people from the heart of the empire truly ever witnessed. For the uninitiated, it was harsh and brutal. For Stiger, the sight was all too common. As he stood looking around, he knew without a doubt that the people of the valley would look to him to right this wrong. The Cyphan would have to wait until this was resolved. The orcs would have to be punished.

Stiger's gaze was drawn back to the centurion and the woman. Vargus looked up at him, tears in his eyes. His face was a mask of anguish. The woman had her head buried in his shoulder, her sobs convulsing her body. Vargus struggled a moment to compose himself and blinked away his tears.

"Now, Della," Vargus said soothingly as he pushed the woman back. "I must talk to the legate. We will get Jenna back. That I promise."

"Vargus," she pleaded, between sobs, "you must get our daughter back. You know what she has been through. She deserves better. Please, for the High Father's sake, bring her home!"

"I will," he said with a heated look in Stiger's direction. "Have I ever promised something I've not delivered on?"

"No," she said and immediately began crying once again. "I don't want you to start now."

Vargus stood and handed his wife off to one of the legionaries, who led the crying woman away. Vargus cleared his throat and approached Stiger.

Eli had dismounted next to Stiger and was studying their surroundings. His face was grim, and he said nothing as Vargus stepped nearer. Stiger understood that, to an elf, every death was tragic, even the lives he took himself.

Father Thomas rode up and dismounted. He was followed by Sergeant Arnold, who remained on his horse with a sad look. Stiger suspected that Arnold had seen his own horrors.

"Sir," Vargus reported, "the orc raiding party struck without warning just after sunset. It was not a large party. It seems they set fire to the western end of the town as a diversion so they could snatch some captives. The militia, when they understood what was happening, were able to drive them off."

"What do they want with captives?" Stiger asked, scratching at the stubble on his jaw. "Ransom?"

"No," Vargus chuckled bitterly. "Orcs care nothing for ransom. The only value captives have is to their priests, who practice ritual killings. It is how they honor their gods."

"Sacrifice?" Stiger asked. "They practice the rite of sacrifice?"

"Yes, sir," Vargus answered grimly. "We must go after them and retrieve our people."

"How many did they take?" Stiger asked.

"We think around ten, including my daughter, Jenna."

Stiger had suspected as much from what he had already overheard. He had to tread carefully here. He needed Vargus on his side, and that would require some effort. If he could sway Vargus, who appeared to command much respect in the valley, the rest would likely come with him. They had to see him as more than just some mythical hero who had been reborn, but a leader whom they could implicitly trust in battle.

"Do you know where they took them?"

"Forkham's Valley," Vargus replied. "It's a small dead-end valley a few miles from here. There is a pass that leads to it. It is orc territory and likely where they will take them."

"I don't recall seeing it on any of the maps."

"I would be surprised if it was listed. No one in their right mind would want to go there. The orcs consider the valley a holy site. All that is there are the remains of an orc temple that General Delvaris destroyed."

Stiger was surprised to hear that. He wanted to find out more about his ancestor, but now was not the time.

"A temple, you say?" Stiger growled, thinking on Castor.

"Yes, the ruins of one anyway," Vargus said. "They worshiped the Twisted One there. It was the reason why Delvaris tore it down."

"Are you sure that is where they went?" Stiger asked, taking in a deep, unhappy breath. He suspected that the orcs still practiced their religion at that site.

"The orcs were spotted heading off in that direction, sir," Vargus explained. "They also had one of their priests with them."

Stiger glanced to the south. A few miles beyond this town, the slope climbed steeply up into the mountains. The clouds, dark and brooding, hid the tops of the snowcapped mountains. Stiger thought it was increasingly looking like there would be more snow. He turned to Eli, who had been listening. Taha'Leeth had also joined them, though he had not heard her come up.

"Find their trail," Stiger ordered to the two of them. "Follow them to this valley. I want to know where they went and where they are holding the captives."

"Are you sure you trust me?" Eli asked Stiger, switching to elven. Taha'Leeth shifted uncomfortably, a concerned look passing across her face as her eyes shifted from Eli to Stiger. He thought he detected a pleading look in her eyes.

Stiger's anger blazed hot as he rounded on Eli, whom he found with a smug look plastered across his face. The elf's eyes twinkled with amusement and mischief. The heat and anger left Stiger in a rush. He had difficulty staying angry with his friend. For that was what Eli was, his one and only true friend. He would put his anger aside for the sake of their friendship. They would work this out later, when time permitted.

"Is Marcus up for this?" Stiger asked in common, declining to take Eli's bait, but softening his tone.

"After spending much of the day miserable in the saddle, he is much recovered," Eli said with a grin. "The aftereffects of the drink have mostly left him. It will not slow him down."

"Good. I want the four of you, Aver'Mons included, on their trail."

"We will leave the horses here," Taha'Leeth said. Her bow, like Eli's, was slung over her back.

"Do you need supplies?" Stiger asked them. "Food, water?"

"No," Eli said. "We have enough rations and we filled our canteens in Tedge."

"I expect that I will be following shortly with Second Cohort."

"We must be after them now!" Vargus protested.

"No," Stiger growled, turning to look back at Vargus. He had had enough of the centurion's attitude, but he still restrained himself. "We are going to do this right. I will not rush headlong into a possible ambush. We don't know what's out there. For all we know, they launched these raids to get us to chase after them."

"I had heard you were a man of action," Vargus countered hotly.

"Centurion," Stiger barked, outraged at the man's implication. "Have you seen those other fires? The ones beyond this town? There were other orc raiding parties out last night. We do not know their size or location. Can you tell me where they are?"

Vargus's jaw worked. He clearly wanted to say more, but saw that Stiger was right.

"We will wait for the cavalry to arrive. Once Cannol's command gets here, we march. The cavalry will scour this end of the valley. They will provide a screen to warn us, so that when we do go up into the mountains and after the bastards, we don't get trapped in that dead-end valley. Understand me?"

"I must see to my wife," Vargus said stiffly. He saluted, his body full of tension, and stalked angrily off.

"Watch out for that one," Eli said quietly. "He is over-whelmed with emotion, and when it comes to making decisions, that can be a bad thing."

"I will see you in a few hours," Stiger said. "Be careful. We do not know what we are dealing with."

"I am the absolute soul of caution," Eli said with a grin. "You should know this by now."

"If I recall correctly," Stiger said with a grin of his own, "you were almost brained to death recently. That was you, right?"

Eli glanced over at Taha'Leeth. "I was a little distracted and did not see the blow coming."

"An interesting flower again?" Stiger asked. He turned to Taha'Leeth. "Make sure he stays focused. I would hate to lose him . . . again."

"I will endeavor to do so," Taha'Leeth said with a wink. "However, he is young and impetuous. It may prove somewhat difficult."

Eli looked scandalized by this. "I never mentioned your advanced age, did I? Think you can keep up with this youngster?"

"See what I mean?" Taha'Leeth said to Stiger as she turned to leave, leading her horse off.

Eli watched Taha'Leeth for a moment and then shot Stiger an amused look.

"Try not to have too much fun," Stiger said. Eli only looked more amused as he turned away and led his horse off after Taha'Leeth.

Shaking his head slightly, Stiger watched the two head off. Eli loved nothing more than a challenge. His friend was now presented with one, tracking a new enemy over unknown ground. Between the three elves and Marcus, there was no doubt in his mind that they would find the orcs and the captives.

He turned away and studied the devastation around him. Stiger breathed in deeply through his nose and immediately regretted it. The stench of the burned town was overpowering. He sneezed a moment later. The Cyphan were waiting. How long would it take to put down the orcs? He did not know, but it was one more obstacle to overcome on the road to reestablishing contact with the empire.

Did he not have enough on his plate already?

A detail of legionaries off to his left drew his attention. They were carrying something into the common. Stiger turned. They carried a body. Several bodies, at least a dozen or so, were lined up. Some were badly burned. Others had not a mark on them. Stiger sucked in an angry breath. A couple of the bodies were small, clearly children. The anger began to grow as he walked over to examine them. One of the children, perhaps five years of age, had been cut down by a blade. The anger gave way to rage and his hand went to the sword hilt. The accustomed, comforting tingle was a roar of energy. Stiger's head snapped up. Where a moment ago he had felt tired and worn from the long journey, he was now wide awake and alert.

Forged for a purpose, forged for a reason, forged for a will. Your will is my will and mine is yours,

the sword hissed malevolently in his mind. *Together we will make them suffer . . .*

NINE

"Sir, Lieutenant Cannol's company arriving."

Stiger turned at the legionary's call. He was gesturing toward the road back to Tedge. Stiger had finished walking through the town, examining the damage. The more he had seen, the greater his anger grew. He wanted very badly to punish the vermin who had done this. His only consolation was that the Cyphan had not broken into the valley.

Stiger walked toward the road, his hand occasionally touching the hilt of his sword, enjoying the feeling of the electric tingle. From the earlier rush of power, he still felt wide awake and alert. The sword had somehow sensed his tiredness and washed it away. Stiger felt as if he had gotten a full night's rest. He glanced down at the sword and wondered on its power. What else was it capable of doing?

Before he had gone more than ten steps, Cannol's cavalry company in a double column trotted into the town common. Bundles of tightly bound hay, along with feedbags, had been strapped to the backs of the horses. They also carried extra saddlebags, which likely contained precooked rations for their riders. The men were prepared for an extended campaign.

Cannol rode at the head of his company, and beside him rode Centurion Quintus from Third Cohort, which was a pleasant surprise. Stiger had expected the centurion to arrive with his cohort. Prior to leaving for Old City, Stiger had spent several hours with Quintus. He liked the man's forthright manner and practical way of looking at things. Quintus, like Vargus, was also a councilor of the valley.

"Good day, sir," Cannol greeted, snapping off a salute as the first of his two hundred troopers began riding onto the common. The lieutenant glanced around. "A right terrible mess, this is."

"Quintus, where is your cohort?"

"About two hours behind, sir. I thought to ride ahead in the event you wished to consult."

"Good thinking," Stiger said. Such initiative was what Stiger expected from competent officers. "We have our work cut out for us."

"Tilanus said orcs." Cannol jerked a thumb behind him. "And we saw that big fellow as we rode in. I must admit that is not what I was expecting."

"When did the 85th march?" Stiger asked, curious to hear about his company.

"They were forming up as we rode out, sir," Cannol said.

"What's taking so long?" Stiger asked.

"Ikely insisted on supply wagons," Cannol answered. "He made sure we had enough precooked rations for a week."

Stiger nodded. It had been the correct move. Armies fought on their stomachs. Without food, there would be little action, and he had no idea how long they would be out here, putting the orcs down. Stiger reminded himself that he had to start thinking like a general, planning beyond simple troop movements.

"About time," an angry voice snapped from behind Stiger.

"Vargus," Quintus greeted with an unhappy look. "We will make them pay for this."

153

"They took Jenna," Vargus announced, striding up.

"Gods no," Quintus breathed, looking back to Stiger. "Legate, we must go after them before the moon rises to its fullest. That is when the bastards traditionally honor their gods."

"We will," Stiger said. "First I will have an officer's council."

"What?" Vargus fairly roared. "You had us wait on the cavalry and now you want to delay us further?"

"Vargus," Quintus snapped sternly, before Stiger could reply. "The legate is correct. We must plan before we step off. You of all people should know this."

This was followed by a moment of silence, as Vargus looked like he would protest, then his shoulders sagged.

"Let's get this over with then," Vargus said sullenly.

Stiger pursed his lips at the irate centurion. The man's attitude was unbecoming an officer of his rank. Things could not go on this way for much longer. If it continued, Stiger would be forced to take some action, and then winning the man over would be impossible.

"Give me five minutes to see to my company, sir," Cannol said, dismounting. He began shouting orders to his sergeants to see that the horses were watered and the men given a rest.

Stiger and his officers were gathered in one of the few buildings to survive the fire, a tailor's shop. They stood around a beaten-up wooden table, heaped with discarded scraps of cloth. A fire crackled in the fireplace, warming the room. Outside, snow had begun to fall, coating the blackened and charred ruins.

"Second Cohort will march for the pass. Our scouts should be hot on the raiding party's trail. Once found, they will send word to the Second, who then can both conduct rescue and take punitive action if able."

Stiger paused, looking around the table. He did not have a map, but did not need one. He turned to Cannol.

"The cavalry will sweep this side of the valley. You are to locate any additional raiding parties and deal with them. If you come across anything too large, steer clear and send word immediately. We cannot afford to have Second Cohort trapped in Forkham Valley. Is that understood?"

"Yes, sir," Cannol said. "If they are out there, we will find them, sir."

"Sir?" Quintus spoke up. "Might I suggest Lieutenant Cannol's command also check in on any isolated farmsteads and plantations. It may not be a bad idea to advise anyone they come across to head to Tedge for protection. At least until the threat is contained. If this is a prelude to extended trouble with the orcs, there will be safety in numbers."

"Very sensible," Stiger agreed and looked to Cannol. "See that it is done."

"That means Tedge will have to be reinforced," Vargus said unhappily. "There will be plenty there who can fight, though a century will provide additional strength and security so that no one else can easily be taken."

"I agree with Vargus, sir," Quintus said. "With your permission, I will dispatch a century from my command to Tedge."

Stiger thought it through. By dispatching a century, it would reduce Third Cohort's strength by eighty men. With the men he had on hand, it was not a big drain. Besides, the 85th would be arriving soon. Including the cavalry, he would have more than twelve hundred men on this side of the valley. It was a considerable force, and he felt comfortable detaching the century.

"See to it," Stiger said, turning toward Quintus. "In fact, I want every civilian left in Riverton sent to Tedge for their safety. There are too few buildings to protect them from the elements and we will need them for our own use."

"The century that will march back to Tedge can escort them," Vargus said. "We can unload a couple of the supply wagons to help move any who are wounded or too infirm to walk that far."

"Unload the wagons? Good thinking." Stiger gave a curt nod of acceptance. He thought for a moment more and then addressed himself to Quintus. "I want Third Cohort to dig in here. Build a rampart around the town. We may need a strong defensive position to fall back on." Stiger realized that Riverton might become a long-term base of operations and thought some defenses would be more than welcome.

"Sir, where will you be?" Quintus asked.

"I will be leading Second Cohort after the raiders to recover our people." Stiger noticed that Vargus looked less than pleased with that. The centurion was red-faced and seemed like he was having difficulty keeping his tongue.

"Yes, sir," Quintus said with a glance at Vargus. "And the 85th, when they arrive, what of them?"

"Send them up after us. We may need their support."

"Sir," Lan spoke up. "I request permission to accompany Second Cohort."

Stiger looked over at Lan with some surprise. He studied the lieutenant for a few seconds. Once before, when they had first set out for Vrell, Lan had requested permission to get in on the action and Stiger had denied him that. Studying his lieutenant, Stiger did not know what had prompted Lan to speak up. Perhaps the lieutenant saw it as his duty to family and empire.

"Please, sir," Lan said, drawing his chin up. "It is important to me."

"Very well," Stiger said with a wave of his hand. "You may accompany us. Your troop will be assigned to Cannol's company for the duration of your absence."

"Thank you, sir," Lan said, looking immensely relieved.

"Anything further?" Stiger asked, looking around the table. No one said anything. Stiger turned to Vargus. "Assemble your men."

Vargus did not need any further encouragement. He managed a salute before storming out of the building, the door banging closed behind him. Vargus could be heard in the street, shouting harshly for his men to fall in.

"I need you to be my eyes." Stiger turned to Cannol, feeling he needed to reinforce the man's orders. Cannol was still a junior and inexperienced officer. He and most of his men had also sat out of the recent fighting, and, in effect, his command, like Second and Third Cohorts, were unproven. "If there is a larger force out there, I don't want to discover it blocking our path out of that valley."

"If there is a larger force, sir, you will have your warning well in advance of such an eventuality."

"Good." Stiger was pleased. "See to your men."

Cannol saluted and stepped out of the building.

"What do you think we will find up there?" Stiger asked of Quintus.

"I fear you will find a lot of orcs," Quintus said matter-of-factly. "More than came out to raid."

Stiger let out a deep breath. "That is what I am thinking."

"This cannot be a coincidence," Quintus continued. "You restore the Compact with the dwarves and assume the mantle of Delvaris. A hostile army is besieging the valley, and now the orcs, who have been peaceful for a good long while, launch a series of raids on our valley. No, I do not think this is a coincidence at all, sir."

"Again, we agree," said Stiger quietly.

"My people have remained vigilant for this time, the restoration of the Compact and your return. I fear there is worse to come."

Stiger was quiet for a pregnant moment. "I am not Delvaris reborn," he said. It bothered him that people thought of him so.

"No . . . of course you are not." Quintus sighed heavily. "Vargus is a good man, a good soldier, and a fine officer, sir."

"Good soldiers follow orders," Stiger replied more harshly than he had meant. He softened his tone. "When it matters, will he follow my orders?"

Quintus looked down. An uncomfortable silence settled around the table.

"I will fortify this town, sir," Quintus said, changing the subject and looking back up. "We will be here waiting for you."

"All right then." Stiger turned to Lan, who had followed their exchange without a saying a word. "Let's go."

"Lieutenant," Quintus said, grabbing Lan's arm as Stiger was halfway through the door. "She is a pretty girl, but see that you don't die for her."

Meaning passed between Quintus and Lan as the centurion released the lieutenant's arm. Stiger stepped out into the street, followed a moment later by Lan, who looked a little shaken. The snow was coming down heavier than before. If it continued, their climb up the pass would prove difficult, and Stiger did not relish fighting in the snow. The elements complicated military operations immensely. Stiger pulled his cloak about him and clipped it closed against the cold.

Vargus's men were formed up, waiting to march out. Stiger and Lan made for the formation. As the snow fell, Stiger could hear the occasional sizzle as the large snowflakes fell onto timbers that were still smoldering.

Once Stiger had joined the Second, the order to march was given, and the cohort, some 480 strong, with armor jingling, began to march out of Riverton. Each man carried a javelin and a haversack stuffed with rations. The shields had been removed from their canvas bags. Amongst the legions, that was always an ominous sight, for it meant the men were going into battle.

"What girl?" Stiger asked as he fell in alongside the formation, with Lan to his right. The lieutenant looked uncomfortable and for a moment did not speak. Stiger glanced over at him in question.

"Jenna," Lan said.

"Vargus's daughter?" Stiger asked with some surprise.

"Yes, sir," Lan admitted. "I first saw Jenna when I met with the Valley Council. She came to the castle to help treat the wounded from the campaign. I was able to get to know her better, and I would be grieved if something were to happen to her, sir."

"I see," Stiger said. "Does her father know?"

"No, sir, I believe he does not."

"Probably not a bad thing considering," Stiger said with a chuckle.

"A fine afternoon for a rescue," a voice boomed from behind.

Stiger started in surprise, stopping to find the paladin hustling up to join them with Sergeant Arnold following. Father Thomas offered the legate a broad grin. Stiger struggled to control himself. He wanted to ask what the paladin thought he was doing and then just shook his head. He already knew the answer and ground his teeth in frustration. Wherever a paladin went, there was sure to be trouble involving the interests of the gods.

"Right then," Stiger said, turning to resume his place alongside the column of marching heavy infantry. "Let's get to it."

TEN

The snow deepened the higher they climbed. There was no path or trail. Vargus explained that there had never been one, at least as long as anyone could remember. Forkham's Valley was orc territory, and no one in their right mind wanted to go there. The route they took was tree- and brush-choked. The men not only had to fight against the deepening snow, but also the brush, pushing it aside as they went.

It was a difficult climb, and within a short time everyone was wet and miserable, Stiger amongst them. Not only was he cold and wet, but the wind was also beginning to pick up, whipping through the trees and blowing the falling snow about, which made for poor visibility. Stiger was becoming concerned about accidently stumbling into a party of orcs.

A short while after starting the climb, they came across a large area that had been trampled by many feet. It was impossible to miss, almost as if whoever had passed through did not care that someone might follow them. The falling snow was only just beginning to fill in the tracks. Blood could occasionally be seen in small splashes where it had fallen, darkening the fresh snow that lay atop it. The blood was red. The captives had been brought this way.

The century continued to struggle up the slope, following the tracks that the orcs had blatantly left through the forest.

It bothered Stiger more than he cared to admit. If what he had been told about the punitive expedition were true, and he had no reason to suspect otherwise, the orcs were inviting another go of it by the valley cohorts. Savages they may be, but Stiger understood these creatures were intelligent. They surely would have remembered. The behavior the orcs had exhibited so far indicated to Stiger that they had nothing to fear. It was this that worried him the most.

The effort at climbing had Stiger and the legionaries sweating and breathing heavily despite the wet and cold. There was very little talking. The climb was made worse by the fast pace that Vargus had set. It took a great deal of effort to simply keep slogging along. Occasionally a man would curse as a tree showered snow down upon him or trip on roots or rocks concealed by the snow. Stiger kept himself focused on where he placed his feet as he climbed, each footstep crunching as he made his way higher.

Vargus stopped unexpectedly and turned to look down on Stiger a few feet below. "Our climb is over. This is the beginning of the pass."

The centurion was breathing heavily but looking relieved. Stiger scrambled up the last few feet and over the edge to the pass itself. He stopped and looked around as the men spilled out into the pass. Where he was standing was level ground. It looked, as near as he could tell through the trees and falling snow, as if two mountain slopes had sprung upward from this spot, almost exactly V-shaped, with the bottom of the V being a flat thirty-foot-wide base that widened the farther it went. The slopes of the two mountains were incredibly steep, so much so that it would require some effort to climb. He could not see how far the pass traveled, as the trees and falling snow obscured his vision.

Stiger wiped sweat from his forehead and turned as Father Thomas came up. Like everyone else, the paladin was breathing heavily from the exertion.

"I would not want to have to make that climb every day," the paladin said with a glance back down the slope.

"Hopefully we will not have to," Stiger replied. "Getting supplies up here would require some work."

"It would not be easy," Father Thomas agreed.

Vargus scowled at their exchange.

"How far does this go?" Stiger asked Vargus.

"The pass travels that way for about a half a mile before it opens to the dead-end valley," Vargus continued. "I understand it's a drop-off of perhaps two hundred feet in a gentle slope down to the base of the valley. Nothing like what we just had to climb. Forkham Valley itself is around five miles in length and perhaps two to three wide. Last time we sent scouts up here, they reported it was all forest with no visible orc settlements."

"How long ago was that?" Stiger asked.

"About five years gone," Vargus responded after a moment's thought.

"Sir!" A legionary called their attention to the slope on their right. From amongst the trees, Eli had emerged and was trotting toward them, his bow slung over his back. Stiger noted sourly his friend looked to be enjoying himself. Eli was in his element, confident, relaxed, and appearing like he had not a care in the world.

"We've found them," Eli announced. Lan came up the slope at the same time and joined them. "The orcs are holding the captives at a ruin about four miles south of here, near the southern end of the valley."

"That should be where the ruins of their temple are located," Vargus said.

Eli knelt down in the snow and quickly drew an outline of the valley with his finger. "This is where we are and this here is where the captives are. They are being kept in a rough wood enclosure that looks like an animal pen. We were able to count twelve captives. There are some rough huts and a good number of orcs about. Several are standing guard."

"Any women among the captives?" Vargus asked anxiously. "My daughter is a young woman."

Eli glanced up at Vargus and tilted his head slightly. "I saw three women, all youthful. They were alive and looked relatively well. Marcus, Taha'Leeth, and Aver'Mons are watching them from a safe distance."

Vargus let out an explosive sigh of relief. He bowed his head a moment in what looked to be a prayer.

"We found a number of cave entrances along the slopes of the valley," Eli continued. "There is evidence of considerable activity around these."

"They live underground, only occasionally coming to the surface to hunt," Vargus explained. "We've had reports in the past of them putting their hand to farming too, but not here. This valley is holy ground for them."

"So there could be a lot of them out there?" Stiger looked at Eli. It was likely why the orcs were not concerned with the valley cohorts. There could be hundreds, if not thousands of the creatures about. Stiger ground his teeth in frustration. This was one headache he had not asked for.

"Yes, I believe there to be a good number of orcs about," Eli answered. "We should be cautious. I do not believe it to be a good idea to take the entire cohort beyond the pass."

"Why?" Vargus demanded. "We push right through and take our people back, then punish the bastards."

"That, I believe, would be a mistake," Eli said firmly. "A large body of men would be much more easily discovered. Once the alarm is sounded, we could find ourselves badly outnumbered and cut off."

"I take it you found a lot of tracks?" Stiger looked at Eli grimly.

"A surprisingly large number," Eli admitted in a grave manner. "I feel the prudent move, once the sun goes down, would be to send a small force forward. This force could free the captives, while the rest of the cohort holds the pass."

"Sneak in, strike quickly, and then run?" Stiger nodded. He liked that approach much better.

"Rubbish," Vargus said dismissively. "These are orcs we are talking about. We quashed them easily enough years ago."

"Have you personally faced an orc?" Eli asked with a raised eyebrow.

"No," Vargus admitted sullenly. "The punitive expedition occurred a year before I joined up. My father, however, did. He said they were no better than bandits and rabble."

"Eli's approach makes sense to me," Stiger said.

"We should take the entire cohort in there, free the captives, and then punish them for their arrogance."

Stiger studied Vargus for a moment. The man was very emotional, as this was personal for him. Stiger knew there was no way he could take the centurion along to free the captives.

"We are here for the captives," Stiger said firmly. "Punishment will have to wait 'til we know more about what we are dealing with."

"Bah! You are being too cautious."

"I will take a century with me," Stiger said, "along with Lan. The rest of the cohort will remain here with you and wait—"

"No." Vargus pointed a finger at Stiger's chest. "I am going."

"Excuse me?" Stiger returned the centurion's intense look, his anger growing by the moment. Lan and Father Thomas shuffled uncomfortably at the confrontation. Eli simply said nothing.

"I am going," Vargus said hotly.

"You are staying here and will do as ordered," Stiger said, keeping his voice calm.

"My daughter is out there! How can you ask that of me?"

"Gentlemen," Father Thomas interrupted, attempting to calm things down before they got out of hand. Some of the men had begun to notice. "Is this really the time?"

Stiger ignored the paladin. He leaned toward Vargus, doing everything he could to keep his temper in check.

"Am I legate in name only?" Stiger demanded of Vargus. "Are you a centurion or not? We need to establish this now, not later."

Vargus clenched his jaw. His pointed finger clenched into a fist, which he shook momentarily in Stiger's direction, then hesitated. The heat abruptly left his eyes and his shoulders slumped.

"You are the legate," he said in a choked voice. "I will follow your orders, sir."

"Will you hold this pass?" Stiger asked calmly. "I need to know you will be here no matter what comes at you."

"I will hold it, sir," Vargus said. "You just get my daughter back. I will be here . . . waiting."

"What century would you recommend I take?"

"Fourth Century," Vargus said without hesitation. "They are the best I have. The centurion in command is Pansa Ruga. You can rely upon him to get the job done." Vargus turned and called to a nearby centurion. "Ruga, over here."

A short, trim, muscular centurion jogged over. Ruga was a little older than Vargus and looked hard as a nail. He had a thick scar running down the right side of his face. His hair was cut short, exposing his balding scalp, and he carried his helmet under his right arm.

"Ruga," Vargus said, "Fourth Century will be going out to rescue our people. The rest of the cohort will remain here to hold the pass for your return. The legate will be personally leading you."

Ruga's eyes snapped to Stiger, but he betrayed no hint of emotion. "Yes, sir."

"We have located the captives at the base of the valley," Stiger said. "As soon as darkness falls, we will set out."

"Yes, sir," Ruga replied and glanced up at the sky. It was still snowing. "I thought I had seen the last of this valley."

"You have been here before, then?" Stiger asked with interest.

"Yes, sir, twenty years back." Ruga reached up to touch his scar. "An orc gave me this, sir."

"How do you feel about being back?" Stiger asked.

"Can't say that I like it all that much," Ruga said. "Orcs are not stupid. They can be downright vicious when riled up by their priests." Ruga paused for a moment, then added, "They would not have raided our valley if they did not think they could challenge us."

"You think this is a challenge, then?" Stiger asked.

"Orc warriors live to challenge each other," Ruga replied. "They recognize strength only, which is why they've not troubled us for the last twenty years. Yes, this is a challenge to see who is now stronger, us or them."

"I see," Stiger said thoughtfully. It seemed that Ruga viewed the orcs a little differently than Vargus.

"Looks like we have about thirty minutes or so, then?" Ruga glanced up at the sky, judging the waning light.

"That's seems about right."

"Then, with your permission, sir, I will see that my men are fed and watered before we leave."

Stiger nodded his permission, pleased with Ruga. Though he wished that the 85th were here and he could take them instead, he suddenly felt much better.

"Mind if I tag along?" Father Thomas asked with a cheerful air. "I think you might have need of me."

Stiger looked over at the paladin and felt his mood darken. He closed his eyes a moment and then reopened them. "I was afraid you would want to join us."

ELEVEN

The men moved as quietly as they could through the darkened trees. The falling snow had the effect of muffling the jingling of armor and the crunching of many feet. Eli led the line, guiding them forward. Each man had a hand on the shoulder of the legionary ahead. As near as Stiger could tell, Eli was leading them up and around the east side of the valley, sticking to the slopes. The going was slow, difficult, and taxing.

Several times they came across well-trodden trails. Stiger eyed these carefully as he passed them by. They were not simple deer tracks, but instead the snow had been crushed down by many large booted feet. The fact that they still looked somewhat fresh despite the falling snow concerned him.

Stiger was following Eli, with Father Thomas behind him. Ruga, along with Lan, was bringing up the rear of the line to ensure there were no stragglers. Anyone who became separated from the group at this point would end up on his own. That would not be a good thing, Stiger thought as they crossed yet another well-trodden and packed-down trail.

Marcus emerged from the gloom ahead of them. Eli stopped, and one by one the line came to a halt as well. Marcus slowly made his way to them, keeping low as he moved. The trees in this part of the valley were older and taller. There was very little undergrowth. Stiger felt exposed, particularly now, as the falling snow was beginning to let up.

Ruga and Lan came up from the rear to find out why the column had stopped.

"Sir, there has been no activity on this side of the hill for several hours. We observed a large number of orcs making their way down to the base of the valley. Since then, no others have come. The captives were removed from the pen they were being held in, but are still in the same general area. Aver'Mons and Taha'Leeth are keeping a close watch on them. We also saw what appeared to be two orc priests. It looks like they are preparing for some sort of a religious service."

Marcus paused for a moment, looked off to his right, and pointed down the slope. "If we move forward another hundred yards, we should be even to the ruins downslope. At that point, there is a thick line of brush between us and them as you near the floor of the valley. It should provide plenty of cover to advance, concealing us right up until the last moment."

"I suggest we move forward and line the century up for assault," Eli said.

"I would prefer to see the ground before we go in." Stiger had long since learned that it was better to know the ground you were going to fight on. "Ruga, move the men forward and get into position. Eli will give you a hand. Marcus, I want to see the captives and the ground."

"Yes, sir."

As the column began to move forward, Marcus led Stiger away and down the slope. To Stiger's slight annoyance, Father Thomas came along. The paladin had left Arnold with the main body of the cohort. The three kept low and slowly worked their way down the slope. Within a handful of minutes, the tall, older trees gave way to younger ones and then thick brush. Every few feet, Marcus paused and listened. No one spoke. In a short time, Stiger was able to smell wood smoke, and through the trees and gloom, he could see the dim glow of firelight.

"Through this stand of brush here, sir," Marcus whispered quietly, motioning to a tight grouping of brush just ahead. Where the brush grew, the trees had been cut down, leaving a number of snow-covered stumps haphazardly about. "You should be able to see the captives."

Stiger used the sign language Eli had taught him to acknowledge Marcus, who seemed genuinely surprised by the finger talk. After a moment, he grinned in obvious understanding of how the legate had learned the language of the rangers.

Stiger carefully started forward, working himself slowly through the brush. Marcus moved up on Stiger's right and Father Thomas on his left. The brush was thick and heavy with snow. They had to be careful to not disturb it too much, lest the falling snow be a dead giveaway. The farther they moved into the brush, the more firelight Stiger could see on the other side. Voices could also be heard, and it sounded a bit like chanting.

Reaching the edge of the brush line, Stiger was provided with a near-unobstructed view right down to the base of the valley below, perhaps twenty yards away. The snow-covered ruins were the most prominent feature in view. Judging from the debris field, the building must have once been quite large. The outline of the stone foundation gave Stiger an indication of the true size of the structure, which would have rivaled some of the more impressive temples in Mal'Zeel.

There were a handful of broken columns that had remained standing, but like a set of bad teeth, these varied in height. Stone blocks, walls, and pillars lay where they had been pulled down. Stiger realized he was looking on his ancestor's work, for the building had clearly been razed. It chilled him to know that Delvaris had pulled the building down.

Six large bonfires had been built on the foundation. The fires lit up the scene in an eerie and almost frightening light. A few hundred orcs were gathered. They were kneeling in loose rows before what appeared to be a makeshift stone altar. Two orcs, looking outlandish in dress, stood by the altar. These two wore fur robes that had been painted with what appeared to be multi-colored designs that Stiger supposed were meant to help make them look impressive and mystical. They also had on elaborate animal headdresses, topped with antlers from a large buck. Stiger guessed these were the priests. He had to admit they looked a little frightening.

There, Marcus signed, pointing. Stiger looked. The captives were being held together in a group. They had been forced to kneel, and their hands were bound behind their backs. Two large orc warriors were standing menacingly over them. As Stiger watched, one of the captives was hauled to his feet and dragged forward toward the two priests by one of the orc warriors. A priest picked up a club and brained the captive, rendering him unconscious. As the man collapsed in a heap, the other priest stepped forward and dragged him bodily over to the altar, where he was laid roughly across. The priest produced a knife and, in a swift motion, sliced open the man's chest.

Stiger mentally recoiled as the orc priest ripped out the heart and held it up high for those assembled to see. Blood and gore dripped down, staining the snow, as the priest shook his prize at his audience. The worshippers broke out into a rough song of joy. The priest turned his back on them and tossed the lifeless heart into a burning brazier next to the altar. The remaining captives wailed and cried out in horror at what they had just witnessed. Without a doubt, they understood they were next.

Stiger began to slowly back out of the bushes, his anger raging. He checked his movement, forced himself to calm down, and then studied the ground more carefully, committing it to memory. Having done so, he slipped backward with the others.

"Those are priests of Castor," Father Thomas whispered once they were clear of the brush. "We need to kill them, and quickly. I have seen this religious rite before. With each life they take, the priest gains in strength. It is the victim's soul that feeds their unholy power. If they manage to take all of the hostages tonight, I may not have the strength to overcome them."

"What happens when we kill a priest?" Marcus asked with concern, fingering his bow. "Does it free the soul?"

"Killing a priest will release the soul," Father Thomas confirmed, "which will then be free to cross over the river and into the afterlife."

Stiger was horrified by this new information, and his anger swelled even further. He directed Marcus to lead them back. Behind, the orcs sang in religious celebration, a harsh sound that, had Stiger's rage not been up, would have left him unsettled.

"The buggers have started killing the captives," Stiger announced quietly, once they had rejoined the century. The officers and Father Thomas had gathered around him. "We are going to attack immediately. Eli, take Marcus and go find Taha'Leeth and Aver'Mons. Once we launch the assault, you are to eliminate those guarding the captives. Kill anything that makes a move to threaten them. You have five minutes to get into position before we go in."

Eli and Marcus did not wait for further encouragement. They immediately started down the slope, the darkness swallowing them up within moments. Stiger paused and glanced up at the sky through the leafless canopy. The snow had stopped falling for the most part and was now just spitting the occasional snowflake. He could now see the faint glow of the moon behind the clouds as they thinned. It was possible the clouds would soon give way and there would be some additional light. Stiger hoped that would not happen, at least until after the assault went in. With the number of the orcs gathered below, he was badly outnumbered. The only thing he had on his side was surprise, and Stiger did not want to waste it.

"We will advance down the slope as quickly as we can," Stiger informed them, outlining his plan. "We will be outnumbered. However, they will not be expecting us. I am counting on shock and surprise to carry the day. Lan, you have the responsibility to free the captives. Ruga, assign men to help him."

"Yes, sir," Lan replied grimly. "I will see that they are freed."

"There are two priests," Stiger said, intentionally neglecting to mention that they were priests of Castor. "They must not escape. We have to kill them. Is that understood?"

Ruga and Lan nodded somberly.

"Once the prisoners are free and the priests are dead, we reform the men and move as quickly as we can toward the pass and safety. Ruga, make sure the men understand this."

"I will, sir," Ruga said with a curt nod. "This valley is cursed. I have no desire to remain any longer than required."

"Very good. Any questions?"

There were none.

Stiger glanced back down the slope in the direction Eli and Marcus had disappeared. He had the uncomfortable feeling that this would be a difficult fight. His hand involuntarily found the hilt of his sword. The comforting electric tingle once again became a surge. It warmed him to the coming action. His aches and pains from the long climb up the steep slope to the pass faded and the night seemed to lighten a little. He glanced down at the sword and felt somewhat grateful he had the weapon.

"Form the men for battle," Stiger ordered, his voice harsh but low. He was still angered by what he had seen. With effort, he forced himself to calm down, closing his eyes to help relax. They were about to go into battle. He had to keep his head. The men were counting on him.

Ruga moved back to his men. Quiet words were spoken and passed up and down the line of battle. Stiger bowed his head to pray, as was his custom prior to going into battle. He offered a brief prayer to the High Father, asking for success and a personal request to spare as many men as possible. He then made sure to commend his spirit into the keeping of the High Father's hands. Prayer complete, he stood from a crouch. His legs felt stiff in the cold. Lan stood up with him, as did the men. Stiger tightened the straps on his helmet before drawing his sword and turning to the century.

"Let's get our people back," Stiger said quietly, but loud enough so for the entire line to hear him clearly. "Draw swords."

With a hiss, the swords of the century came out. They had left their shields behind with the cohort to avoid entanglement with the brush and making too much noise. He did not like going into battle without them, but felt it was necessary. Once the captives were freed, they would need to move as quickly as possible back to the safety of the cohort. The men would move quicker without their shields. Stiger looked over at Father Thomas, who had not drawn his sword.

"Remember the priests," the paladin reminded him. "They must not escape."

"We will visit justice upon them," Stiger growled, struggling to contain his anger, which had bubbled up again. Grim-faced and determined to do his duty, he then gave the order to advance.

The men moved down the slope toward the base of the valley, carefully stepping around trees, large rocks, and brush. They struggled to stay in line. The pace was not too fast, nor too slow. Stiger felt pressure to rush because the orcs had begun sacrificing the captives, but he resisted that impulse. He wanted the men to arrive together and as one group. So far, the orcs had no idea they were coming and Stiger aimed to keep it that way. When the legionaries arrived, the orcs would have precious little time to respond.

They came upon the stand of brush Stiger had peered through just minutes before. He turned and carefully scanned the line of battle. Everything appeared to be in order. This was it. He was committed now. Looking forward, he pushed his way through the brush, the men following in a double line of battle behind him. The base of the valley was immediately visible. The orcs were still singing away, oblivious. Their priests were performing some sort of ritual, butchering the body of the man they had just killed. Stiger saw with relief that they had not killed any more of the captives.

Seconds later, the century was through the brush. None of the orcs had noticed the advancing line emerging from the darkness. Stiger saw no need to draw attention and continued the steady, silent advance, not wanting to give away the assault until the last possible moment. He studied the orcs, many of whom had on only furs. Very few appeared armed or wore armor. They were clearly not expecting trouble.

They are in for quite a surprise, Stiger thought grimly and glanced over at Lan, who was at his side. The lieutenant was ashen with a grim but determined expression. Then there was a shout from one of the orcs, who stood, pointing over at the legionaries. Others turned and stood in astonishment. A ripple of surprise spread rapidly through them.

"Charge!" Stiger roared and thrust his sword toward the enemy. Setting the example, he broke into a run.

The legionaries behind him shouted their war cries and charged forward, eating up the last of the ground to the enemy. Orcs scrambled to their feet, many backpedaling. A number of those few who had weapons stood and bravely made ready to receive the charge.

Running the last few feet with his men, Stiger picked out an orc who hefted a large war hammer, the end studded with nasty-looking spikes. The anger and rage Stiger had been struggling to hold back exploded. He screamed as he closed the last few feet. The creature snarled, bearing its animal-like teeth at him. Stiger's sword flared into blue brilliance as he attacked, which he hardly noticed as he ducked the orc's powerful swing and planted his armored shoulder into its midriff, his momentum adding to the strength of the blow. The orc huffed from the impact and staggered backward as Stiger brought his sword around, striking out.

The sword sank with ease into its side, and the orc screamed with agony. There was an intense sizzling, like an egg frying in a pan, and with it the creature's eyes glazed over, the light of life extinguished. Stiger pulled back, and with a groan of escaping air from its lungs, the orc dropped like a child's discarded doll. The creature's greenish-looking blood sizzled, popped, and hissed, smoking as the power of the sword burned it off of the blade.

Suffering, the sword hissed with what seemed like a deep feeling of exultation in Stiger's mind. Stiger stood transfixed as the last of the blood rapidly burned and boiled off of the blade. Then the legionaries from the Fourth Century pushed past him, slamming into the disorganized body of the enemy with a loud crash, intermixed with screams and cries of pain as short swords struck home to deadly effect.

Reason returned and, with it, the sword's brilliance dimmed, returning the blade to its normal appearance. He put the sword from his mind and instead glanced around to get a better sense for the fight, for battles frequently needed direction.

The vast majority of the orcs were running. A small number stood their ground, fighting desperately against the legionaries. Some had weapons; others did not and fought with their teeth and bare hands.

"See to that knot," Stiger shouted, pointing with his sword at ten orcs who had banded together and were encouraging others to join them.

"Take them down," Ruga's optio, an equivalent to a corporal, shouted. The optio led several men forward, with more joining them.

A few feet away, Stiger saw a legionary knocked bodily down by an unarmed orc, who had thrown a powerful punch to the side of the man's helmet. The legionary's sword went flying, landing in the snow. The orc stood over the legionary, reaching down toward the man's neck. Stiger charged the orc, who, seeing the legate coming, straightened back up, eyes wary. Stiger jabbed out with his sword and the creature nimbly danced back. The orc roared as a sword was unexpectedly thrust into its back by another legionary. Injured, it turned toward the legionary. Stiger lunged forward and stabbed deep. The orc staggered and Stiger struck again, cutting it down.

Recovering, he turned and quickly glanced around. The momentum of the charge had carried the fighting beyond him. The legionary who had been knocked down had pulled himself up to his knees. Stiger helped the young man to his feet. He appeared shaken, but no worse.

"Come on, son," Stiger encouraged. "Go get your sword and get back in the fight."

"Thank you, sir," the legionary said, reaching up to feel his helmet, where he had been hit. Stiger saw a good-sized dent there. The man's eyes went wide as he felt out the dent.

"Your sword," Stiger snapped with irritation to get the legionary's mind back on what mattered. He bent down and picked up the discarded weapon. "Those orcs aren't going to kill themselves."

"Yes, sir." The legionary took his sword and moved off in the direction of the fighting.

A flash of intense light drew Stiger's attention to his right. Father Thomas, wielding the large golden battle hammer that Stiger had seen before at Castle Vrell, was confronted by several orcs. The paladin was working his way toward the first of the priests. Five warriors barred his path. There were no legionaries nearby to help. The paladin swung the mighty battle hammer with ease, and it connected with an orc. There was an incredible flash of intense white light and the orc was thrown violently backward. It landed in a heap several feet away and did not stir. Stiger could hear Father Thomas speaking in an impassioned tone as he fought. It took Stiger a moment to realize the paladin was quoting scripture as he laid into the enemy.

Realizing the danger, the orcs spread out, edging around the paladin. They were looking to come at him from all sides. Father Thomas recognized the danger and swung his hammer in wide arcs to keep them at bay. It was only a matter of time before one of them got behind the paladin. Stiger decided to not let that happen. He sprang into action, jogging over and attacking a large orc edging around behind the paladin, who turned at the last second and saw him. Their swords clanged against one another's as the orc blocked Stiger's opening strike, thrusting his sword violently aside. The impact set Stiger's fingers tingling.

Before the orc could effectively swing his large sword to block a second time, Stiger stepped closer and jabbed. The blade sank deeply into its stomach. The creature bellowed in pain and brought its sword down at Stiger, who barely ducked the blow, which scraped along his shoulder armor. The blow stung and Stiger twisted away, pulling his blade out as he did so. His sword did not glow or burn off the creature's blood like it had moments before, and the orc did not give him time to wonder on this as it lashed out, forcing him to duck once again. This time the large blade whistled inches over his head. Without missing a beat, Stiger stepped in close a second time and punched his sword again into the creature's stomach. The sword sank deeply and struck bone. He gave the weapon a vicious twist and then yanked it back. Blood, gore, and intestines came out along with the blade. As he stepped back, Stiger felt the hot, wet spray of blood on his face.

The orc groaned and dropped its sword. Hands holding its ruined belly, it collapsed backwards to the ground, thrashing about. Stiger stepped forward and drove the point of his sword into its throat, bringing the creature's life to a premature end.

Motion to his side caused him to turn. Another orc lashed out with a sword. Stiger barely managed to get his sword up to parry the strike. He took a step backward to allow himself space to recover as the orc warrior lashed out again. Stiger caught the blade with his own, turned it aside using the creature's own momentum, and then stepped forward, thrusting upward into the orc's unprotected breast. Stiger felt his blade slip between ribs and bite deep. The creature gasped, immediately dropping to its knees. Locked between its ribs, the hilt of Stiger's sword was ripped violently from his hand as the orc fell onto its side, stone dead.

An arrow twisted by Stiger's head to thud with a meaty thwack into something directly behind him. He turned to find an orc, war hammer held high above its head, frozen in shock. It had been about to bring the weapon down on his unprotected back. The orc stared dumbly down upon an arrow protruding from its chest. Before Stiger could react, another arrow buried itself in the orc's neck. The creature slowly toppled backwards, letting go of the hammer as it fell.

Glancing back around, he saw Taha'Leeth up the slope, bow in hand. She offered him a thumbs up and a smile before turning her attention to her left, drawing a fresh arrow, nocking the missile, and loosing so quickly that the entire action seemed a blur.

Recovering, Stiger quickly looked around to get his bearings. Father Thomas was in the process of killing the last orc that blocked his path to the priests. Reaching for his sword, Stiger tried to pull it free. It seemed wedged in tightly between the creature's ribs and would not easily come loose. He placed a boot on the orc's chest and gave a mighty pull. With a sucking sound, the sword finally came free.

Stiger turned back toward Father Thomas, who was now advancing upon the two priests with deadly intent. The priests of Castor, with their strange dress of painted patterns, had a wild and outlandish look about them that sent shivers down his spine. They were creatures that worshipped and had been blessed by a dark and evil god, the stuff of nightmares.

One of the priests held a staff and pointed it in the paladin's direction. Inky, spidery black lines materialized in the air and rapidly snaked themselves toward Father Thomas, who raised his golden battle hammer. The spidery black lines struck the hammer in a shower of black sparks that in a flash turned golden. The paladin grunted with effort and thrust his battle hammer forward, as one might a shield. The hammer shimmered, wavering with multicolored light before solidifying once again to gold. Where they touched the paladin's hammer, the black spidery lines that stretched from the priest's staff turned golden, flaring brilliantly in the darkness.

Stiger saw the priest's eyes go wide as the golden light rapidly worked its way back toward the priest. The orc snarled something at the paladin, but it was cut short as the golden light reached the staff. There was a flash of light and the staff began to melt. The priest released the staff, but it was too late. The golden light had spread to its hands and then arms, slowly consuming the creature in its entirety. Stiger watched in fascination and horror as the priest dropped to his knees and began to convulse violently, screaming as if the golden light were burning him alive.

Motion drew Stiger's attention to the other priest, who held out a gnarled hand toward the paladin. Black lightning leapt forth. Father Thomas's gaze was upon the convulsing priest. He did not see the attack coming. Somehow, Stiger found himself at the paladin's side, though he did not remember moving there. His sword was up and it flared with light as he put himself between the paladin and the attacking priest. Stiger raised the glowing blade, instinctively moving to block the black lightning that crackled and hissed with power as it exploded forward. Why he did this Stiger did not know, but it somehow seemed the right thing to do. Stiger pushed down his fear as the black lightning impacted upon the sword with a powerful blow that almost knocked him from his feet.

His hand and arm went completely numb from the impact, but he did not release the weapon. He wasn't even sure he could have had he wanted to. His hand seemed locked to the hilt, almost as if another will held it in place. The blade crackled and hissed as the black lightning exploded with power upon the glowing steel. Stiger's arm shook from the impact, which abruptly became painful. It felt as if his bones were being torn apart. The painful sensation rapidly spread from his arm throughout the entirety of his body. He tried to scream and found it difficult to breathe. He struggled to suck in a breath and could not. Tears welled up in his eyes. His vision began to blur. The attack seemed to last an eternity, but was in reality only a handful of heartbeats.

With shocking abruptness, it was gone, and Stiger found he could breathe once again. The pain lancing through his body dissipated and he almost collapsed to the ground as his strength fled. He closed his eyes, but then his strength returned in a rush and the pain faded to a mere memory.

He blinked, feeling fresh and alert, and looked up at the priest, who backed up. Stiger thought he read fear in its eyes, and the creature bared its teeth at him, snarling something that he did not understand.

"All right, sweetheart," Stiger growled, advancing upon the creature. He felt a terrible need to end its life. The drive to kill it was nearly overpowering, like a great thirst that he was dying to quench. "It's my turn now."

The priest continued to snarl at him, speaking words in its own language that Stiger did not understand. It stretched forth its hand once again. Though he could see nothing visible, Stiger felt an intense coldness settle about him and found he had difficulty moving, almost freezing in place. An arrow struck at the priest and bounced off with a crack, as if repelled by an invisible force. A second arrow rapidly followed the first with the same result. The orc barred its teeth again in what was a gruesome smile of rotten and yellowed teeth. It laughed at him. Struggling, Stiger found no matter how hard he tried, he simply could not move. The orc stepped closer and drew a vicious-looking black obsidian dagger from the folds of its painted robes.

It cannot end this way!

Stiger's rage blazed anew as the orc made to strike him down. The sword flared with a brilliant light and abruptly he was free, able to move. In a flash he struck, the sword snapping out, smacking the hand with the dagger, severing fingers and sending the priest's dark weapon flying. Howling in pain, the orc fell backwards. Stiger was on it in an instant, driving his sword deeply into its chest, where it slid home, slicing through bone and tissue with unbelievable ease.

Suffer . . . the sword hissed, and for a moment, Stiger thought he could feel the creature cry out in his mind, a deep, terrible sound that only he heard. It was rapidly replaced with the sizzling of the sword. The anger and rage left him in a rush as he pulled the sword out, which dimmed and then stopped glowing altogether. The priest of Castor collapsed to the ground, very much dead and completely soulless. How he knew this, Stiger did not know, but the sword had done something with the creature's soul. Of that Stiger was sure. He looked down upon his blade. It was clean, with no hint of blood or gore marring its polished surface. He stepped back, breathing hard as a hand came to rest gently upon his shoulder. He turned and found Father Thomas.

"That was incredibly brave of you, my son," the paladin said, looking older than his years. His eyes flicked to the sword in Stiger's hand. "In the future, a little more caution may be advisable. You should not have survived your encounter. I suspect that artifact you carry had a hand in it."

Glancing down at his sword, Stiger felt incredibly drained. A shout of fear drew his attention. He turned and saw the remainder of the orcs fleeing the field. As they ran, some were pointing and shouting at him and Father Thomas. In moments, there was not a live orc in view. He saw movement to his left. Lan and several legionaries were freeing the captives, cutting their bonds. Stiger saw Lan cut a girl free, and she threw her arms fiercely around him. Stiger knew she must have been Vargus's daughter.

"Is it evil?" Stiger asked, turning back to Father Thomas and fearing the paladin's answer. "The sword, is it evil? Through it, I think I felt the creature die."

Father Thomas closed his eyes briefly and then opened them. "I sense no evil, but that is no guarantee with such a powerful artifact."

"I feel like it is almost—" Stiger said and then hesitated. There was a shout and his attention was drawn to Centurion

Ruga, who was calling for his men not to pursue the orcs into the trees.

"Ruga!" Stiger shouted, turning away from the paladin. The centurion looked over to the legate. "Reform the men. Get a quick head count. No one living gets left behind."

"Yes, sir." The centurion began shouting orders.

A shrill horn blared out from the slopes, somewhat muffled by the trees. Another horn from the opposite side of the small valley answered the first.

"That cannot be good," Stiger said, glancing around at the trees. The alarm had just been sounded. He looked back toward Ruga. "We need to go, now."

TWELVE

Lan helped Jenna up from where she had tripped and fallen in the snow. He brushed her off, even though she was already thoroughly wet and soaked through. Taking her arm, he helped her move through the deep snow and trees in the direction of Second Cohort and safety. A horn blast sounded harshly from the darkness behind them, urging them on.

The orc horns seemed to be getting closer. In his youth, Lan had spent time hunting with his father on their extensive lands outside of Mal'Zeel. He had enjoyed the thrill and excitement of chasing down driven game. Now he knew how the prey felt. The sandal was on the other foot. They were the prey and the orcs the hunters. Lan understood he would forever feel different about hunting.

"Come on," he encouraged Jenna and the other freed captives. "Keep going. The cohort is just a ways ahead."

The century had formed a loose screen around the freed captives as they made their way back toward the pass, moving as quickly as they could, no longer concerned about stealth. The men called to each other, watching the darkness for any hint of movement. Orders were snapped by both Stiger and Ruga, shifting the men about as they saw the need. Two of the captives had been seriously injured and were being helped along by a pair of legionaries.

An agonized howl split the night air with a shocking abruptness. Lan's head snapped to the right, searching the trees in that direction as he tried to pierce the veil of darkness. The moon poked out through a cloud and he saw a figure emerge with a bow in hand. Lan recognized Eli, who raised the weapon and loosed an arrow back into the trees. A large orc came out of the darkness at a run and into the moonlight, stumbling before crashing to the snow-covered ground, Eli's spent missile having pierced its throat. Eli slipped his bow over his back and drew both his sword and a wicked-looking dagger. He turned and stepped beyond sight, moving gracefully back into the darkness of the trees. The moon retreated behind a cloud, and what little light there had been was suddenly gone. A moment later, the clash of steel sounded from the direction Eli had gone. This was followed by another howl of pain and then silence.

To the left and very close, a high-pitched, agonized squeal drew his attention. Then came again the sound of sword meeting sword, which was once again followed by silence. Lan had heard stories of how deadly the elven rangers could be when in their element. They were well-known for being guardians of their people's forests, always present but never seen, hunting and killing those who violated their borders. He had never truly believed until now.

Lan stepped around a large tree, helping Jenna as he did so, and saw Stiger up ahead, leading the century onward. Two orcs charged from the trees. Sword drawn, the legate dropped one of the orcs in a move so fast and smooth it looked impossibly unnatural. The other orc charged a distracted legionary, who fell under a savage blow from its hammer. The two nearest legionaries immediately attacked the orc, cutting it brutally down with a rapid series of sword strikes.

Centurion Ruga knelt down next to the fallen legionary and after a moment shook his head sadly. Jenna looked down with horror as they stepped around the man whose head had been crushed by the blow.

"Don't look," Lan said, turning her head away with a firm hand. "Just keep going."

A clash behind them drew his attention. Lan turned and saw that several orcs had emerged from the darkness and were battling away with the rearguard. Sword drawn, Ruga pushed his way back to them, shouting orders and joining in on the fighting himself.

"Marco, Max," Ruga shouted as he waded into the fight. "On me, on me."

The two legionaries, who had been moving along the sides of the century, helping to cover the freed captives, stepped back and joined their centurion. The fighting intensified as additional orcs emerged from the darkness and threw themselves forward, snarling and howling like wild animals as they came.

The century continued on toward the safety of the pass, with the rearguard fighting as they moved back, one step at a time. It was vicious and hard work, with neither side willing to show the other mercy. A man screamed and fell as a sword cleaved deeply into his thigh. Bleeding out in a gush of blood, the legionary thrust his sword up and into the belly of the orc that had just dealt him a mortal wound, punching the blade as deep as he could. The point emerged from the creature's back. The orc gasped and choked. The legionary's strength abandoned him and he released his sword as his lifeblood flowed away. He collapsed into the snow. A moment later, the orc fell dead over top of him.

Jenna tripped on a tree root that had been concealed under the snow and fell hard. Lan lost his grip on her arm. She rolled down the slope to his right before coming to a stop in a tangle of limbs a dozen feet below.

"Jenna!" Lan shouted in dismay and quickly made his way down to her side as she struggled to her knees. Reaching her, he helped her up, and together they started up the slope and back toward the security of the century.

The sound of movement behind him caused Lan to turn. Something large was crashing through the brush. Though he could not see, he knew it was an orc. Lan gave her one more push ahead and up the slope, then drew his sword and turned to face whatever was coming out of the darkness. An orc with an incredibly large sword stepped around a tree. Their eyes met, and for a moment both stood frozen. Then the creature roared and charged the lieutenant.

Lan braced himself and prepared to block the attack. The parry rang in his ears and left his hand hurting. He attempted a counterstrike, but in the darkness failed to see the orc lash out with a fist from its free hand. It connected with the side of his helmet, and Lan went down into the snow, sword flying from his hand and landing several feet up the slope. Dazed, he picked himself up on his hands and knees and was surprised to find the orc had focused its attention elsewhere. To his growing horror, Lan saw that it was advancing on Jenna. Struggling up the slope, she looked back and screamed. There was no one near enough to help. The closest legionaries were over ten feet away above them and fighting desperately for their lives.

"No," he shouted, scrambling to his feet. He drew his dagger and launched himself at the orc's back. His first attempt scraped across the creature's armor, but his second caught it in the back of the leg, digging deep. The orc roared in pain and slammed Lan backward with an elbow to the face. He tumbled down the slope, only coming to a stop when a tree painfully broke his plunge. Dazed and hurting, Lan picked himself up and saw the orc limping back toward him with the clear intention of finishing him off.

Lan had lost his dagger and was defenseless. He tried backing up, but the tree was behind him and he stumbled back onto his butt, landing in the cold snow. The orc bared its teeth and raised its sword for the killing blow. Unexpectedly, the orc jerked violently, and then a sword point emerged from its neck, hot blood spraying over the lieutenant.

The creature fell heavily, face first into the snow next to him, twitching and quite dead. Eyes wide, Lan looked up from the corpse. Jenna was standing there with his sword in her hand, trembling and looking quite shocked at what she had just done.

Lan slowly dragged himself to his feet. His entire body was one big painful ache. Jenna was trembling and looking at him wide-eyed. He carefully took the sword from her, feeling incredible relief at still being alive. He looked back up the slope. The fighting had intensified. The rearguard was backing up just a few feet above them. He realized they needed to get moving or both of them might get left behind.

"My father taught me how to use the sword," she said, staring down at the dead orc as the moon peeked out from a cloud and bathed the land below in a pale light. "I . . . I never thought I would need to know how."

"I love you," he said. The words spilled out, and at that moment, he realized that he truly did love her. It went beyond simple infatuation. He stood looking at her stupidly. Standing there in the moonlight, Jenna's hair was a wet, tangled mess. He thought he had never seen anyone look so beautiful or be so brave. She had saved him, after he had set out to save her.

"I know," she said with a little smile. The trembling stopped. She bit her lower lip, glanced up the slope and then grabbed his hand, tugging him toward the safety of the century and the rearguard. Ruga saw them climbing up and called for the rearguard to stand firm. As soon as the two were safely up, he gave the order to begin falling back again. Lan and Jenna continued ahead of them. After several minutes of hard fighting, the last of the orcs pressing the rearguard were killed. Ruga, taking advantage of the opportunity, ordered the rearguard to catch up with the rest of the century, which was twenty feet ahead.

The slope of the valley began to increase as they climbed up toward the pass, the century struggling onward. Orcs in ones and twos burst from the darkness, savagely throwing themselves at the legionaries, roaring as they did so. The legionaries worked together, efficiently cutting them down.

At the rear of the century, Ruga squinted into the darkness as the moon went behind another cloud. The front was pulling ahead once again, and he barked an order to increase the pace. In the trees and darkness on either side of the struggling century, screams and roars of pain once again began to sound, with the occasional clash of steel.

An orc burst from behind a tree, charging toward a legionary just ahead of the lieutenant. Lan made to shout a warning, but a shadow detached itself from the darkness, closing on the creature with frightful speed. There was a meaty thwack and a grunt, and the orc went crashing down into the snow. The shadow disappeared back into the darkness so rapidly that Lan wondered if he had imagined it. It had been one of the elves.

There was a roar and several orcs charged from the trees to the left. A flash of white lightning that was followed by a solid-sounding crack caused Lan to jump. Father Thomas, wielding his large golden war hammer, fought alongside several legionaries there. The war hammer glowed with a holy light, illuminating those around him. The paladin had a fierce and determined expression on his face as he stepped forward and out of the press of men to confront another orc. He swung his hammer in a downward arc, and when it struck the creature, there was another brilliant flash of light, followed by a crack that momentarily blinded Lan. When his vision cleared, he saw the orc dead, rolling back down the slope like a tossed bag of potatoes.

Jenna stumbled. Lan gripped her arm firmly to keep her from falling again. The climb was becoming much steeper and at points required some scrambling, which meant they were nearing the mouth of the pass. Helping Jenna, he almost did not see an orc explode from cover and charge toward them. A legionary to his left stepped before Lan, sword coming up to block the orc's blow as the creature swung its long sword in a vicious arc. There was a deafening clash as the two swords met and sparked in the darkness. The legionary recovered quickly and jabbed his sword into the orc's unprotected belly. The creature howled in pain and fell back, a hand over the wound, disappearing into the darkness from whence it came.

"Thank you," Lan said gratefully to the legionary.

"You would do the same for me, sir." The legionary was breathing hard. They were all winded, wet, and nearly exhausted.

Abruptly, the column came to an unexpected halt. Lan actually bumped into the man before him and was about to say something, but instead stopped. Just ahead, he saw a line of orcs blocking their way. There were at least thirty of them, and they stood shoulder-to-shoulder. All wore armor, including helmets, and carried shields. They looked like an organized military formation.

"Prepare to charge!" Stiger's voice shouted from ahead, near the front. Those legionaries who were forward had been formed up by the legate into a hasty line of battle. Stiger stood just behind the line, his attention wholly fixed upon the enemy formation. "Give them some legionary steel, boys!"

"High Father, lend us your holy light," Father Thomas shouted in what sounded like a desperate appeal. There was a hissing, followed by an incredible crack, which thundered high above. A moment later, the valley exploded into light, as if the sun had risen early. Lan stared upward as the crack echoed around the mountains. A massive golden ball of light hovered perhaps two hundred feet above them, shedding its radiance down upon the small valley.

Lan glanced back toward the line of orcs. They appeared to be stunned, all of them gaping upward at the light, with several even taking an unsure step backward. One of the orcs, taller than the others, recovered quickly and barked what sounded like an order.

"Charge!" Stiger roared, and the legionaries at the front surged forward directly into the orc line.

"Move!" Ruga shouted to the rearguard and the freed captives. "While we can, hurry now."

They scrambled forward as quickly as they could. The charge hit the orc line, which immediately buckled under the pressure and drove through it. Lan tried to steer Jenna through the confused melee of fighting and found himself facing an orc. He let go of Jenna's arm and punched his sword into the orc's side, but it scraped harmlessly against the orc's breastplate. The creature snarled at him as an animal would, baring its teeth and swinging a fist in his direction. Lan ducked it and punched out again, stabbing toward the orc's unprotected leg. The sword punched deep and the leg buckled. The orc fell heavily to a knee as Lan pulled his sword out. Another legionary to Lan's right stabbed with his sword and drove it down through the creature's neck, killing it with one strike.

A half second later, a war hammer wielded by another orc slammed into the legionary's side, driving him violently into Lan. They collapsed together in a heap. Managing to hang onto his sword, Lan struggled to free himself, scooting backward. He was partially pinned. The legionary who had been hit with the hammer was clearly dead; his armor and chest had been caved in from the force of the blow. The sight of it shocked Lan more than he cared to admit as he rolled the dying legionary off of him.

The fighting swirled around the lieutenant as he pulled himself to his feet, looking for Jenna. Lan saw a freed captive brutally cut down by a sword that nearly cut the young boy in half. There were orcs all around the century. It occurred to him that they were heavily outnumbered, and he began to panic when he could not see Jenna. He finally found her down in the snow. She had been pushed backward by a legionary, who was shielding her from an orc warrior. The orc's large sword swung around, knocking the legionary's sword aside and slicing deeply into the man's neck. He collapsed, unmoving, his blood pumping out in squirts onto the snow.

Lan, seeing that the orc wore a breastplate and helmet, lunged forward before it could recover, aiming his sword for the unprotected armpit. He missed, but his momentum knocked the orc down. Managing to remain on his feet, Lan pulled his sword back to attack again and found himself facing another orc. A powerful fist caught him in the face. Vision swimming, he managed to slam the sword as hard as he could into the creature's exposed neck. Warm blood sluiced over his hand and sword as the orc fell forward onto him, knocking him down. He rolled out from underneath the creature as it kicked its death throes and got to his feet, once again looking for Jenna. She had pulled herself to her knees and was looking around in wide-eyed fear. He made his way to her side, staggering slightly.

The paladin's light illuminated the desperate struggle. Lan blinked, trying to get a sense for what was occurring around him. It was chaos, but he was now sure they were losing. His mind screamed that he had to get Jenna away and to safety, but he did not know where they could go. The century was completely surrounded. Stiger had formed the men into a defensive ring and was calling out encouragements, his sword glowing with magical energy as he struck down orc after orc in a mad frenzy. It was clear to Lan that there was no longer any thought about struggling forward toward the pass and safety. Without their shields, Lan knew there was no way the century would last long, as the orcs threw themselves forward with reckless abandon at the human legionaries.

Lan took a step toward Jenna, realizing with a deep sadness that they would die together, when a tremendous shout rang out to his right. This was followed by the sound of many feet thundering through the snow and a resounding crash. Lan rubbed at his eyes with his free hand. He was not quite sure he believed what he was seeing. A wall of charging legionaries, shields to the front, slammed into the orcs from behind. In just seconds, they pushed through to the survivors of the century and then past them, throwing the orcs violently back.

Exhausted, battered, and bloodied, Lan helped Jenna to her feet. Concern in her eyes, she reached a tender hand up to his face, which he could feel was beginning to bruise. She touched his lip, which had been split open. He winced at her light touch and then grinned through bloody teeth. They were saved. They were going to live.

"I love you," she said in a low voice and then tucked into him in an embrace, leaning her head against his armor.

"I know," he replied with a smile that rapidly turned into a wince. His split lip hurt too much to continue smiling.

There was much shouting as the orcs were chased off into the woods. Officers were blowing whistles and calling for their men to reform. Lan glanced around at the survivors of the century. He was painfully aware that there were very few, perhaps maybe thirty of the original eighty left. It had been a close thing. He saw Stiger and Ruga speaking with another centurion. They were gesturing back up the hill toward the pass, which Lan realized was only thirty to forty feet away.

"Fourth Century," Ruga shouted, coming back their way. "You've had your fun, you lazy bastards. Time to get back to some real soldiering. Fall in. We're moving up to the pass."

Ruga stopped when he saw Jenna holding fiercely onto Lan. "I understand your father is waiting for you just up there," he said with a slight smile at the girl and then sent a wink, which was directed to Lan.

"Yes, Uncle Ruga," Jenna said. "I would expect nothing less from Papa."

The older centurion reached out a hand and fondly tousled her hair, as one might a child. He then stepped off, shouting at his men as if they had done something wrong.

"Uncle?" Lan asked, slipping from her embrace. He wiped his blade clean on his soaked tunic and sheathed it.

"My favorite uncle," she said with a grin. "He always brought me a toy or sweet when he stopped by the tavern."

"Favorite uncle?" Lan asked, looking back at the mean-looking centurion and seeing a different side of the man.

"And most protective," she said with a playful smile, clearly relieved that they would both live another day.

Lan saw the elves and Marcus emerge from the woods as the holy light that Father Thomas had conjured dissipated, plunging the valley back into darkness illuminated only by the pale glow of moonlight. Eli was making a beeline for Stiger.

"I think we had better get up the pass." Lan turned, and together they continued up the slope to safety.

THIRTEEN

Stiger struggled up the last few feet of slope to the top of the pass with a feeling of vast relief. He felt like dropping to the ground and resting, but instead surveyed the scene before him. Thirty to forty feet ahead, Second Cohort had built a small improvised barricade, neatly blocking the pass. While he had been gone, the men had not been idle. The barricade had been constructed using a small berm of snow that they had built up and then packed down. A number of tree trunks had been placed atop the snow berm in a criss-crossed fashion, creating a crude but serviceable barrier for the men to fight behind.

Stiger glanced over as Ruga clambered up next to him. The centurion's armor was dented and scratched. One of the chin guards on his helmet was missing. Blood, both green and red, had spattered across his armor and dried. The centurion looked as wet, cold, and miserable as Stiger felt. Fighting under winter conditions was a terrible experience that tended to significantly increase casualties. It was why most fighting stopped during the winter months and armies typically went into quarters 'til spring.

Ruga took in the scene before throwing Stiger a sardonic look. "With you in command, sir, I must confess I never once doubted we would make it."

Stiger stared back at the centurion for a moment before exploding with laughter. He clapped the older man on the shoulder. Ruga was a man he could like. The centurion laughed with him.

"After this is over, we will share a jug of wine and drink to those we lost," Stiger declared.

Vargus walked up to the two men. The centurion's eyes ran over the both of them. Stiger was sure they looked a sight.

"It was a little spirited," Ruga commented as the harsh blaring of a horn sounded behind them, some distance off in the valley. The centurion glanced backward. "Just a little."

"My daughter?" Vargus asked.

"Alive and well," Ruga said. Vargus's shoulders sagged in relief.

The survivors from Ruga's century and the freed captives were scrambling up the last few feet of slope to the level ground of the pass. Behind them, Third and Fifth Centuries followed, keeping a watchful eye out for any additional orcs.

"I expect they will follow soon enough," Stiger said to Vargus. The centurion looked doubtful.

"Father!" Vargus turned, and his daughter threw herself into his arms. He hugged her tightly as she broke down in tears. Lan came up behind them, eyeing Vargus a little uncertainly. The lieutenant had had a rough time of it. The side of his face was bruising badly, his lip was split, and his armor was scratched, pitted, and badly dented in places. He was also covered in a lot of dried greenish blood.

"Thank you for saving my least favorite niece," Ruga said, offering his hand to the lieutenant.

Lan took the centurion's proffered hand and winced with the effort.

"Least favorite?" Jenna exclaimed with mock indignation, pulling herself away from her father and rounding on her uncle. Her eyes were red with tears, but she could not suppress a smile. "You big liar."

She hugged Ruga and gave him a kiss on the cheek. "Thank you for coming back for me."

"He will make a good addition to the family," Ruga commented after she released him, jerking a thumb in Lan's direction. "At least after he cleans up a bit and takes a bath. You really do drag home anything, don't you?"

Jenna's eyes snapped to her father, who looked over at Ruga first with a questioning look and then at the battered lieutenant. The centurion's eyes narrowed dangerously. Stiger glanced curiously between the two. Lan was so battered and tired that he seemed not to care what her father thought.

"What?" Ruga asked innocently as Jenna turned a fiery look upon him. "You should thank me. It's out in the open now. Besides, if your daddy objects, well, he and I will just have to have a long talk. Over the years we've had a few of those, you know."

Vargus threw a scowl at Ruga before turning to his daughter. "We will speak of this later."

"I expected nothing less," Ruga said with a tired nod directed at Vargus. "Don't you worry none, girl. Your daddy will come around. Trust me on this."

"Sir," Marcus called from down the slope, interrupting them. He scrambled up and saluted Stiger. "A lot of orcs are heading this way. At least several hundred. The lieutenant said to expect an assault."

Stiger looked back down toward the darkened valley. The moon had come out again. He was extremely worn out, wet, and cold. He felt miserable and his body ached from the exertion. It had been a long, hard day and was already proving to be a more difficult night. When he had started out from Thane's Mountain, he had not envisioned his day unfolding in the way it had.

He took a deep breath, and his hand found the hilt of his sword, seeking its comforting electric tingle. Instead, he received a jolt that flared through his arm and into his body. Time seemed to slow in the middle of the breath he was taking. Vargus blinked, and it appeared to take an eternity for the man to complete the action. Stiger trembled as the power of the sword flared through him and then abruptly was gone. He staggered back a step.

"Are you all right, sir?" Ruga asked with concern, reaching out a hand to steady the legate.

Stiger blinked. The weariness and sense of cold were gone. Though he was still completely soaked through, his body no longer ached from his exertions of the last few hours. It wasn't like before when his aches and pains had faded. This time they were completely gone. He felt rejuvenated, better than if he had woken up from a great night's sleep. The moonlight shining down on the snow also seemed a little brighter than it had a moment before. Stiger glanced down at his sword and shook his head in disbelief.

"Sir?" Ruga asked again, stepping closer.

"I'm fine, just a little tired is all," Stiger replied, recovering.

"What do you intend for us to do?" Vargus asked, looking for direction.

Glancing over at Marcus and then the valley again, Stiger rapidly thought things through before turning back to the makeshift barricade. There was only one option that made any real sense to him.

"We hold here."

"Hold, sir?" Vargus asked. "If they are coming, as you say, then why not march back to Riverton? Then we would have the strength of both cohorts, instead of one. We could give them a real pasting with such strength."

Stiger considered the centurion's words a moment before replying.

"The ground here lends itself better to defense," Stiger responded, gesturing at the confines of the pass. "They can only come at us from a narrow front. We will be able to hold them, bleed them, and then push them back into their valley. If we give them a good enough bloody nose, perhaps it will stop further raids, at least until we can hit them back properly."

"Will you bring up the Third?" Vargus asked, clearly not happy with Stiger's answer.

"No, I don't think so," Stiger responded. "If we need to, we will call upon them. However, the 85th should be arriving soon. That, I think, will provide us sufficient reinforcement."

"Sir, if I might offer my advice?" Vargus shifted his feet.

Stiger looked to the centurion and nodded for the man to speak, as if Vargus suddenly needed his permission. The man had never really held back before, and Stiger wondered what was coming.

"After we stop the orcs, we come back with all three cohorts and the dwarves and clean these animals out good. They must be taught a lesson."

The last of Ruga's weary men stepped by the four officers. The cohorts that had just come to their rescue were beginning to scramble back up to the level ground of the pass.

"I am afraid we're going to have to," Ruga commented with a sour expression, and Stiger agreed with that sentiment. Before he turned his attention back to the Cyphan, the orcs would have to be dealt with, and harshly. Stiger could ill afford to leave an enemy at his back.

"You two." Stiger turned to Lan and Ruga. "Make for Riverton. See that the captives we freed get there safely. I want them out of here as soon as possible. Ruga, your century can provide escort."

"Yes, sir," Ruga said.

"Excellent work, Ruga. You and your men did well."

"Thank you, sir," Ruga said, drawing himself up and offering Stiger a smart salute. Lan did the same, though the effort clearly hurt, as he winced somewhat painfully.

Stiger watched them go. Jenna was helping to support Lan as the cavalry trooper hobbled off with Ruga. Stiger then turned to Vargus, who was looking at his daughter and the lieutenant with a hooded expression.

"The lieutenant is a good man," Stiger told him.

"If you will excuse me," Vargus said in reply, his voice harsh, "I will see to my men, sir."

Vargus stepped off toward the makeshift barricade. Stiger noticed that Marcus had remained behind. The scout looked tired and weary. He had good reason. "Go get some rest. You've more than earned it."

Marcus saluted and left Stiger alone, standing at the mouth of the pass. He looked out over the moonlit valley and took a deep breath. From his vantage point, the small valley seemed peaceful, almost serene. Under the moonlight, the snow both on and amidst the trees gleamed brightly. The view was magnificent. It was also deceptive, for this was a place of evil and death. Somewhere out there were a lot of orcs, his friend, and two other elves.

Stiger breathed out slowly before he turned his back and walked to the defensive line, prepared to do his duty. He would hold this pass and bleed the orcs. Every orc he dealt with now was one less he would have to contend with later.

"85th coming up," a legionary called out, drawing Stiger's attention almost as soon as he had climbed over the makeshift barricade. He looked toward the other end of the pass and, sure enough, saw a body of men marching through the trees. The distinctive standard of his company draped in a tiger's pelt was held up proudly at the front.

Stiger could not help but feel a sense of relief. These were his men, whom he had personally trained. They had been tested in the fires of combat and proven themselves again and again. If asked, they would walk through the seven levels of hell and do it with pride. They were good men. They were his men.

"What kept you?" Stiger asked of Blake when the sergeant came up and saluted. The sergeant's eyes flicked over Stiger's bedraggled and battered appearance and he raised a curious eyebrow.

"You know how it is, sir, always waiting on someone else to do their bloody job," the sergeant said in a lighthearted manner. "That is the way of the legions."

"I see," Stiger said, suppressing a smile. It was good to have the old veteran sergeant back at his side. "Where's Ranl?"

"Lieutenant Ikely kept him at the castle," Blake said. "You will just have to put up with me instead."

"I guess I will have to," Stiger said, flashing a smile at the sergeant. "What was Third Cohort up to when you passed through Riverton?"

"Digging in, sir," Blake replied, looking beyond Stiger toward the makeshift barricade. "Expecting some trouble, are we?"

"You could say that," Stiger replied, following the sergeant's gaze. "Orcs, and a lot of them."

"Had a run-in with a band of them buggers when I first joined the legions," Blake said, which actually surprised

Stiger. "At the time, they scared the hell out of me, but like anything else that walks or crawls the land, they can be killed just the same."

"Make sure the men know that," Stiger told him as a shout of alarm sounded behind him. Stiger glanced over to see Vargus hurrying toward the center of the line.

"Where do you want me and the boys?" Blake asked him.

"The 85th will act as a reserve. Break the company up into files and position them at intervals just behind the line."

"Yes, sir," Blake said and then eyed Second Cohort. "They look good, sir, but how are they? How are they really? Ranl and I have been wondering."

Stiger was silent a moment as he considered his answer before speaking.

"A century of them just fought like veterans to rescue a handful of captives," Stiger said. He paused a moment as Ruga and the survivors of the Fourth marched by with the civilians and Lan. The centurion saluted Stiger. Blake eyed them neutrally as he took in their battered appearance. All of them looked as if they had gone through the grinder. Then they were gone, swallowed up by the gloom of the night. "If the rest of the cohort fights as they did, then I expect they will handle themselves well."

"That is mighty good to hear, sir." Blake looked back at the 85th, which had halted and stood waiting for orders. "With your permission, I will get the men into position."

"Very well." Stiger watched as Blake turned and began shouting orders. The men of the 85th rapidly began separating into files, and as each file moved by him, they gave Stiger a cheer. He smiled and nodded back at them as they passed.

An orc horn blared harshly. It seemed uncomfortably close. Stiger knew that the enemy would be coming shortly.

He thought on his decision to hold the pass, considered the possibility of pulling back, and then immediately dismissed the idea. He was in command of a powerful defensive position. This was good ground, damn good. Glancing up at the steep, craggy slopes that hemmed in the pass, Stiger knew there was no easy way to flank his position. Under the circumstances, it was the very best he could ask for.

If he pulled back to Riverton, there was no guarantee the orcs would attack his fortified position there. They could simply ignore him and bypass the defenders, spilling out into the valley itself. Stiger would then have to chase them down. Such a possibility did not appeal to him. With the 85th on hand, he had a little over six hundred men defending an extremely narrow front, with steep slopes to either side.

Yes, he thought. Holding was the correct decision. Let them come.

Stiger joined Vargus. The centurion was in the center of his line, studying the trees to the front of the barricade. He gave the appearance of being calm and unconcerned, but vigilant. It was what was expected of a legionary officer.

"A couple of orcs showed themselves a few moments ago, sir," Vargus informed him, pointing to the drop-off. "They have since disappeared."

Stiger nodded, but said nothing.

"Thank you," Vargus said, without looking over at Stiger. He was clearly uncomfortable, and Stiger suspected that it took a lot for the man to make such an admission. "Thank you for bringing my daughter back."

"No thanks are necessary," Stiger replied. "A lot of good men gave their lives for the captives."

"Yes, they did," Vargus agreed, turning to Stiger, sudden passion in his tone. "Those men died willingly. They died for their families. They died for our home. The Compact is much more than just an alliance. It is our way of life, a sacred trust. Yes, our forefathers came here to protect and guard the World Gate, yet today we defend our home."

Stiger remained silent as he returned Vargus's gaze. He did not feel the need to respond, as it was clear Vargus believed fully what he had just said and Stiger likely suspected that it was true. The men fought now to protect their home, the valley.

"Sir, look!" a legionary shouted, pointing. Three shadows emerged from the darkness at a dead run for the defensive barricade. Stiger immediately recognized the elves.

"Let them through," he shouted, so there could be no mistake. "They are friends."

Eli, Taha'Leeth, and Aver'Mons scrambled up and over the improvised barricade. All three were out of breath. Stiger and Vargus hurried over to them.

"They are coming," Eli said, catching his breath. "A lot of them."

"How many?" Vargus demanded.

Stiger glanced off in the direction the three elves had just come. Though he could see nothing, the elves would not have been running unless the threat had been dire. From the improvised barricade to the point where the pass dropped toward the valley was perhaps forty feet. Vargus's men had cut down many of the trees to the front of the barricade, which provided additional visibility. Under the moonlight, which reflected brightly off of the snow, Stiger could see right to the edge of the drop-off.

"Hundreds . . . at least," Eli said, struggling to catch his breath.

"Perhaps a thousand or more," Taha'Leeth added in elven. Her hands on her knees, she was bent over, breathing heavily.

"An abomination too," Aver'Mons added in elven, which brought Stiger's head around to the elf, as he could speak their language quite well. "I caught sight of it, though it was not moving toward the pass with the orcs."

"What did they say?" Vargus asked of Eli and Taha'Leeth.

"He said there is a minion of Castor out there," Stiger explained gruffly. It seemed Castor was not done with the valley. Stiger had known this from the moment Father Thomas had told him the orc priests were of the Twisted One's ilk.

"A minion is evil incarnate," Father Thomas said. The paladin had come up. "It represents the direct will of the dark god Castor."

"Like you?" Vargus asked. "But for a dark god, a dark paladin?"

Father Thomas nodded slightly. "You could think of it that way, if you like."

Stiger had heard enough. The orcs were coming, and it was as simple as that. He would deal with whatever came his way when it arrived. Besides, he had Father Thomas with him, and together they had already defeated one of Castor's minions. If need be, they would do it again.

"Prepare to receive assault," Stiger said to Vargus, cutting off further discussion. "We must hold."

"Yes, sir," Vargus acknowledged and turned to another centurion who was standing nearby. "All centuries to the line."

Orders were quickly passed. The men took their shields and moved up to the line, falling into neat, orderly ranks. The legionaries in the front rank carried a single javelin. Those behind carried two or more. They had been unable to take the wagons up to the pass, which meant that their supply of javelins was limited. Vargus had apparently sent men back for more, which meant that they had enough for perhaps an extra toss or two. Behind them, the 85th was moving into position at spaced intervals behind Second Cohort.

"Here they come!"

What looked like a wave of darkness rose up to their front as a mass of orcs climbed up over the lip of the pass. The orcs shuffled forward several steps and then stopped. They stood silent and unmoving, simply gazing at the legionaries. Unlike many of the orcs they had faced down in Forkham's Valley, these had come prepared, with plate armor and helmets. Weapon drawn, they were ready for a fight. Stiger had to admit even to himself the orcs presented an unnerving sight. It was then he noticed his legionaries. He could sense their uncertainty and unease.

"They can be killed like any other," Stiger shouted, moving up to the line and climbing atop the barricade so that all could see and hear him. "Those bastards thought they could come into your valley. Yes, your valley. They killed. They burned. They took captives." There was some grumbling at that. It was what Stiger wanted to hear. "Ruga's century showed them they can't come into our valley and take our people!" The legionaries roared heartily at this.

"We are the Thirteenth! We are the legion. From Delvaris's time to now, we are the shield that protects the empire." Stiger remembered what Vargus had just told him about the sentiment of the valley cohorts. "We stand to protect the valley behind us and your families. We stand and we hold the line!" The legionaries roared their approval at this, working themselves up.

"We hold the line," Stiger shouted again and paused, about to go on, but Vargus beat him to it.

"What do we do?" Vargus roared at his men, and at that moment, Stiger loved the cantankerous centurion like a brother.

"HOLD!" the legionaries roared as one. "HOLD . . . HOLD . . . HOLD!"

Stiger took one more look around. The men looked determined and angry. The unease and uncertainty was gone. He punched his fist up and into the air.

"HOLD . . . HOLD . . . HOLD!" the men continued to shout.

Satisfied, Stiger climbed down off of the barricade and turned toward the orcs. During his short speech, their numbers had continued to swell, filling up the other end of the pass. They seemed more of a mob than an organized fighting force, yet their numbers were considerable.

Stiger wondered why they just stood there watching. It was almost as if they were waiting for something. The orcs were easily within javelin range, and he was about to call for a toss when something began to happen. A gap formed in the center of the mob, and then two large orcs stepped through. One was a warrior, carrying a battle hammer loosely in one hand. The other was one of their priests, for he wore black robes with brightly painted designs and carried a wooden staff. The priest's headdress was made from the skull of a tiger, and when combined with his dress, he looked otherworldly. The gap closed up behind them. Stiger's legionaries quieted down. It seemed that all eyes on both sides were on the two orcs.

The large warrior regarded the legionaries for a brief moment, spat on the ground, and then turned his back contemptuously on them. He began addressing the orcs in what seemed like an upbeat tone. Stiger recognized it as a morale boosting speech, kind of like the one he had just delivered. The orcs began shouting back in reply to what the warrior was telling them.

"Eli," Stiger snapped, looking back and around for his friend. Both were in arrow range. "Deal with those two."

Eli and the other two elves did not even hesitate. They pushed through the line of legionaries, climbed the improvised barricade, and were over in a flash. Sprinting ahead a bit, they each drew an arrow, aimed, and released. It happened so quickly and unexpectedly, it was shocking. All three arrows bit home. The big warrior stopped in mid-speech and dropped like a felled tree. The priest staggered, turning an angry glare on the legionaries. He made to raise his staff, but three more arrows struck him in rapid succession. He let out an anguished cry and collapsed into the snow, dead.

A stunned silence settled over the field. Then an orc roared its animal-like rage at the legionaries. This was taken up by the entire group of them. The legionaries countered with a hearty cheer of approval. Eli, Taha'Leeth, and Aver'Mons sprinted back to the safety of the barricade, which they rapidly scrambled over.

"Nice job," Stiger commented to Eli, once his friend had made it back over.

"Always pleased to serve," Eli said, exposing his needle-like teeth.

"It was an honor," Aver'Mons said in elven, disgust lacing his tone. "Those of the Horde have no place here."

"It's not every day you have the opportunity to remove such filth from this world," Taha'Leeth commented as she slung her bow over her shoulder.

"I suppose you have done your good deed for the day," Stiger said to her. She flashed him a dazzling smile in reply.

"I fear there will be more good deeds needing some doing before long," she said, her look turning feral, almost wild.

Stiger frowned.

"I do not want you and Aver'Mons taking any risks in the coming fighting," Stiger said quietly to her in elven. What was coming would be brutal and ugly, standup legionary fighting. He could not afford to lose such valuable rangers before his campaign against the Cyphan had even begun. "You are both to hang back and stay out of any direct fighting."

"You would hobble us?" she asked Stiger back in elven, an angry look in her eyes.

"You will not fight on the line."

"Yet you humans can?" Taha'Leeth narrowed her eyes. "We are not good enough to fight alongside you? Is that it?"

Her anger made her suddenly look even more beautiful to Stiger's eyes. Her face had flushed and her eyes, especially intent upon him, had a depth to them that he found surprising. At this moment, her fiery red hair matched her personality. Stiger sighed deeply.

"This is what the boys train for," Stiger told her. "You and Aver'Mons are rangers. Your place is not in the line."

"I told you he liked you," Eli said with a huge grin. Taha'Leeth's eyes turned to Eli, shooting daggers at him. "He only means you are too skilled to risk losing you and," Eli hesitated a second and his gaze flicked to Stiger, "Aver'Mons in the brutality of the line."

She turned back to Stiger, her look softening. "Is that so?"

He nodded.

"Very well," she said. "We will take no unneeded risks."

Stiger figured it was the best he was likely going to get and so he nodded, turning his attention back on the orcs. They had worked themselves up into a proper frenzy, but had yet to move forward. Scanning them critically, Stiger could detect no officers, sergeants, or really any type of leadership or organization amongst them. By killing the warrior and priest, Stiger had hoped to decapitate their leadership. Perhaps it would pay off?

"Would you check on Marcus?" Stiger asked of her. "I do not want him in the line either. I told him to get some rest."

Taha'Leeth nodded, and with a gesture to Aver'Mons, they both went in search of the scout-turned-ranger.

"That could have gone better," Eli said with a chuckle. "You were lucky I was here to translate your thinking to her."

"Second and third ranks," Stiger shouted, electing to not respond to his friend, "javelins at the ready. First rank, hold!"

The centurions repeated his orders up and down the line. The second and third ranks took several steps back to make room for a toss.

"You take the left side," Stiger said to Vargus. "I will take the center and our right. Don't hesitate to call in a reserve file from the 85th."

"Yes, sir," Vargus replied after a moment's hesitation and left for his position on the line. Stiger imagined it was hard for the centurion to take orders from someone else, especially after having had sole command over his cohort for so long.

"I do believe you may want to consider sending some men up those slopes," Eli suggested as Vargus moved off.

Stiger looked up at the steep, rocky slopes on either side of the pass and could not help but agree. It was unlikely any serious fighting would occur there, but the orcs, once they figured out that they could not break his line, might try to get up and around behind him.

"Blake!" Stiger shouted to the sergeant. Blake jogged over. "Send a file up both slopes on either side of us. Make it clear to the corporals that, should they get seriously pushed, they are to send for aid. Also, pass your javelins forward to the Second."

"Yes, sir," Blake said, glancing at both sides of the line. "Might I suggest two files on each side? That way they can hold longer . . . at any rate, long enough for aid to arrive."

Stiger considered the suggestion. It made sense, but it also meant that his reserves would be weakened. He nodded in acceptance. "See to it, centurion."

Blake turned away, then stopped and looked back at Stiger with a quizzical look. "Sir?"

"You heard me," Stiger said with a straight face. One of the perks to being made a legate was that he now had the authority to promote men from the ranks. In the old days, before Emperor Midiuses's reforms, men could move from being a regular to an officer based upon merit alone. Now it was an exceedingly rare occurrence, as the officer corps was reserved for the nobility and those who could afford to purchase a commission. It was one of the things that Stiger felt the legions had lost and ensured that useless men made it into positions of authority that they were ill-suited for. "I am promoting you to centurion, effective immediately. Ranl too, when I next see him."

"Me, sir? An officer?" Blake asked in astonishment, almost as if he had been struck by lightning. "Ranl?"

"Yes," Stiger replied. "I have decided we are going to reorganize the 85th and the garrison companies under the banner of the Thirteenth and form another cohort. You will command that cohort."

"Uh, yes, sir," the sergeant-turned-centurion replied uncertainly.

"We will speak more on this later," Stiger said, his eyes returning to the roaring and shouting of the orcs. "Now, if you would kindly get those files moving, I would appreciate some semblance of security along my flanks."

"Yes, sir." Blake snapped off a salute and hurried off.

Stiger called the standard bearers for Second Cohort and the 85th to him. "You two stay near me at all times."

"Yes, sir," they replied in unison. In the north, he had seen General Treim keep the legionary standards with him. During the chaos of battle, you could always tell where the general was located by simply looking for the standards. Though this would not be a large battle, it was dark out. Should someone need to find him, it would be easier with the standards following him around.

A great roar went up from the other side of the pass, and the mass of the orcs surged forward toward the legionary line. The ground trembled with the thunder of their feet. Stiger thought it sounded like a cavalry charge. The confined slopes of the pass amplified the sound, making it seem more ominous.

"First rank, present shields and javelins!" Stiger roared. Shields came up, and javelins were leveled as men braced themselves to receive the charge. It was time to soften the orcs up. "Second rank! Javelins release!"

With grunts of exertion, the second rank threw their javelins. It was an exceptionally good toss. The missiles arced upward and fell with deadly accuracy amongst the charging orcs. The air was filled with the sound of screams, animal-like roars of pain, and the clatter and crash of the javelins striking armor. Orcs fell by the dozen, tripping those behind them. Totally unfazed, the mass continued forward, heedlessly trampling their fellows who had been struck down or fallen.

"Third rank! Javelins release!" Stiger watched as the volley of javelins flew upward and then slammed down amongst the charging orcs, who were just a few yards shy of the improvised barricade. Dozens more fell, and still the mass of them came on. The time for organized volleys was over. "Second and third ranks, release at will!"

Javelins in ones and twos began to be thrown, and then a steady stream of missiles arched up over the line and into the enemy. Several heartbeats later, the charge slammed into the defensive barricade. More than a few orcs were thrown flat as they attempted to scale the barricade, only to have pressure from behind knock them down. These first few were trampled and crushed as their fellows behind climbed over their bodies, eager to get at the humans. They were met by shield and javelin. The legionaries of the first rank jabbed, punching their javelins forward, seeking soft spots. Wounded orcs screamed their pain, fell backward, and were swallowed up by the press.

Stiger understood the javelins of the first rank would only last a short time. While they did, it would help to keep the orcs at a distance. However, the shanks of the weapons were intentionally designed to be soft so that they bent after being thrown, which rendered them useless after the initial toss. The enemy would not be able to throw the weapon back. In direct combat, the same would eventually occur, and the shank would bend, usually after a javelin struck armor instead of flesh. When rendered useless, the legionary would be forced to discard the weapon to draw his sword. Then the fighting would get close and difficult.

Under the bright moonlight, Stiger watched as the fighting raged up and down his line. The cacophony of the battle was near deafening, but his men were holding. The improvised barricade was not an ideal defensive wall, but it had effectively broken up the charge.

Having scaled the barricade, the orcs found themselves at a disadvantage. Orc armor consisted of protection for the head, chest, abdomen, and arms. Their legs were not protected, meaning that they were exposed to the legionary swords and javelins. Using their shields for protection, the legionaries struck upward at the orcs with quick thrusts, bringing down many.

The struggle continued unabated in its ferocity as the orcs threw themselves at the legionaries. An orc dived off of the barricade and into the ranks of his men, easily leaping over the first rank. Another orc did the same, and in a matter of seconds, more were diving forward. Most were rapidly cut down by the second rank, but a few managed to regain their feet and fight. Those few did not last long and were cut down under a flurry of swords. Stiger shook his head in dismay. He had never seen anything like it. The orcs were throwing themselves at his men with reckless abandon.

He kept swiveling his head left and right, looking for signs of trouble, but so far the men were holding. He was taking casualties, but nowhere near as many as the orcs were suffering. The fighting was almost one-sided as his men slaughtered orcs by the bushel. Legionary discipline, training, and fighting as a cohesive unit were winning the day.

Whenever a man was wounded, another immediately took his place in the line. The injured man struggled or was helped back to the aid station. The cohort surgeon was there with a couple orderlies. Stiger glanced back and saw Father Thomas was also there, attending to the wounded. It was reassuring that the paladin was here to help tend to his men. Without a doubt many more would survive as a result of Father Thomas's presence.

Turning back to the action, Stiger frowned as he saw another man on the front line fall, his shield ripped away from him by one orc, even as another brought a hammer down on the man's helmet. The man dropped like a rock.

Without missing a beat, a legionary stepped forward and into the fallen man's place.

Stiger watched the fighting, the minutes ticking by as his men fought the tide of orcs pressing forward. He grew concerned. There had been no letup in the fighting since it had started. The orcs were continuing their assault on his line without regard to their losses. Stiger could not understand it. Where human soldiers would have eventually pulled back to regroup before testing his line again, the orcs just kept coming. Were they trying to tire his men out? It was a troubling thought, as Stiger had no idea how many orcs there were beyond what he could see to his direct front.

A centurion near Stiger blew hard on a whistle, signaling the changing out of the first rank for the second. It was efficiently done, and the fresh rank took their place on the line. Those who had just come off formed up and took their position as the third rank, breathing hard from their exertion and taking stock.

Stiger glanced first to his left and then to his right, checking on his flanks along the slopes. There was no action there or even a hint of a potential fight developing. In fact, the orcs were only striking at the direct center of his line. The centuries manning the last twenty feet on either side, right up to the mountain slopes of the pass, were not even engaged. He could not believe what he was seeing. The files he had dispatched to the slopes had only climbed up around ten to twenty feet. They stood with their shields resting on the ground, watching the show below.

Stiger turned to Eli, who had remained by his side. The elf looked troubled and Stiger suspected they were having similar thoughts.

"We cannot continue like this," Stiger said to him as another whistle was blown and the ranks rotated again.

"Agreed," Eli said. "The continued pressure on our line will tell."

Stiger thought for a minute, rubbing his jaw. He had felt compelled to hold this position, as it was so formidable. That aside, he had never liked simply holding a line, as it surrendered the initiative to the enemy. He had always preferred a battle of maneuver over a static defense, where he could dictate the terms.

"I am thinking of reforming the 85th," Stiger told him, sounding out the plan he was putting together in his head, "and sending half to either flank. Once in position, they push forward over the barricade and then collapse toward the middle."

"Striking the orcs along their flanks." Eli raised an eyebrow, considering the plan. "It might work, depending upon how many of them there are beyond what we can see."

Stiger thought through his plan again and then sent a runner for Blake and Vargus.

"This cannot go on," Vargus said when he arrived just after Blake. "My boys will eventually tire."

"This is what we are going to do," Stiger informed them. "The 85th will reform. Half will go to the right flank and the other half will move to the left. Blake, you will command the left and Eli the right. Once both sides are in position, you will push over the barricade, sweeping whatever enemy is before you. When you are over, I want you to swing around and push into the sides of the enemy, boxing them in. Once those bastards react and the pressure along our center eases, Second Cohort will go over the top and push hard into the enemy. We will have them on three sides."

"That will give up the advantage of the defensive line," Vargus protested, not looking terribly excited by the prospect of the action Stiger had laid out.

"The orcs have the initiative," Stiger said, hammering a fist into his open palm. "If we do not take it back, the pressure along our front will tell."

"Should this move fail," Vargus added, "we will see the same result."

Stiger could detect no heat or resentment in the man's voice. He was simply expressing his opinion and not challenging Stiger directly. It was what a good officer should do, and Stiger decided to take it as such. He wanted his officers to speak their minds.

"Those are my orders, gentlemen," Stiger informed them, ending debate. "Any further questions?"

"Sir, I have a suggestion."

Stiger looked at Blake and nodded for him to continue.

"If we take the last rank from the Second and divide them boys up evenly along the flanks, it would add greater weight to our push."

Stiger looked to Vargus. "If we do as he suggests, can you hold with two ranks?"

"I can hold," Vargus said with a grim look.

"Very good." Stiger did not desire to waste any more time. "Let's get to it."

The officers split up, and within minutes, the 85th was on the move. A short while later, part of the Second Cohort was moving toward either flank. Stiger had placed himself just behind the line, in the center, literally within spitting distance of the struggle and enemy. The standard bearers followed him. It was good that the men saw him near the front.

Taking a step back, he looked to his left and then right. The men were forming up into assault lines. It was painful to watch, as they seemed to move slowly, but Stiger understood that movements like this took time to prepare and execute.

He calmed himself and waited, all while the fighting to his front continued with unabated ferocity.

Eli's side pushed forward first, driving up and over the barricade, the men giving a "HAAAH!" as they drove forward. At the same time, the force up along the slope pushed forward and down. Stiger looked to the left and saw a similar scene. Within a few seconds, both assault prongs were out of sight, hidden by the fighting to his direct front. He had known this would happen, but his anxiety increased regardless. Stiger had no idea how the assaults along his flanks were faring. He struggled to detect any change to those orcs attacking the defensive barricade directly in front of him. It seemed as if the cacophony of the fight increased somewhat in intensity, but Stiger considered that it was likely just his imagination. He reminded himself to be patient and wait.

He returned to what he could see and deal with. Vargus was pacing up and down a portion of the line, shouting out encouragement and, when needed, orders. The other centurions were either doing the same or had placed themselves in the thick of the fighting, as an example to their men. Stiger moved toward Vargus, with the standard bearers dutifully following him.

"Nothing yet," Vargus said as Stiger came up.

Something should have happened, Stiger told himself. It had been almost five minutes and he was beginning to wonder if too much time had passed. Perhaps both flanks had run into trouble as they pushed forward.

"What about a push now?" Stiger asked, having to holler above the noise of the fighting.

"I don't think we could effectively push up and over the barricade without some lessening of the pressure," Vargus informed him. "We are just too thin. If we failed, the line might collapse."

Stiger nodded in understanding. The orcs were throwing themselves at the legionaries. It was incredible to witness and worrying. The creatures fought as individuals with no regard for themselves and no coordination with their fellows. Each seemed to have the exclusive goal of getting at the human legionaries and killing one.

"Sir." One of the standard bearers drew his attention to the far right. Where moments before the pressure had been intense at that spot, the orcs there had taken a step back. That part of the barricade was no longer under direct assault. The orcs there had shifted their attention away from the legionaries to their front along the barricade, to their rear.

"It's working," Stiger breathed to himself. He immediately knew what had to be done, before the orcs to his front could adjust to the assault from the sides. "Send Second Cohort forward."

"Shouldn't we wait for more of a reaction?" Vargus asked him. "The line—"

"There may not be time for that," Stiger said. "We need to push them from all sides and do it at the same time."

"But, sir—"

"It must be now," Stiger insisted, feeling more than ever it was the right move as he watched more orcs shift their attention. To create the panic he wanted to generate amongst the enemy, he needed to apply intense pressure on all three sides at the same time. "Before it is too late!"

"Second Cohort, prepare to advance," Vargus bellowed, drawing his sword and stepping up to the line. Centurions up and down the line repeated the order. Vargus waited another moment to give the men time to prepare. "Forward!"

A great shout went up from the legionaries of the Second, and they pressed forward, pushing back against the orcs. Shields to the front, with short swords darting out, they hammered against the enemy. Stiger drew his sword with the intention of joining them.

Kill them all!

A pure, white-hot rage flowed into him from the sword. Stiger felt the anger in his breast explode with an astonishing intensity toward the orcs. It threatened to overwhelm his ability to reason. He felt an almost unreasonable urge to spill as much blood as possible. He wanted nothing more than to kill all of the orcs before him. Stiger took a halting step forward and almost threw himself into the ranks, but managed to just barely control himself. The sword was glowing a brilliant blue, so bright it was almost blinding in the dark of the night. It was hard to think, to reason.

What was happening to him?

Kill them all!

Stiger felt an incredible push, urging him forward and into the fight. He was stunned by the power of it and staggered slightly. Instinctively, he knew it was wrong. He had to remain in control of his faculties to direct the fight. He struggled forcefully against the push. Sweat beaded his brow and his hand holding the sword shook violently. The struggle was intense, with Stiger fighting back. It was almost as if the sword were trying to take control of his body.

"I rule here, not you," Stiger growled, forcing his will into the thought and fighting down the rage. There was a moment of resistance, then the pressure relented and the sword dimmed. Reason returned. His anger and hate diminished in intensity.

"Sir?" one of the standard bearers asked, looking at him with concern written across his face, eyes warily on the glowing sword.

"I am fine," Stiger said, wiping the sweat from his brow with the back of his arm. "I am fine."

Blinking, Stiger glanced at the sword in his hand with more than a little worry. The weapon clearly had a will of its own, despite what it claimed.

I rule here, Stiger thought at the sword, reinforcing his will over it. Not you.

For now . . .

Stiger felt chilled by its words. Then, abruptly, the line before him surged forward as the pressure against the legionaries crumbled. Stiger had no more time to spare on the sword. Second Cohort was advancing as the orcs fell back. Putting the sword and its chilling words from his mind, he followed, climbing the barricade after the legionaries. It was tricky work, as Stiger found that he had to climb over a pile of orc bodies. The standard bearers followed him.

Reaching the top, Stiger could see the entirety of the fighting. He stopped to get his bearings. Both assault prongs had pushed through and into the flanks of the throng of orcs. The attention of those on the sides was firmly fixed upon both Eli's and Blake's commands. The assault prongs were still pushing steadily forward, using solid shield-work as they cut their way ahead. Watching them, Stiger felt incredible pride in the 85th.

Second Cohort continued the push forward as well. They were cutting a bloody swath straight down the center, leaving numerous bodies in their wake. The orcs were having difficulty coping with the legionary shield wall and the deadly short swords that jabbed out. Stiger's eye was drawn to the end of the pass, where the drop-off began. He could see fresh orc warriors climbing up to the pass. These stood uncertainly, taking in the growing disaster. He wondered how many were behind them and decided that he did not care to find out.

Stiger looked for Vargus and saw him. The centurion was with his men, directing the fighting. Stiger climbed down off of the barricade, careful where he put his feet so that he did not trip. There were bodies and discarded weapons lying all around. It would not do to trip and find oneself accidently impaled. Stiger jogged over to the centurion.

"You were right, sir," Vargus said in excitement, a huge grin on his face. "Look at my boys! By the High Father, we have them now."

"Spread the word. We push them right up to the end of the pass, but no farther," Stiger ordered. "We have no idea how many of the enemy are down in the valley."

"You think there could be more?" Vargus asked, showing surprise, some of the excitement fading from his face.

"Your people know the orcs better than I do." Stiger raised his voice. "The numbers we have seen today, do they represent more than one tribe of warriors?"

Vargus glanced around, eyes going wide. "Yes . . . yes, they do, and the tribes would rather fight each other than work together."

"So," Stiger said, though he had already surmised this, "we have something to worry about then."

"This is a concentration of the mountain tribes," Vargus breathed as it dawned upon him. "The last time that happened was against Delvaris."

Vargus turned and bellowed out some orders to his centurions, instructing them to not advance beyond the end of the pass. These orders were quickly passed to several runners, who went in search of the cohort's centurions, as well as Eli and Blake, who were beyond sight or hearing.

"We will stop our advance at the end of the pass, sir," Vargus assured him and then stepped back to the fighting of his cohort.

Within minutes, both flanking assault prongs linked up with the main body of the Second. The drive continued, pushing the orcs right up to the end of the pass. There the legionaries stopped as the last of the orcs finally broke and ran down into the woods below, disappearing from view.

Stiger looked up at the sky and saw the first tinges of dawn, and with it, he suddenly felt extremely tired. There were hundreds of bodies in the pass, mostly orc, though he knew a fair number would be his legionaries.

A horn sounded from the trees down in Forkham's Valley. This one was joined by another. Stiger knew with sickening certainty that the orcs were reforming. They would be back and likely would come at him again, this time with greater numbers. After what he had just witnessed, he knew he could not hold them, not here in the pass. Second Cohort and the 85th were tired. There was also the matter with the abomination of Castor. Where was it?

Stiger called for his senior officers, which included Vargus, Blake, and Eli.

"I fear there are more coming," Stiger announced. "I do not think we can hold, not without more men. It would take Third Cohort at least two hours to reach the pass, perhaps too long a time. Does anyone disagree with me?"

No one did.

"Then we will withdraw as soon as practicable. Our wounded go down first. We will hold the center of the pass, just long enough for them to get a head start."

"What of the dead, sir?" Vargus asked with an unhappy look.

"They stay where they fell," Stiger responded, knowing his answer would not be a popular one. "We will come back for them when we can."

Vargus looked as if he wanted to argue, but then nodded in acceptance. It was the right decision. Stiger could read it in the man's eyes.

"Make sure there is no looting of bodies," Stiger added, looking at Vargus and Blake. "We know a minion of Castor is involved. I do not want the men picking up some item that is contaminated. Is that understood?"

"Yes, sir," they replied almost in unison.

"Eli, as we withdraw, I would like you to observe the enemy. I need to know what comes after us."

"It will be done," Eli said. "Taha'Leeth and Aver'Mons will join me, as well as Marcus."

"Good." Stiger turned back to Vargus. "Get a runner ready. I intend to send a dispatch back to Riverton with details on what has happened here. I will order the cavalry concentrated and to alert Quintus to expect possible trouble on our heels."

"Yes, sir." Vargus looked suddenly weary. "What of the First?"

"I will order them to march as well." Stiger met the centurion's eyes. "I will also alert Braddock that we may require his assistance."

Vargus untied his helmet and removed it. The centurion cracked his neck, stretching it out, before running a hand through his matted hair.

"Your men did well," Stiger told him. "Extremely well."

"Thank you, sir," Vargus said wearily.

Another horn blew in the distance, drawing their attention.

Stiger took a deep breath of cold mountain air and let it out slowly. He had no idea how long the orcs would give him before coming again. He would not waste the time he had just purchased with the blood of his men.

"Let's get to it then."

FOURTEEN

The sun had been up for several hours. It provided little warmth. The tired, wet, and weary column arrived at Riverton to find a fresh trench and five-foot rampart surrounding the town. Legionaries from Third Cohort were hard at work expanding the defenses. The men stopped working to watch as the Second and 85th marched into town. One of those watching began to clap, which was taken up by all of those nearby. The clapping became a cheer, which brought a few tired heads up. Though they had fallen back on the town, the men of the Second had taken the measure of orcs beyond their number and won a hard-fought fight.

"Hold your heads up proudly now, boys," Vargus called out to those of his men. "Second Cohort arriving!"

Stiger was pleased at the reception the men were receiving. They deserved it. Stiger was wet and tired. The effect of the sword had worn off, leaving him, he suspected, more drained than he should be. Rubbing at his eyes, he stifled a yawn. Quintus stood waiting just inside the town, on the common.

"Had a hard time of it?" Quintus asked, taking in Stiger and the men as they marched in.

"That is an understatement," Stiger said.

Vargus joined them and shook hands with Quintus. He then turned to Stiger, drew himself up, and saluted smartly.

"Thank you, sir," Vargus said with a firmness that Stiger had not expected, "again, for rescuing my daughter."

"You would have done the same, were she my daughter."

"I will follow your orders, sir," Vargus added, after recovering. "I swear it."

"As long as you continue to give me your thoughts, I would welcome them," Stiger replied, recognizing that he had earned the man's respect. He had hoped to win Vargus over. Stiger had seen him in action, and though he was difficult, the man was a good leader.

"You can count on that," Vargus assured him. "I will not let you down."

"I expect nothing less," Stiger replied. "Get your men fed and rested. It is likely we will need them fresh soon enough."

Vargus nodded and stepped off.

"Has the cavalry reported in?" Stiger asked Quintus.

"They are still arriving in troops. I've put those who have come in to work on the fortifications," Quintus answered. "They don't take to manual labor."

"They wouldn't," Stiger growled unhappily. "Most are spoiled second and third sons of the lesser nobility."

"Lieutenant Cannol has yet to report in," Quintus added. "He took a troop to a village a good distance east of here."

"I expect he will turn up before long." Stiger stifled another yawn.

"I did detach two troops to patrol in the direction of the pass," Quintus said.

"Yes, we encountered them. I borrowed one to send a dispatch to the castle." Stiger glanced around at the snow-covered ruins of the town. It no longer smoked, but still stank badly. "I need a place to sleep, at least for a few hours." He needed some rest to be fresh when the orcs came again.

"I have a room for you," Quintus said, gesturing for Stiger to follow. "It is quiet and dry, with a fire."

"Sounds perfect." Stiger followed the centurion through the ruins. They passed several intact buildings where wounded from the Second were being tended to. Stiger made a mental note to check on his losses.

"I ordered First Cohort to march," Stiger said. "I would expect them to arrive sometime today."

Arm in arm Lan rounded a corner with Jenna, heading in the direction Stiger and Quintus had been moving. The lieutenant had cleaned up since Stiger had last seen him. His face was still badly damaged with a split lip and bruised cheek, but he was moving much less gingerly than before.

"Lieutenant, where is your troop?" Stiger demanded. Though the lieutenant had had a rough time of it, Stiger suspected the man was neglecting his duties in favor of spending time with Vargus's daughter. It was time to remind Lan of his responsibilities.

"They just came in, sir," Lan reported, straightening up into a position of attention and offering a salute.

"Have they been assigned to work on the fortifications?"

"Ah, no, sir, not yet."

"Shouldn't you be seeing to that?"

"I had intended to," the lieutenant replied a little guiltily. "I was escorting Miss Jenna here to her father."

Stiger looked to Jenna. She had also cleaned up, though was sporting a nasty bruise to her neck and a black eye.

"Your father is seeing to his men. I believe you can find him on your own. The lieutenant here has his duty to attend to."

"Yes, legate," she said with a firmness that seemed beyond her years. Taking the hint, she left them. Stiger noticed that Lan's eyes followed her. Once she was out of earshot, he stepped up close to the lieutenant and lowered his voice.

"You must focus on your responsibilities. Personal matters come after. Is that understood?"

"Yes, sir."

"I expect we will not have to speak of this again?"

"Ah, no, sir."

Lan stepped off with a purpose.

Quintus watched him go and then turned to Stiger. "Before you and your men arrived, that girl was horribly wronged by members of the garrison."

"So I have heard," Stiger replied and recognized surprise in the centurion's eyes. "The lieutenant reported on the details of his meeting with you and the council. He was very detailed in his description of what occurred. I rather suspect he felt responsible for making it up to her."

"He appears to be a good man."

"He is young, yet has the makings of a fine officer," Stiger said, then stopped again and turned to Quintus. "Make sure the rest of those we freed, including Jenna, are moved back to Tedge. They will be one less distraction."

"I will see to it after you're settled."

Quintus led Stiger to a small one-room building that had escaped the fire. The room was bare of furniture, with the exception of a camp cot in a corner. Stiger suspected that the cot belonged to Quintus himself. There was a small crackling fire in the fireplace, which was a welcome sight. Stiger added a couple logs and poked it up. He turned back to the centurion.

There was a knock at the door. Quintus answered it and spoke briefly to a legionary, then closed the door.

"This just arrived for you," Quintus said, handing over a dispatch.

Stiger opened the dispatch. It had been written earlier that morning. Ikely reported that the First would march with their accompanying artillery train and supply wagons. The train and wagons would slow them down, but when they got here, he would have close to two thousand men on hand, with the added bonus of some light artillery. He was cheered by the news.

"Very good," Stiger said, taking off his wet cloak and hanging it on a hook by the fire. He removed his sword, still in its scabbard, careful not to touch the hilt, and leaned it against the wall near the cot. He did not desire a surge of unexpected vigor. "Have a dispatch rider sent to me, along with some food and the saddlebags from my horse. I could really use a dry tunic."

"Yes, sir," Quintus said. "I will see that you are not disturbed, unless it is absolutely necessary."

"Thank you."

Quintus closed the door behind him. With the door closed and the fire building, the room warmed considerably. Stiger sat on the cot and took his boots and socks off. They were soaked through. He placed them by the fire to dry. He removed his armor next and stacked it neatly against a wall. It was a mess. He would have to spend some time later cleaning it.

Stiger then pulled a dispatch pad from a pocket in his cloak. The pad was damp, but not too terribly wet. He wrote out a quick note to Braddock. This was his second dispatch to the thane. Stiger explained in terse details what had occurred. He told Braddock that he expected to be attacked at Riverton. He requested that Braddock's army be made ready to march should he need them. He folded and sealed the dispatch, then wrote out another to Ikely. As he finished, there was a knock at the door.

"Come."

The door opened and two legionaries filed in. One held a ration canteen and half a loaf of bread wrapped in a towel. The other had Stiger's saddlebags. Stiger took the saddlebags and gestured for the legionary to place the food on the cot. He handed over the dispatches, along with instructions, thanked them, and the two legionaries left. Stiger opened one of his saddlebags, removed a fresh tunic, and changed into it. The feeling of wearing dry clothing felt good. He hung the one he had been wearing on a free hook by the fire.

Sitting on the cot, he looked down at the bag, which contained his pipe, and briefly considered having a smoke, but he was too tired and hungry. He opened the canteen and groaned when he saw salted pork inside.

"It figures."

"Sir?"

Stiger's eyes snapped open. There was a hard knocking at the door. It was dark in the room. The embers in the fireplace provided the only light, and that was not much. Stiger sat up on the cot. He realized with alarm he must have slept through the day. Why had they not woken him?

"Sir?" The knocking resumed again, determined.

"Come." Stiger swung his legs over to the floor.

The door opened and in washed a blast of cold air. Quintus stepped in, followed closely by Vargus. Quintus carried a lamp, which immediately lit the room. Taha'Leeth stepped through the door and closed it after her. Her beauty alone brightened the dreary room.

Stiger rubbed at his eyes and stood stiffly. His body ached terribly. From their grim expressions, he knew it must be bad news. He moved to the fire, grabbed one of the last remaining logs, and tossed it in. He turned back toward them and prepared himself for the worst.

"Well?"

"The orcs took a while, but they are coming and in greater numbers than before," Taha'Leeth informed him. "The equivalent of an army."

"An army, you say?" Stiger asked in disbelief, thinking suddenly on the World Gate. "An army?"

"That is not all," she told him. "The minion marches with them, along with many priests."

"Any idea as to numbers?"

Taha'Leeth shook her head. "They are still emerging from the pass, many thousands at the least. Eli and Aver'Mons remained behind with Marcus."

"How long until they get here?" Stiger asked, running a hand through his hair.

"Two hours, maybe a little longer?" she replied with a shrug. "They do not seem much concerned with speed."

Stiger's thoughts turned inward. He had learned from Vargus on the march out to the pass that the orcs lived across the southern end of the mountain range. They had to have been gathering this army for some time, he realized. Had the raid on the valley been planned? Or had it been a few restless and ill-disciplined orcs prematurely tipping their hand?

Stiger's raid to rescue the captives and the ensuing fight in the pass might have caught the orcs off guard. He might have forced a fight that the enemy was not prepared to engage in. The more he thought on it, the more he became certain this was what had occurred.

What would have happened if there had been no warning? Stiger went cold at that thought, for he knew the orc army would have spilled into the valley before he or anyone else would have known there was even a danger. The orc raid on the valley had been a blessing in disguise. Now what to do?

There was a knock at the door, which Vargus opened. Father Thomas and Lieutenant Cannol entered.

"You have heard?" Stiger asked of them, and they nodded grimly.

"I sent Cannol to find Father Thomas," Quintus admitted.

"We are facing a dire threat," Father Thomas said quietly. "I can feel it."

Stiger rubbed at his jaw. The unshaven stubble felt rough under his hand. Everyone in the room was looking to him. He took a deep breath and thought about what he needed to do. It was obvious he could not hold here, even with the First. His eyes narrowed.

"Where is Sabinus?" Stiger asked, wondering why the man was not present.

"They were delayed by a band of orcs," Quintus informed him. "They should be here in about an hour and a half."

Stiger thought furiously. He could not fall back on Castle Vrell. There was not enough room in the castle for all of his legionaries and the dwarves. He had no concerns about the castle being able to hold. The fortifications were just as strong on this side of the valley as the other facing the Cyphan encamped in the Sentinel Forest. Besides, he thought, the enemy would not likely go for it. Their objective had to be the World Gate, and as Stiger saw it, the only option that came to mind was to fall back in the direction of Thane's Mountain. If the dwarven army joined up with him at some point, then he could turn and, perhaps, with Braddock, offer battle.

"We are going to abandon Riverton," Stiger announced. "We cannot hold against such a force, even were First Cohort here."

"What do we do then?" Quintus asked. "And what of the people of the valley? What of our families?"

"We spread the word for everyone to make for Old City," Stiger announced. He would have to send a dispatch to Braddock asking for the civilians of the valley to be permitted to shelter within his city. He would also send his casualties to the city. There was no doubt in Stiger's mind that the thane would agree. "We evacuate the valley."

"And then what?" Vargus asked.

Stiger began to pace in the small room, thinking on what he knew of the valley. He abruptly stopped and turned to Vargus. "Remember that river we crossed with the wooden bridge? The one on the way to Thane's Mountain?"

"The Sai'ko River?" Vargus asked.

"Is that its name?"

Vargus nodded.

"Are there any crossings or places to ford other than the bridge?"

"No," Vargus said, thinking it over. "Not for over two or more miles in either direction, at any rate. The river is rather deep."

Stiger thought for a moment more before speaking. "The terrain on the northern side of the bridge is perfect for defense. We will take that small ridgeline and fortify it. I will ask Braddock to join us, and together, I believe it will be extremely difficult for the orcs to dislodge us."

"You realize that is where Delvaris fought a battle," Quintus said quietly, and the room stilled. Stiger did not miss the significance of that.

"Yes, I know," Stiger replied, thinking on what Braddock had told him.

"Will there be time to fortify the ridge?" Quintus asked.

"Wait . . . you mean to allow them to cross the bridge?" Vargus had a look of astonishment on his face.

"Yes," Stiger explained. "We will fortify that low ridgeline just beyond the bridge. The area to the front of the ridgeline is a confined space, allowing only a couple thousand across at a time. If we can get those heights fortified, then they can throw themselves against us all day long in limited numbers. We will bleed them dry."

"What if they attempt to flank us?" Quintus asked. "Orcs are not stupid. They could explore out along the river and locate the crossings to the north and south. We could find ourselves outflanked."

"We have the cavalry to watch the crossings," Stiger countered, looking over to Cannol. "If they make such an attempt, we will either contest it or fall back on Thane's Mountain. If the worst happens, then we can help the dwarves hold the fortress of Grata'Jalor."

Stiger paused for a moment. He had begun pacing again and then stopped, looking at those assembled in the room. "This move can only be a bid for the World Gate."

"I agree," Father Thomas spoke up. "We cannot allow Castor to possess the World Gate."

"We will stop them," Taha'Leeth said fiercely, drawing their attention.

"I will entertain any other ideas if you have them," Stiger said, looking at his officers.

"Over three hundred years ago, this position worked well enough for Delvaris and the original Thirteenth," Quintus said after a pregnant moment. "Perhaps it will work just as well for us."

"Form the men up," Stiger ordered. "We need to march as soon as possible. If we have to leave supplies here, so be it. Burn them, but make sure we take all of the shovels and pick-axes. We are going to need them." Stiger turned to Cannol. "Send me a dispatch rider. I will have orders for Sabinus to change the direction of his march." Stiger stopped. He had just had an interesting idea. He smiled tightly as the idea blossomed further. "I will also have a message for Braddock. I want a full troop as escort, to make sure the dispatches arrive."

"Yes, sir," Cannol said.

"Cannol, detach two troops to begin spreading the word for people to evacuate the valley to Thane's Mountain. Make it clear to all that the legion will be falling back to the river at Bridgetown. We will be unable to protect them should they elect to stay."

The lieutenant nodded his understanding. "My men will see to it."

"Good." Stiger glanced around at those assembled. The looks were grim. "We will meet this test and overcome it," he said firmly. "Dismissed."

The officers began to file out of the room.

Stiger stopped Vargus, catching the centurion's arm, and asked him to stay a moment.

Taha'Leeth hesitated as if she wanted to say something, but then saw that he wanted to have a word with Vargus. She shrugged, offered Stiger a mischievous smile, and followed the others out. Stiger wondered what she meant by that. He pushed the thought aside and turned to Vargus.

"How many men did you lose?"

"Eighty-four." The centurion had a sad look about him. These were people he had lived alongside, worked with, and known since they were born. Stiger reflected that it would be much different losing such people than in a typical legion-ary unit, where its members came from across the empire. Vargus would have to face their families and loved ones, a few of whom might even place blame upon the centurion for their loss. "Does it get any easier?"

"No," Stiger breathed, realizing that the centurion had likely never lost a man before. "It most certainly does not."

"You have lost many men?" Vargus asked, looking up.

"Yes," Stiger admitted. "Far too many."

"How do you man...?" The centurion's shoulders sagged briefly as he trailed off.

"We do the best we can and try not to make too many mistakes that cost additional lives."

"You have made mistakes then?" Vargus gave Stiger a look, as if he very much doubted such a thing.

"Yes," Stiger admitted. "You will make mistakes too. You must learn from them, so that others may live. Vargus, we are not perfect in what we do. Our profession is amongst the hardest there is, for there is only a very fine line between life and death. As officers, we do everything we can to load the dice for our side, and yet the enemy does not always play by our rules, even when we cheat. No matter how well you plan or train your men, there will always be a cost. We work to limit that cost, while at the same time discharging our duty to the best of our ability."

"What if discharging our duty costs more lives?"

"Then we do what is necessary." Stiger paused a moment, looked the centurion firmly in the eye. "Never forget those you lost along the road of service. That is how you honor them."

"I see, sir," Vargus said, thinking for a moment. He frowned. "Thank you."

"Good, now go get your men ready to march."

Vargus turned away and then stopped, looking back at Stiger. "What if this is a mistake?"

"Falling back on the Sai'ko?"

"Yes, that," the centurion confirmed.

"Then a lot of good men will die," Stiger growled, "and I will have to live with that."

Vargus nodded in understanding and left without uttering another word.

FIFTEEN

Stiger surveyed the defensive works before him. He had marched his men hard through the night to get to the ground he had chosen for his stand. The men had been at it for a little over three hours and had achieved a great deal in that time. They toiled with shovels and pickaxes, digging away. At first, they had difficulty breaking through the top soil, which had frozen, but after that hard crust had been penetrated, the ground had yielded up earth quickly enough. Thankfully, winter had just begun and the ground had not frozen deeply.

A trench had been excavated along the top of the small ridgeline on the north side of the river. The dirt from the excavation was piled up and packed down to create a serviceable rampart. Exposed to the cold air, the moist, unearthed dirt had rapidly frozen solid.

Stiger would have loved to have had defensive works that included sharpened stakes and caltrops, but none had been brought when his men had marched from the castle. There had been no time to assemble such supplies. So, there was no wooden barricade, and it was not a very impressive defensive wall. However, when combined with the trench, which was around five feet deep, it made his position strong and would be difficult to overcome.

Fishhook-like in shape, the ridgeline bent outward from the bridge at the middle and gradually ran back on the flanks, almost to the water in either direction. The defensive works followed the top of the ridge, all the way to the river's edge. He had taken great care to make sure the ends of his line were more heavily fortified and anchored, as he could not allow the enemy to overcome him there and roll up his line. The bowl in the center of the hook helped to create the perfect killing ground, as it was not a very large area. To complicate things for the enemy, the bridge and river would act as a chokepoint. So basically, no matter how large the enemy host, the orcs would only be able to assault his positions with a near-equal number of warriors to those defending. Stiger's men behind the defensive works would have a decisive advantage in such a struggle.

Stiger had not destroyed the bridge, because he meant to allow the orcs to cross to assault his line. The ridgeline was good ground and the terrain lent itself naturally to defense, which allowed him to position his forces in such a way that the enemy could only assault him along the narrow front of the bowl. Only around the bridge, where the silt had built up by the wooden pilings, could one easily ford the river. He considered himself lucky that it was not yet cold enough for the river to have frozen over. A few feet beyond the bridge, either up or downstream, the water deepened significantly. Stiger knew this, because he had personally checked. Unless the enemy had brought their own bridging equipment, they would be in for a rough time.

Stiger looked out across the bridge. All he needed was for the orc army to come to him and fight him here. If the enemy turned away toward one of the other crossings, he would be in a difficult spot. His cavalry was out shadowing the enemy's line of advance, keeping an eye upon them.

Thankfully, the enemy did not have cavalry of their own and were unable to hinder his eyes. Stiger was receiving regular reports on their movement. He had also instructed Cannol to hit any orc scouts that moved in the direction of the two nearest crossings. He hoped by doing this to keep the enemy ignorant of them for as long as possible.

Based upon the latest report, which had come in a short while ago, the enemy was making right for the bridge and his position. The orcs who had traded with the valley undoubtedly knew of the bridge, but Stiger wondered if they knew about the other crossings to the east and west. Out of habit, Stiger absentmindedly rested his hand on the sword hilt and felt the reassuring electric tingle. He glanced down at the weapon for a moment and contemplated it.

What else can you do? Stiger silently asked the sword, wondering on its abilities and the potential risks of continuing to use it.

Not unexpectedly, the sword did not answer. Stiger resolved to speak to Father Thomas to seek the paladin's guidance just as soon as time permitted. He had meant to do so before, but something always seemed to come up. His thoughts returned to the coming battle and he looked out across the river. Though the enemy was not yet in sight, it was only a matter of time now.

A hammering behind him drew his attention. A platform was being constructed right behind the defensive rampart. In fact, six platforms were under construction. Each would hold one of First Cohort's bolt throwers. Unfortunately, the cohort's catapults had been placed atop the walls of Castle Vrell. It would have been impossible to rapidly disassemble and move them, so Sabinus had brought the bolt throwers. All things considered, Stiger was well pleased he had the deadly machines on hand. When used properly, they were very potent weapons.

"Artillery," Sabinus said at his side, following the legate's gaze. "Every soldier's friend."

"As long as you are not on the receiving end," Stiger said dryly.

"Very truly said." Sabinus glanced up at the sky. The first hints of dawn had appeared.

Stiger glanced over at the centurion, who suddenly grinned back at him. Sabinus was one of the original members of the Thirteenth, magically preserved for well over three hundred years. He was a hard-bitten, nail-eating fire-breather of a veteran, who had put in over twenty-five real years of real service to the empire before coming south with Delvaris. Before he had been placed into stasis, he had achieved the coveted rank of primus pilus, the most senior centurion of the legion and commander of the First Cohort. The primus pilus, a career soldier, was also an advisor to the legate. A smart legionary commander would always listen to his most senior centurion.

"What was it like?" Stiger asked the man. "What was it like being held in magical stasis for centuries? How did it feel?"

Sabinus chuckled. "I felt nothing, just closed my eyes one moment, and the next opened them to find myself here in your time. It was like waking prematurely from a nap, and feeling anything but rested. It took me a day to recover to the point where I could walk steadily, and another 'til I felt somewhat normal. At first I had difficulty believing that any real time had passed, but then . . . " Sabinus gestured around him at the fortifications. "I believe now, I can tell you that. Why do you ask?"

"Just curious is all," Stiger said and was silent for a time. "You fought here before, didn't you?"

"That I did, sir." His expression became clouded. He started to say something further and then hesitated.

"Go on," Stiger encouraged him. "Tell me about it."

"Last time, we brought more men and artillery. We also had time to properly dig in. The river was fuller too, as it had rained."

"Tell me more," Stiger ordered when Sabinus had trailed off, clearly lost in his thoughts and memories. He wanted to hear about what Delvaris had done and how the fighting here had gone down. Perhaps there was something he could learn that might prove useful in the coming battle.

"We fortified this same ridgeline, though to be honest, I remember it being some feet higher. I recommended we destroy the bridge here, but the legate thought otherwise and insisted that we do no such thing. Brogan, that is Braddock's father, and the legate wanted to have the battle here on this side of the river." He paused and pointed down toward the bridge. "That was a nice big stone bridge back then, dwarf-built, not the flimsy thing below." Sabinus pursed his lips as he looked down at the wooden bridge below them. "So much has changed since my time, sir."

"This is now your time," Stiger said, sharing a sympathetic look with the man. He could not guess how much Sabinus had left behind. What had he given up . . . a family, a wife, children, friends? There was no going back for Centurion Sabinus.

"There were," Sabinus continued, "two other bridges, some miles to the east and west, that we destroyed though. The enemy swept down the valley to this point, nearly double our strength. They poured across the bridge. Funny thing, though, they only crossed the bridge and made no attempt to ford the river itself. Perhaps the water was moving too fast or high. Regardless, they still made it across. The enemy filled up this here bowl before the ridgeline and came right at us . . . bold-like. All day we held and they kept coming. The bulk of the dwarven army, which was late, finally arrived. With the dwarves holding part of the line, the legate sent several cohorts, along with a contingent of dwarves, down the river a ways to sneak across and flank the orcs on the other side, who were waiting to cross. The flanking movement was handled and executed perfectly. Caught the orcs flat-footed, it did. We went over the top and into them hard. After a tough time, the orcs fell back to the south, where the next day we fought another battle and properly defeated them."

Stiger was silent as he thought this through. "That second battle . . . is that where General Delvaris fell to the minion of Castor?"

"General?" Sabinus asked and then nodded. The centurion looked at him in a funny way that made Stiger more than a little uncomfortable. "That is right, you call legates generals now. Yes, Legate Delvaris fell in that battle, but not before he took down the minion."

They were silent several minutes. Stiger found himself recalling the vision the sword had shown him back at Castle Vrell, of the fight between Delvaris and Castor's minion. Stiger took a breath and slowly let it out.

"The orcs seem a pretty determined bunch," Stiger said, moving the subject off of Delvaris.

"As long as priests are present, they can be very stubborn," Sabinus said. "Take them away and they crumble easily enough."

"When they were flanked here at the bridge, did their morale break? Is that why they fell back to the south side of the valley?"

"No, sir," Sabinus answered. "They fell back in good order. Truth be told, both sides were exhausted. We did not even attempt to pursue until the next day."

"I see," Stiger said, chewing his lip as he thought on what the centurion had just said.

"Sir." A legionary hustled up to the two officers and hastily saluted. "Dispatch here for you."

Stiger took the dispatch and opened it, scanning the contents. "Thank you. I will not have a reply."

The legionary saluted and left. Stiger handed the dispatch over to Sabinus. The centurion read the contents and then looked up at Stiger with no little amount of surprise. "You asked Braddock to do this?"

"Yes," Stiger admitted. "He was to march just as soon as the orc army passed him by."

"Then he will not arrive in time to help us hold?"

"No, he will not," Stiger said. "Braddock will come up behind the enemy after they are fully engaged in assaulting our line. At that point, the orcs will be trapped. It is my intention to destroy the enemy and not give them an opportunity to escape."

"How large is the enemy army?" Sabinus asked.

"We will be outnumbered." Stiger surveyed the work around him.

"How many are there?" Sabinus pressed.

"Somewhere between twenty-five and thirty thousand, perhaps more."

"Between the three cohorts, the 85th, and the cavalry, we will have a little over two thousand to hold the line?"

"We have five hundred militia who joined us," Stiger reminded him. "I estimate our current strength to be around three thousand."

"Old men." Sabinus spat on the ground.

"Those most recently retired, the ablest of them," Stiger replied. "I sent the rest on to Old City to look after the civilians. Should we fail to hold, they can join Hrove's warriors and any survivors in defense of the mountain and the World Gate."

As Stiger had expected, Braddock had opened the city to the people of the valley. Wagons, horses, mules, livestock, and families, some walking and some riding, were still streaming over the bridge below, up the ridge and by legionaries, who were digging in. The line of people and animals stretched out of sight behind a series of small hills on the other side of the river.

Stiger understood that people were taking other routes, using river crossings both to the north and south. He felt responsible for them all, and it made him more than a little uncomfortable at the risk he was about to take. But that was warfare in a nutshell. Without risk, and the occasional bold stroke, there could be little reward.

Stiger gestured toward the naturally shaped bowl before them. "I expect the enemy will only be able to get, at most, around three thousand across the river at any one time. This is a powerful position. We should easily be able to hold, at least long enough for Braddock to arrive with his army."

"Yes, sir," Sabinus said.

"You have given me an idea though." Stiger looked around and spotted Vargus fifty yards away, inspecting the construction of the defensive works. He was moving along the line with Quintus at his side. Stiger started over toward the other two centurions, with Sabinus following.

Vargus saw Stiger and nudged Quintus, who turned. The legate noted that both men looked tired. Stiger felt just as weary, but it did not stop him from his duties. They braced to attention and saluted.

"How far is the nearest river crossing?" Stiger asked as he joined the two officers.

"That would be Milman's Ford," Quintus said, pointing. "About two miles east. If you are concerned about the orcs crossing the river, we have a troop of cavalry watching for that."

"I am not concerned about that," Stiger said with a wave of his hand. "What I am worried about are the dwarves."

Both centurions looked at him with questioning expressions. Stiger explained his plans for the battle and what he had arranged to happen with Braddock. The two centurions looked at each other for a moment, as if thinking the same thing, before turning back to Stiger and Sabinus.

"Sir." Quintus spoke up first. "That would then put the river between us and the dwarves."

"I am fairly confident that when the time comes we can clear this side," Vargus added. "However, that bridge will become a chokepoint. We may be unable to get sufficient men across in time to aid our allies."

"Having given it some thought, that is also my thinking," Stiger informed them. He glanced around his defensive works and mentally calculated the minimum number of men he needed to effectively defend this line. He nodded to himself and then turned back to his officers. "I intend to send First Cohort to make a crossing at Milman's Ford. Once the cavalry comes in, they will follow and join up. That would put over eight hundred infantry and two hundred cavalry over the river and free to strike the enemy at will."

"I," Quintus said carefully, "am not sure I'm comfortable stripping our defensive line of nearly a third of our strength, even before the enemy has arrived."

"What if the enemy angles toward the crossings or even splits off a force to take one?" Vargus said.

"Then the cavalry will alert us and we fall back toward Thane's Mountain . . . at least long enough for Braddock's army to engage the enemy's tail," Stiger said. "If they don't move for one of the crossings and continue on straight for us when the dwarves hit them, then Sabinus, moving along the water's edge, will attack them on their flank. We will push over the top and clear this side of the river out and then cross the bridge and link up."

"Sir." A legionary approached the officers, interrupting. He saluted. "Dispatch from Lieutenant Cannol."

Stiger took the dispatch and then dismissed the legionary.

"The enemy is less than an hour away," Stiger summarized, looking up at the brightening and cloudless sky. Soon the sun would be warming the land and bringing some much-needed warmth. The night had been bitterly cold. "They have yet to detach a force for any of the crossings. The lieutenant feels they are coming here, to us."

"Well then," Sabinus said, "I had better get my boys formed up."

"Are you committed to this course of action?" Quintus asked Stiger, clearly hoping to change the legate's mind.

"I am," Stiger growled. The more he thought on it, the more it made sense. He turned back to Sabinus. "When Cannol arrives, I will give him orders to ride and join up with you. You are in overall command of this expedition, though when you go in, I want Cannol's company slashing at the enemy's flanks. Don't waste them away as dismounted infantry."

"What if the dwarves are late?" Sabinus shifted, running a hand through his hair. "The longer we are across the river, the greater likelihood my command will be discovered. How do you wish me to proceed under such circumstances?"

"I rather suspect that in such an eventuality we will be under tremendous pressure," Stiger said. "My order to you, sir, is to do what you think practical. If that means falling back to the ford, then do so. If you feel you can attack those enemy forces before you on your side of the river with a prospect of success, then do so. We shall post lookouts for you. When you go in, we will go over the top. You will be the man on the spot. So, ultimately, it will be your decision to do what you think best."

"I see," Sabinus said, and a hammering nearby drew his attention to one of the bolt throwers. "I will leave behind the men assigned to the bolt throwers. They are experienced in the operation of the machines. You, I think, will need them more than I."

Stiger nodded in agreement. It was what he had been thinking as well.

Sabinus cracked another grin at Stiger. The centurion gave him what Stiger thought to be an odd look as he snapped to attention and saluted smartly. Stiger returned the centurion's salute and then offered his hand.

"Just like old times," Sabinus said, taking his hand warmly. Stiger felt chilled by the man's words.

"Ones I unfortunately did not live through."

Sabinus looked as if he wanted to say something, but instead settled for a simple, "Good luck, sir."

"To you as well."

Stiger watched Sabinus stomp off and then turned to the other two officers. "Quintus, reposition your men to hold the left, and Vargus, take the right. The militia will hold the center, while the 85th acts as a ready reserve."

There was an uncomfortable moment of silence. Stiger decided to break it. "Gentlemen, we only need to hold the line. The dwarves will come. When they do, we must be ready. Understood?"

"Yes, sir," Vargus said.

"I understand, sir," said Quintus. "You can count on our men. They know that they are all that stands between the orcs and their families."

"Then let us show the orcs what the legions are made of."

Stiger turned away from the officers, allowing them to get back to work. He wished Eli were with him, but his friend was out with the cavalry. He moved up to the edge of line, carefully crossing over the trench and climbing the rampart. On top, he surveyed his entire line and began to wonder if he had made the right decision. As usual, the self-questioning and second-guessing of his own plans had begun. Stiger knew it would torment him right up until the fighting began. He slapped his thigh in irritation.

First Cohort had already begun pulling off the line. He watched them for a moment before turning back to the bridge and the bowl beneath his defensive works. Once the orc army arrived, they would pour across the bridge, down into the bowl below him, and then up the slopes of the ridge to test the defenses. In his mind, he could see the battle developing as if it had already happened. Would it go as he had planned? He hoped so, but in war, nothing was certain.

Alone, Stiger began to walk the line. Wherever he went, men were busy preparing for the enemy. Water carriers with buckets drawn from the river were making the rounds. Details were also distributing rations. Eyes came up, tracking him as he passed. Many called out a greeting or gave him a spontaneous cheer. Stiger replied with a simple nod and continued on his way. How many of the valley cohorts viewed him as Delvaris reborn? The thought made Stiger uncomfortable, as if he were someone other than himself, which he knew he was not.

If they fight better for it, so be it. I will play the part.

"Sir?" Blake had come up and interrupted Stiger's thoughts. The newly-made centurion saluted. The only change Stiger noted about the former sergeant was that he now wore his sword on his left side, as befitted an officer. "I understand the 85th is to act as a reserve? Is that correct, sir?"

"Yes, that is right."

"Where do you want us then?"

"Directly in the center of the line, behind the valley militia. I want you formed up behind them and ready to step forward or deploy to either flank if required. I expect that this line will come under heavy assault. Once it does, the 85th will be our only reserve."

"Is that First Cohort forming up to march?" The centurion was pointing to their right, behind the line.

"First will be marching to a river crossing with the intention of flanking the enemy," Stiger informed him.

"When I signed up, they never said life would be easy, sir," Blake said cheerfully.

That brought out a chuckle from Stiger that was cut short by a horn blaring in the distance. Both Stiger and Blake turned to look. Across the river, they could see the cavalry moving in one large body toward the bridge. Behind them, a screen of riders was clearly keeping watch on the approaching enemy host.

Well, Stiger thought to himself, it is about to begin.

The stream of civilians below began to panic, cramming themselves onto the bridge and pushing and shoving their way across. Watching them, Stiger knew that it would only get worse the closer the enemy got.

"Send two files of men down to the bridge," Stiger ordered Blake, pointing. "Sort that business out. I want it orderly."

"Yes, sir." Blake saluted and hustled off.

Stiger continued his walk along the fortifications. He stopped near a bolt thrower and looked it over. The crew had been stacking the deadly bolts, placing them within easy reach. They snapped to attention.

"Is your machine ready?" Stiger asked the optio in charge.

"Aye, sir," the optio replied. "This nasty bitch is ready to fire on your orders."

"What's your name?" Stiger asked the man, who looked to be old enough to have put in at least ten years of service. That was typically the length of time a legionary would have to serve to be considered for promotion.

"Lucius Cornelius Alexander, sir."

"Well, Alexander, I hope your aim is good."

"Dead on, sir," the optio replied. "You can count on me and my boys to give it to them bastards hot and hard, sir."

There were nods all around. Stiger liked their attitude.

"Done this before then?" Stiger asked.

"A time or two, sir," Alexander replied laconically.

"Carry on then," Stiger said and stepped past them, deciding to return to the center.

There was a gap in the center of the line where boards had been run out over the trench for people, wagons, and animals to cross. The rampart also had a gate in the center. The gate was currently open. Stiger wanted to be there when Cannol came through. As he reached the center of his line, the first troop of cavalry was riding over the bridge. The civilians had clearly been told to wait until the formation was across. Both of Blake's files were just starting down into the bowl.

Stiger looked across the water. The screen of cavalry in the distance was getting closer, riding into sight as they crested a small hill and then disappearing again as they cantered down it. The sun was shining now and it was much easier to see them. The screen stopped occasionally. Stiger could imagine them studying the advancing enemy army and then moving on to a safer position from which to watch again.

A marching army normally kicked up a good bit of dust. This time, there was no sign of that. The snow kept the ground wet, frozen, and muddy, so there was no dust in the air. As he stood there, he saw what at first appeared to be smudge in the distance. Stiger squinted, knowing what it was: the vanguard of the enemy army. He watched for a few minutes.

Stiger turned to watch the first of his cavalry as they made it to the top of the small ridge and the defensive line. They dismounted and, one by one, walked their mounts over the planks and through the gate. They looked tired and weary. The horses looked to be in good condition, though, which was a comfort.

"Sergeant." Stiger called the trooper in charge over.

"Sir?" The trooper dismounted and offered a salute, looking up at the legate on top of the rampart.

"Hold your men ready just behind the line," Stiger ordered. "Your company will be moving out as soon as they all come in. Make sure as the others arrive, they do the same."

"Yes, sir."

Stiger waved the tired sergeant on through the gate and watched the last of the formation move through. Several other troops rode through the gate in the next few minutes. Only the thin screen on the other side of the bridge remained. That and the civilians, who were now abandoning anything that slowed them down, including bags and packs. The last of them rushed across the bridge, Blake's legionaries making sure that things did not get out of hand. Beyond them, the smudge had become a large host of orcs, of which Stiger could now differentiate individuals. The enemy were perhaps a mile and a half away now.

"There sure are a lot of them." Stiger turned to find Quintus.

"That there are." Stiger took a deep breath. "Would you be kind enough to have the recall sounded for our cavalry?"

Quintus turned to a legionary standing a few feet from him. He had been watching the approaching enemy, as had everyone else along the line. The centurion snapped an order, and the man dashed off to find a horn blower. Within moments, another man with a horn mounted the rampart and sounded the recall. He blew on it hard, three rapid blasts. The cavalry across the river wheeled about and galloped toward the bridge. There they stopped and waited for the last of the civilians to rush across. They followed, along with the two files from the 85th, and began making their way up toward the defensive line.

Stiger recognized Lan and watched the lieutenant lead his troop up the hill. From their blood-spattered armor, they had clearly seen some action.

"Lieutenant," Stiger called to him, "looks like you've had some excitement."

"Surprised a few orc scouts," Lan said, pulling up below the legate. His men continued, dismounting before crossing the planks and passing through the gate. "I am pleased to report no casualties, sir."

"Very good," Stiger replied. "Lieutenant Cannol's company will be heading out shortly. Your troop is to remain. Detach three men to act as personal messengers for Vargus, Quintus, and Blake. You will take your position with me, and the remainder of your men shall act as messengers. Questions?"

"No, sir," Lan replied.

"Then get yourself through the line and fed, and then report back to me as soon as practical."

The lieutenant saluted, dismounted, and walked his horse through the gate. He was still limping slightly from the battering he had taken on the way back to the pass in Forkham's Valley. Stiger watched him go before turning back as the last of the riders made their way up the ridge. He was pleased to see Eli, Marcus, and the other two elves, along with Lieutenant Cannol. Eli offered him a grin as he dismounted. His friend was clearly enjoying himself immensely.

"You live for this, don't you?" Stiger accused.

"I suppose a little excitement makes a long life tolerable."

"See to your horse," Stiger told him, suspecting that there was some truth in what Eli had just said, and for some reason Eli's longevity reminded him of their argument back in Old City. A bit of the anger returned. He forced it down. "Once you've done that, come and join me if you would."

Eli nodded and led his horse away, with Marcus and the other elves following him.

"Sir," Quintus spoke up, "I wanted to report that all of the bolt throwers are ready."

"Excellent," Stiger said. "They are to go into action once the enemy passes the middle of the bridge, not before."

"I will pass that along."

"Join your men," Stiger said and returned the centurion's salute before Quintus stepped off, climbing down the reverse side of the rampart. Eli had already passed through. Taha'Leeth caught his eye. He winked at her, surprising himself. There was a small twist to her lips as she flashed him a smile, and then she was gone.

Aver'Mons caught the exchange and turned away. Stiger suspected the elf was offended by him. Taha'Leeth was essentially elven royalty. Had Stiger been in elven lands to the north, his behavior toward her would have been much more reserved. Then again, she was from the south, and up until recently, her people had been slaves. Who knew what was considered acceptable behavior amongst her own? Stiger pushed such thoughts from his mind. He had more important things to worry about.

Last to pass through was Cannol. Stiger had made his way down and stood by the gate and waited for him.

"Lieutenant." Stiger stopped him with a hand.

"Sir?" the lieutenant asked, looking at Stiger.

"I have another job for you. First Cohort marched for Milman's Ford, which is located a couple of miles east of here. I want you to ride and join Sabinus. He will be crossing the ford and then falling on the flanks of the enemy on the other side of the river. Once you cross, screen for his force. You will be his eyes. After he engages the enemy, slash their flanks."

"I understand, sir," Cannol said, glancing back through the gate on the enemy host approaching the bridge, just on the other side of the river. "Do you think you can hold long enough for us to flank them, sir?" the lieutenant asked. "That is quite a large force out there."

"Don't worry about us holding. You and Sabinus get across the river and strike them good and hard just as soon as you can."

"Yes, sir," the lieutenant said, turned to go, and then checked himself. "Oh, the last word I had from Braddock was that his army had marched and is trailing a few hours behind the orcs. I left a few men out to stay in contact with him."

Stiger felt encouraged by the news.

"See Vargus before you go and take along a local guide so you don't miss the ford. Also, once you cross the river, I want you to send a rider to Braddock. Kindly ask him to hurry."

"I will see to it."

"Good luck, Lieutenant."

"Thank you, and to you too, sir."

The lieutenant stepped off, leading his horse toward his men. Several legionaries stepped forward removed the planking bridging the trench and then dropped the heavy gate into place as Stiger climbed back up the earthen rampart. A detail then began shoveling a waiting pile of dirt over it, with the clear intention of filling in the gap. When they were done, there would be no hint the gate had ever existed.

Turning toward the enemy, Stiger took a deep breath. It was almost time.

SIXTEEN

Stiger returned his attention to the enemy, who were nearing the bridge. Across the river, Bridgetown burned furiously, sending huge columns of smoke up into the sky. The enemy host had stopped around a hundred yards from the wooden span. The size of the orc army was frightening. Priests in their wild outfits could be seen moving before the enemy, along with a handful of warriors who wore better armor and were clearly leaders of some sort. One orc warrior, who was far larger than any other that Stiger had seen, stepped forward. Several orcs moved with him. They advanced to within twenty-five yards of the bridge and were clearly surveying the legion's position along the ridge, of which they could only see the defensive works.

Stiger imagined that the large warrior was the main orc leader. Nowhere could he see the minion of Castor. The group talked amongst themselves for some time, with the leader gesturing at Stiger's position. An orc detached itself from the group. It walked onto the bridge and casually glanced over both sides before turning back.

Stiger heard footsteps behind him, climbing the rampart. Apart from himself and a few others, he had made sure that no one could be fully seen; only the tops of the heads of the men were visible as they peered out over at the enemy. The legionaries were on the reverse side of the earthen rampart, waiting for the order to move up. Stiger glanced back to see Lan, Eli, and Father Thomas joining him. He idly wondered where Taha'Leeth and Aver'Mons had gone off to.

"Bless me," Father Thomas said, once he had joined Stiger.

"I rather think we could all use the High Father's blessing about now," Stiger said to the paladin. Father Thomas laughed at that, startling some of the nearest legionaries, who had been looking grimly on the enemy below.

"You sent off First Cohort?" Eli asked.

"Yes, I sent them on a wide flanking movement to the east. Cannol's company will be joining them as well."

"An interesting move," Eli added as he surveyed the orc army. "Gets you more men across the river around the time Braddock's army strikes."

"Let us hope it works out that way," Stiger said. It all came down to timing, and Stiger was concerned. For all he knew, the enemy could be aware of Braddock's advance and was preparing to turn on the dwarves.

"I am sure Braddock understands the gravity of the matter." Eli's attempt at reassuring him had the opposite effect. This fight before him would be the largest battle that Stiger had ever commanded, and he was worried, though he was doing his best to keep it from others. He had bet large on this battle.

The orc leader abruptly turned, having seen enough, and walked back to his army. He began pacing in front of his orcs, apparently giving a speech, his arms gesticulating wildly as he talked to them. Though Stiger could not hear what was being said, the orc army roared approval. It was clear the leader was stirring them up.

"Man the wall!" Stiger shouted, and all along the fish-hook defensive line, men stepped up to their places. To the enemy, it would look like an army had sprung up from the ground. Stiger meant it as a show to get their attention and also to interrupt their leader's morale-building speech.

Across the way, the orc army stopped cheering as the legionaries came into view atop the rampart. The enemy leader turned, saw Stiger's men, then apparently said something, for the orc army roared their rage and hate at the legionaries and began to chant something that Stiger could not quite hear clearly.

"I think they are chanting a word, perhaps even a name. It sounds like Sovat, whatever that means," Eli suggested and shrugged when Stiger looked over at him. "I don't speak orc."

"What?" Stiger asked, with some amusement. "Not enough time on your hands, after learning dwarven?"

"I think I will add it to my list," Eli said dryly.

"That way," Stiger grinned at him, "next time you can be more useful."

Eli grinned back, amused.

Stiger looked around and spotted Centurion Tilanus from the militia. He beckoned the man over.

"Legate?"

"Are your men ready to hold the center?"

"They are at their positions," Tilanus replied. "We will hold, as Delvaris himself held at this very spot."

"The 85th is just behind you," Stiger said with a gesture. "Do not hesitate to call for aid if you need it. I expect the center shall be their focus."

"I will, sir," Tilanus assured him.

"I am counting on your men."

"They are good men, sir, just retired within the last couple years."

"I know. That is why I put them at the center. According to Vargus and Quintus, they are the most experienced and seasoned on the field this day. I needed the best."

"Thank you, sir." Tilanus puffed up at the compliment.

"Resume your post," Stiger ordered as the orcs roared again from across the river.

Tilanus saluted and returned to his men, just feet away. Stiger knew his words had been overheard and would be passed to each man under the centurion's command, which had been his intention all along. They would fight harder knowing that he was counting on them.

Stiger turned back to the enemy and caught Eli's eye. His friend well knew what he had just done, and why he had done it. Eli had seen him manipulate men to his will before. Though he suspected Eli disapproved, it was nothing new. A good leader knew how to get the best out of his men. A poor leader did not. It sounded a bit coldblooded, but it was necessary. Stiger shrugged.

A harsh horn sounded from the enemy, followed by a tremendous battle cry that dwarfed the others so far. The orcs surged forward toward the bridge. It rapidly became a chokepoint, chock full of the enemy as they fought each other to be the first across the wooden span. A few of those who could not get onto the bridge through the press, after a slight hesitation, splashed into the water, where they carefully began to negotiate the shallows around the support pylons.

Stiger had expected some of the enemy to attempt to swim across the river, but the orcs seemed to shy back from the fast-moving water, keeping to the silt-filled shallows around the bridge pylons. An orc ventured too far, lost its footing, and disappeared beneath the surface. Another slipped and quickly followed the first. Moments later, a handful more were rapidly swept away and under the surface. Surprisingly, no other orcs ventured into the water after that, the remainder electing to cross using the bridge. Stiger wondered if orc armor was simply too much dead weight to be easily countered. Perhaps, Stiger considered, they could not swim?

CRACK!

Stiger almost jumped as the nearest bolt thrower released. The bolt slammed into the middle of the throng of orcs crossing the bridge. A series of cracks from the other machines sounded as they also fired. Stiger saw one bolt pass clean through the chest of an armored warrior and strike the creature behind, dropping them both and knocking down a third. One orc near the railing of the bridge was hit so hard, the missile's energy carried him over the side and into the water, where he disappeared from view. The bolt thrower crews sprang to work reloading. Stiger had seen bolt throwers in action before, and knew a good crew could fire two to three rounds per minute. In the old days before Emperor Midiuses's reforms, each imperial legion had carried around sixty such machines with them. These days, a legionary company carried two machines, either bolt throwers or small catapults. Again, Stiger had the feeling that the legions had lost something with those reforms.

Under continual fire from the bolt throwers, which were cracking away at the enemy, the orcs poured out into the bowl and started up the slope of the small ridgeline toward the legionary positions. All along the line, the men prepared themselves. Watching the orcs climb, Stiger suddenly felt helpless. It was a terrible feeling and one he had not truly experienced until this moment. He became very still. Stiger had never commanded so many men on the field of battle. In the north, against the Rivan, he had taken part in battles that were larger in size and scope, but this was different. He was the ultimate authority on the field. It was a sobering thought, and the weight of his responsibility had suddenly come to rest heavily upon his shoulders. Should he fail, how many would die? Conversely, Stiger wondered, what would the cost be should he succeed?

Most of the fight was now out of his hands. He had placed his men in a superior position, given the necessary orders, and had reserves standing by, ready to be fed into the battle. He even had Lan and his troop available to act as messengers. The truth was that Stiger's command had grown beyond him. He was no longer responsible for a single company and fighting his own men, but a small army. Others who were on the spot would have to make the critical decisions about how best to fight their units. He could not do it for them. For the first time in a great long while, he abruptly realized he would have to rely upon others to do the job he was accustomed to doing himself. The thought depressed him. *Is this what it's like to be a legionary commander? Does General Treim feel as helpless?*

A volley of javelins, thrown from a century to his right, arced up in the air and slammed down into a group of orcs charging up the ridge. The javelins, for the most part, were well-thrown, and a number of orcs were struck down. Another volley followed that one.

"Sir?"

Stiger turned to Lan and raised an eyebrow in question.

"I am afraid . . . " The lieutenant jabbed a thumb at an optio who looked a little uncomfortable. " . . . they would like you to step back behind the rampart, sir, so that they can properly do their job."

Stiger looked at the militia optio and several legion-aries nervously waiting for him to step back and behind the protection of the earthen rampart. They stood ready with their shields resting on the ground to the sides. Stiger took a deep breath and glanced around once more before stepping down. He gave a nod to the optio and his men, who moved up to the rampart. The tops of their chests were visible from the other side, providing them partial cover for when the enemy arrived. There had been no time to erect a wooden barricade atop the earthen mound, and even if there had been, there were no trees within easy reach. This battle would be fought on pastureland.

Sabinus had brought the legion's eagle with him. Legionary Beck stood there, proudly holding the Thirteenth's eagle, point resting in the snow. It glinted brightly under the sunlight and would be visible across the entire field. Stiger had instructed Beck to stay close and fol-low him wherever he went. Two legionaries from the 85th had been assigned as guards for Beck and the eagle. It would not do to allow the enemy to capture it.

Stiger glanced one more time around his line. He could see other unit standards held up high, men standing to the line, shields presented forward in anticipation of receiving the first orcs. Along his line, javelins flew through the air, raining down on those below, who were climbing the ridge. The first ranks retained their javelins, while the second and third ranks threw for all they were worth. Every few seconds there was a CRACK from a bolt thrower as the light artillery released. From his spot—he had selected it due to it being the highest point on the field—Stiger could see the entire line and the bridge below, though much of the bowl was concealed from his view. Stiger looked around for a higher vantage point but did not see one. He did see an empty open-top supply wagon parked several feet away. The wagon was still hitched.

"Lieutenant." Stiger turned calmly to Lan. "Would you be kind enough to bring that wagon closer to the line? I would prefer a better view of the battle."

"Yes, sir," the lieutenant said as the first of the orcs hit his line.

Stiger turned away to watch the action. This was the moment of truth. He moved up behind the militia holding this portion of the line. In their armor, they were mostly indistinguishable from other legionaries, though in some cases, it fit poorly. The first orcs scrambled up the rampart, only to receive jabs and thrusts from javelins seeking soft, unprotected flesh. An orc howled in agony as a javelin punched through its left leg. Hefting a stone hammer, it dropped the weapon and snatched the javelin with both hands before it could be pulled back. The creature ripped the javelin free from the legionary and began to slowly draw the weapon out from its leg, when a jab from another legionary thrust through its throat. Yanking back, the legionary completely ripped the creature's throat open. The orc staggered backward before it was pushed aside by a fellow. It tumbled back down the slope and out of sight.

Another orc, hefting a large sword, took its place. The creature batted away at the numerous javelins that were thrust in its direction. Despite the orc's efforts, one found purchase in its belly. The legionary wielding the javelin thrust deeply and then jerked the weapon back, inadvertently pulling the orc forward. The creature grunted and fell into the mass of tightly packed legionaries. It died under a flurry of sword strikes from those in the second rank.

"Lock shields," Tilanus shouted to the front line as a wave of orcs crested the top of the rampart. The shields snapped together with an audible thunk, legionaries thrusting over them with their javelins at the orcs. Those in the second and third ranks stood close behind the first, ready to enter the battle when needed or called to do so.

The struggle was intense and hot work. Stiger watched. He itched to draw steel and join them, but refused the urge. He needed to stay focused on the battle as a whole and look for opportunities. A clatter behind him signaled the arrival of the wagon. Lan pulled the heavy supply wagon up, just behind the last line of men, before engaging the brake. Stiger immediately made for it and accepted Lan's hand. The lieutenant pulled the legate up and into the bed of the wagon. He then helped Eli up.

From the wagon's bed, Stiger could see the entire battle. Nearly the whole line was engaged, with the exception of those men nearest the water. The orcs seemed to be ignoring them, where he had made sure to make his defenses the strongest, the trench deeper and the rampart rising to a much greater height. Looking down at the enemy in the bowl, Stiger was stunned at how many orcs were crammed down in there, waiting their turn to get at his legionaries. They were literally standing shoulder to shoulder. The bridge was packed tight. On the other side of the river, the orc army had also spread out, coming close to the riverbank, but not quite to its edge. They were watching the fight across the way.

One of the railings on the bridge gave way, collapsing under the press, and a number of orcs went tumbling into the fast-moving water. They sank from sight and were not seen again. Those who had been nearest to the collapse shied away from the edge, though the press of bodies inevitably sent additional orcs over the side and into the water.

"Lieutenant." Stiger pointed out the ends of his lines, which intersected with the water. The orcs were still avoiding them, which was odd, but could be explained by the difficulty of overcoming the defenses there. "Send a rider to Vargus and Quintus. Inform them to strip the ends of their lines by half and use those men as a reserve wherever they might need them."

"Yes, sir." The lieutenant beckoned two waiting dispatch riders over to him and spoke to them, passing along Stiger's orders. They mounted up and galloped away.

Stiger was pleased. So far his line was holding. The orcs were having trouble scaling and overcoming both the trench and rampart. Once they reached the top of the dirt wall, they were being rapidly cut down. Stiger noted that his legionaries had thrown the last of their javelins. Only those in the front rank still had theirs, and of those, there were fewer and fewer, as the weapons were either snatched away or bent and rendered useless. His men were increasingly forced to draw their short swords. It meant that the fighting would become more dangerous.

"Look at that," Eli said, drawing Stiger's attention to the rear. Coming down the mountain were a number of small figures. They were leading a team of oxen pulling what appeared to be a medium-sized catapult. Behind the catapult were several large supply wagons that lumbered along slowly.

"Those are gnomes," Lan said. "Where did they come from?"

"I would imagine Old City," Stiger said and turned back to the action. The gnomes were still some ways off, and one catapult, though welcome, would not make a material difference to this battle, but any assistance was welcome. He hoped that more help was on the way.

Stiger saw the first of his men fall, one of the militia, just a few feet away. A war hammer crashed over the top of the man's shield and down on his helmet, crushing the skull like an overripe melon. Without missing a beat, the man behind him stepped into the gap, striking at the orc that was celebrating its kill. He caught the orc in the thigh and then slammed his shield into the creature's body, sending it back over the other side of the rampart and knocking down several orcs scrambling up the slope. It was so smartly done that Stiger wanted to congratulate the man, but there was just no time. He forced himself to keep perspective. There were little dramas like the one he had just witnessed playing out across the battlefield.

CRACK!

The bolt-throwing crews were keeping up a steady fire. Though they could be incredibly accurate when the operators wished, by simply firing as rapidly as they could into the bowl where the enemy was tightly grouped, it was difficult to miss. The crews were focusing on speed.

Stiger had a sudden thought. "Send a rider to each bolt thrower," he said, drawing Lan's attention. He pointed toward the bridge, where the enemy was still crossing. "I want all of them focused back on the bridge. Pour it on them."

"Yes, sir," Lan replied, then turned and shouted to two more of his troopers. They galloped off to spread the word. Within five minutes, all of the bolt throwers were spraying fire on those tightly-packed orcs who were stuck on the bridge, waiting their turn to move forward. A panic ensued. Orcs pushed and shoved to get forward, forcing others over the side, while a number tried to get as low as possible. There was no protection for them. The bolt throwers had the elevation and could fire right down into their midst.

There was simply nowhere to go, as the bowl was packed tight. It was carnage on the bridge, which was what Stiger had wanted. Those who now made it over the bridge would know what waited for them on this side of the river. The message was clear. Death waited.

"You . . . you . . . look," a small, insistent, squeaky voice called up to them. "Look."

Stiger, Lan, and Eli looked down and into the black, beady eyes of a gnome standing beside the wagon. It was gesturing at them and was hard to hear over the noise. Having gotten their attention, it hissed at them with a displeased look.

"There," the gnome pointed to the catapult around twenty-five yards away. The team of oxen had been unhitched and led away. Gnomes swarmed over the machine, making it ready to fire. Other gnomes were unloading with ludicrous care what appeared to be large clay jars from the wagons and stacking them next to the catapult. The clay jars were half the size of a gnome, and four of them were required to carry one.

"Boom." The gnome pointed toward the orcs, as if requesting permission to join the fight. "We go boom?"

"Okay," Stiger said, gesturing at the orcs. "Fire away."

The gnome snickered, turned, and ran back the catapult, yelling in its own language.

"What do you think are in those jars?" Lan asked, eying the gnomes curiously.

"Lead shot, likely," Stiger said with indifference. "Though, with the size of that artillery piece, it should surprise the orcs when it fires. I suppose it could reach clear across the river."

"That would be nice to see," Eli said, glancing over at the catapult. "I wish they had brought more than one piece though."

"Let's be grateful for what they did bring."

Tilanus blew hard on a whistle and swapped out the first rank of his militia. They stepped to the rear, breathing heavily. Stiger glanced along his line. It was a common theme. The ranks were getting swapped out. An aid station had been set up to the rear. Several wounded were being helped. A few were even being carried. Stiger looked back at the aid station and saw Father Thomas and Sergeant Arnold there helping the surgeons as the number of the wounded began to grow. It pained Stiger to see men he commanded bloodied, maimed, and terribly injured. It was always the same. He ground his teeth in frustration.

There was a deep creaking to his right, followed by a heavy thud. Stiger looked over just as the gnome catapult released, launching a large clay jar high into the air, where it arced up and then came down smack in the center of the bowl. The result was a terrific explosion of smoke and sound that ripped the enemy bodily apart where the jar had landed. The concussive blast knocked those within fifteen feet down or into their fellows.

Stiger was so surprised that he almost fell backward out of the wagon. Eli caught him by the arm. Lan had almost done the same, but managed to remain on his feet. Silence abruptly settled upon the battlefield as everyone froze in shock.

The gnomes were using magic!

After a moment, the orcs came to their senses when there were no further explosions and threw themselves forward once again at the legionaries. The fight was back on.

Stiger's head snapped around to the gnomes. They were celebrating, thumping each other on the back with glee. He saw the gnome he had just spoken to doubled over with laughter.

"Bring me that gnome," Stiger ordered of Eli, pointing out the one he wanted. The elf jumped down from the wagon, dashed over to the gnome in question, and lifted the stunned creature off its feet. Eli ran back to Stiger and unceremoniously dumped the gnome into the bed of the wagon. It climbed to its feet, glaring at Eli while it brushed itself off.

"You." Stiger demanded its attention. "What is your name?"

"Name?" the gnome parroted and looked up at Stiger with a frown on its face.

"Yes, your name. I am Stiger." He tapped his chest with a thumb. "Stiger."

"Cragg," the gnome responded, patting its chest with a hand.

"You are Cragg?" Stiger confirmed and pointed at the gnome.

The gnome nodded, its intense, beady eyes fixed upon Stiger.

"Look there," Stiger said, pointing toward the bridge. "See that bridge?"

"Boom?" Cragg asked, looking from the bridge back up at Stiger. "Go boom?"

"Yes," Stiger said, gesturing at the bridge. "Make the bridge go boom!"

The gnome nodded vigorously, an evil smile spreading across its small face. "Go boom!"

"Go boom," Stiger said, pointing once again toward the bridge.

Cragg scrambled down from the wagon and ran over to the catapult. The other gnomes had stopped to watch. Cragg began shouting what seemed like orders and cuffing those who did not move fast enough for his liking.

"Do you think this is a good idea, sir?" Lan asked. "We will need that bridge to cross when the time comes."

"Don't feel like a swim?" Stiger asked him in jest, then sobered. "When it comes time, we can cross the shallows around the bridge pylons."

Stiger turned back. The ends of his lines were still free from assault. Despite the strength of his defenses there, it was a logical place to hit Stiger's line, and that had gotten him thinking. The orcs seemed somewhat wary of the water. Stiger had a suspicion that it wasn't the cold or the weight of their armor that was keeping them from it, but something else, perhaps even an aversion to water. He wanted to test it by destroying the bridge.

There was a deep creaking groan, followed by a solid thud to his right. Stiger watched as another clay jar sailed up into the air. It missed the bridge entirely, landing on the far side of the riverbank in the middle of the mass of the orc army. There was another deep explosion filled with smoke that tore a hole through the enemy.

The gnomes hooted and hollered with glee at the destruction they had wrought. Cragg, on the other hand, did not seem too pleased. He screamed at them, gesticulating wildly, becoming red in the face. The gnomes seemed to think his rage was hilarious and collapsed, doubled over in fits of laughter.

Slowly, almost painfully, the catapult was rearmed. The gnomes scurried off of the large machine, and Cragg barked an order to a gnome standing to the side, who was holding a rope. The gnome yanked hard on the rope and launched the next jar. It flew true, landing smack in the middle of the bridge. The explosion was terrific. Boards, timbers, body parts, and splinters shot in all directions as the wooden construction came apart. With a groan, the entire middle span of the bridge collapsed into the water. In seconds, it was ripped apart by the current. Then the entire structure was concealed by the smoke from the blast.

When the smoke cleared, Stiger saw that the bridge was a mangled wreck, with the river pulling large chunks downstream. A few orcs had managed to cling to floating timbers. They, too, were being carried away by the current.

The orcs on the other side of the river backed up, looking none too eager to come near the water. They showed absolutely no interest in crossing. Bridge or no bridge, Stiger could not understand why they would not push forward. The fighting on the north side of the river continued to rage on, but those on the south side held their ground. The minutes wore on. No move was made to cross. Stiger wondered how long that would last.

"How many do you estimate are down in the bowl?" Stiger asked Eli, looking over at his friend.

"Perhaps six, maybe even seven thousand," Eli postulated. "It is a considerable portion of their army."

"Why don't they cross?" Lan asked the question that was on Stiger's mind. "It is almost like they are afraid of the water."

"There are monkeys in the forests of my homeland that cannot swim," Eli said. "If they fall into the water, they are so heavy they sink right to the bottom and drown. Their bones are very thick."

"Like those monkeys that live on Tela'vGar Island?" Stiger asked him. "The ones you showed me that time, shortly after we first met. They can't get off the island."

"Yes, those are the ones."

"You are suggesting that the orcs, like those monkeys, are too heavy to swim. Is that it?" Stiger looked over at his friend. "That perhaps they are even too afraid to cross the wreckage of the bridge and shallows for fear of being swept into deeper water?"

"That is a distinct possibility," Eli admitted, "one I think that is not beyond reason."

Stiger looked down into the bowl. The orcs trapped there still seemed intent upon breaking his line, though he did not see how they could do it. Stiger's position was just too strong. The enemy north of the river did not appear to be too concerned with being cut off. As Stiger watched them continue to throw themselves against his line, he began to wonder if he should let them continue to do so. His line would only be breached when either his men tired or their ranks thinned, and that was unlikely. On the south side of the river, the majority of the orc army stood watching the struggle silently. Would they get up the courage to cross? Stiger expected that if he gave them enough time, they would. He had a feeling the priests would see to it.

There was another explosion in the bowl as the gnomes fired off a clay jar from their catapult. Stiger looked over at the gleeful little creatures dying with mirth at the destruction they had just wrought on the enemy. They seemed to be having the time of their lives, whooping, hooting, and hollering as they set to work rearming their deadly machine.

Stiger looked back to the bowl and scratched at his jaw. He then looked beyond the bowl, to the other side of the river. First Cohort had not yet made their appearance. By his calculation, they should have crossed the river and been well on their way marching west toward the enemy.

"Right," Stiger said aloud to himself. He turned to Lan as he climbed down from the wagon. "Get me Blake."

Stiger did not wait to hear the lieutenant's response. He jogged over to the catapult as it fired another clay jar, which sailed up into the air before falling out of view on the other side of the rampart. There was an explosion, this one muffled. Stiger could feel the vibration of the explosion through his boots. He searched for Cragg and found him with several other gnomes, doubled over with laughter. Seeing Stiger, Cragg straightened up, pointed toward the catapult, and grinned.

"Boom!" Those around him exploded into another bout of laughter, as if Cragg had made a terrifically humorous joke.

"Funny," Stiger agreed without mirth and knelt down in front of Cragg. In the snow, he sketched out their defensive line, the bowl, river, and the enemy on the other side of the river. Cragg followed with interest. Stiger last pointed at the catapult, which loomed over them, and made a dot in the snow. "Catapult . . . go boom here."

"Boom," Cragg pointed at the catapult, and then at the spot in the snow.

"Boom, fire over the river," Stiger said, pointing at his snow map. Then he shook his head. "No boom in bowl. Shoot at the other side of the river where the bridge was. I want to keep the enemy from crossing. Understand?"

Cragg frowned, his black, beady eyes on the crude map in the snow. Stiger repeated himself once again and Cragg stepped forward, climbed up on the catapult where he could see better, and pointed out across the river.

"Boom," Cragg said and then climbed back down, drawing a path in the snow from the spot that represented the catapult over to the other side of river where the bridge had been. He then looked up at Stiger in question.

"Boom," Stiger said with a pleased nod. They seemed to understand one another.

The gnome's face broke into a smile and he turned to his fellows, unleashing a torrent of words that Stiger did not understand. The gnomes swarmed over the catapult, making adjustments as they rearmed the machine. He watched for a moment before returning to the wagon and climbing back up into the bed. Eli helped him up with a hand.

"If I was successful, our little friends here are going to begin hammering the other side of the river across from where the bridge was."

Sure enough, with a creaking groan, followed by a deep thunk, a clay jar arced up into the sky. It sailed over the river and landed amongst the densely packed orcs on the south side, some four hundred yards away, landing exactly in the middle of the causeway that had at one time led up to the bridge. The explosion echoed back to them. The reaction on the far bank was profound. The orcs began to back up from the river and spread out. Those who had been wounded by the explosion writhed on the ground, with no one coming to their aid.

"I want the bolt throwers shooting across the river," Stiger told Lan. "They are to focus on the other side of the bridge where the gnomes are now firing. I want to discourage the orcs from attempting a crossing."

"Yes, sir." Lan hopped down off of the wagon and spoke to two of his waiting troopers.

"Sir?" Blake spoke up from behind the wagon. Stiger turned, looking down on the centurion. He gestured for him to climb up.

"The enemy, though they do not seem to realize it, are trapped in the bowl below us," Stiger said when the centurion had joined him.

"Why don't they cross the river?" Blake was studying the far bank.

"We think they cannot swim," Eli told him.

"They could wade across," Blake said, pointing toward the ruins of the bridge.

"Perhaps their fear of the water is too great to attempt that without sufficient motivation?" Eli postulated.

"Regardless of their reasons," Stiger said, "all of our artillery will be firing on the far bank, hammering the causeway. With luck, it will deter any consideration for a crossing."

"You mean to go over the top," Blake realized with dawning comprehension.

"Yes," Stiger confirmed. "Bring up the 85th to the center of the line. I want an assault formation. After the 85th pushes forward, the entire line will go over the top."

Blake glanced at the furious assault on the defensive works before them and then down into the bowl, studying it carefully. Finally, he looked back at Stiger.

"This is going to be bloody hot work, sir." Blake looked grave.

"I expect so," Stiger agreed. "As long as we keep formation and drive to the river, we should have the advantage. It is downhill, and the orcs fight as individuals, not as a cohesive formation. Our organization will be our strength, and their weakness."

"I will bring up the 85th, sir." Blake climbed down off the wagon.

Stiger took out his dispatch pad and, using his charcoal pencil, began to scratch out orders for Vargus and Quintus. He finished each with "confirmation requested." Sealing the orders, he handed them over to Lan. "See that Vargus and Quintus each get one as soon as possible."

"Are you sure about this?" Eli asked Stiger as Lan stepped off to his dispatch riders, who kicked their horses hard, hooves thundering.

"No," Stiger said, after a slight hesitation. "But I feel it must be done. First Cohort should be on the other side of the river by now, and well on their way. At some point, we were going to have to go over to the attack anyway."

"We can wait until the First engages," Eli suggested, "continue to whittle away at those on our side of the river."

"Yes, we could do as you suggest," Stiger admitted as another explosion ripped across the river, sending clouds of smoke, snow, and dirt into the air. The orcs there had begun to back up even farther. "However, we have these before us. They are trapped, and the enemy on the other side of the river does not seem inclined to send additional aid. Should we delay, they might decide to risk a crossing, denying us the opportunity to destroy those of the enemy before us. If we can take this side of the river, it is unlikely they could take it back from us. Do you disagree?"

Eli considered Stiger's words and then shook his head.

"When the First hits them, we need to be ready to cross at that time, not after," Stiger continued. "Considering the enemy's current disposition, I think it might possibly prove detrimental should we have to fight our way through to the river after First Cohort engages. It would be far better, I think, to be in a position to assist them immediately. Don't you agree?"

Eli nodded again. "What if the dwarves are late?"

"Then we are in trouble," Stiger admitted to Eli as the first files of the 85th began to move around the wagon and up to the line. "I am going forward with the men. I want you to stay here."

"I will," Eli said unhappily. He was not wearing armor like Stiger and clearly understood his friend's intention.

"Find Taha'Leeth, Aver'Mons, and Marcus. If this is successful, I will likely have work for you later."

Stiger jumped down from the wagon. As he did so, the men from the 85th, Stiger's Tigers, cheered their commander. He felt nostalgic at seeing their faces. These were his boys. He had trained them, and they were good. Stiger knew he could rely upon them. He was going to send them into the meat grinder, and the least he could do was join them. He knew he should stay back, but the 85th was going to be the point of his spear. There were times when examples had to be set, and Stiger knew without a doubt this was one.

He went looking for Tilanus, who was manning the line with his men, fighting furiously against the orcs. Behind him, the corporals of the 85th were beginning to arrange the men into ranks for the assault.

Stiger stepped around to a pile of shields that had been stacked behind the line and out of the way. These were from the injured or dead, who no longer had a use for them. There were far more than Stiger would have liked to see. He bent down and grabbed a shield for his own use. An expert on such things, Stiger decided the shield was made well and had been maintained with care. It would prove suitable.

"The 85th will be going over the top," Stiger informed Tilanus, who was eyeing Stiger's company as it moved into an assault formation. Tilanus's eyes flicked to the shield in Stiger's hand. This close to the line, the noise generated by the fighting was deafening, and Stiger was forced to shout to be heard. "When I give the order to advance, pull your men aside. Once we are over, form them up and follow us at a distance of ten yards. Do not let any orcs get between our two formations. We are going to drive right down to the river to where the bridge used to be."

"Yes, sir," Tilanus said, looking a little uncomfortable with the idea of what Stiger was proposing.

"Make sure you follow rapidly. Do not allow too much of a gap to form."

"I will be right behind the 85th, sir."

"Good man," Stiger said, clapping the older centurion on the shoulder good-naturedly.

A rider galloped up to Stiger, bent down, and handed over a dispatch. Stiger took it and opened it. Vargus had confirmed his understanding and would be looking for the 85th to go over to the assault. Another rider galloped up a few seconds later.

"Sir," the trooper reported, saluting, "Centurion Quintus said to inform you he will go over the top after the 85th."

"Very good."

It was time. Hefting his shield, Stiger stepped to the front of the 85th. He turned and surveyed his men. The tiger pelt standard was held high and all eyes were upon him. Legionary Beck carried the eagle forward. Blake had placed Beck in the center of the formation. Stiger knew that the men would fight like devils to keep the eagle safe.

Stiger caught Corporal Durggen's eye and nodded. All eyes were upon him. He thought about giving a rousing speech, but this close to the line, the noise was deafening and only those nearest would hear him. Instead he pulled forth his sword. The tingle ran rapidly up and down his arm and then was gone. There was no surge of vigor. He held the sword high. Two hundred men drew their swords and gave a mighty roar.

"Advance!" Stiger roared, turning and pointing with his sword toward the rampart.

"HAAAH!" the men shouted and started a slow and steady march toward the defenders on the rampart. Stiger allowed the men of the first rank to move by him.

"HAAAH . . . HAAAH . . . .HAAAH!"

Tilanus, seeing the 85th move forward, pulled his men back to both sides, temporarily opening a gap in the line along the rampart. The orcs, clearly thinking the legionaries were abandoning the defensive works, surged forward and over the rampart, only to catch sight of the wall of armored men advancing upon them, shields forward and swords held at the ready. The orcs hesitated, unsure what to do, before pressure from behind pushed them forward. A moment later, Stiger's forward line met the orcs with a loud crash as shields slammed violently into the orcs, who fought back with hammer and sword.

Stiger, between the first and second rank, saw an opening form in the shield wall and stepped forward to stab at an orc, which had been pushed off-balance by another from behind the creature. Stiger's sword caught the orc in the neck, ripping it open. The orc fell back and collapsed. The line continued to advance. Stiger stepped over the twitching body, moving up to the rampart. The man to his direct front was cut down by an orc sword that had reached over his shield and stabbed downward. A legionary to the fallen man's side stabbed the creature in the leg. Stiger immediately stepped into the man's place and slammed his shield into the orc before jabbing out with his sword, which found the soft tissue of an unprotected forearm. The orc roared in pain and swung its sword wildly with its uninjured arm, even as it staggered to a knee, leg buckling.

Stiger easily blocked the clumsy strike, which clanged off of his shield boss. In the cold, he felt the blow communicate painfully with his arm but did not let that stop him. His next jab took the creature in the exposed armpit. He felt the sword grate off bone. Badly wounded, the orc fell back but had nowhere to go, as it had backed up to the rampart. The next thrust by the man to Stiger's right ended it.

"Over the top!" Stiger shouted at his men. An orc above swung downward at him with a sword. Stiger brought his shield up to block the blow. Splinters flew in a spray from the shield as the sword bounced off of the top. Before the creature could recover, Stiger jabbed upward, striking at an unprotected leg. He felt the sword sink home and slammed forward with his shield, knocking it back and over the other side of the rampart. It fell backward, taking several others with it to the trench below.

"Over the top!" Stiger scrambled up over the rampart, legionaries on both sides of him doing the same. "Get at them! Come on now!"

Atop the rampart, an orc in the trench below swung a hammer at Stiger, which he blocked. Before the orc could recover, a legionary jumped down in the trench next to it, hitting it with his shield, knocking the creature aside. Stiger jumped down and hammered his sword down into the orc's belly. Another sword struck the orc, killing it.

Almost immediately, Stiger was slammed backward as an orc hit him in the chest with a sword, which bounced painfully off his armor with a piercing screech. Managing to hang onto his sword and shield, Stiger attacked, his sword scraping across the orc's chest armor. Snarling, it struck him again, this time in the shoulder. Hurting from the stinging blow, Stiger's rage exploded, and with it his sword began to glow hotly. Stiger's aches and pains vanished in a flash as fresh power and vigor flowed into him. His tiredness fled. Everything around him seemed to slow as he struck out toward the enemy. His thrust slid easily through the orc's chest armor and immediately began to hiss and sizzle as it cut into skin, sinew, and bone beyond. The orc twitched before falling backward, stone dead.

KILL THEM ALLL!

With a surge of rage, the sword encouraged him onward. Stiger lashed out at another orc, and the sword once again stabbed through armor. It was like cutting through a fresh loaf of bread. Stiger found his anger and rage mounting as he helped to clear the trench around him, cutting down one orc after another.

Stiger blinked. Where a moment before orcs had filled the trench, it was now chock full of legionaries. There were no more of the enemy within easy reach. The anger and rage called on him to find more and he turned toward the other side of the trench, even as additional legionaries jumped in behind him. He started to climb out of the trench, intent at finding additional orcs to slay. He abruptly stopped and glanced down at his glowing sword.

"Stop it!" he growled at the sword and tried to force the rage back. It was a difficult thing to do, but after a moment, it passed and he was able to think rationally again. The glowing blade dimmed somewhat. A few of his men were eying Stiger and the sword warily.

I want more, the sword hissed.

Stiger ignored it and glanced around the trench. Several legionaries were looking up at the other side of the trench with hesitation. They knew what awaited them.

"Out! Get out of the trench! At them, boys!" Stiger yelled at his men. "Get moving. Don't stop. We must keep advancing."

Setting the example, Stiger began climbing out of the shallow trench. As he did so, he glanced to his left and right and was relieved to see his men moving forward with him. They crested the trench and were back in contact with the mass of orcs in the bowl. To Stiger, they appeared to be surprised that the legionaries had come out from behind their defenses. It was likely the reason why no more orcs had piled into the trench. He could almost read the growing doubt in their eyes as the tide of the battle began to flow against them.

Stiger found himself abruptly confronted with an orc priest, garbed only in a long black robe, face heavily tattooed, and white-dyed hair limed back with no headdress. The priest snarled its hate at him and punched a dagger forward. Stiger easily deflected the strike with his shield. He stepped forward and jabbed his sword into the robes, where he estimated the orc's belly to be. The priest issued a groan as Stiger's sword slid deep.

The sword flared, and like before, there was an awful sizzling sound. Time seemed to stop. It was as if he had taken a deep breath and was holding it. The world around him was waiting for him to release it. The hilt felt uncomfortably warm in his hand. The priest's eyes flashed with an unearthly light and a mist poured out of its mouth, as if a last breath were escaping a dying body. Stiger exhaled, and the world around him began moving once again. The sound of the battle crashed home with a suddenness that was jarring.

In that instant, the priest's body fell backward off of Stiger's sword and into the orcs behind him. Horrified, they either looked on Stiger or at the fallen priest. Several squealed like pigs, turned, and pushed by their fellows. They rushed toward the river, disappearing in the crush of bodies.

A large warrior looking down on the priest roared in rage, turning his eyes on Stiger. The orc wore polished armor that was of better quality than most. A large gold torc was fitted around its neck. Bearing its oversized canines at Stiger, it advanced, hammer coming up into the ready position. Stiger knew without a doubt this had been the orc he had seen across the river. This was the leader of the enemy army.

"Grats'sag," the orc spat at Stiger, who leveled his shield in preparation.

"You want to dance with me?" Stiger yelled back at the creature, crouching down into an individual combat stance. He felt incredibly calm and in control. Gone were the feelings of rage and anger. The sword no longer glowed. "Come on, big boy."

Roaring, the orc charged Stiger, swinging the hammer for all it was worth. Stiger raised his shield to deflect the blow. As the hammer struck his shield boss, the force drove the hammer upward. The top of Stiger's shield splintered, sending a shower of wood slivers into the air. Stiger staggered backward.

"Grats'sag thags," the orc spat again and advanced, its eyes upon the human prey before it.

Still feeling that same sense of calm and control, Stiger leapt forward. The leader swung the hammer, which crashed into Stiger's shield, completely shattering the remains. Stiger released the shield, even as he stabbed upward with his sword. It punctured the orc's right forearm, digging down to the bone. He dragged the sword around, completely opening up the arm. The orc roared with pain, bearing its teeth at him. Stiger stepped back and out of reach, offering the creature a huge smile.

"There's more where that came from," Stiger growled.

The orc looked down at its ruined arm, which it brought up to its mouth, where a long pink tongue snaked out to lick at the green blood, which was escaping in a rush. Stiger took the opportunity to glance around and realized the other orcs were giving the two of them space. Somehow he had become separated from his men. There was a ring of orcs around him and their leader, keeping everyone else back, including Stiger's men. Behind him, Stiger could hear the legionaries fighting their way to him.

"Come on, big boy!" Stiger shouted to the orc. "Want some more?"

Stiger threw himself forward as the orc drew its hammer back and swung. He ducked. The hammer sailed over his helmet with less than an inch to spare. Stiger struck forward, jabbing his sword into the warrior's groin. The orc grunted and fell backward, dropping the war hammer. Stiger followed it, striking his opponent again, this time in the left thigh, eliciting another grunt. A powerful fist lashed out, hammering him in the chest and knocking him back on his butt. He struggled to catch his breath for a moment and then stood and glanced nervously about him at the ring of orcs. They were staring down with stricken expressions at their leader.

Bleeding profusely, the orc leader had fallen and was struggling to get to its feet. The wounded leg failed, and it instead rolled onto all fours, with one hand reaching for the dropped hammer. It was time to end this. Stiger approached the orc as it crawled away from him toward the hammer. He drove his sword down into the back of the leader's exposed neck, giving the blade a vicious twist, feeling bone crunch through the hilt. The creature collapsed into the muddied and bloodied snow, unmoving.

There was a collective moan from those orcs who had been watching. Stiger looked around nervously, expecting to be rushed, but the fight seemed to have gone out of them. They stood in shock. Several turned and ran toward the river. The fighting behind Stiger abruptly intensified, and then there were legionaries about him, moving by and charging into those stunned orcs who had remained. Stiger's shoulders sagged in weary relief.

"That is a right plum big bastard," Blake commented casually, coming up next to Stiger. The two of them were looking down on the orc Stiger had just killed in personal combat. "For a moment there, I thought we'd lost you, sir."

Stiger said nothing.

"Might I humbly offer the legate some advice?"

Stiger looked over at the centurion and nodded, having a feeling of what was coming.

"You set a good example for the boys, sir, but nearly gave me a heart attack. Next time would the legate kindly let the men go first?"

Glancing down at the dead orc, Stiger knelt down and removed the blood-spattered gold torc from around its neck. He hesitated a moment, examining his trophy. Stiger idly wondered if the torc was contaminated by evil. He certainly felt nothing wrong with it. He would have the paladin look it over later he decided and tucked the trophy into his armor. He then glanced around at the fighting. His legionaries were spread out. The vast majority of orcs were still fighting ferociously, though many were now making for the river crossing where the bridge had been.

"We need to reform the men," Stiger told Blake. "This isn't over. We need lines."

"Durggen, Beni, get those men organized into a line," Blake thundered as he grabbed a legionary and physically propelled him in the direction he wanted. "Come on, son, fall in."

"Fall in!" Stiger shouted. "Fall in! Reform!"

In short order, between the corporals, Blake, and Stiger, they were able to reform the men into several ranks. Space had formed around the 85th. Those orcs nearest had fallen back several paces. Stiger looked around the bowl and saw both Vargus's and Quintus's cohorts were out over the rampart, fighting their way down the slope toward the river.

Tilanus's men were just now moving out of the trench and down the hill toward the 85th.

"We push forward all the way to the river," Stiger shouted at the men. "We carve a path of death to the river!"

The men roared in reply.

"Lock shields!" Stiger called. With a resounding thunk, the shields snapped together. "Advance."

The men moved forward toward the orcs with a determined step. A number of orcs who had been warily watching as the legionaries reformed threw themselves at the line. Swords jabbed out, taking them down. The advance continued, and then the entire line was back in contact. Stiger, with Blake at his side, followed behind the lines. Tilanus's men had formed up and were now also advancing. They were only thirty yards back and moving rapidly to close the gap. There were no live orcs between the two legionary formations.

"Keep that line steady," Blake shouted at the men. "Remember your training. Use your shield properly now."

"Legionary Teg," Stiger called. "Good sword work. Remember, boys, real killers like Teg jab and stab."

The line slogged forward. The orcs came at them as individuals and in small groups. Stiger suspected that orcs placed a great deal of emphasis on personal glory and prowess on the battlefield. Today it was costing them dearly, though it was not entirely one-sided. His legionaries were falling with alarming regularity. There were just too many orcs who were ready to throw themselves mindlessly at the human legionaries.

The fighting was hot and heavy as the 85th carved a path through the orcs. Several times, Stiger was tempted to help those in the front rank, but he restrained himself. He had already set the example. It was no longer his job to fight in the ranks. Blake had reminded him of that. His place was to lead.

Blake pulled out a whistle and blew on it hard, two strong blasts, indicating that the first rank fall back and the second rank step forward. It was smartly done, and the orcs to their front found themselves facing fresh men.

"Keep going, boys," Blake encouraged. "No one stops Stiger's Tigers, not today nor any day!"

Stiger glanced back to see Tilanus and his militia covering as the company continued to advance ahead of them. He estimated that the centurion still had around four hundred men, which was good. The militia would be needed once they reached the river.

It seemed to take forever, and then suddenly the river was before them. Orcs were fleeing to either side. Blake called for the company to halt on the riverbank. Breathing heavily, the men caught their breath and rested their heavy shields on the ground.

The ruined bridge was to their right by around thirty yards. It was time to take the causeway and secure their side of the crossing.

"Reform to march on the remains of the bridge," Stiger ordered Blake, pointing with his sword at the causeway. It took a few minutes. Blake repositioned the company, aligning it along the riverbank. Stiger restrained himself from intervening. He knew it would not speed things up. Besides, it was Blake's responsibility now, and Stiger would not undermine the man.

"Advance."

At least a hundred of the enemy were clustered around the causeway to the ruined bridge. For a moment, it looked like they would flee across the shallows where the bridge had been, and as Stiger watched, several orcs did just that, splashing into the water. A few more joined those working their way across the river, but that was where it ended. The remainder looked torn with indecision, jabbering and gesticulating amongst themselves, almost seeming more afraid of crossing the water than the approaching legionary formation. Incredibly, the vast majority of them stood their ground and roared their hatred rather than flee to safety just a few yards away.

The line continued a steady advance. The two sides came together with a crash. The fight was brutal and over in a handful of minutes. Stiger called for a halt once his formation was sitting along the causeway and ramp that had once led to the bridge. The bridge itself was a twisted ruin of torn boards, bodies, and rushing water, which Stiger judged to be thoroughly crossable. Those few orcs who had fled across had just proved it.

It was time to take stock. First he studied the situation in the bowl. Both cohorts were making good progress toward the river, though there were still a lot of orcs in front of them. The orcs were looking more and more desperate, especially with Stiger sitting on their only way across the river. Many were trying to work their way around the two cohorts, to climb the slopes and escape through the now unguarded rampart. For every one that managed to escape, five looked to be cut down. It was very efficient and violent. The legions were nothing if not proficient at their craft.

Stiger studied the opposite riverbank. There were a lot of orcs there, perhaps fifty yards away from the river's edge, staring silently at the slaughter. He idly wondered where First Cohort and the dwarves were. He saw no evidence of either. Once the valley was cleaned up, the real fight awaited him across the river. That would be the challenge for the day.

"Tilanus," Stiger called the centurion over.

"That was some fine fighting, sir," Tilanus exclaimed. "I never thought to see the like."

"There is more ahead," Stiger said. He glanced back around the bowl. He felt pressure to wrap up the fighting here as quickly as possible so that he could prepare his men to cross the river. It was most assuredly going to be a contested crossing.

"Yes, sir," Tilanus agreed, eyeing the other side of the river and the remainder of the orc host. The older centurion looked winded but unfazed by the action he had just been through.

"The 85th will hold the bridge. Take your men and go to the aid of Second Cohort," Stiger ordered, pointing. "They seem to be having a more difficult time of it than the Third. Cut your way through to them and then together go to help Quintus. Understood?"

"Perfectly."

The centurion saluted and Stiger watched him go. He considered for a moment going with him, but the most important spot on the field was where he was now standing. Should the enemy across the river decide to advance, Stiger would have to hold them until the bowl had been cleared and the other two cohorts could assist.

Stiger wiped his sword clean on his tunic and sheathed it. Once again, he found himself an unhappy spectator.

SEVENTEEN

"Half of my men are down," Vargus informed Stiger, who mentally winced at the news. The centurion was formal in his report, but Stiger could see the anguish in the man's eyes. Stiger's other senior officers looked on.

"And you?" Stiger asked of Quintus. The centurion was nursing a shallow cut to his hand.

"I've lost around a quarter of my men," he said with a pained look. "Then again, we've hurt the orcs much more than I thought possible."

Stiger glanced around the body-strewn bowl. Even now, before the bodies had had a chance to cool, the carrion birds had begun to circle. It was a sickening sight, but one he had become all too familiar with.

It was a good victory, Stiger decided, but the battle was only partially won. Across the river, Sabinus had hit the orc army and was currently locked in an intense fight. The muffled sound of the battle, though they could not see it from their current position, reached them across the water. Stiger had sent someone up to the ridge to get a better view. The man had reported that the First was heavily engaged just beyond a small hill that blocked their view, perhaps a quarter mile away.

To the intense frustration of the gnomes, the orcs had moved out of range of their catapult. Unable to get the machine over the earthen rampart and trench, they were hauling it back the way they had come. Stiger had managed, however, to move four of his bolt throwers through brute force down to the banks of the river, where their crews were awaiting his orders. There had been no time to move the others.

"Your cohort will lead the assault across the river," Stiger informed Quintus.

It was clear to Stiger Quintus had been expecting as much and nodded in grim understanding. His eyes wandered over to the ruins of the bridge and the orcs waiting beyond. Stiger could well imagine the man's thoughts at what was about to be required of him. It stood to reason that some incredibly difficult fighting lay ahead.

"The 85th will follow the Third, and the Second will come after. Tilanus, you will hold this side of the crossing in the event we are compelled to fall back."

"Yes, sir," Tilanus said with a grim nod.

Stiger looked at Quintus, Blake, and Vargus. "Gentlemen, it has been easy going until now. The real fighting is ahead, across that river. We must push through the orcs and link up with Sabinus. With any luck, the dwarves should be moving into position to seal the trap. The enemy will be caught between both of our forces. If we succeed, the orcs should trouble the valley no more, and we will be free to turn our energies to the Cyphan." Stiger paused a moment, allowing what he had said to sink in. "I know you will do your duty."

The officers broke up, trotting to their men. Stiger turned to look once again at the orcs on the other side of the river. They did not seem be concerned about Stiger's legionaries. Their attention was focused wholly on the fighting that was just out of his view.

Stiger walked over to the 85th, which was off to the side of the ruined bridge. Blake was organizing the men, getting them up on their feet and calling them to fall in. Stiger found Eli and Taha'Leeth speaking quietly in elven. He noticed that their bows were slung over their backs, quivers empty.

"Where are Marcus and Aver'Mons?"

"They are checking the riverbanks to the east and west," Eli informed him. "Despite the cavalry watching the crossings, I thought it in our best interests to make sure nothing had been missed."

"Good thinking," Stiger said and turned to watch as Third Cohort marched by, making toward the shallows around the ruined bridge.

"I dislike river assaults," Eli said, his eyes on the Third, which had halted before the water and was dressing ranks in preparation for a crossing.

"We've done more than our share," Stiger said, looking over at his friend. "At least we have some artillery to soften the enemy up."

Quintus snapped an order to the artillery crews on both sides of the ruined bridge, and there was an immediate CRACK as all four bolt throwers fired, nearly simultaneously. The deadly missiles tore into the nearest orcs, who were at extreme range just over a hundred yards away. A number went down or crashed into their fellows, propelled forward by the kinetic energy of the missiles. The orcs, whose attention had been on the fighting on their side of the river, turned in shock at the unexpected attack.

"Advance," Quintus hollered, and the Third started forward, splashing into the water. They worked their way around obstacles, helping each other as they moved through the twisted and torn remnants of the wooden bridge. It was hard going. The progress was slow, but they were managing.

"Both of you remain here," Stiger ordered, at which Eli looked over at him in surprise. "I want you both to check on the refugees in Old City."

It was a flimsy excuse, and Eli saw right through it. He studied Stiger for a moment and then firmly shook his head in the negative. "I am crossing with you."

"As am I," Taha'Leeth informed him. She placed a gentle hand on his forearm, which was grimy and dirty. It was a tender gesture and one Stiger had not expected. "Our place is with you, as is our path."

CRACK! A bolt thrower fired.

Stiger let out a breath of frustration. He was trying to spare his friend and Taha'Leeth what was coming. He seriously doubted that he could lose Eli again and he had no wish to see Taha'Leeth come to harm. Neither of the elves wore armor, and he feared for their safety in the potential crush of melee that waited just yards away, but he could see the determined look in Eli's eyes. There was no mistaking it. Eli'Far, elven ranger and lieutenant in the imperial legions, would be at his side for this fight. Taha'Leeth looked just as firm.

CRACK!

"Very well then," Stiger gave in, as the 85th began marching up to the water's edge. Stiger turned and moved forward with them, his eyes on the Third, which had just reached the other side and was forming a line of battle on the far bank. So far the orcs were watching the humans, incredibly making no move to interfere. Stiger had expected the enemy to vigorously contest the crossing. Why they did not make a move to do so puzzled him.

Then, a priest pushed his way out of the crowd of uncertain orcs and began shouting, working them up. One orc stepped forward several paces, holding aloft a large sword and roaring. A second orc joined him, and suddenly the mass of them charged the legionary line.

CRACK!

Stiger had no more time for watching, as Blake gave the order to advance. He had moved himself to just behind the front rank and took a step into the frigid water. The cold immediately cut to the bone. It was a shock to be sure, but Stiger kept on going, easing himself around a ruined support beam. The depth of the water rapidly went from his thighs to his chest. It was so cold his fingers ached with an intense agony, and he shivered. The pressure of the water rushing past made it a challenge to keep his footing. Several times he was forced to grab for a handhold on the ruins of the bridge, lest he be swept away. Stiger glanced behind him and saw Eli and Taha'Leeth just feet away, following.

There was a loud crash just ahead as the orcs slammed into the legionary shield line. The sound of fighting, complete with screams of rage, pain, and animal-like roars, drifted over the water toward them. Stiger looked up to get a view of what was happening. He was gratified to see Quintus's men advancing, shields locked together, moving one half-step at a time, creating additional room on the bank for the men who were still crossing. To the right of Quintus's positon, the ground rose up into a small hill. It was bare of the enemy.

"When we come out of the water," Stiger said to Blake, pointing to where he wanted the 85th, "I want you to take Quintus's extreme right. Make a double line from that point there."

"Yes, sir," Blake said as they continued to struggle through the rushing water.

"Once formed up," Stiger continued, "we will swing forward up toward the hill, extending our line as we do so. Think of the meeting point of the Third and the 85th as a well-oiled hinge on a door. When you are in position, the 85th will be the door slamming closed down upon the enemy flank. Got me?"

Blake nodded his understanding. Moments later, the 85th began emerging from the water.

"Corporal Beni, form up there next to the Third, smartly now." Blake gestured, showing Beni where he wanted his file.

Soaked through, Stiger emerged onto dry ground and moved over to Quintus, who was right behind his double line of men. Stiger got his first real look at the orcs taking on the Third. There were several hundred of them in a great big unorganized mass. For a fleeting moment, Stiger wondered what the orc army would be like if they fought as a trained and cohesive unit. How much more effective and dangerous would they be? He forced the thought aside, as he did not really want to find out.

Beyond the orcs to his front, there was a growing gap between this bunch and the rest of the enemy army, which seemed to be moving away, as if they had somewhere else to be. Stiger was surprised that they were ignoring the fight that was playing out here at the river's edge. Had the dwarves finally arrived? The bulk of the enemy army was marching away from where First Cohort was reported to be, so it clearly wasn't Sabinus that had their attention. It had to be the dwarves.

Despite the pressure against the line, the Third was steadily pushing forward a half-step at a time and forcing the orcs back, inflicting heavy casualties as they did so.

"The 85th is forming up on your right," Stiger said to Quintus. "As soon as we are in position, they will swing forward, hinging on you, and push into this bunch's flank."

"Do you want me to bring my boys to a stop before they swing forward?" Quintus asked him.

Stiger considered the idea for a moment and then discarded it. "If you stop, the enemy may spread out, making it more difficult for the 85th to swing into them."

Quintus frowned as he thought it through and then gave a curt nod. Stiger stepped back toward the right. Almost all of the 85th was out of the frigid water. Blake was slotting each file into line as they came up. It took time, but it was well done. The enemy was focused on the Third and had as of yet not reacted to the 85th's presence as it extended the legionary line. Stiger looked behind him. The Second was just starting across. After a moment's consideration, he made for Taha'Leeth, who was just behind the 85th's growing line.

"When Vargus comes across, tell him to follow the 85th up. I want them right behind my company."

Taha'Leeth nodded her understanding.

Stiger then turned to Eli and pointed at a tall hill to their right. "Get on top of that hill and see if you can locate the First."

Eli turned and set off.

"All set, sir," Blake announced, and Stiger turned back to see that the 85th was in line and ready.

"Give the order." Stiger drew his sword and felt the electric tingle. He had not thought to grab a free shield prior to crossing. He was sure one would be made available soon enough should he need it.

Blake gave the order to draw swords and then to advance. The company formed up into a double line and began to swing forward slowly toward the orcs, bending around as they did so. At first, the enemy was wholly focused on the Third, but then several noticed the advancing legionaries and began to shout a warning. Heads turned to face the swinging door as it formed a near-perfect angle on Third Cohort. Stiger studied the enemy before him and realized he had to hit them hard, before they became organized against his swinging door.

"Give the order to charge," Stiger said to Blake.

"Charge!" Blake roared at his men, who, after a moment's hesitation, exploded into a run, shields held forward, swords at the ready. The 85th slammed into the orcs with a loud crash, screaming as they came. For several seconds, it was mass confusion as the impetus of the charge carried the legionaries forward in amongst the orcs, who reeled backward. Many of the enemy fell to the short swords, which jabbed out from behind the protection of the shields. Then the fighting became more difficult as the enemy's will stiffened, and the orcs turned and fought with a ferocity that was surprising.

Corporals began calling their files to form up into shield lines. Stiger and Blake shouted orders and encouragement as the line came back together. Shields thunked into place. Stiger gave the order to push. The legionaries shoved forward as one, slamming their shields into the enemy and then unlocking them to jab outward for a quick stab before locking them back into place. Under incredible pressure, the orcs held. They looked as if they would hold firm. Then, slowly at first, they began to give ground. In moments, both the Third and the 85th were driving the enemy steadily back, the pace increasing with each step.

Stiger looked up and around for the rest of the orc army. He spotted them and felt a great sense of relief. Unexpectedly, they were still moving away from him, completely ignoring Stiger and his men.

"Where do you want me?" Vargus said, having come up. Stiger turned and saw Second Cohort was marching up behind the 85th.

"Double time it to my right," Stiger pointed with his sword. "Extend your line and use mine as a hinge to slam into the back side of this bunch, like the 85th just did, hinging on the Third. If done quickly enough, we will have them penned in on three sides and it should be a bloody massacre."

Vargus understood in an instant what Stiger wanted. He turned back to his cohort, calling orders to his men. Armor jingling, the Second began to trot by in good order, moving into position where Stiger wanted them.

Stiger turned back to the fight. It seemed to him, though he could not tell exactly what made him feel this way, that the orcs were beginning to get edgy. He could see no officers, sergeants, or corporals amongst them, only the occasional priest or what he took to be a tribal chief, who seemed better outfitted. The orcs fought as individuals. They were deadly and motivated, to be sure, and they outnumbered Stiger's men, but the orcs were up against a highly trained and organized force. Stiger had the initiative here.

There was a deafening shout to his right. The Second swung around, closing the door perfectly, as if they had practiced the maneuver regularly. The orcs were now boxed in on three sides and the killing began in earnest. Under such pressure, the orcs lasted less than a minute, long enough for the priest he had seen earlier to be cut brutally down by several jabbing short swords. The orcs gave a great groan at this and ran for it, with the legionaries pursuing. The slaughter was terrible to see, with the legionaries taking their revenge upon the creatures for daring to come into the valley. No mercy was shown. The legionaries expected none in return.

Stiger's shoulders sagged in relief. The crossing had been easier than he had expected it to be. Looking, he could see the bulk of the enemy army still moving south and away. They were actually angling slightly southwest. He spotted something to his right and saw Eli jogging toward him.

"First Cohort is a quarter mile that way." Eli pointed back toward the hill. "It looks as if they have overcome a small enemy blocking force. The cavalry is with them. To the south I can see the entire dwarven army. They have positioned themselves to prevent the orcs from retreating. Braddock is already heavily engaged. If I had to guess, I would say the orcs are trying to break out."

"We have them," Stiger said with sudden excitement.

"It would seem so," Eli replied.

"Can you make it to First Cohort and tell them to hold off from advancing? I want us all together when we hit the enemy's backside."

"I can," Eli said and started off at a run, with Taha'Leeth following him.

"We have them," Stiger said to himself, hammering fist to palm. He turned away, calling for Vargus, Quintus, and Blake. It was time to get the men reformed.

EIGHTEEN

Braddock looked over the battlefield and felt a great sense of satisfaction. It was littered with thousands of corpses. Between him and the humans, it had been a great slaughter, a battle worthy of some serious drinking and song. There were both dwarves and humans moving among the bodies, looking for those still alive and injured. Whenever any were found, they were helped to the aid stations. Orcs found alive were dispatched.

The work of dealing with the bodies had also begun. Thankfully it was winter and not the middle of summer. They would be spared the unbearable stench of rotting flesh. Legionary and dwarven dead were being moved aside for proper care of the remains. The dwarves would be sent back to Garand Thoss, where kin from their clans would inter them in the tombs beneath the city. Of the legionaries, Braddock understood that their dead would be burned. The orcs would likely be buried in mass graves. No funeral rites would be given to them, as they worshiped and served the dark gods.

Braddock walked toward the river, surveying this side of the battlefield. His bodyguard, not wishing to interrupt the thane's contemplations, followed at a respectful distance. Garrack was also a step behind him. This portion of the field was where the legionaries had fought. Braddock climbed a small hill and was able to get a vantage that overlooked the river and the remains of the bridge. The number of orc bodies on the other side of the river, beneath the legionary fortifications, was astonishing. He had never seen so many corpses in such a confined area.

"Though human," Garrack said, "they are tenacious fighters."

"Yes," Braddock agreed. "They are worthy allies. Especially the legate. He I can respect."

"Stiger is the one the Oracle prophesized," Garrack said. "Did you seriously doubt he would be worthy of respect?"

Braddock looked over to Garrack, a scowl on his face, which softened after a moment. "No, I had no doubts, but after this," Braddock held his arms out, "my esteem for the legate has increased."

Atop the hill, Braddock turned in a circle, surveying everything. He could see his army less than a quarter of a mile away. They had reformed and gone into a temporary encampment. The legionaries had moved back to their original position along the fortified heights across the river, where their supply wagons were located. He could see their sentries posted at the river crossing and along the low ridge-line. Several riders appeared and made their way down from the defensive works, splashed into the water next to the ruined bridge, and carefully crossed.

Braddock had no difficulty recognizing the legate as he, his elf, and a guard detail worked their way up the hill. The thane assumed that one of the human sentries had spotted him and sent word to Stiger. Though they had exchanged numerous messages, the two had not met since leaving Old City.

"Well met, Thane Braddock," Stiger greeted as he rode up and dismounted.

"A fine victory, this," Braddock said and offered his hand, which was accepted. "Together we work to fulfill the terms of the Compact."

"This is a good victory," Stiger agreed, "though I fear one not without cost."

Braddock knew the humans had taken the brunt of the fighting and suffered heavily. The legate had suggested the strategy, which Braddock had endorsed. Both had known that by Braddock staying his hand and waiting for the orcs to pass him by, the legionaries would pay a heavy price. Yet because of it, the orcs had suffered terribly. Perhaps as many as a thousand of the vile creatures had managed to escape from the trap. Even now, the human cavalry was running them down and chasing them back to their own territory to the south.

"All victories come with a cost," Braddock said, attempting to ease the legate's burden. Though Stiger looked pleased at what they had accomplished, the thane thought he detected a sadness in the human's eyes.

"That they do," Stiger said, barely above a whisper.

"A punitive expedition need to be mounted," Garrack said. "Orcs need to be dug out of caves and mines and pushed farther back into mountains."

"I should think that two war bands and a contingent of gnomes will be sufficient," Braddock said, looking over at Garrack for confirmation of his assessment.

"I take it that my legionaries will be included in such a venture?"

Braddock narrowed his eyes at that. "If you think it necessary."

"I do." Stiger's tone suggested that he would brook no disagreement on this point. "We will do this together or not at all."

Braddock took a deep, calming breath. He had to remember that this was an alliance of equal powers. The legate, far from trying to be offensive, was simply reminding him of that reality. Braddock had never been part of an alliance before, and it was proving to be a learning experience. He reminded himself once again that he had to think of the alliance as a whole.

"We will do this together," Braddock affirmed. "Human, dwarf, and gnome."

"That sounds more like it," Stiger said. "We each pull our own weight."

"Is strange," Garrack said, changing the subject.

"What is?" Braddock asked.

"Orcs fighting aboveground during day."

"How do they normally fight then?" Stiger asked, eyes narrowing.

"Orcs are creatures of the earth," Braddock answered. "We class them as one of the lesser races because they almost exclusively shun the sun and prefer the dark depths. Though they have their own lands, we occasionally find them on the fringes of our territories. Most encounters occur in mines and caves. When they come to the surface, they do not normally fight or raid during the daylight hours, as their vision in the sun is quite poor. Orcs prefer the shadows and night."

"Battle should have happened under our feet," Garrack added.

"What do you mean?" Stiger asked, eying Garrack intently. "How can the battle have taken place in the earth?"

"I would think that obvious," Braddock said. "My people long occupied this land, and even though much of it cannot be seen, their legacy is all around us. This entire valley and the surrounding mountains are honeycombed with mines and caves."

Braddock saw Stiger pale.

"Then there could be orcs beneath our feet?" Stiger asked, glancing down at the ground, as if he might be able to see them through the earth. "Could this have been a diversion to get at the World Gate?"

"This was no diversion," Braddock said. "The orcs sent too many."

"We have warriors patrolling caverns and mines," Garrack said. "They warn us if such a thing happens."

"Good," Stiger replied, seeming somewhat relieved.

"Still, it is strange that the orcs chose to fight out of their element, during the day," Braddock said.

"What of the minion of Castor?" Stiger asked. "Has it been spotted?"

"No," Braddock answered.

"Then it is still out there."

"We will have to find it," Braddock agreed. "It will likely have to be rooted out of a cave when we send forth the punitive expedition. It is a good thing you have the paladin and Rarokan."

Braddock saw Stiger glance down at his sheathed sword. If he was not mistaken, the thane recognized unease. There was always a cost to wielding such a powerful artifact. Braddock wondered if Stiger had realized that yet.

"Is that gnome work?" Braddock asked, intentionally changing the subject, and gesturing toward the ruined bridge.

"Yes," Stiger replied. "They fired clay jars from a catapult. It was impressive magic."

"Hardly," Braddock said with a wave. "They used blasting powder, very dangerous stuff. We use it to break tough rock in our mines. It is made from the droppings of bats and other things."

"I would be interested in this blasting powder," Stiger said, looking over at him. "Its effect on the battlefield could be profound."

"It is very unstable," Braddock warned. "Gnomes have no common sense. It is a wonder they did not kill themselves or others while launching it from a catapult. I would recommend against it."

"Still," Stiger persisted, "I believe that it should be studied further."

"Very well." Braddock heaved a heavy sigh. "I will have the gnomes explain how to make it and properly care for it. Will that do?"

"Do any of them speak common better than Cragg?"

"Cragg?" Braddock asked with mild surprise. He reminded himself to speak with the mean little bastard. Cragg had no business revealing dwarven secrets to the humans. If Braddock had his way, the humans would never learn the secret behind blasting powder, let alone how to make it. Alliance or not, the secret of blasting powder would remain with his people.

"Yes," Stiger said. "Though he barely speaks common."

"I would be surprised if any of the little shits speak common better," Braddock stated. "Cragg is an anomaly amongst gnomes."

Braddock noticed Stiger stiffen and his eyes narrow. The legate was looking past him, in the direction of the Braddock's army. The thane turned and saw a human rider galloping at full speed toward them, horse kicking up clods of snow mixed with dirt in its wake. A horn calling the dwarven army to alert sounded from Braddock's army encampment. The thane glanced at Garrack, wondering what could have happened. Braddock noticed that Stiger shared a look with Eli.

"Sir, I am glad I found you!" the rider said to Stiger, pulling his horse up sharply and offering a salute. The horse was all but blown. Foam dripped from its mouth as it breathed heavily. "The orcs . . . they have another army, and it's coming here, sir."

"How large?" Stiger demanded, taking a half step forward. "How far out are they?"

"Four hours at least, and they number twice as many as what we just faced. Lieutenant Cannol is shadowing them now, sir."

"Damn," Stiger said, slapping a palm against his thigh.

"What we fought must have been the vanguard," Eli commented ironically. "They must not have expected us to wipe it out so quickly."

"You mean they hoped to draw us into battle and fix us in place?" Braddock asked, having some difficulty believing that the orcs had stayed their hand and held back a second, larger army. It was almost unbelievable.

"Perhaps they just planned on whittling us down," Eli suggested, "and then hitting us with overwhelming force."

"I think it is clear we cannot remain here," Stiger said. "With the sun setting soon, I am not terribly keen on a fight in the dark."

"What if we pulled back and held our fortified line?" Eli suggested. "They may not wish to cross the river like the others."

"Orcs fear water, but they will cross," Braddock said firmly.

"How can you be sure?" Stiger asked. "After the bridge was destroyed, they showed no interest in crossing the river."

"Perhaps leaders were on your side of river?" Garrack suggested. "No one left to push them across?"

"I believe I killed their leader," Stiger said with a slow nod. "It could be as you say."

"If they are bringing such large numbers," Braddock said, "they will most assuredly cross. Their priests will see to that."

"Then it is safe to assume that they would eventually cross at other points as well," Stiger said. "With such numbers, and crossings at other points, our fortified position would not long remain tenable, and we may find ourselves involved in a fighting retreat."

"Why come for it now?" Garrack asked. "Is not time yet. Gate cannot be opened."

"What if they are sending a like-sized force beneath our feet?" Stiger asked with concern.

"Then we will have warning of that," Braddock assured him. "The tunnels and mines are old and dangerous. It would be madness to move a large force like that underground. That is why they come aboveground. Besides, Hrove is holding Grata'Jalor with over two thousand warriors, and the only way into the citadel is across the drawbridge. There are no tunnels or mines into it."

"Suppose they did send a force through the mines," Stiger pressed. "Would we get warning with sufficient time to pull back to Grata'Jalor?"

"Not unless we moved closer," Braddock said, not liking the possibility of giving up such a defensive position across the river. "We would have to fall back upon the mountain itself."

"Could we hold from Grata'Jalor?" Stiger asked.

"Though we have some months' worth, our food supply would run out long before they could break in," Braddock answered with a frown, thinking on the logistics. "We have to resolve this now. A prolonged siege would prove problematic."

"The ground before the entrance to the mountain is good ground. Even though we would be unable to dig in, we could make a stand there," Stiger suggested.

"Yes." Braddock considered, and then nodded in acceptance. "That would be a good place to hold. Between us, it would be difficult for them to break our lines. If it goes badly, we can pull back into the mountain and bleed them with every step, then counterpunch when the time is right."

Stiger took out a dispatch pad and began writing furiously. Braddock watched for a moment and then turned to one of his bodyguards.

"The army is to march for the mountain," Braddock said in dwarven. "Those are my orders."

"Yes, my thane." The dwarf bowed and then started at a run for the army.

"Can we hold them there?" Garrack asked in the Dvergran language.

Braddock took a deep breath and slowly let it out, considering his reply. "We have to."

"Perhaps one of the dragons will consent to help us," Garrack suggested hopefully.

"And leave the Gate unguarded?" Braddock scoffed, astonished at the suggestion. "I should think not."

"It does little harm to ask Menos," Garrack pressed. "He might intercede on our behalf."

Braddock studied his childhood friend for a moment. "You are correct. Go and ask the First One. Perhaps some good will come of it."

Garrack nodded his acceptance and started back for the dwarven army encampment, where their ponies were kept.

Braddock watched him go for a moment and wished his friend success. He knew that Menos was unlikely to help in any meaningful way, at least until the Gate itself was directly threatened.

"Take this to Lieutenant Ikely," Stiger said, handing a dispatch to the rider. "It informs him what has occurred and orders him to hold the castle at all costs. Don't kill your horse getting there. Travel along the river until you hit the slopes of the mountains and then carefully work your way back and around to the castle."

"Yes, sir." The trooper saluted.

"Good luck, son."

"Thank you, sir," the trooper said and led his nearly blown horse away toward the river.

"It appears our job here is unfinished," Eli said with a sudden grin. "Perhaps when we are done here, I will finally see this peace you have mentioned. You know, the kind when the legions are done? Is it called legion peace?"

Stiger rolled his eyes, but said nothing.

Braddock looked between the two of them. Human and elf, they seemed an unlikely pair to form a friendship. The thane idly wondered if he would ever call Stiger a friend, and then immediately dismissed the idea. He was thane of the dwarves. He had no friends.

A dwarven horn sounded out, and all three turned. Braddock's eyes found Stiger's. He knew without a doubt, and could see the same in the legate's eyes, that the coming fight would test them both.

Stiger sat on a rough-cut log before his campfire, wearily gazing into its depths. The flames crackled and popped, sending a spray of sparks up into the night air. He took a pull on his pipe and looked over at Quintus. The centurion sat across from him and appeared as weary and spent as Stiger felt. Around them, thousands of campfires lit up the night, with dwarves, gnomes, and humans alike huddling close for warmth. Exhausted, most had turned in for the night, sleeping on their arms and getting what rest they could under the dark shadow of Thane's Mountain.

Quintus leaned forward to warm his hands against the bitter cold. Stiger blew out a slow stream of smoke, regarded his centurion, and then took another pull on his pipe. In battle, the man had proven himself a capable and steady leader of men. Stiger was well-pleased to have him as one of his officers. Quintus was a man he could rely upon.

"This waiting is the most difficult part," Quintus said. The centurion looked up from the flames and met Stiger's gaze. "Isn't it?"

"It always is," Stiger agreed. "Especially made more so when there is nothing to do."

Quintus did not reply. Stiger could only imagine the man's thoughts. Today was the first time the centurion had lost men under his command, and Stiger knew there was precious little he could say. He thought about giving what comfort he could, but then changed his mind. Like Stiger himself, Quintus was a practical man. Stiger rather suspected the centurion understood that in war men were bound to die, no matter how well you planned or led them. Practical or not, Stiger had always found the deaths of men under his command a difficult burden to shoulder. He could almost read the self-doubt and recrimination in Quintus's eyes, the self-blame and guilt at having survived when others had not.

"We should count ourselves lucky," Stiger said, instead settling on diverting the man's thoughts a little.

"How is that, sir?" Quintus looked up, running a tired hand through his short-cropped hair, which was starting to gray around the temples.

"The men needed rest," Stiger said, exhaling smoke as he spoke, "and the enemy has given us sufficient time to make that happen."

Quintus rubbed his chin, considering Stiger's words. "By not crossing the river, they are unwittingly giving us time to recover."

"Yes," Stiger nodded slowly. "A wise commander takes whatever the enemy gives and, when possible, turns it to his advantage."

Taking another slow pull, Stiger spared his pipe a sour look. The tobacco had a bitter taste to it. He wished he still had the good smooth eastern tobacco that he had brought with him when he had come south. Unfortunately, he had long since smoked that fine stuff away. Instead, Stiger had to content himself with the poor quality stuff that had been liberated from the Cyphan after one of his many ambushes in the Sentinel Forest.

"Yes, sir," Quintus said, and glanced around. "I am sure you are right."

Stiger followed the man's gaze to the nearest campfire, where men from a century of the Second slept, huddled under blankets. There were no tents, but the gnomes had delivered extra blankets from a supply that Braddock's dwarves had brought with them. Every layer helped. By the centurion's look, Stiger could tell that Quintus cared deeply for his men, who were undoubtedly shivering under their blankets.

Braddock and Stiger had made the decision to have the army sleep outside of the shelter of the mountain. Both he and the thane had been concerned that it might not be possible to get the entire army out in time to deploy and meet the enemy when they finally came up. Their decision, an unpopular one, had translated into a cold night for all involved.

Stiger's men had at least three days' rations left, so food was not an immediate concern. Rest, however, was. The army had been exhausted after the battle. The subsequent march to Thane's Mountain had only added to the deep fatigue. At the time, Stiger had been seriously concerned that the enemy would push right across the river and immediately march upon the mountain. Instead, the orcs had hesitated and stopped at the river before the ruined bridge.

"Once the crossing begins," Stiger said, "it will take some time for them to move their entire army across and then assemble before marching upon our position." Stiger paused and glanced up at the moon. Bright and full, it had slipped out from behind a passing cloud. "Assuming they cross tonight, we can expect a battle sometime around midday, perhaps even late afternoon or evening tomorrow for that matter."

"That long?" Quintus asked, raising his eyebrows.

Stiger reminded himself that Quintus was of the valley cohorts and had not served openly with the legions. The man had never been on a true campaign. He had no idea the effort and time it took to move an entire army. Though the orcs operated differently than a human army, they still had the same difficulties when it came to moving such numbers over any serious obstacle. Stiger nodded in confirmation to the centurion.

"The enemy will find us fresh," Stiger said firmly. He puffed on his pipe and blew the smoke out slowly. "They will discover us ready for them."

Sabinus approached the fire, carrying a mug of tea. "Sir," he greeted. "I just finished settling my men in for the night. May I join you?"

Stiger nodded, and Sabinus took a vacant seat upon a rough-cut log.

Freshly made, the mug steamed in the cold air. Quintus sipped it and sighed softly. "That is good."

"Sabinus," Stiger said, "what is the one thing serving in the legions teaches you?"

"That would have to be patience, sir." Sabinus chuckled, and Stiger nodded.

"Quintus," Stiger said, directing himself back to the centurion, "you will find that patiently waiting, whether it be for the enemy or for someone else to do their job, is an unofficial requirement of serving in His Emperor's legions."

"You know," Sabinus drawled, "I once waited over three hundred years for someone. I do believe that must have set some kind of record. Don't you agree, sir?"

Stiger frowned back at the centurion, who burst out with a laugh at the legate's expression. Quintus managed a chuckle also, and the mood around the fire lightened considerably. Stiger's expression softened.

"I see that spirits are up," Eli said, striding into the firelight. He took a moment to warm his hands by the fire before unslinging his bow from his back and settling down on a free log. He looked at the amused expressions on the two centurions' faces, and then at Stiger with a raised, questioning eyebrow.

"Where have you been?" Stiger asked curiously. He had not seen Eli for several hours, which was nothing unusual. Eli and the other elves had quietly separated from the column as the march to the mountain began. Eli had explained vaguely that he wanted a look around and would rejoin him later. Stiger wondered what his friend had been up to.

"We were down by the river watching the enemy," Eli said. "I encountered a few dwarven pioneers doing the same. They are skilled, though nowhere close to a ranger's level of competence."

Stiger raised his eyebrows at that. He had heard Braddock speak of his pioneers but had yet to see them in action. Stiger had wondered how good they were. If Eli had been impressed, then they were very good at the business of scouting.

"What are the enemy up to?" Stiger asked.

"They were quite intent on constructing a series of primitive bridges," Eli told him plainly. "You know, I find it surprising to admit that orcs can be quite industrious, and are possibly more intelligent than they have so far demonstrated."

"I see." Stiger took another pull on his pipe as he regarded the elf. There was hidden meaning in Eli's words. Stiger decided that it was a gentle reminder not to become complacent. The enemy were more than just animals. They were thinking beings, even if they did resemble animals.

"When do you think they will begin their crossing?" Sabinus asked.

"They have already sent across a number of scouts," Eli said. "The pioneers spent a little bit of time skirmishing with them before pulling back to simply observe from a position of safety. By now, though, I would imagine the enemy should have begun to cross with considerable force."

Sabinus sat back on his log. He nodded absently to himself as he turned his gaze to the flames. Then he looked back up at Stiger. "I wonder how the cavalry are faring."

"No way to tell," Stiger said. The cavalry were just one of his many concerns. He wished Cannol well on his mission.

319

"I still can't help but feel," Quintus said, "that it might have been wiser to have them fall back on the mountain with us. Before this is done, we may wish we had their swords at our side."

"And have the cavalry fight as dismounted infantry?" Sabinus scoffed with a tone of some disgust before taking another sip of his tea. Like most other infantry officers Stiger had known, Sabinus harbored a deep distrust of the cavalry and their reliability. "I think the legate was quite right to send them off and around behind the enemy."

"With luck," Stiger said, steering the conversation to safer ground, "Cannol will have some success harassing the enemy's communications and cutting any supply."

"At least our men will be fed and rested," Sabinus said brightly. "We can thank the High Father for that."

"We will be ready for them," Stiger agreed. He, too, worried that he had made a mistake by sending Cannol's men off. He changed the subject. "Any word on the refugees from the valley?"

"Yes, sir," Quintus said. "I sent an officer to check on them. He arrived back a short time ago. The dwarves have been very accommodating and set them up in Old City. The conditions are not ideal, but our people have access to fresh water. Centurion Malik—I believe you know him—well, he has taken charge."

"I know Malik," Stiger confirmed with a nod, recalling the scarred tavern keeper from Bridgetown. The man's tavern was now nothing more than ashes. The entire town had been torched by the enemy, and all along their line of march, the orcs had burned a swath right through the center of the valley. The destruction was such that Stiger suspected it would take years for the valley to recover.

"Vargus mentioned you had met him. He's a good man," Quintus said, scratching at the stubble on his cheek. "They have a good-sized guard, even if it is only old men and those too unfit to march, all of whom are retired legionaries. Malik reports that a good number brought food and livestock with them. He is seeing to it that they share and ration what they have. He says it should be enough to last around two weeks, perhaps a little longer. The dwarves and gnomes are also helping, but," Quintus spread his hands out, palms up, and shrugged, "well, any assistance our allies are capable of providing is extremely limited in nature."

"I see. At least they are secure," Stiger said. It was some comfort that the civilians were safe and one less immediate thing to worry on. "After this business is finished, we can worry about how to feed them."

Stiger was deeply concerned about the coming battle, and he fell silent as his thoughts turned to it. Would he and Braddock be able to hold? Could they fight off this vast orc horde? Braddock seemed confident and optimistic enough, but Stiger was not so sure. He had his doubts. A great deal would be decided on the morrow, perhaps even the fate of the world.

"If you will excuse me, sir," Quintus said, having apparently sensed Stiger's mood. He stood. The centurion stifled a yawn with the back of his hand. "I believe I will check on my men and then turn in myself. I expect tomorrow will be rather busy."

Stiger absently nodded, and the centurion stepped away. Sleep sounded like a very good idea. Stiger was so tired and spent that his eyes periodically shed tears, which he occasionally wiped away with a hand. His upper left eyelid twitched a little in an annoying manner. Stiger had endured longer periods without much sleep while serving in the north, during a siege, and knew without a doubt that he had to get some sleep. He well recognized the symptoms of growing exhaustion and was now sure that use of the sword had made them worse. The fatigue he felt was incredible. He intended to turn in himself shortly. Hopefully, he would be able to catch a few hours of rest before he was needed.

"Taha'Leeth?" Stiger asked, glancing over at Eli.

"Sleeping," Eli responded with an open-mouthed grin. The elf's eyes twinkled with mischief. "Aver'Mons and Marcus too. You have kept us all a little busy of late. Even elves need sleep, you know."

"That was not up to me," Stiger growled. "You know that."

"I suppose so," Eli said with a shrug, and the smile disappeared. No one spoke for several minutes as they sat around the campfire, each lost in his own thoughts.

Sabinus eventually stood and stretched before dumping the remainder of his tea into the fire.

"Good night, sir," Sabinus said, turned to go, and then stopped, looking back. "Today's fighting was some of the most difficult and challenging I have ever seen." The centurion frowned and seemed to want to say more, but hesitated, clearly uncomfortable.

"I understand," Stiger said with a wave of his hand, preempting the man before he could say anything further. "You and your men fought hard today."

"Thank you, sir," Sabinus said, looking down at the snow. With his foot, he moved aside an inch to reveal the wet paving stone below. He took a deep breath and straightened up, an intense look in his eyes. "The Thirteenth could not be commanded by a better man. Legate Delvaris would be pleased to know his legion is in good hands, sir."

Stiger at first said nothing, feeling more than somewhat uncomfortable with the centurion's sentiment. He was not sure how to answer, nor did he trust himself to. After a moment, he nodded, accepting the compliment for what it was. Despite the mind-numbing exhaustion that he felt, Stiger was greatly moved. He had to clear his throat before he was able to speak. "I appreciate the kind words. Now, see that you get some sleep."

"Yes, sir." Sabinus stepped away.

"Do you think," Eli said, with a glance over at Stiger after Sabinus was out of earshot, "he will feel the same way after tomorrow's battle?"

Stiger scowled at Eli but chose not to reply, instead returning his gaze to the flames.

"Sir." A legionary approached, saluting, and then handed over a dispatch. "A dwarf brought this for you."

"Thank you," Stiger said, dismissing the man. He opened the dispatch and scanned its contents, tilting it toward the fire to better catch the light. "The enemy is crossing in strength at several points along the river," Stiger reported to Eli. "At the current rate, Braddock estimates that it will take the orcs at least six hours to get the bulk of their army over to our side of the river." He paused a moment, looking over at Eli. "If that remains true, the men will have the night to sleep."

It was good news, but Stiger was still worried about what the new day would bring. He crumpled the dispatch and threw it into the flames, where it immediately caught fire and burned brightly.

"Castor seems very determined to have the Gate," Eli said.

"The Twisted One must have been planning and gathering his forces for years," Stiger said, shaking his head slightly. He wondered why the High Father had not planned in the same manner. Then again, here he was with a dwarven army and parts of the Vanished, the legendary Thirteenth Legion. Perhaps the High Father had prepared for this after all? The thought was not a comforting one, as the odds still seemed very stacked against him.

"It seems so," Eli agreed.

"I," Stiger said quietly, "do not much like this burden that has been given over to me."

"It is how you humans say," Eli said, thinking, and then, flashing a closed-mouth grin, "the hand you have been dealt?"

"Yes." Stiger glanced at the fire, and then back to Eli. "And it is a terrible hand."

"It's not so bad," Eli said.

"Oh?"

"You have more than a little help." Eli gestured around at the campfires beyond their own. "And, of course, you have me. What more could you ask for?"

"I never asked for this," Stiger said very quietly so that he was not overheard by men sleeping at nearby fires, "nor what is coming . . . "

"And yet you are here," Eli said simply, his voice hardening. "You are meant to be here. Of that, there can be no doubt."

"Yes," Stiger said, taking another pull on his pipe and blowing out a stream of smoke. "I am here."

"It is where you need to be, are meant to be," Eli said firmly, and then his expression clouded into one of sadness. "Tomorrow, many gathered here tonight will see their last sunrise."

Stiger rubbed at his tired eyes. What Eli had just said was true. The coming battle would be brutal, ugly, and very hard. Stiger worried about it, as he did everything else. He had his doubts, but that was not what really concerned him.

"If," Stiger said, "we pull off a miracle and are victorious tomorrow . . . how then will we confront the Cyphan?"

Eli did not reply, and so Stiger continued.

"We have already lost so many . . . too many."

There was a pregnant moment of silence.

"I don't know," Eli finally said. "But I think you will manage to find a way. You always do."

"I don't know anymore," Stiger admitted. If it were anyone other than Eli, he would have said nothing, and would have never voiced his doubts openly. "I just don't know."

"Well," Eli said, flashing Stiger another grin, "you will succeed, and one day, you will fulfill your promise to show me this legionary peace you keep speaking of."

Stiger rolled his eyes, and a soft chuckle escaped his lips. Eli had always been able to show him the lighter side when things looked especially dark. He regarded his friend for another moment, then nodded as he took one more pull on his pipe. He then tapped it clean against the cut log and stood. It was time to turn in for the night. He had to be fresh and ready for the enemy.

NINETEEN

"They are pushing the dwarves back," Quintus said grimly to Stiger. The centurion was calm and collected, though Stiger thought he detected concern in the man's tone. The sun had set several hours ago, and a full moon illuminated the snow-covered battlefield in an eerie, almost ethereal light.

"I know," Stiger growled, not liking what he was seeing. Both he and Quintus were atop one of the thick stone trading buildings that were located before the massive gates of Thane's Mountain. Solidly built, the buildings were slowly surrendering to the ravages of time and lack of maintenance. Several of the buildings had collapsed in upon themselves, with only the walls remaining. The one upon which they were observing the battle was surprisingly intact. It was so tall, perhaps twenty feet in height, that a ladder had been required to ascend to the roof.

Braddock's army was arrayed just beyond the woods, nearly twenty thousand strong. They were organized in ranks, five deep. The thane's battle line bulged outward at the center, with his flanks bending leisurely back toward the mountain itself. The dwarves were heavily armored, more so than a legionary. They carried large oval shields that, if rested upon the ground, reached nearly to their bearded chins. Each was armed as they individually preferred with a variety of weapons, which included axes, hammers, and swords. Dwarven armor covered nearly their entire bodies. They were like some of the armored horse warriors that Stiger had encountered in the north. Though they fought in ranks, they were not as coordinated or well-drilled in formation fighting as the legions.

The heavy armor and shields meant the dwarves were incredibly difficult to take down, but from what Stiger had seen, they were also slow to react and maneuver as a body. In comparison, Stiger's legionaries were lightly armored and much more maneuverable, meaning his men could react quicker to the changing conditions on a battlefield. Stiger supposed it all came down to what worked best for the dwarves, not the empire.

The thane had insisted upon having his dwarves meet the first waves of the enemy assault, which had begun with the full moon high above. Stiger, recognizing that his men needed additional rest, had listened to Braddock's impassioned appeal that this was hallowed ground for the dwarves, and Legend required that they meet the orcs in battle first, and before the humans. Stiger had graciously given in. He had used the time to further rest and feed his men. Massive bonfires roared toward the rear of the dwarven lines, where in the frigid cold his men waited, ready to be called upon to form up. From the pressure upon the dwarven lines, Stiger understood that time was fast approaching.

There were three gnome catapults that were firing away. Only one used the clay jars that exploded upon contact. Stiger suspected the nasty little creatures only had a limited supply of the blasting powder. Braddock had explained that the stuff was incredibly hard to make. Stiger also had his six bolt throwers in action. These had been mounted atop of the trading buildings and were firing over the heads of the dwarves, cracking away to deadly effect.

Stiger was drawn to a sound behind him. He turned and looked to see a formation of gnomes marching out through the gates to the mountain. They wore highly polished armor that caught and reflected the moonlight brilliantly. Unlike a legionary unit, the gnomes had no standard. There seemed no end to the formation as it continued to march through the gates. He estimated that there were at least several thousand of them, and they marched out with a precision that would have made a legion proud.

"Will you look at that," Quintus breathed, marveling.

One gnome marched at the head of the formation with two others, who were out in front, clearly officers. The gnome stepped aside when it spotted Stiger and removed its helmet to look up at him. They all looked the same to Stiger, but he suspected that he knew this one.

"Cragg?" Stiger called down in question.

The gnome nodded vigorously and said something back in his own language, which Stiger could not understand. When it became evident that he was not making himself understood, Cragg pulled out his sword, which was only a little shorter than a gladius, and pointed it at Stiger and then in the direction of the enemy. The message was clear enough.

"Quite right," Stiger said, knowing that even though Braddock had not yet called for his men, it was time. The dwarves had more than satisfied their Legend. They now needed help, and Stiger would provide it.

"Quintus." Stiger turned back to the centurion. "Get the men formed up. I am going to find Braddock."

"Yes, sir."

Stiger climbed down the ladder. His feet crunched into the snow as he stepped off the last rung. Once Stiger was clear, Quintus started down the ladder himself. Blake had assigned Corporal Durggen's file to act as Stiger's personal escort, and they were waiting for their legate. Stiger found Cragg also waiting. The gnome smiled sadistically at him before giving Stiger a mocking legionary salute, followed by a snicker, and then rejoined his fellows, who were still marching past.

"Cragg," Stiger called. The gnome turned. "Give it to them hard."

The gnome got the general meaning and nodded vigorously before turning away. Stiger watched the little creatures march by. One gnome began to sing, and within moments, the entire formation broke out into a song. Stiger could not understand the words, but it was a rousing melody that was meant to lift spirits. At least he hoped so. Knowing the gnomes, whatever they were singing was in all probability not fit for polite society.

Stiger started toward the dwarven lines, with his escort following close at hand. The sound of the fighting intensified the nearer he got, but Stiger found he could not see the actual fighting, as the lines were too deep. Stiger passed the last of the abandoned trade buildings and stepped out onto the snow-covered meadow. He reminded himself it was actually not a meadow. There was paving stone underneath the snow.

"Where can I find Braddock?" Stiger asked a passing dwarven officer, who pointed off to the left in a vague manner.

Stiger stepped off in that direction and eventually found the thane. Braddock was surrounded by his officers and aides. A camp table was before them, with a map spread out on top. Messengers came and went with surprising swiftness. The thane's bodyguard created a ring about them. Naggock spotted Stiger and waved him through without even a passing hesitation.

"Well, that's progress," Stiger said to himself and indicated that his escort remain behind after Naggock shook his head at them.

Braddock was having an intense discussion with Garrack and a clan chief Stiger recognized as Tyga. He had been introduced to the dwarf when they had left Castle Vrell. Stiger was surprised to find Ogg was present as well.

"Legate," Braddock greeted with a grim expression, looking up from the map on the camp table. "I was just about to send for you."

"My men are forming up as we speak," Stiger told the thane. "What is the situation?"

"It is not good," Braddock admitted. "Though we are taking a terrible toll on the orcs, I fear it is only a matter of time before they force us back to the gates of the mountain. The enemy has several trained formations that are fighting with a surprising amount of coordination."

"Really?" This was something that Stiger had not wanted to hear.

"Yes," Braddock confirmed. "Thankfully, those formations are few in number, and the vast majority of the enemy are fighting as individuals. Lucky for us, orcs, for the most part, have difficulty thinking beyond themselves."

Stiger looked down on the table to see several wooden blocks set strategically on the map, which was a rough-drawn depiction of the ground before the gates to Old City. Braddock noticed Stiger's gaze and pointed at the blocks.

"I have had to give ground and extend my line out to here and here. Thankfully, beyond the ends of our line, the terrain is completely impassable. Extending my lines, though, has created a new problem."

"You have thinned your depth." Stiger nodded, understanding the problem. Braddock's warriors would have less time to recover when the ranks were rotated. It also meant that a breakthrough at any one point would be more difficult to contain. "How are your reserves?" Stiger asked the thane.

"Dwindling."

"If I bring up my entire command, we can assume a portion of the front. That way you can add depth back to your lines."

"Yes, that is what I was thinking." The thane ran a hand through his beard and paused a moment before continuing. "I do not think it will be enough, though."

"It will not," Ogg said. The wizard was leaning heavily upon his staff and looked to be in a disagreeable mood.

Garrack said something harsh in dwarven to Ogg, who cast Garrack a withering look, but said nothing.

"What would you have us do?" Braddock demanded of Ogg.

The wizard shifted his gaze to Braddock.

"Pull the army back into Old City and Grata'Jalor," Ogg said, which was followed almost immediately by a mad giggle. "They are here for the World Gate. That is all."

"Is it time then?" Braddock asked of the wizard.

"No," Ogg said. "We still have a few months. The time is not right for the planes to align."

"Then the World Gate cannot be opened to Tanis yet?" Stiger asked.

"The World Gate cannot yet be opened," the wizard confirmed with a strained look over at Stiger.

"Ogg, I will not turn the army around and march through those gates like a dog with its tail between its legs," Braddock said with some heat.

"Give the order, Braddock," Ogg implored. "The World Gate is all that matters."

"It's not that easy. It will have to be a fighting withdrawal, and that will be costly. Not to mention the cost to Legend . . . "

"What does Legend matter when the fate of our world is at stake?"

Garrack barked something at Ogg in dwarven. It did not sound pleasant.

"Is there no point or hope of holding then?" Stiger growled. "I am getting tired of falling back."

"We are dwarves," Garrack said, switching back to his rough common. "Nothing we cannot do."

Braddock glanced over at Garrack and then back at Stiger, running an idle hand through his tightly braided beard. "If you can put your men into the line, that might give us the depth and strength we need to hold, at least for a time. There would be very few reserves once you are committed. Should the line falter, it could mean disaster."

"Then we must make sure the line holds," Stiger said with firmness.

"Ogg." Braddock turned to the wizard. "Can you do anything to help?"

"No." The wizard looked uncomfortable and for a moment did not meet his thane's gaze. "I dare not. I fear before this night is done I will need all of my strength and the power I've been holding onto for months."

"You speak of the Twisted One's minion, perhaps?" Stiger asked the wizard.

"I do not know," Ogg admitted hesitantly and then a distant look came over him. "I can feel something building. I . . . I just do not know . . . "

"That's not terribly helpful," Braddock said with a scowl of frustration thrown in Ogg's direction. He then turned back to Stiger. "Castor's minion has not been sighted for several hours. We have no idea where it is."

"The creature is masking its presence," Ogg said. "Neither I nor the dragons can sense it. We assume it has had some help, magical."

Stiger ignored Ogg. The missing minion was the least of his concerns. Instead, he looked around at the ground they were defending and then back up toward the gate, thinking furiously. Simply assuming a position in the line was not enough.

"We need to pull back to the trade buildings," Stiger said suddenly. "Their walls are thick, and high. We defend the spaces in between the buildings."

Braddock glanced back toward the ancient buildings and his eyes lit up, seeing the possibilities for defense.

"I like it," Braddock said. "It will allow us to deepen our lines and also create a new reserve."

"It would," Stiger agreed, surprised he had not thought of it earlier. The space between the buildings was confined, really just small streets that were large enough for a wagon or cart. It meant that they would not have to hold the entire front, only the streets between the buildings. It would also channel the orcs. "Where do you want us?"

Braddock was silent as he contemplated Stiger's question. The thane glanced down at the map and said something to Garrack in dwarven and then Tyga, clearly consulting the two. The three spoke some more, and then Braddock looked back up at Stiger.

"I would like to place you in the center of the line," Braddock said, looking down again at the map and tracing out the new battle line. "That way I can peel my warriors back from the center to both sides and, at the same time, reinforce my wings."

"I was rather hoping to take one of the wings," Stiger told him, "and not have to split your army in two."

"It is my wings that are in trouble, not my center," Braddock explained. "My best warriors are in the center. By giving up the center, this way I can add steel to each flank rather quickly."

"Okay," Stiger agreed, studying the map. "I will bring my boys up. Once we are in position, you can begin falling back."

Stiger made his way back toward his men, his escort closing up around him. He found his senior officers, including Taha'Leeth and Father Thomas, gathered together. Sergeant Arnold stood behind the paladin. The men were formed up into marching ranks, at ease, but ready to move. Many pairs of eyes from the ranks shifted toward Stiger as he approached his officers.

"We are going to move up and take the center of the line," Stiger informed them. "The dwarves are having a hard time of it. This will allow them to reinforce and add depth along both wings."

"This is an uncommonly good night for a fight," Blake said cheerfully. "A tad bit cold, but 'least it's not snowing."

"Now that you've put words to such thoughts," Sabinus growled, "the gods are bound to curse us with adverse weather."

"Think happy thoughts," Blake responded. "Happy thoughts, my friend."

"The First and the Second will take the right, and the 85th and Third the left," Stiger continued. "Once we are in position and engaged with the enemy, the entire line will begin falling back to the first set of buildings. We will take up defensive positions amongst the buildings. Once there, assume street fighting formations. This will allow us to deepen our own ranks and create a reserve. The narrow confines of the streets will limit the number of enemy that can be sent forward at any one time. Along with our tactics, discipline, and shields, it should combine to make the perfect environment for killing them."

"What of my boys?" Tilanus asked as a contingent of dwarves, perhaps twenty strong, marched by them.

Stiger recognized Hrove amongst them. The clan chief cast Stiger a disdainful look as he passed. Hrove was not dressed for battle. The chieftain's look bothered Stiger more than he cared to admit. There was something off about him. Stiger could not say what exactly, but he knew an enemy when he saw one. Hrove was one dwarf who just did not like humans, and probably never would.

"How many men do you have left?" Stiger asked Tilanus.

"Around two hundred and fifty able to march," Tilanus answered.

Thinking on Hrove got Stiger considering the residents of the valley, who were safely holed up in Old City. What would happen to them if the army failed to hold? What would happen if Grata'Jalor fell?

"How many of the militia are with the refugees from the valley?" Stiger asked of Quintus. "Do you know?"

"Maybe two thousand men in armor and under arms," the centurion responded. "To be perfectly fair, most are too old to march and put up a good fight. They are a shadow of their former selves."

"The majority of our people will be armed though," Vargus countered. "We train everyone to fight, and I mean everyone."

"I would feel better if they had some additional steel," Stiger said to Tilanus, concerned that the battle might go badly. "I want you to send two hundred men to protect the civilians, yourself included. Until otherwise ordered, you will be in overall command. Leave fifty men at the gates to the mountain, under a capable centurion. They will act as a rearguard—added insurance, if you will—should things go poorly here."

"But, sir," Tilanus protested, and Stiger stopped him with a raised hand.

"This is not a debate," Stiger told him firmly. "You will do as ordered."

"Yes, sir," Tilanus said stiffly, with a concerned look directed to Quintus. The other centurion was stony-faced.

"I concur," Quintus said after a pregnant pause and addressed himself to Tilanus. "Your men will not make much of a difference here if things go badly. However, they may make a difference in protecting our families."

"Can I rely upon you?" Stiger asked of Tilanus. He was grateful for Quintus's support.

"You can," Tilanus said, giving in. "What if the dwarves take issue with us placing men at the gates to the mountain? From what I can see, they already have more than two hundred there."

They all turned to look. Hrove's warriors stood around the gates, waiting.

"Tell the dwarves that I ordered it and if they have a problem to speak to Braddock," Stiger told him and then paused, thinking. There was nothing more to say. "With any luck, in a few hours' time, we will have a fantastic tale to tell our grandchildren."

There were polite chuckles from the officers. Eli also looked amused, but Stiger noted a grimness to his normally implacable facade. It matched what Stiger was feeling inside.

"Well then," Stiger said with a clap of his hands, "let's get our men up and into the line."

❧ ❧ ❧

Stiger had his men formed into a line of battle, four deep. They were arrayed behind the center of the dwarven line. Stiger stood with Garrack and the chieftain, Kiello. Sabinus, Vargus, and Quintus had joined them, along with Eli and Blake.

"He says he peel off the last ranks and allow your men to move forward," Garrack translated what Kiello had just said. "He leave only first rank. Says you must hurry when happens."

"We will move forward as soon as it is done," Stiger said and then turned to his officers. He had to yell to be heard over the fighting. The dwarves had been steadily pulling back. "Got that?"

There were grim nods all around.

"Good luck, gentlemen."

Stiger watched as each centurion went his way. Once again Stiger felt like a helpless spectator. It was something he knew he would have to become accustomed to. Stiger moved back through the ranks with Blake and Eli. Behind the 85th stood Father Thomas, with Sergeant Arnold at his side. Both looked calm and collected, which was something Stiger did not feel but as usual worked hard to keep from those around him. Prior to a fight it was always the same for Stiger. The enemy badly outnumbered them, and Stiger was deeply concerned. The battle was not going as well as would be hoped. Studying the two men, he wondered if they were also presenting a false façade, concealing their worries. Or were they just naturally confident? Stiger wondered if they thought the same of him. Were they all frauds? It was an interesting thought.

"Legate," Father Thomas greeted him.

"I had thought you might be at the aid station," said Stiger, as Sabinus, to the right, shouted the order to move up. First and Second Cohorts began to move forward.

Quintus barked the order to advance. The Third began moving up. A second later, Blake, just a few feet away, ordered the 85th to advance. In steady step, Stiger's entire line moved forward, right up to within five feet of the last dwarven rank.

"Not this time," Father Thomas said. "I feel the call to be here."

"Oh great," Stiger replied, though he was honest enough to admit to himself that he did not begrudge the paladin's presence. Tonight Father Thomas was welcome and, Stiger suspected, would be badly needed.

"Draw swords," Blake ordered, and the company's blades came out. An order that Stiger did not hear was snapped by dwarven officers, and the dwarves to the legionaries' front began streaming backward through his ranks toward the rear. The retiring dwarves were battered and bloodied, most of it green. The dwarves were so wide that the legionaries had to step aside to let them pass. Some kind words were exchanged, and more than one legionary was clapped in a friendly manner on the shoulder. Stiger found it heartening to see.

"I feel the call as well," Sergeant Arnold announced quietly, as if he were almost afraid to admit it aloud.

Stiger looked sharply at the sergeant. The man was far from the beaten shell of a person he had been just weeks ago. Arnold stood straight, tall, and, surprisingly, with a dignified air. His uniform was well-maintained, armor highly polished. Arnold was also clean-shaven. The sergeant then looked over at Father Thomas in surprise at the admission he had just made and received a nod of approval and confirmation.

"Two paladins?" Stiger asked.

"No," Father Thomas replied. "Arnold has his own personal trials to endure and overcome before he can be considered one of the High Father's holy warriors. I was blessed and honored to be his mentor and the conduit of the High Father's will. In short, I was his guide. His path lies on a different road than mine. Though, the High Father willing, I think he will one day make a fine paladin."

Arnold looked surprised at that, but said nothing further.

"I guess I should count myself lucky then," Stiger said, and found that he meant it.

"Lock shields," Blake shouted, which was followed by a loud thunk as the company's shields came solidly together. "Steady there, boys."

"As you should, my son." Father Thomas drew his saber and looked over at Stiger with a solemn expression. It was the first time Stiger had ever seen him draw it. The saber was an incredibly beautiful weapon that seemed to have been polished so well, the blade's surface was perfectly mirrored, catching the moonlight in striking flashes. Stiger, appreciative of fine weapons, could not guess at the saber's value. The weapon must have been made by a master smith of unparalleled ability.

"Upon ascension to service, the High Father presents each of us with a personal gift," Father Thomas said, having caught Stiger's look. "This was mine. Each paladin receives something . . . unique."

"Like Father Griggs's horse?" Stiger snapped his fingers in sudden realization of his time in the north. He well remembered the magnificent stallion Father Griggs had owned. Stiger had never before seen a better-looking animal. Not only was the paladin's horse pure white as untouched mountain snow, but it had also been incredibly intelligent, almost frighteningly so. When Father Griggs had passed from this world, the general in command of Stiger's legion had attempted to claim the horse as his own, but the animal had disappeared from the legion's stables. The general had thought the horse stolen and a search had been mounted, which proved fruitless. To Stiger's knowledge, it had never been found. Had the High Father taken it back?

"Yes," Father Thomas said with an understanding smile. "That was a wondrous gift and a worthy companion for Father Griggs."

"Steady now," Blake shouted. "Get ready to let the last of the dwarves through."

A light drew Stiger's attention to his left, where Arnold was standing. The sergeant was holding forth his hand, a surprised expression upon his wrinkled and weather-beaten face, as a ball of light began to coalesce in the air. The hand was held palm up and the ball of light was growing rapidly in size.

"Now," Blake roared, unaware of what was happening behind him with Arnold. "Brace yourselves."

The light continued to grow in brilliance until Stiger was forced to look away, shielding his face with his hand. The light grew brighter than the sun, lighting up all around him. It was so bright, Stiger could see the outline of the bones in his palm. Then there was a hiss and a pop, and the light source exploded skyward, where it blazed like the morning sun, lighting up the entire battlefield. There was a moan and Sergeant Arnold collapsed, Father Thomas catching the man and lowering him to the ground. Like an old dishrag, Arnold looked spent.

The last of the dwarves that had been holding the line in the center streamed back through the ranks. Once through, the legionaries immediately brought their shields up, expecting an attack, but the light shining down from above had stunned the orcs into immobility.

"Advance!" Stiger shouted, recognizing an opportunity when he saw one. "Advance!"

The legionaries jumped, not expecting the order. After their hesitation, they moved steadily forward, taking up the position the dwarves had vacated, and then pushed into the orcs. Shields to the fore, they slammed them into the stunned enemy, swords darting out, jabbing and thrusting with deadly effect.

"Rip into them, boys!" Stiger shouted in encouragement. He looked toward the Third and was gratified to see that cohort moving forward as well. The First and Second were also advancing. In fact, from what he could see all up and down the line, the dwarves were pushing forward, tearing into the stunned orcs. Stiger did not know what Arnold had done, but it was nothing short of miraculous, and for that he was grateful.

The orcs just stared upward, completely stupefied, not even moving to defend themselves as the legionary swords stabbed and punched into them. The legionaries doggedly cut their way forward through the unresisting masses of orcs. Hundreds fell, and then the light slowly began to fade and, with it, the paralysis of the enemy. The orcs shook themselves, as if becoming aware of their surroundings once again. Then, they attacked with a viciousness that was shocking.

"Halt!" Stiger shouted, and the advance of the 85th ground to a stop, with the legionaries bringing their shields together. "Straighten that line there!"

To his left and right in the moonlight he saw that Vargus, Quintus, and Sabinus had stopped their cohorts and were carefully aligning on the 85th.

"I am going to check on the Third and Second," Stiger informed Blake after he was sure the line before him was going to hold. He then turned to Eli. "Stay with Blake and lend him your assistance."

"I will do as you ask," Eli told him, and it was clear from his tone that he felt his place was at Stiger's side. Stiger would have brought him along, but Blake was new to fighting the company. Stiger needed the 85th to hold, and Eli would help him do that.

Stiger moved over to Vargus's side of the line first. He had given up his escort to strengthen the ranks for the 85th. He estimated that, since marching from the castle, he had lost close to half of his combat power. The thought was painful, and Stiger quickly pushed it away. He had to focus on the here and now. Vargus had just blown hard on a wooden whistle, switching out the first rank, which, Stiger was pleased to note, was nicely done.

"Sir," Vargus greeted him tersely, without taking his eyes off of the action to his front. Stiger saw him wince as one of his men was brutally struck down. The man in the next rank stepped right over the body and took his place at the front rank. The men behind dragged the body out of the way, which left a stained trail of blood in the snow. "These are good boys, very good boys."

Stiger was not sure if the comment was directed at him, but he got the centurion's meaning. "They are all good boys. They should not be treated so."

"Very truly said, sir." Vargus glanced over at him for a moment before returning his attention to the action. Stiger stayed with Vargus for a few minutes before moving over to Quintus. He found the centurion helping a gravely wounded man to sit down behind the line.

"Stay here," the centurion told the soldier, who was mortally wounded. "When you can, move yourself back to the aid station. All right?"

"Yes, sir," the young man said, hands trembling, eyes wide as he worked to put his slippery insides back into his belly.

Quintus patted him in a fatherly fashion on the shoulder and, with a sad look, stepped back to the line. He eyed Stiger as he came up.

"I knew that boy since he was a baby," Quintus said in a hard tone. "I will not enjoy telling his mother of his last moments."

Stiger said nothing as he watched the action to the Third's front. All across his line, they were holding. The legionary shield, the one piece of kit that was more hated and loved than the helmet, was making an impressive difference. The eager press from behind was forcing the enemy up close against the shield wall, which did not allow them much room to swing their weapons, whether it be the longsword or hammer. This was creating the perfect combat environment for Stiger's men as his boys threw their shoulders into it, pushing the shield wall into the enemy while periodically jabbing out with the short sword. The orcs at the front were getting pushed from the front and pressed from behind as well. They had almost no room to move and fight. Stiger's legionaries, on the other hand, were in their element.

Quintus stepped up to the rear rank. He had placed his wooden whistle loosely in his mouth and was watching the action closely. Occasionally, he or one of the other centurions called out some advice or a profanity-ridden threat. Gripping the whistle tight in his teeth, he blew two hard, short blasts. The first rank stepped back and the second rank took their place, throwing their shields forward and into the enemy.

Stiger's previous doubts about the valley cohorts were gone. Vargus and Quintus had done their duty and maintained the high standards of the legions, even though neither had actually served openly. He understood that these standards had been maintained down through the centuries from the original members of the Thirteenth Legion. In the last few years, after the legions had returned to Vrell, in secret the valley cohorts had continued to train and drill their men, even as the corrupted Captain Aveeno had begun spreading terror across the valley.

Stiger moved over to Sabinus next. First Cohort was the last of the original men from Thirteenth, magically held in stasis through dwarven magic for over three hundred years. These men had served and seen a lot of action. They moved and fought better than the other cohorts, but the difference between them was slim. Looking on the men of the Vanished before him, Stiger could not help but feel awed. They had fought under the direct command of his ancestor, General Delvaris. These were men of legend, and they were fighting like it, struggling valiantly against the dark tide of the enemy.

Despite such feelings, Stiger's critical eye began to notice things that alarmed him. Sabinus had almost completely rotated through his ranks. If the pressure continued, it was only a matter of time until the men tired to an extent where the cohort would begin to suffer an increase in casualties. The losses so far were few, but that was bound to change.

Stiger studied his line and those of the Second and Third, trying to think of some way to break the current dynamic. The dwarves along the wings were steadily pulling back. In a few moments, the center of the line, the position Stiger's men were in, would start falling back as well toward the trade buildings. Until then, there was really nothing he could do, other than encourage the men to keep fighting. They would just have to hold for a bit more.

Abruptly, several men to his direct front dropped like a handful of stones that had been thrown into a pond. The men in the second rank dropped a half second later. Black lightning reached for those in the third rank. A legionary in its path dove to the side, the lightning snapping harmlessly over him, only to connect with the man behind.

Before Stiger knew what he was doing, his sword was in his hand and he was pushing his way through the ranks. The rage exploded and with it his sword flared to brilliance. The men nearest drew back from him.

The black lightning flickered from existence, fading from view before he could reach it. Stepping over the bodies of his men, Stiger saw an orc priest through the gap in his line. The priest snarled when it saw Stiger and bared its teeth, tusks on prominent display. Holding forth a gnarled claw-like hand, black lightning leapt out from the fingertips, crackling and hissing with power as it reached for Stiger.

The rage drove Stiger forward, sword held before him, to which the lightning seemed drawn. It struck against the sword in a massive blow. It was as if Stiger had just deflected a powerful sword strike. The blade crackled and hissed as the black lightning exploded on glowing steel. Pain shot through his body, and though he was better prepared this time, it still felt like his bones were being torn apart. The rage drove him onward, and he took a shuddering half-step forward and then another. Tears welled up in his eyes. Everything around him became a blur. He was beginning to have difficulty breathing, and then abruptly the attack ceased. The lightning faded from existence in an instant. Stiger found himself standing before the priest, shaken and weakened from the ordeal. His strength returned in a rush and he was able to see clearly once again.

The priest's eyes blinked with evident shock as Stiger punched his blade into its chest.

Suffer, the sword hissed in Stiger's mind. The priest's eyes lost their focus as the blade hissed and sizzled. Stiger jerked the weapon back, and it came away pristine. The priest tottered for a moment before collapsing in a heap at his feet. Stiger abruptly felt incredibly drained, as if he had aged a decade in mere moments. He staggered drunkenly backward. The nearby orcs stood mute, either looking down at the body of their priest or up at Stiger in horror.

A pair of hands grabbed Stiger from behind and roughly dragged him backward. The hole in the line closed up as the centurions shouted orders and threats at their men. The legionaries moving forward presented their shields toward the orcs as they pressed forward again, this time more carefully.

"Sir," Sabinus said, and Stiger realized it was the centurion who had pulled him back. "Are you all right?"

"Yes," Stiger answered, blinking. He shook his head and felt somewhat better, more himself.

"Would you be kind enough to leave the priests to me?" Father Thomas said. "That is the third one so far."

Stiger sheathed his sword. The incredible rage he felt was gone, as if it had never been. In its place, he felt an emptiness, as if a hole had opened up in his soul. Stiger glanced down at his sword. He understood that some of the rage came from him, but much of it was coming from the sword. He wondered if perhaps they fueled each other's fury.

We are made for one another, the sword hissed in reply to his thoughts. *Your fate is mine, and mine is yours.*

Ignoring it, Stiger rubbed the back of his neck. "Did you say a third one?"

"That's right. I dealt with one. Arnold took care of the other."

"Arnold?" Stiger asked.

Father Thomas gestured behind him. Arnold was making his way toward them, clearly recovered from the miracle he had performed earlier. The sergeant was holding a great golden hammer, like the one that Stiger had seen Father Thomas wield. It pulsed and throbbed with a golden light. Arnold had clearly found his purpose in life. If Stiger had any doubts before, it was clear Arnold's future lay elsewhere. It would not be with the legions.

"Will there be more?" Stiger asked.

"Most assuredly, though I would recommend you avoid them if possible. You carry a weapon of some considerable power, yet you may come across something that you cannot handle alone." The paladin paused a moment and eyed Stiger's sword with a contemplative look. His eyes sought out Stiger's. "As I have become fond of you, I would not want to lose you to an agent of evil."

"Sir," Sabinus called his attention to a party of dwarves that had hurried over. Still feeling unbelievably worn out, Stiger drew himself up. He recognized Garrack.

"Braddock says he pull back to shorten line some more," Garrack explained in broken common. "It be quick."

"How far?" Stiger asked. The lines on the flanks were already twenty-five yards closer to the trade buildings than they had been just minutes before.

"Up to buildings," Garrack informed him and pointed behind them.

Stiger immediately understood. "When?"

"We sound horn, you fight back towards buildings."

"Once we hear the horn, we will begin pulling back in order."

"Yes," Garrack said and left, hurrying off.

"Send word to the other cohorts," Stiger said to Sabinus. "We will pull back in good order and match the withdrawal of the dwarves on either flank."

Sabinus turned to two legionaries and snapped out orders. They dashed off into the night. A few minutes later, a series of horn blasts sounded over the cacophony of the fight. Almost immediately, the dwarves on both sides began to step backward at the quick. Orders were barked and the legionary line fell back with them.

The enemy seemed surprised by the sudden movement and for a moment did not advance. Then, as a wave lapping up on the shore, they surged forward and the two armies were back in contact. Stiger watched silently as his legionaries pulled back fighting as they did so. Within a couple of minutes, they had reached the foundation on which the first of the trade buildings had been built, a type of terrace about two feet in height. Stiger glanced around at the buildings. There was approximately ten feet of street space between each building, enough for a wagon or cart to easily negotiate, which he assumed had been its purpose.

Stiger stepped up onto the terrace and moved back to make sure he was out of the way. As the lines backed up, centurions snapped orders. One rank at a time stepped back and up onto the terrace, jogging back to nearly the end of the building and cross street before the next terrace, where they reformed. Stiger watched as one rank after another moved by, until finally the first rank was left alone, facing the enemy. The orcs understood what was occurring and threw themselves forward with an intensity that was frightening. The centurion standing before Stiger ordered the first rank back.

One legionary was not quick enough. His shield was ripped away and a war hammer slammed him in the right shoulder, driving him down to the snow. Another orc stepped forward and stabbed downward with a large sword. The power of the strike punched through his armor, digging deep into the man's chest. He flailed like a fish out of water as the orc removed the sword by placing a large boot on his chest. The orc with the hammer gave a savage roar of rage and brought the weapon down on the dying man's head, driving it into the snow. Stiger felt sickened.

The rest of the legionaries made it back and up onto the terrace. Holding their shields before them, they were able backpedal to safety. A fresh rank was waiting for them. Shields parted to let them through.

The trade buildings had been constructed in neat, even rows. The centurion commanding this century had moved up and placed his line almost midway down the first row of buildings. The street between buildings permitted five men to stand shoulder to shoulder. The space served to limit the number of orcs who could fit through the gap between buildings. Stiger glanced upward. At around twenty feet in height, the buildings looked too tall for the orcs to easily scale. The walls were made of large stone blocks fitted so well together that there were no easy handholds. There was no way that the enemy would be able to easily batter their way through the walls, as they were quite thick. The orcs would have to fight from an inferior position.

Behind the line, fresh ranks waited their turn to become the first rank. It was a good defensive position, and it reminded Stiger of some of the city fighting he had taken part in a few years before, where the combat had occurred in the narrow confines between buildings. In that instance, Stiger's men had been the aggressors, when they had helped to take the city of Certa from the Rivan. The sandal was on the other foot now, and Stiger was the defender. It was an uncomfortable thought, and Stiger hoped the outcome of this fight tuned out better than it had for the Rivan, who had been nearly slaughtered to a man.

Stiger felt confident his men would be able to hold for some time. He went to the back of the building to the cross street between rows. He quickly made his way along the line of buildings, checking on his entire line. The only potential trouble spot was the very center, with the main thoroughfare that was much wider and moved between buildings directly up to the main gates of the mountain. When he arrived there, Stiger was surprised to discover his legionaries resting and not in direct contact with the enemy.

To their direct front, the gnomes were throwing themselves at the orcs. Surprisingly, the mean little creatures were ripping the enemy to pieces. They were small enough that they barely came up to an orc's knees, where they struck at the unprotected legs of their enemies, hacking away, until the larger creature fell, and then they swarmed over and efficiently dispatched it.

Stiger found Quintus watching them calmly. His men were formed up into six ranks of twelve across and were waiting calmly for orders, shields resting upon the ground. Quintus had a small reserve that he had created. These waited a few feet behind. To the Third's left and amongst the buildings on the other side of the road, the dwarven line began, extending all the way to the far flank.

"Sir, I was just about to send a runner," Quintus said. "Braddock extended his lines to this road. We only need to hold this stretch here and back the way you came, at least until you hit the other wing of the dwarven army."

"I can see that," Stiger said, still watching the gnomes fight just twenty feet ahead.

"They are going to pull back in a moment," Quintus informed him.

"How can you tell?"

"We've done this dance a couple of times now," Quintus told him. "Watch."

The gnomes, on some signal Stiger could not detect, broke off what they were doing and ran as quick as they could, little legs pumping hard toward the legionary lines.

"Ready shields," Quintus called as the gnomes raced through the legionary ranks. Once the last of the gnomes were through, the shields came up and swords were leveled toward the orcs.

"Advance."

Quintus led his cohort about ten steps forward before bringing them to a halt. The orcs advanced warily toward them. It was the first time Stiger had seen them show any kind of real caution in this battle. Judging from the number of bodies left behind by the gnomes, the orcs had been handled roughly. He glanced behind at the gnomes and saw them celebrating, thumping one another on the back. Their high-pitched laughter echoed along the walls of the trade buildings to either side.

"They will rest a few minutes and then come charging through our lines at the orcs. We will pull back a ways. They have their fun, and then we repeat it all over again."

Stiger shook his head, but it seemed to be working, though judging by the number of small bodies left on the field, the action had not been completely one-sided.

"Tell you the truth, sir," Quintus said, "I don't think those vicious little shits have any fear."

"It is a good thing they are on our side then," Stiger said. "Do you know where Braddock is currently?"

"I was told he had set up a command post somewhere near the gates to the mountain."

"Kindly send word to the other cohorts that is where I will be. I do not plan to be long."

"Yes, sir."

Stiger found Braddock around fifty yards from the gates. Hrove and several aides were leaving as Stiger arrived, heading in the direction of the gates to the mountain. Hrove gave Stiger a nasty smirk as he brushed by him. Ignoring the surly dwarf, Stiger continued on and was waved through the screen of bodyguards by Naggock. He saw that Braddock was surrounded by aides, including Garrack and Ogg. Tyga was also present. Garrack saw Stiger and made his way over to him.

"Not very friendly, is he?" Stiger said, jerking a thumb at the back of the retreating chieftain.

"Hrove?" Garrack asked, furrowing his brow and looking. "Do not trouble yourself. No one likes Hrove, but is loyal. That is all that matters."

The thane looked up and spotted Stiger.

"Legate," Braddock greeted, beckoning him over. "How are your legionaries?"

"We're holding," Stiger informed him. "And your dwarves?"

"The same," Braddock told him. "Our situation has improved somewhat. I feel fairly confident that we can continue to hold the orcs for some time, perhaps until morning."

Stiger glanced up at the position of the moon. By his reckoning, dawn was at least four hours away. He agreed with Braddock's assessment. In amongst the tight confines of the trade buildings, his men should have no trouble holding, though with time they would begin to flag and tire. Then again, the orcs would have the same problem. It was quite possible both sides would fight themselves to a stalemate.

"The enemy has taken heavy losses, and still they come," Braddock said with some frustration in his voice. "They willingly sacrifice ten to take down one. I have never seen the like."

"I suppose they will eventually tire themselves out," Stiger replied.

"Tyga feels we should pull back into the mountain and close the gates," Braddock told him bluntly. "It would give us a chance to recover and rest before taking the fight back to them."

Tyga looked up as his name was spoken by his thane, though it was clear the chieftain could not follow the discourse, which was in the common tongue.

"They not get through gates easy," Garrack said, struggling over the words. "We rest and then attack out through tunnels."

"It sounds reasonable," Stiger said as he thought it over. Though their lines were holding, he was becoming more concerned by the minute. He could not put his finger on it, but something just was not right. It was almost as if he were sensing some impending doom. Stiger pushed the dark thoughts away. He could not allow his imagination to run wild on him. A military leader who let that happen was inviting disaster. Stiger had learned a long time ago to think things through reasonably before making decisions.

Stiger's attention was drawn to Ogg. The wizard seemed preoccupied. He was pacing back and forth, ignoring them. Stiger was about to say more when he saw Braddock turn with a look of surprise in his eyes. Ogg's head snapped around too. Menos, the caretaker, was approaching.

"Menos," Braddock greeted, inclining his head. Those dwarves around the thane bowed deeply.

The caretaker ignored them all and instead walked a few feet farther before stopping. His gaze was upon the fighting. The dwarves around Braddock all had their eyes upon the caretaker, even Braddock's bodyguards.

"What's wrong?" Stiger asked of Braddock.

"The caretaker has never been known to leave the Gate room," the thane explained tersely. "I do not understand why he has come."

"I asked for help from dragons," Garrack said in barely a whisper. "Why caretaker is here himself I not know."

"Can he help?" Stiger asked.

"I am not sure," Braddock admitted, and then glanced up at the dark sky, searching. "If he brought one of the dragons, it could prove decisive."

Stiger looked up at the sky and saw nothing.

"A dragon or two," he said, "might just come in handy. Don't you agree?"

Menos began to pace, first walking ten feet to the left and then back to the right, his robes barely moving, giving him the impression that he was gliding across the trampled snow. Menos began to speak in a language Stiger had never heard before. It was smooth and beautiful-sounding, but also at the same time angry in tone. Stiger shot Braddock a questioning look, not sure what was happening. The thane appeared just as perplexed.

Stiger was about to ask a question when movement to his left caught his attention. A small double column of ten dwarves was marching up to them. They had clearly come from the direction that Menos just had, which was undoubtedly from the gates to the mountain itself. In the moonlight, Stiger saw that they were from Braddock's clan, all wearing the thane's purple cloaks. Perhaps they were the caretaker's escort?

Putting them from his mind, he turned back toward Braddock and then stopped himself. The dwarven formation was making a beeline right for the thane, not Menos, who had paced off to the right a ways. They were almost to the protective ring of Braddock's personal guard and were not slowing. Stiger frowned and was about to question Braddock when they drew steel.

Distracted by the caretaker, Naggock's guard were caught by surprise and unprepared as their attackers charged into them. Three of the guard were cut down before they knew they were under attack. Two of the attackers charged right for the thane. Stiger was between them and Braddock. He shoved Braddock aside as he drew his sword. Stiger brought his blade up, blocking a sword as it came down on where Braddock had been a half second before. The two swords came together in a crash. In the bitter night air, the impact jarred Stiger's arm and left his hand stinging. He spun around to the attacker's side, pulling out his dagger and drove it into the dwarf's neck before the traitor could recover. Releasing the dagger, Stiger turned to face the second dwarf, but before he could bring his sword back up, they crashed violently together and went down in a heap. Stiger's helmet smacked the ground hard, and for a moment he was dazed. The felt padding inside had done little to absorb the impact. The wet and cold snow on the back of his neck was a shock and Stiger came to his senses quickly. He struggled to untangle himself.

The dwarf had lost his sword but continued to fight, punching Stiger repeatedly. Having held onto his weapon, Stiger hammered the hilt of the sword down on the attacker's helmet. It rang with a dull metal clank and did no injury. A hand grasped his neck. Stiger tried to force it away, but the dwarf was too strong. A second hand reached for his throat and Stiger found himself unable to breathe as the dwarf began to choke the life out of him. Stiger kicked and tried to roll the attacker off of him, but the dwarf was too heavy. His lungs began to burn and his vision swam. Then there was a sickening crunch, and the dwarf went rigid. The hands strangling him relaxed, and went slack. Stiger gulped sweet cold air and it felt wonderful.

The body of the dwarf was rolled off of him. Blinking, Stiger looked up and saw Naggock standing above him, holding a bloodied sword. The expression on the dwarf's face was one of hot anger. Naggock stepped away. The clash of swords, grunts, and dwarven curses was close at hand. Stiger got to his feet. Most of the traitors were down. So were a number of the thane's personal guard. He saw Ogg backing up and away from the fight, intent on staying clear. Braddock had his sword out and was trading blows with one of the attackers. Tyga, several feet to Stiger's right, swung a sword in a level arc and neatly cut through the throat of his opponent, blood flying in the wake of the sword. Without missing a beat, the chieftain took a step to his left and slammed a mailed fist into the face of a dwarf fighting with one of the thane's guard. The dwarf crumpled.

Stiger took a step toward Braddock with the intention of helping the thane, but it was unnecessary. Braddock deflected a blow, took a step inside his opponent's reach, grabbed the other's sword arm—preventing it from being brought back around—and slammed his sword into his attacker's belly, sword point punching right through the armor. The mortally wounded dwarf groaned, dropped his sword, and collapsed to his knees.

Placing a hand on his attacker's chest, Braddock pushed back and withdrew his sword, then threw his opponent down to the ground with a look of disgust. The thane turned his back on the traitor and left him to die. The fighting was over.

Braddock looked toward Stiger and gave him a nod of thanks before his eyes spied a body lying on the ground. It was Garrack, sightless eyes staring up at the darkened sky. The thane stepped over to him and knelt down. Ogg moved up behind his thane, staring down at Garrack in a look Stiger would have described as complete dismay. The wizard's shoulders had slumped and he took a shuddering breath.

Braddock said some anguish-laden words in his own language before reaching forward to close Garrack's eyes. Tyga stepped forward and rested a hand upon the thane's armored shoulder and then oddly moved it from Braddock to Ogg. The wizard looked over at the chieftain, and Stiger was surprised to see tears in his eyes.

Tyga did not say anything, but just stood there, clearly sharing their moment of grief. Braddock took a deep breath and then stood. There was anguish in his eyes, but also a look of hardness and resolve.

The thane turned and saw Ogg. His face twisted with loathing and he snapped something at the wizard, who shrank back. Tyga's face hardened, and he spoke to both of them in dwarven. Braddock stepped toward Stiger, his eyes hard and full of anger.

"He won't even use his magic to save his own father," Braddock told Stiger, switching back to common, fury lacing his tone. "He allowed the one who gave him life to be butchered . . . "

"Garrack is Ogg's father?" Stiger asked with some surprise.

"What I do," Ogg said, grief clouding his voice, "I do for the good of our people, and this world. I dare not waste my power . . . even to save . . . my father."

A loud groaning behind them drew their attention. The massive gates to the mountain started closing. In the torchlight, a struggle could be seen. The dwarven guard, Hrove's warriors, were attacking the legionaries that Stiger had posted there as a rearguard. The fight was furious, but clearly one-sided, as the dwarves outnumbered and overwhelmed his surprised men.

"NAA!" Tyga shouted, drew his sword, and charged the gate. The gates were closing too quickly, swinging shut with a speed Stiger would have thought impossible due to their size. There was no way Tyga would make it before the mountain was sealed. After running ten feet, Tyga seemed to come to the same realization. He stopped and simply watched.

"Hrove," Braddock whispered. The gates closed a few seconds later with a resounding boom that momentarily drowned out the sound of the two armies fighting. The thane's shoulders slumped with what Stiger read as defeat. With a sickening feeling, Stiger knew that they were in deep trouble.

Tyga turned and slowly walked back to them, looking more than dejected. He looked utterly dismayed, beaten even. Tears ran down the dwarf's cheeks and into his braided beard.

Braddock took a deep breath, squared his shoulders, and said something in dwarven to Tyga, which elicited an unhappy bark of grim laughter, followed by a curt shake of the chieftain's head.

"What did you say to him?" Stiger asked.

"He and Hrove have a long-running dispute over the ownership of a mine that borders both of their territories. I told him that if we survive this, the silver mine is his."

Hearing the black humor, Stiger's heart sank even further. With the mountain sealed, they were trapped.

"We no longer have any choice. Hrove saw to that," Braddock said, anger trembling his voice. "We either defeat them or fight to the last. Between us, I am thinking it will be the latter."

"There is no other way into the mountain?" Stiger asked, unwilling to accept that they were doomed, for he could not see a way to defeat the orc army. It was simply too large.

"We are trapped," Braddock said, seeming resigned to fate. "The orcs are to our front, and the mountain behind us. There is nowhere for us to go."

Tyga said something in dwarven to Braddock.

"Yes," Braddock said with a nod at Tyga, "We will make the orcs pay dearly for each life they take tonight."

Stiger could not believe what he was hearing. There had to be a way out. There must be something he could do. There always was. He glanced around, thinking furiously. Never before had he felt so helpless. He would not fail his men this way. He could not.

The caretaker said something. Stiger turned toward Menos, having forgotten about him. The caretaker's voice rose in tone, and a moment later, he was screaming and spitting with rage. Menos seemed oblivious to their situation, to being shut out of the mountain, the hopelessness of their position. The caretaker's rage was directed at the orc army assaulting their lines. He screamed his hatred at the enemy. Stiger did not know why the caretaker's rage captured his attention, but it did. Absently, he rested his hand upon his sword hilt and felt the familiar tingle.

"—dare come here!" Menos raged, and Stiger jumped in surprise as he suddenly could understand what the caretaker was saying. "Vile, evil, unclean orcs, followers of the dark gods . . . after all these long years, you dare to test me?

You dare to return? You forget the wrath of my people. For that I will make you pay."

"I . . . think it might be prudent that we should take a step or two back," Ogg suggested, and Stiger did not need to be told twice, as something in the air began to happen around Menos.

The caretaker's form shimmered, blurred, and grew rapidly in size. Braddock and the others stumbled backwards. Stiger backpedaled quickly, not daring to take his eyes off of the changing form of the caretaker, who no longer held any recognizable shape, and then in an instant, it coalesced. Stiger blinked.

An indescribable earsplitting roar of rage drowned out the fighting across the entirety of the battlefield. The power of the roar drove Stiger to his knees. He and everyone else trembled with instinctive fear.

Where Menos had stood moments before, a massive black dragon had taken the caretaker's place. It was nearly twice as large as Currose. The dragon snaked its head back and roared up into the night air. A massive gout of flame shot upward. Stiger held his hands clapped over his ears as the dragon roared its rage to the world. A feeling of indescribable, utter fear spread through Stiger, and from what he could see, everyone else was similarly affected. Stiger had never known what it was like to be a coward, but now he wanted to do nothing more than run and hide, only his legs would not work.

The dragon spread its wings and took to the air with a massive flap. The backwash of wind pushed Stiger down and onto his side. He rolled onto his back and watched in awe mingled with fear as the black dragon climbed up into the dark sky and was briefly silhouetted against the moon before disappearing into the night.

A stillness settled over the battlefield as both armies looked skyward. The dragon could not be seen, but its powerful wings could be heard. After a few seconds, there was silence as the wings stopped pumping the air. Then, on the far side of the field, a long blast of flame swept downward onto the orc army as the dragon swooped low. The blast of flame exploded across a hundred yards of the enemy line. Instead of climbing back up into the sky for another attack, the dragon landed amongst the orc horde. Claws ripped and tore, jaws snapped, and its long tail lashed about, crushing orcs into the ground or throwing them bodily into the air.

Black lightning reached out from half a dozen orc priests and struck at the dragon. The lightning seemed to have no effect on it. The dragon turned its head, opened its mouth, and spat silver lightning at one of the priests, who was struck down in an explosion of light and sound.

Stiger staggered to his feet. The crushing wave of fear was gone. From his current position, he could see the dragon's fire continuing to burn furiously where it had been sprayed. The magnificent creature was expending its rage upon a portion of the orc army, which seemed transfixed by the spectacle before them. It was incredible to behold. Stiger watched the dragon for a few moment and then abruptly knew what he had to do. He rushed over to Braddock, who was picking himself up.

"We need to attack, now." Stiger shook the thane, who looked at him blankly for a moment. "We could not ask for a better distraction."

"Yes," Braddock said, recovering his wits, "you are quite correct."

Stiger turned and ran for his men. He found Vargus first. The centurion, like the rest of the army, was watching the dragon rip into the enemy. There was a blast of flame from the creature, and orcs died by the hundreds. It let out a tremendous roar that seemed filled with satisfaction.

"Send the men forward," Stiger ordered. Vargus looked at him blankly for a moment before the centurion's eyes narrowed.

"What about the dragon?" Vargus asked him. "What if it goes after our men too?"

"Centurion Vargus, now is our chance," Stiger said, feeling the urgency of the moment. Sending the men forward with the dragon in a complete rage was a risk, but Stiger felt it was one worth taking. "We must attack. Send the men forward."

"Ah, yes, sir." Vargus glanced around. Everyone on the field of battle was watching the dragon or, in the enemy's case, cowering and drawing away from the frightful beast. Stiger left the centurion to look for Sabinus. Behind him he could hear Vargus calling his men forward.

"Sabinus," Stiger shouted, when he found the centurion. "Send the men forward!"

"Forward!" Sabinus roared to his men, snapping many out of their shock. This was why the legions trained and drilled so hard, for the men instinctually responded to obey orders. "Centurions, forward. We are attacking."

And then, Stiger's entire line moved and went forward with a great shout. Stiger drew his sword and went with them. The dwarves to either side of the legionaries surged ahead, along with the gnomes, and slammed into the enemy. It took only moments, but the orc army broke, running for the tree line, hotly pursued. The dragon snaked its head, following the flight of the enemy, and then unfurled its wings. Roaring with rage at the fleeing orcs, it took to the air.

TWENTY

Stiger stood next to Braddock, Tyga, Ogg, and Sabinus. Braddock's bodyguards were around them in a protective screen, much more vigilant than before. Naggock had taken the attempted assassination of his thane very personally and, Stiger suspected, hard. It had almost succeeded, but for Stiger's intervention in shoving the thane aside.

They were studying the sealed gates of the mountain, and had been for the last thirty minutes. The sun had risen, though they were still in the shade of the mountain. With the night giving way to day, the temperatures had begun to climb, but a chill wind reminded everyone that winter was just beginning.

Behind, elements of both armies combed the battlefield, carefully looking for wounded to save and living enemies to dispatch. Stiger had sent the elves and Marcus to find his cavalry, with orders to drive any enemy survivors that made it down into the valley to the other side and back from whence they had come.

The dragon was occupied scouring the forest beyond the meadow, hunting for orcs that were in hiding. Every now and then, a terrible roar of exultation could be heard when the dragon found a fugitive.

Menos, it turned out, had always been the second dragon, Sian Tane. According to Ogg, a Noctalum's true form was that of a dragon. It had been a secret that only the wizard had known and kept to himself. Stiger reflected that Currose's terrible anger back in the gate room might have arisen from the ranger nearly discovering the secret little game the two dragons had apparently played for centuries with none other than the wizard the wiser.

The problem was now the mountain. They were about fifty yards from the sealed entrance. A detail of a hundred dwarven warriors had been brought up in the event the gates unexpectedly opened. They stood around looking bored.

Stiger was deeply concerned about the valley refugees who had gone to Old City. Were they fighting for their lives against Hrove's warriors? He was somewhat comforted that he had made the decision to send the bulk of Tilanus's men to augment their defensive strength. Though he was now wondering if Tilanus had even made it. Those he had sent to help act as a rearguard and hold the gates to the mountain certainly had not.

"Well," Stiger said, thinking that if Braddock did not get to the disloyal chieftain first, he would, "we have to get in. How do we do it?"

"The long way," Braddock said unhappily and kicked at the snow. "We go through the mines and tunnels."

"How long will that take?"

"At least a half day to get to the nearest entrance," Braddock said, letting out a deep explosive breath, "and another full day before we can make it to Old City. However, we need to rest the army first."

Stiger agreed. Braddock's army, and his legionaries, were exhausted. They were spent and not going anywhere, at least for several hours.

"Would those approaches be left unguarded?" Sabinus asked.

"No," Braddock answered. "Hrove will move to secure the tunnels and mines."

"So we will have to fight our way in," Sabinus said.

Stiger sighed. It was not an ideal situation, but what could he do? They could not march until the army was rested. That meant even more time wasted while the civilians of the valley potentially fought for their lives. There was no doubt in Stiger's mind that Hrove would do his best to do away with them. They represented a threat to the chieftain. The civilians he had sent to safety were most probably fighting in the confused confines of a long-dead city as he and the others stood here calmly studying the gates. Though he could not have foreseen it, Stiger felt terrible just the same.

"Yes," Braddock said. "We can start out tomorrow morning."

It was as Stiger had suspected. Then a thought occurred to him. "Do you think the dragon might consent to forcibly open the gates?"

They all turned to look at him with some surprise. Ogg giggled. "Yes, a dragon could easily get through those gates."

"He flew off," Braddock said, with evident frustration directed at the wizard. "How do we get him back?"

"We don't," Ogg said. "Sian Tane will return when he is ready. We can just wait."

"How long will that be?" Sabinus wondered, and Ogg shrugged as if to say he had no idea.

"Why?" Stiger asked the question that had been on his mind. "Why would Hrove betray you?"

"Hrove has always suffered from ambition, though I never imagined it to be so great," Braddock said. "Without this army, there would have been little to stop him from proclaiming himself thane and returning to the nations with a tale of our ignominious defeat."

"The truth would eventually be learned," Ogg said.

"By then it would be too late," Braddock replied. "Hrove would rule with an iron fist."

"Hrove." Tyga, unable to follow the conversation, had picked up the name. He spat on the ground with evident disgust and then kicked at the snow.

Stiger saw Father Thomas approaching. The paladin was without Arnold, who he had last seen at the aid station. Stiger glanced down at the sword. It was well past time he had a talk with Father Thomas about it.

"I had better see to my men," Stiger said, excusing himself.

Braddock nodded in a distracted sort of way. His attention was still on the gates, which barred him from entrance to the mountain. Stiger gestured for Sabinus to follow and started off to intercept Father Thomas.

"It is time to recall the men," Stiger said to Sabinus as they walked. "Let's get them fed and rested so that we can move out before sunrise."

"Another night sleeping on their arms," Sabinus said, gazing up at the sky. "It will do them no harm after what they've been through." Sabinus paused, thinking. "Sir, I would like to send back to the castle for additional supplies and tents. We can also bring out the prisoners and put them to work. They can help dispose of the bodies."

"See to it," Stiger said, feeling suddenly weary. He needed rest. "Make sure you get some sleep yourself."

"I will, sir," he said.

"Also, later this evening," Stiger added, "I would like strength counts."

"Yes, sir," Sabinus said. "Though, if I had to guess, we have lost nearly two-thirds of our strength from what we marched with."

"That bad?" Stiger stopped and closed his eyes, feeling miserable. It was a terrible price to pay, and they still had the Cyphan Confederacy to contend with, not to mention the traitorous Hrove. How was he going to manage?

"It could have been much worse, sir."

"It can always be worse," Stiger replied, feeling somewhat numb at having lost so many good men. "We could have very easily lost everything."

"But we didn't, sir." Sabinus scratched an itch on his arm. Both of them were grimy and dirty. They badly needed to clean up. "We fought through, sir, and without you, I doubt we would have done as well."

Stiger took a deep breath and let it out slowly. He considered Sabinus for a moment before nodding in grudging acceptance of the words meant to lessen the burden for losing so many. It helped, but then again, it did not. He wondered for a moment how generals like Treim came to terms with large-scale losses. One day, perhaps if he survived long enough to see his mentor again, he would ask.

"Legate," Father Thomas greeted him. The paladin looked worn and tired. He was just as grimy and dirty as the rest of them. His armor was scratched and in some places pitted, in others splashed with both red and green blood. "I can find no evidence of the minion."

"As usual, you are just full of cheerful news," Stiger said sourly. "I was hoping the dragon would have at least gotten it."

"I doubt a dragon could have taken it down," Father Thomas admitted. "Though I admit I am not quite sure how such an encounter would play out."

Stiger's hand came to rest upon the hilt of his sword, and he felt the comforting electric tingle. Stiger took a deep breath and was suddenly less tired than he had been a moment before. Glancing down at the weapon, he began to wonder again on the full extent of the sword's power.

Ask, the sword hissed sullenly in his mind. *Our fate is linked . . . it is past time for you to know . . .*

Stiger felt a chill run down his back. His gaze shifted over to Sabinus. "Would you see to the men? I would like to speak with Father Thomas alone for a moment."

"Yes, sir." Sabinus saluted and stepped off.

Stiger felt uncomfortable and wasn't at first sure how to start. Stiger glanced down at the sword again. Though he feared what it represented, it had become a part of him, almost as if it were now tied to his soul. If it turned out to be a weapon of evil intent, Stiger was unsure he could manage to give it up. Father Thomas appeared to sense his unease.

"You wish to speak about Rarokan?"

"Yes," Stiger said, relieved that the paladin had broken the ice. "I—"

The ground trembled beneath Stiger's boots. He glanced around, wondering what could have caused it. Sabinus, only a few feet away, had stopped and was looking around as well. The ground trembled again, this time lasting for several seconds. Small rocks higher up on the slopes began to shift and crash downward. Then the ground really shook and the mountain seemed to ring like a bell. Stiger looked back toward Braddock. The dwarves were looking up at the mountain and the gates.

"Come on," Stiger said to Father Thomas, and they rushed over to Braddock. "What's going on?"

"The Gate," Ogg whispered in horror. "It is being opened."

"Let's get the army up, then," Stiger said and waved for Sabinus to join them.

"Not that gate," Ogg snapped. "The World Gate."

"What?" Braddock demanded. "I thought you said it was not time."

"It is not." The wizard looked worried.

"Then how can it be opened?"

"The Gate is a conduit to time, and space." The wizard had a wild look to his beardless face. "Space meaning another world or place, like Tanis. Time meaning the instantaneous travel over a great distance without the passage of a single moment. This is, in all probability, beyond your feeble intellects, but theoretically, it can also manipulate time not simply for travel over long distances, but to either move forward or backward."

Braddock looked at the wizard with a frown.

"You are talking time travel?" Stiger asked, not quite sure he was following Ogg's meaning, but sensing somehow he was correct. "Going to either the future or past?"

"Yes," the wizard said in a whisper, and the ground shook again, this time violently.

"Who is opening the World Gate?" Braddock demanded.

"Only a wizard of sufficient power can manipulate the World Gate," Ogg replied.

"What about a minion of Castor?" Stiger asked, beginning to get a very bad feeling about what was coming. Delvaris had confronted a minion. Was it planning on going back in time? Or forward to the day when the Gate could be opened to Tanis? "We never found it."

"I suspect that a direct representative of a god could manipulate the Gate," Ogg replied with a sharp look at Stiger. "Though I believe a wizard would still be needed."

"It must have gone through the mines and tunnels," Braddock postulated, glancing back on the battlefield, and its many dead. With the shaking of the mountain, the carrion birds had taken panicked flight. "This was all an elaborate distraction, a ruse. We were meant to see only the orc army, not the real threat to the World Gate."

"Unless Hrove let it in?" Stiger suggested, thinking on the chieftain's betrayal.

"Even he would not be so foolish," Braddock said with a sharp look.

"I am not so sure," Ogg replied with a distant look, scratching at his beardless chin.

"How do we get to the Gate?" Stiger asked. Before anyone could reply, the mountain shook violently. It was as if a struggle were taking place under their feet. An ear-splitting roar of rage sounded from the air behind them. A massive black shape streaked down from the heavens. The dragon opened its mouth, and a silver lightning bolt shot forth, impacting the gates that barred access to the mountain a split second before the dragon slammed into them, claws extended like a great bird of prey. Stiger was thrown from his feet by the collision, as was everyone else. Smoke and dust exploded into the air, followed by an incredible cracking and rending sound. Large rocks and boulders began to rain down around them. One of Naggock's dwarves screamed, and then went silent as a piece of tumbling stone crushed him. Then it ended. The dragon screamed again, and this time it sounded different, as if the dragon were calling from a distance or from inside a well.

Stiger dragged himself to his knees. The dust and smoke began to clear. The gates had been battered inward and shattered. There was no sign of the dragon, though he could hear it inside the mountain. It sounded like the dragon was doing battle. The dwarven detail before the gates, which moments before had been standing around bored, recovered first and went charging into the mountain. Their movement spurred Stiger to action. Standing,

Stiger turned to Sabinus, who looked just as stunned as everyone else.

"First Cohort is the closest?" Stiger knew the dwarven army was dispersed across the battlefield, as were the Second and Third Cohorts. The 85th was also in the field. Only the First was organized where they had made their stand the night before.

"Yes, sir," he replied.

"Bring them immediately," Stiger ordered. "Send word to the other cohorts. We have to take the mountain back."

Sabinus jogged off in the direction of the First.

"We need to get to the World Gate," Ogg said, regaining his feet. There looked to be fear in the wizard's eyes. "Currose is fighting a losing battle. She is fighting the minion. I can feel it. Braddock, we must get there now, you and the legate."

"What?" Braddock asked, gazing on the ruined entrance to the mountain.

"I will take us there," Ogg insisted. "Step closer to me. Quickly now."

"I am coming too," Father Thomas said. Ogg looked as if he wanted to argue, but then nodded his acceptance.

"Why?" Braddock asked.

"The Oracle's Prophecy," Ogg replied. "We must stop Castor."

Braddock paled at the wizard's words. Naggock said something to Ogg, who replied in the negative.

"Braddock, tell him to guide Sabinus and First Cohort to the World Gate," Stiger said hurriedly, realizing that Ogg had told the bodyguard he could not come with them. "Can he be their guide under the mountain?"

Braddock spoke rapidly. Naggock seemed to want to argue, but then curtly nodded his acceptance.

The mountain shook again, this time more violently. Larger boulders and parts of the intricately carved cliff face crashed down, and then suddenly everything was still.

"We must hurry!" Ogg fairly screamed. "The World Gate is opening. Stand close to me."

Stiger, Braddock, and Father Thomas stepped closer to the wizard.

"Prepare yourselves," the wizard snapped and brought his staff down hard on the snow-covered stone. The oddly shaped crystal flashed brightly, momentarily blinding them. There was an earsplitting crack, as if the world had been torn asunder. An unearthly fog enveloped them, and then they were somewhere else. Disoriented, Stiger staggered slightly. He found himself in the Gate room, where he had first seen Currose. This time, though, a scene of chaos, destruction, and disorder greeted him.

Twenty-One

The setting Stiger found himself in was almost indescrib-able. Smoke was thick in the air, making visibility poor. An orange glow off to the right told him something burned, for he could feel the intense heat. Rock from the ceiling lit-tered the once-smooth stone floor, which was cracked like the surface of a frozen lake during the spring thaw. The floor was littered with bodies, all orcs, with lots of green blood and large splashes of a dark reddish blood that was neither human nor dwarf in origin.

Stiger drew his sword, and immediately it began to glow a soft, pale blue. He quickly glanced around to get his bear-ings. Braddock, framed by the orange glow from the fire, was to his right. The thane had pulled out his sword. Ogg was slightly behind the two of them, and Father Thomas was to Stiger's left. A dark, inert shape lay directly ahead.

Stiger approached it cautiously and discovered an enor-mous, lifeless dragon tail. Obscured by the dense smoke, he could barely make out the shape of the rest of the dragon. Stiger guessed it was Currose.

"This way," Ogg whispered, pointing ahead past the dragon tail. Stiger could see the others stifling the urge to cough. Ogg held part of his robe up to his face and breathed through that to help filter out the smoke.

Stiger climbed over the tail of the dragon. Ahead through the smoke, he could hear something shuffling, moving amongst the debris, and beyond that a chanting in a language he did not know. The acrid stench of smoke burned his lungs, and he struggled against the urge to cough, but failed and began to hack. Stiger cursed himself as someone ahead shouted a warning. Footsteps pounded in their direction, and from the smoke emerged four large orcs.

The mountain suddenly shook, and in the distance a dragon roared. It was all Stiger could do to keep his feet as rock rained down from above. One of the orcs tripped and went crashing to the floor. The shaking stopped, and Stiger braced himself as one of those still standing attacked him, swinging a massive hammer for Stiger's head. He dodged back at the last moment, and the hammer sailed by, with just inches to spare. Stiger stepped forward, jabbing with his sword before the orc could recover. Aiming his strike carefully, the blade point dug into its hip, just below where the plate armor ended. He felt the blade strike bone and continue forward with more resistance.

The orc bellowed in pain and fell backward, a hand going to the wound. Stiger gritted his teeth and pressed his attack. The orc swung the hammer back around, and Stiger ducked the wild swing, coming up and jabbing again, this time into the groin. The orc screamed in agony and fell to the ground, where another jab silenced it permanently.

Stiger glanced around. The other two orcs were also down. Father Thomas was just pulling his saber back, having neatly severed the head of his opponent. Braddock had killed the one he faced and was now pressing on to the orc who had fallen. It had regained its feet and was looking at the four of them warily, eyes narrowed, and longsword held before it.

Something flew past Braddock and struck the orc hard in the chest with a pop, flinging it backward to where it crashed down in a heap. Ogg dropped his hand, which had been held forth.

"We're wasting time," Ogg snapped and gestured through the smoke. The message was clear, and they continued forward. They came to the edge of the ring of stone pillars, which glowed in a vibrant, pulsing purple light. With each pulse, the ground seemed to throb. Stiger could feel the vibration through his boots. The smoke had thickened. The acrid stench burned Stiger's lungs. All of them were hacking, struggling to breathe. Stiger could barely see two feet in front of his face.

"Don't touch the pillars," Ogg warned.

Stiger had been about to and snatched his hand away. He could still hear the chanting just ahead. It had risen in pitch. The mountain shook once again. A dragon roared off in the distance. Stiger knew it was Sian Tane. It sounded as if the dragon were fighting its way to them. With each roar, it seemed to be getting closer.

After stepping past the pillars and into the circle of stones, the smoke inexplicably cleared. It was as if the smoke could not pass beyond the glowing ring. Stiger took a deep breath of fresh air and found himself staring at the back of what could only be another abomination. The creature was so misshapen that Stiger's mind had difficulty processing it. There was another present, and this one was human. He wore a maroon robe and carried a staff with a crystal similar to the one Ogg carried. Both were facing the two enormous central pillars, which were throbbing rapidly with an intense blue light. The two pillars emitted a high-pitched hum. Lightning flashed and crackled between them in what seemed to be a rapidly increasing series of discharges.

The crystal on the wizard's staff flared with light, and he stepped back and away from the abomination. Where the lightning had been flashing back and forth between the two pillars, a patch of white light now stretched evenly out between them. The light was intense, though it faded to blackness a half second later. Stiger found himself looking at what he could only describe as a dark hole slowly coalescing in the air. For reasons that he could not explain, the hole felt bottomless, like looking down into a very deep well. With a shock, he realized he was gazing upon a portal to another time.

Father Thomas, Ogg, and Braddock stepped through the ring of stones. Ogg coughed and sucked in a deep breath of fresh air. The human wizard turned around. Recognition flickered in the strange wizard's eyes as they fixated upon Ogg, and for a moment no one moved. Stiger thought he detected fear in the human wizard's eyes, but it was gone in a flash. Then the wizard struck, holding forth his staff. A beam of brilliant yellow light shot forth. Ogg held up his own staff, and the beam of light shot past them, deflected as if by some invisible force. Its passage through the air left the hairs on Stiger's arms quivering. The beam hit the ceiling and exploded, raining small rocks down to the floor behind them.

Without being told, Stiger knew what he had to do, and advanced. At the same time, the abomination turned around, saw them, and smiled, a disfigured mouth full of mismatched and crooked teeth. The minion was humanoid in shape, but a horribly twisted thing. Its face looked as if it had been mashed so many times that everything was in the wrong place. It met Stiger's eyes before turning dismissively away and back to the still-coalescing portal. The minion held out a gnarled hand in the direction of the portal, and the ever-present, high-pitched hum of the

World Gate intensified. The floor itself seemed to vibrate with power.

The human wizard's attention was fixed solely upon Ogg. He said something that seemed to make no sense, and even though Stiger clearly heard the words, the memory of them immediately slid from his mind. A blue globe flashed from the wizard's staff directly toward Ogg, who batted it away seemingly without any effort. A green globe flew from Ogg's staff to the human wizard, who deflected it toward Stiger. Instinctively, he raised his sword to block it. The globe hit the sword with the sound of a thunder crack. Stiger was staggered by the force of the blow, and his fingers went numb as agony beyond measure tore through him.

POWER, the sword hissed with what seemed to be exultation. The agony faded, replaced by a feeling of incredible strength and ability. Stiger's tired mind felt sharper than it had been in days. *Strike the wizard down! Take the wizard's life force for our own!*

He moved toward the wizard, who took a step back, but it was not far enough. As if Stiger were a bystander, he saw his blade reach out and punch effortlessly into the wizard's chest. The wizard's face contorted in agony, astonishment, and then incredible fear. The sword hissed and sizzled as it went in. The light in the wizard's eyes that spoke of life seemed to flicker before going out, extinguished forever. Stiger felt the sword hilt grow warm and then hot in his hand before suddenly cooling. The body fell backward, landing in a heap amongst the fallen stones and stalactites from the ceiling.

Stiger turned to face the abomination. It was moving toward the portal, and before Stiger could react, it stepped between the two pillars and, incredibly, vanished. Simultaneously, from behind, Ogg said something in the same language the other wizard had used moments ago. Like before, though Stiger clearly heard the words, they slipped out of his mind as if they had never been spoken. The floor shook, and Stiger had the feeling of immense power being released behind him. His hair stood on end. Then everything went incredibly still.

Stiger turned around and saw Ogg standing there weakly, supported by his staff. The wizard was clearly exhausted. Stiger blinked. The wizard's face was now creased by age and he looked to have grown much older, elderly. Stiger's surprise in this change lasted only a moment, for his attention was drawn away from Ogg. Beyond the circle of stones was complete darkness. Nothing, not even the devastation, the dragon's body, nor the smoke, could be seen. Stiger looked back to the portal. It was still there. The two pillars hummed with power. He glanced back to find Ogg's eyes upon him. Stiger had a bad feeling about what was to come.

"You must go after it," the wizard told him.

Twenty-Two

"What do you mean go after it?" Stiger asked incredulously.

"Precisely that," Ogg replied. "You must follow it, and kill it, before it changes history."

"You want me to go through that?" Stiger asked incredulously. "Where does it go?"

Ogg shuffled up to him, leaning heavily upon his staff. The metal guard clicked against the stone floor, and besides the humming of the World Gate, Stiger became conscious of no other sounds. Ogg cast a tired look toward where the minion had gone through, and then his eyes tracked to Stiger's.

"I sense it has gone back to the past," Ogg explained. "I suspect you know where."

"That was the minion that Delvaris fought," Stiger said as a statement, suddenly knowing it to be true. He glanced down in wonder at the sword in his hand.

"Did Rarokan show you that?" Ogg asked curiously. "The sword, did it show you?"

"During the fight against the abomination back at Castle Vrell," Stiger explained. "It showed me Delvaris and the minion confronting each other on a field of battle. I saw my ancestor kill it."

"Perhaps not."

"What do you mean?"

"It has gone back to change our timeline." Ogg gestured toward the blackness beyond the ring of stones. "In fact, it has already done so. You need to go back, find Delvaris, help him confront it, and kill it. In short, fix things."

"You can't be serious," Stiger said, aghast. "Me? Why not you?"

"I am weakening," Ogg said with a sudden shudder. "The magic I just loosed was powerful. I had been storing it for this moment. I cannot hold the portal open for much longer. You must go through the World Gate, and soon. If you do not, I will weaken, and the spell will fail. In that moment, all will be lost."

Stiger looked at the wizard in disbelief and then glanced back toward the Gate. Ogg was proposing to send him back in time, over three hundred years to be exact. It was so fantastic, he was having difficulty wrapping his head around the concept.

Then he stilled, and a hand went to his cloak pocket. He pulled out Delvaris's scroll, hands shaking as he did so. The scroll was damp and smudged. He glanced at the Gate. Delvaris had known . . . it was so clear now.

Ogg coughed and seemed to shrink in upon himself. The wizard looked to be aging before Stiger's eyes, growing older and more frail with every passing moment.

"You must hurry." The words came out as if the wizard were struggling to breathe.

"If I go, will I be able to come back?" Stiger looked up hopefully at Ogg.

The wizard looked him level in the eyes and for a moment did not answer.

"As long as there is a wizard of great power holding the Gate open, travel between both sides is possible. You know what our time holds. I am not exactly sure what you will need to do, but you must help Delvaris kill the creature. Set things right. You cannot tell any, including the dragons, of the future, for it would change things more should they know. You may only confide in Thoggle, my master, teacher, and mentor. Do you understand me? Only Thoggle."

Stiger nodded and turned toward the Gate. The great dark hole in the world beckoned. It called to him. He had never felt so alone in his life. A hand came to rest upon his shoulder.

"I will go with you, my son," Father Thomas said. "You shall not have to walk this path alone."

Stiger felt an immense wave of relief wash over him. He looked back at the paladin, and then at Ogg, who nodded, encouraging him to go.

"I will go also," Braddock announced and stepped forward.

"No," Ogg said with force before being consumed by a wracking cough. "You must not. Only the two of them go back."

"You've known this?" Braddock asked in an accusing tone.

"From the moment my master took me on as an apprentice," the wizard answered. "I have been preparing for this my entire life."

"Thoggle knew also?" Braddock asked.

"Thoggle waits on the other side," Ogg told him, coughing. Blood flecked his lips, which twisted into a sneer. "As does Brogan, your father."

"My father," Braddock said with longing, looking at the Gate.

"You must remain," Ogg implored. "Stiger must go. It is his destiny, his fate. He is the Tiger that the Oracle has spoken of."

"The Tiger's Fate?" Braddock whispered in awe. "No . . . "

"Now you understand, Braddock," Ogg spoke over his thane. "The sword has always been meant for him, forged for his hand alone. He was not simply the restorer of the Compact, but also the direct instrument of prophecy, an important game piece of the gods."

"I . . . " Braddock turned to Stiger, shaken, clearly unsure what to say. He cleared his throat, then nodded, straightening. "At first I thought I would dislike you, but I've since learned you are a man of great Legend. For that, you have my respect. Upon my own personal Legend, I will be here when you return through the World Gate. I will wait for you."

"The sword," Stiger turned to Ogg, alarmed at what the wizard had just revealed. "What of it?"

"You must master it . . . before it masters you," Ogg said, and broke into coughing fit, which wracked his body terribly. The wizard sucked in a ragged breath and almost fell to his knees. "I cannot hold the gate open for much longer . . . You . . . have to . . . go!"

Stiger gazed at the wizard a moment more before he stepped forward toward the Gate. He wished Eli were with him and at that moment realized how much he truly valued and relied upon his friend. Stiger took a deep breath and let it out slowly. Eli was not here, and this was something that had to be done. He shared a brief glance with Father Thomas and then looked back toward the World Gate.

The portal seemed to call him forward. It hummed with power, and he felt mesmerized the closer he got to it. His legs, of their own accord, seemed to carry him forward, and then he stepped through. The world went white, and he felt as if he were falling from a height of some distance. The feeling lasted for only a fraction of a second before he felt solid ground beneath his feet.

Stiger's vision returned, and he blinked in surprise as Father Thomas stepped out of the Gate behind him. They were in the same gate room that they had been in just moments before, but this room was intact, without the destruction that had been visited upon the one in the future. The ring of stones glowed, throbbing brilliantly with purple light, and beyond them Stiger could see both dwarves and humans. Surprisingly, no dragons were present. Stiger took one of the dwarves to be a wizard, based upon the staff he was holding, and another who stood next to him to be thane, likely Braddock's father. The thane wore nearly identical armor to his son, along with a rich purple cape . . . or Braddock will one day wear, Stiger corrected himself, remembering where he was. He had traveled back in time.

Stiger recognized one of the men a heartbeat later as Centurion Sabinus. The centurion was kneeling over a body, a grief-stricken look upon his face. Stiger walked up to both of them. All eyes in the room were upon him and Father Thomas. The body was that of Delvaris. Of that Stiger was sure. With his throat ripped out, Delvaris was very dead. There could be no doubt of the man's identity, as the general was wearing the very same kit that Stiger had on even now.

"This is certainly not what I had expected to find," Father Thomas said quietly to him.

Stiger felt his heart plummet. He had failed. Castor had won.

A thunderclap behind him caused Stiger, and everyone else in the room, to jump. He looked around, and with horror saw that the Gate had closed. The two crystal columns had stilled to a dull glow and soft hum.

"Oh shit," Stiger said and realized Ogg had let the World Gate close. He took in a deep breath and let it out slowly. There was no going back now.

End of Book 3

ABOUT THE AUTHOR

Marc Alan Edelheit has a Bachelor's Degree in Science and obtained a Master's in Education as a Reading and Writing Specialist. He is currently an executive in the healthcare industry, staying up late at night to work on his novels. Marc has traveled the world, from Asia to Europe, even at one point crossing the border at Check Point Charlie in Berlin toward the end of the Cold War. Marc is the ultimate history fan and incorporates much of that passion into his work to bring greater realism to his fans. He is also an avid reader, devouring several books a week, ranging from history to science fiction and fantasy. Marc currently resides in New Hope, Pennsylvania, just miles from where Washington crossed the Delaware.

A Note from the Author

I hope you enjoyed *The Tiger's Fate* and continue to read my books. Stiger and Eli's adventures will continue.

A <u>positive review</u> would be awesome and greatly appreciated, as it affords me the opportunity to focus more time and energy on my writing and helps to persuade others to read my work. I read each and every review.

Grammar suggestions and any spelling corrections are most welcome. Please contact me through email, Facebook or Amazon.

Don't forget to sign up to my newsletter on my website to get the latest news.

Thank you . . .

Marc Alan Edelheit

Coming Soon
Stiger and Eli's Adventures Continue in:

Chronicles of an Imperial Legionary Officer
Book 4
The Tiger's Time

Also Coming Soon
Tales of the Seventh
Stiger
(A Prequel Novella)

Care to be notified when the next book is released
and receive updates from the author?
Join the Newsletter mailing list at Marc's website:

http://www.MAEnovels.com

Facebook: Marc Edelheit Author
Twitter: @Marc Edelheit

Also:
Listen to the Author's Free History Podcast at

http://www.2centhistory.com/

Made in the USA
Las Vegas, NV
24 September 2022